A Quick Sun Rises

A Quick Sun Rises

Book 3 of the Master of the Tane

Thomas Rath

iUniverse, Inc.
New York   Bloomington

A Quick Sun Rises
Book 3 of the Master of the Tane

iUniverse books may be ordered through booksellers or by contacting:

iUniverse
1663 Liberty Drive
Bloomington, IN 47403
www.iuniverse.com
1-800-Authors (1-800-288-4677)

ISBN: 978-1-4502-4845-7 (sc)
ISBN: 978-1-4502-4846-4 (ebook)

Printed in the United States of America

iUniverse rev. date: 07/27/2010

For Teryn, my greatest fan.

Chapter One

Thane caught the early morning wind rising to his call as it took his spirit and lifted him skyward. Looking back, he watched as Jne moved away from their horses and stepped closer to his body where she would keep watch over it while he used his ArVen Tane to ride the winds. Only the day before their mounts had wandered into camp to their great joy and relief. Both had been let out of the city before the dark army reached Haykon, both knowing the city would never hold and the only chance their horses had for survival was to be set free.

They had been three days hard pressed following the eastern shore of the Corrin River traveling south, staying close to the groves of trees that hugged its banks, on their desperate race to reach Calandra before Zadok unleashed his evil host.

Daily, he and Jne had traveled away from the column of refugees to a place where Thane could be alone to use his powers and watch the activities of the enemy that infested the smoldering fortress city, Haykon. His main purpose had been to determine whether or not they had quit the town and were giving chase so as to warn those who had been lucky enough to get out of Haykon with their lives, but he was also concerned about those farther behind.

Most of the townspeople had left through the eastern gates by order of Prince Ranse when the wall blocking the entrance to Nomad's pass had fallen, but they had stuck to the road and were at least two days back unaware of the great danger that might begin its pursuit at any time. Thane had reported such to the prince and Colonel Braxton their first day out but both agreed that none could be spared to go to their aid and hurry them along. They were left to hope and fate that they were quick enough and far enough ahead when Zadok finally ordered his minions forward.

Gaining height while slowing his approach, Thane kept himself well away from the city and the senses of the dragon that he knew could be anywhere looking for him. Having killed another of Zadok's pets, he'd expected the black dragon to be sent to harass and kill as many of the Haykon refugees as possible while searching for him but, to his relief, the skies had remained clear. That did not mean he was going to risk a closer look at the pillaging of Haykon, though. He knew all too well the evil that now filled what was left of the city. He also knew that a multitude of people had not escaped and that the many campfires that now lit the town and surrounding its surrounding area were actually the cook fires for those who'd been killed or captured. No, he had no desire to be witness to such abhorrent depravity.

Stopping at a great height, still a fair distance away, he suddenly felt a strange feeling coming over him as if the air around him was thick with a greasy black oil that invaded his spirit and made him feel dirty. He moved back, as if to retreat from this strange sensation when his eyes were suddenly drawn to the eastern gate that hung in ruin, barely supported by the one remaining hinge. There was a great amount of movement and then like dark puss oozing from a festering wound, a great mass of bodies poured out of the city and spilled onto the road. Others began approaching from outside the wall and joined the main body until the throng swelled in size while snaking forward toward the unsuspecting refugees.

"They're moving."

"That's right," a voice cackled just as a face appeared in the air in front of him. Recovering quickly from the shock of being discovered, he instantly recognized the evil apparition.

"Zadok," he hissed, trying to control the alarm and apprehension he felt at being exposed. Looking about quickly he didn't see the dragon but that didn't relieve his anxiety completely. He still remembered all too well the last time he and Zadok met on the winds. That time he had barely escaped from having his spirit torn apart.

The face wavered for a brief moment, flicking in and out of visibility before finally sharpening back into focus. Zadok's countenance was a mask of rage. "How do you know that name?"

Thane relaxed slightly, feeling he had gained the upper hand for the moment, but still moved his eyes about as if expecting the dragon to appear any instant. He was in a precarious position and he knew it. To return to his body now would only invite Zadok to follow and discover his location or worse still, have the black dragon sent instead. He still didn't know the extent of Zadok's powers, though the fact that he had killed his own brother, Gelfin, one who had the same gifts that Thane now possessed, made him more than dangerous. He had to keep him off balance and think of a way to escape. Now was not the proper time to test his increased capacity with the Tane. More than his life was swinging precariously in the balance.

He gathered more wind, calling out to it to surround him in a silent whirlwind, trying to prepare for whatever Zadok might throw as he answered. "Your brother told me all about you, Zadok."

Zadok's face faded slightly but returned quickly, an evil grin on his face. "I have no brother, Thane. You must be mistaken. But no matter, you can call me whatever you like, it won't change the fact that you will soon be dead."

Thane steeled his nerves, searching for the calm and confidence he found while in battle. He was fighting, though no blows had yet been exchanged, and he knew that to show any fear or weakness would surely turn to Zadok's advantage. He forced a smile. "No brother? Well then, I guess that necklace I took from you belonged to someone else."

He heard a scream and then a blast of oily feeling air crashed into him before both were suddenly cut off as Zadok's face blinked out. Recovering quickly, he smiled, pushing the soiled wind away while calling more to buoy up his spirit. So that was it. He'd found his enemy's weakness. Backing away slightly he watched and waited for Zadok to reappear but his face did not immediately materialize. Was that it? Was he to get away without a fight? But Zadok's face suddenly flashed into existence and rushed forward.

"I will give you one last chance," he raged as he quickly devoured the space between them. "Return my...trinket, and then bow to me and you may yet survive when I am through."

Thane held his ground this time, preparing to unleash his own force of wind as he shook his head and smiled at Zadok's face now mere feet away. "I'm sorry, Zadok, but your trinket no longer exists."

"Impossible!" he screamed, his face flashing in and out in quick succession as he fought for control. "A severed TanIs cannot release fire!"

Thane's eyes narrowed. "That is where you are wrong, Zadok. I have released your brother, Gelfin, from his prison and destroyed the TanIs that held him there. No longer is he yours to torment."

Zadok screamed releasing a tremendous blast of wind that was meant to dissipate the air holding Thane and destroy him in its wake but Thane was ready. Releasing the air that was coiled like a snake around him, it shot out engulfing Zadok's and canceling its power before he sent another might gust at Zadok himself. The blast shot true but missed its mark as Zadok's rage completely cut off his concentration and he disappeared.

Thane didn't wait, this time, to see if he would return. Now was his chance to escape and warn the others. Calling the wind around him he made to turn back but was suddenly held in place when his eyes caught sight of a black mass rising from the ashes of what was once the city of Haykon. Lifting slowly into the air, it released a terrifying cry that instantly filled him with dread.

∗   ∗   ∗

Jack lifted the tent flap and walked out into spring's early morning chill still fighting to gain a foothold over winter. It had rained some the night before leaving the ground just wet enough to turn the camp muddy. Stretching, he surveyed the haphazard formation of bodies strewn across the ground like the dead from a horrible battle. Very few of Haykon's refugees had the luxury of a tent so many had huddled as close as they could to the nearest tree with the hope of keeping dry during the night. Though helpful with the first drops of rain, many now found themselves victims of the larger drops that gathered in the leaves above and fell mercilessly on them soaking them all the same even though the rain had stopped an hour before. Though cold and wet, none was allowed to start a fire for fear that it might be seen and give up their position. Even now, many kept a keen eye to the sky expecting that any moment a dragon might drop down and have them for breakfast.

Jack sighed at the sight. So many lost, and still many who would not make it to the gates of Calandra. Every morning a count had been reported of those who had passed during the night. Most had been the infirmed and aged who were sick or dying before leaving Haykon. But instead of the dignity and peace of dying at home with family and friends gathered around, they were forced to the road to give their last breaths to a foreign land surrounded by unfamiliar and blank faces. Instead of a proper goodbye with the appropriate rites and ceremonies administered, a shallow, mass grave was their final ordinance.

A few hungry babies cried out in the distance reminding him of the stark shortage of food that was to greet the refugees once again this morning. They would all share what was available but none would leave camp satisfied this day. It had been such a desperate race to get away from Haykon with their lives alone that none had time to worry about from where the next meal might come. The promise of reaching Calandra soon was their only real hope.

Looking east, Jack strained his eyes to catch a glimpse of the gleaming towers of Calandra but to no avail.

"Will we make it to the city soon, Master Jack?" a small voice suddenly asked, slightly startling him from his dark thoughts.

Looking down, he found Teek, the small Waseeni boy and only known survivor of his race, sitting on a stump next to the tent. His hands were busily twisting a strange object around in his fingers as he gave Jack a questioning look. Jack smiled and nodded. "Looks like we'll start to the east today, son. We should see the city by late this afternoon and make it there by sometime late tomorrow."

"That is, if the dragon doesn't return," Teek added for him.

He stared at the boy for a moment and then nodded slightly. Teek had seen too much sorrow in the past days for a boy his age; more than anyone should have to face in a lifetime. But these were dark times. None of them should have had to suffer what they had if not for the careless rule of their leaders. Soon, all hope would be lost because those leaders had failed to act quickly or at all.

His focus suddenly turned to the object with which Teek was playing. "What is that you keep fiddling with?" he asked, nodding toward Teek's hands.

Teek looked down at one of the two prized objects he had left in his life. "It's an old medallion my friend gave me before he died."

Jack raised an eyebrow and stared at the Waseeni boy for a moment. "You mind if I take a look?"

Teek shrugged. "Sure," he said dropping the medallion into his outstretched hand.

He grabbed the small chain and lifted it up for a better look. Attached to the end was a gold medallion inlaid with a strange insignia made of silver that curved into different points in the middle and was accented with four various colored gems. His expression changed to one of wonder and surprise.

"Who did you say gave this to you?" he breathed, his voice edged slightly turning his question into an obvious command.

Teek blinked, a little taken back by Jack's obvious recognition of the medallion. Thoughts of the prison in Thornen Dar flashed into his mind and he suddenly wondered if he might soon discover the similarities of prison cells held between dwarfs and humans. "It...it was a gift, Master Jack; a gift from a friend. I swear I didn't steal it."

Jack pulled his gaze from the medallion at Teek's last comment and looked at the boy, registering the concern in his face and realizing he must have frightened him with his demanding behavior. His frown quickly changed to a smile and his manner lightened to a more amiable disposition. "My apologies, friend Teek," he soothed. "I did not mean to startle you. I know that you did not steal this, at least from its original owner." Leaning closer to the boy he looked about quickly as if to discover any unwanted listeners and then whispered conspiratorially, "You see, it was I who gave it away in the first place."

Teek's eyes widened in wonder, his nervousness doubling in an instant. Swallowing quickly at a failed attempt to wet his suddenly dry throat he whispered, "you mean, you're the..."

Jack cut him off, his own demeanor becoming slightly nervous. "Let's not worry about who or what I might or might have been for now. Let's instead concentrate on the question first given. Who gave this to *you*?"

Teek's expression didn't change. "Yes, my Lord."

Jack sighed. "That will never do," he said half to himself. "It's Jack, boy. Just plain Jack. Understand?"

Teek blinked but didn't respond.

Jack's voice took on a slight edge again as his frustration level began to climb. Not so much at the boy, but at his own foolishness in not guarding his words while trying to put the boy at ease. Obviously he had done just the opposite and was now feeling he'd placed himself in a situation he would all together rather avoid. "The name, Teek. Who was it that gave you this medallion?"

"It was Twee," Teek quickly answered and then hurried to add, "your....

Jack cut him off again with a raised finger. "Just Jack."

Teek merely nodded.

A smiled suddenly broke through his rough exterior as the name finally settled into his mind. "Did you say, Twee?"

Teek just nodded.

Jack's smile turned into a joyful laugh, "Well, I'll be a troll's trophy."

Teek was beside himself. "You knew him?"

Jack sobered at the word *knew* suddenly remembering that all of Teek's people had been wiped out by a dragon that left nothing but an empty hole in the Teague swamplands where Teek's race once made its home. "Yes," he nodded, returning the medallion to Teek and then squeezing his shoulder in friendship and sympathy. "I knew old Twee quite well. One of the most trusted of my..." he trailed off as if in deep thought and then flashed a concerned look at Teek as if just realizing the boy was there. "He was a good friend. Someone I trusted."

"He was a father to me," Teek said, dropping his eyes to the medallion in his hands and trying to hide the emotion that was obvious in his voice.

Jack stared at the young Waseeni boy understanding from his own experience what the boy was suffering. "Twee was a great man, Teek." His expression softened and his eyes glazed slightly as if caught in a distant memory. "He was a wanderer; an adventurer. I never knew anyone whose feet itched so much to be out on the road exploring. Got himself into a lot of trouble that way, but he always seemed to escape. I'd venture to say that he saw more places than any yet still alive to tell the tale."

Teek smiled, remembering the stories he loved to hear his old friend tell and the wanderlust that filled him every time they were together. "He told me of one of those places just before he died." Teek's own thoughts raced back as if reliving the tale as he stared at the medallion and spoke. "Something about being lost in the Underwoods Forest and finding a grove of trees."

Jack's eyebrows furrowed slightly. "Trees in a forest, eh? Did you say that was right before he died?"

Teek looked up at Jack as if startled by his voice and then smiled weakly. "No, they were different from the others. They were set apart and beautiful. He said they felt like they were alive."

Jack opened his mouth as if preparing to point out the obvious but Teek put his hand up to stop him.

"I know what you are going to say, I said the same thing. But he explained it like they were alive like you or me. So much so that he thought if they had the mind to, they might just uproot and move on." Teek stopped for a moment, his face suddenly showing some concern. "Do you think he was just telling a story that wasn't really true to amuse a young boy?"

Jack's expression became more serious. Something was scratching at his mind, a memory stored deep long ago that was trying to find its way through the corridors of his brain and into his remembrance but it wouldn't come. "I never knew Twee to speak other than the exact truth no matter what the consequences. No, Teek, if he told it to you, you can be certain it was not made up."

Teek smiled and then nodded.

He wanted to question him more, hoping to regain whatever it was that was agitating his memory, but was interrupted when he caught site of a small group of men carefully picking their way through the camp. They moved toward the tent in a deliberate manner yet careful not to soil themselves by inadvertently coming too close to one of the exhausted, filthy refugees.

Their were five of them total. Two were obviously sent as bodyguards of sorts, their physical size and display of battle gear marking them so, yet anyone accustomed to war would instantly recognize their equipment as showpieces and not extremely functional in a real fight. The other three were dressed in gaudy silks and furs giving them an air of aristocracy but painting them more as those who try too hard to appear as more than they really are.

The leader was gaunt and frail looking, the wisps of his receding hair hanging tenuously to the great bald spot on top of his head that he tried unsuccessfully to cover by combing what little he had over from one side to the other. His nose was large and hawkish protruding from his small head and guarded on either side by tiny black eyes that seemed to never stop darting about. A laced handkerchief was held by a boyish hand under his nostrils as if the smell of the camp were too offensive for his delicate beak. His strut was like that of a peacock, prancing about in a show of superiority, gracing the common folk with the mere blessing of his presence.

Jack spat on the ground, the anger and disgust rising like acid in his belly. "So," he growled barely under his breath, "the ambassadors have finally arrived."

Teek looked at him quizzically. "Ambassadors?"

"Yes," he replied, eyeing the approaching figures with disgust. "Calandra's answer to the slaughter of its people."

Teek stared at the men incredulously. This was what they sent to save them from complete annihilation? He turned to Jack as if to put voice to the questions in his mind when the men finally passed their last obstacle and quickly covered the ground between them. The one in the lead stepped up to Jack while the other two stood back leaving the two guards at their backs. Jack could see now that they were more like pets than protection.

"Who is the one in charge here?" the one in front asked, the thin, whiney voice emitting from his frail frame. Just the greasy sound of it made Jack want to go and bathe.

"Who's askin'?" Jack replied unable to completely disguise the disgust from his voice.

The man's eyes played slowly over him as if trying to determine if he was even worthy of addressing, a small sneer of loathing playing across his thin lips. Finally, as if coming to the conclusion that Jack may in fact be leader of such a dirty infestation of filth as he saw around him, he spoke. "I am Ambassador Prissley of the House of Maggest, Chief Ambassador to his royal majesty and protector of the land, his grace, King Dagan. And who might you be?"

Jack's anger was just at the surface now and he wasn't sure he would be able to hold it in check much longer. He knew all too well the House of Maggest. A more apt name would have been House of Maggots for that was what the truly were. Maggest was a mid-level House of opportunists with their noses constantly to the wind sniffing out any chance to prey on the misfortunes feeding on the financial corpses of their rivals or anyone else that might give them a boost in status. In what he now considered another life, he had had to deal with the Maggest House for a time and the foul stench it left in his nostrils was rediscovered in the form of Prissley Maggest.

"You can call me Jack," he replied, his face getting red with the exertion it required to hold from simply pounding the king's men into the mud.

Although seemingly impossible, Prissley puffed himself even more, his handkerchief covered nose rising still higher in the air. "And from what House do you hale?"

Jack's eyes narrowed menacingly. "No House," he hissed, "just Jack."

The ambassador's demeanor instantly turned from one of self-importance to a frozen wall of disdain. It was all too obvious that one without the significance of a landed House was not worth the air such a person wasted in breathing. As far as Prissley was concerned, their interview had ended and Jack was nothing but a ball of waste rolled about in the mud by a dung beetle.

He couldn't mistaken the instant change and opened his mouth for a verbal onslaught, but just at that moment, the tent flapped open and out pressed Jace followed immediately by Prince Ranse. Both kept to their ranger garb still not giving over to the royal dress deemed appropriate for a prince or that of the king's elite royal guard. Anyone catching a glimpse of the rune markings that had been carved into Jace's hands would mark him for the weapon's master he was. Ranse, on the other hand, would have not appeared to be anything other than a common traveler with his doe skinned pants and hanging green tunic. It had been decided to keep his royalty a secret so as not to cause undo alarm or fuss from the refugees or the meager band of men that were now left of Haykon's armed force.

Prissley, though, was not fooled, recognizing the prince almost immediately. His reaction, however, was not what Jack would have expected from one involved with the royal household. He merely turned away as if Jack were no more than a common piece of manure to be left smoldering in the street and then only nodded slightly to the prince. Being the third son of the king did not afford Ranse much, if any, power but respect still should have been shown to one of his station, especially from the ambassador. Ranse seemed unfazed though and simply nodded back before addressing him. At least Prissley followed that much protocol to allow the prince to speak first. A courtesy he had not afforded Jack.

"Prissley, what brings you here? I'm fairly certain my father has not sent you to welcome us with open arms into the city."

The ambassador smirked at the suggestion as if the prince had said something funny. "Of course not, we were sent to deal with Haykon's embarrassment."

Jack opened his mouth, no longer able to contain his rage but was quickly cut off by the prince. "By embarrassment, I presume you mean the fact that we are here with Haykon's sole surviving refugees and that the thousands of trolls, goblins, and orcs that chase after us should have been dealt with more efficiently."

Prissley smiled sweetly. Jack thought he might throw up. "Never fear, Ranse," he said the prince's name—eliminating the royal title and courtesy he should have given—with weakly masked disdain. "We will take care of the mess that has become of your father's northern fortress. In the meantime, you honestly don't think to bring such dregs," he motioned to the refugees, "to the grand city of Calandra." It was not a question but a statement.

Ranse's eyes flashed for a brief moment but his features remained calm. "That is precisely what I mean to do."

The ambassador laughed out loud this time. "You know that will never do."

It was obvious that Ranse had had enough. "Is that all? I wouldn't want to keep you from your errand, after all."

Maggest smiled at the prince, his lips turning up in a sickly fashion. "We are through here." Turning to the four behind him he motioned them to follow. "Come, let us be gone from such filth before I lose my breakfast from the scent of it." Then looking back at the prince purposefully he added, "We have another mess to deal with." And then he turned about and picked his way back through the crowds.

The four of them watched the ambassador and his entourage retreat, the incredulity clear on their faces, except for Jace's whose face never altered from the stern look he seemed to hold constantly. "Can they really stop those that follow us?" Teek asked in wonder.

Jack and the prince regarded him. Ranse smiled and then shook his head. "They go to their doom my young friend."

"At least there's some good to all of this," Jack added half under his breath before adding, "and that is where we will all end if we don't get this group moving."

*   *   *

Checking the dragon's position, Thane pressed harder gathering the wind to race him back toward his body. It wasn't long before he passed over the refugees who had taken their leisure in their race for Calandra and his stomach tightened. Looking back, he could not see the dragon any longer. Where had it gone? He was certain it had been sent after him when Zadok's rage made him unable to fight on the winds. But then where was it? Had it returned to Haykon? He paused in his flight, checking the sky in all directions. He didn't see it. He looked back at the people of Haykon and it was then he realized what a fool he'd been. The dragon was not sent for him. No matter how fast it flew, it was no longer a match for the speed he could call forth. No, the dragon was after the unsuspecting townspeople. Zadok was chipping away at the HuMan population. The centuries of waiting gave him the patience to slowly and methodically destroy them a little bit at a time. The helpless refugees from Haykon would supply his army with fodder for the last press against Calandra.

Dropping down near the long file of people he tried to find someone who might be able to see him so he could warn them but he knew when he started it was in vain. Only one having the ArVen Tane would be able to see him as he rode the winds. It was no use and he knew it. Even if they could see him and start the line running, they would be no match for the speed of the dragon. They were lost unless he could somehow turn it away. Regaining altitude he turned back the way he came as he continued to climb finally catching sight of a distant black dot gradually growing in size as the dragon ate up the distance between them. Gathering about him all the wind he could hold, he kept going higher as he followed the dragon's path, all the while appearing larger as it came. Then its speed suddenly increase as it caught sight of the unsuspecting travelers below.

He readied himself, knowing he had only one shot at this, his spirit straining to hold the tremendous amount of wind that now swirled about him in a seeming vortex of power. It had to be enough. The dragon was almost directly under him when suddenly, its body shot forward in a dive heading straight for the people below. Thane followed, the vortex of air rushing with him as he arrowed toward the dragon's back.

Gaining speed, he quickly closed the distance and prepared to release the gathered wind. He prayed it would be enough to force the dragon into the ground kill it or, at least, wound it enough to save the line of people still slowly moving along the road and unaware of the danger falling upon them. Holding for a brief moment longer he inched closer and then released the wind, holding back only enough to keep himself from spiraling into the dragon's back.

What had appeared to him as a raging torrent hit the dragon dead on but to his dismay its affects were minor at best. The dragon did drop some but was quickly able to right itself as it passed over the people and rushed toward the front line eliciting panicked shrieks of terror as the people finally understood their fate.

He watched in horror as it swooped down over the front and then turned about to face them. It paused, as if enjoying the moment, before drawing in a great breath and then releasing its foul blood red liquid over the front lines of people and reducing them almost instantly into puddles. Those escaping the initial blast turned back in a frenzy of terror at seeing their friends and loved ones dissolved to nothing before their eyes while the dragon fear wrapped a vice grip around their hearts.

Thane thought he was going to be sick. He needed to help them but what more could he do? It was obvious that his wind powers were useless against the corporeal world while he remained in spirit form. He needed his body but it was still far away, and without it he knew he could not affectively attack the dragon. He watched as it turned about and then dropped in closer maneuvering to make sure none of the chaotic mass got away but instead reversed their direction.

"It's herding them back to the army. They'll all be massacred." He could not save them. The thought was a lead ball in his gut. With all the powers he possessed, he was powerless to save these people. The only thing left was to get back to camp and warn the others. At least he could help the remaining people of Haykon escape. At least that is what he wrapped his mind and emotions around so as not to give into despair. Turning away he raced back to Jne with as much speed as he could gather.

Jne didn't flinch in the least as his head suddenly lifted; she'd become accustomed to his popping in and out of his body in the past few days. "What news?" she asked, catching the look on his face as he quickly rose and turned for his horse. "They come, don't they?"

"Yes," he replied, grabbing Chtey's mane and jumping onto his back. "The dragon has moved out ahead of the people escaping on the road and is now herding them back to the army that has just left Haykon on its way to overtake them."

Jne jumped onto her own horse and turned it south toward their camp. She knew just as well that there was no hope for the others.

"We must make speed if we are to help the rest," he shouted and then pushed his horse into a dead run. Jne didn't answer but urged her mount after him.

Chapter Two

Thane and Jne entered the camp amidst chaos. At first glance it might appear that everyone had gone mad as they seemed to run about without purpose, but they knew better. The camp was preparing to move. At Jack's command, everyone was picking up what tents, bedding, and cooking utensils they had and were preparing for a final push towards Calandra and the relative safety it provided—for the moment.

The pace had been slow and wearisome even in the face of the danger that lurked behind them as a constant threat to their existence. Still, moving such numbers of untrained and disorganized people unaccustomed to such exertions was a challenge in the best of circumstances. The people were tired and hungry and many had let the icy hand of despair find place around their hearts where it slowly robbed them of hope. All that most of them had known was left behind in ruin to the enemy that had destroyed their city and killed so many of their friends and family members. The feeling of despair was a thick cloud over the camp that fell as a choking mist snuffing out on any spark of optimism.

Dismounting so as not to trample any in the crowded mass, Thane and Jne lead their horses as quickly as possible through the throng seeking any who would know Jack's or Ranse's whereabouts. Their going was slow and hampered due to the masses having huddled together like frightened chicks who were now trying to gather their few belongings and move out. Gone was the stigma and fear that was generally associated with the Tjal-Dihn and would have normally opened a large swath before them. That fear had been replaced with the apathy of those who have given themselves over to the inevitability of death.

Thane tried to avoid the eyes of the people on every side as he passed them, feeling stifled by their looks of defeat. He would not give up and he knew Jne would not either. As long as he had one breath still within him he would fight to protect as many of these people as he possibly could. The irony of it all was lost on him now. The very people who had tried to annihilate his own race years ago were now left at his mercy and protection. But that didn't matter to him. Saving them from their enemy was all that occupied his mind now. That and the twinge of guilt that, though unwarranted, was nevertheless always present and pressing that he could have done more. But there was so much that was out of his immediate control. He did not rule or lead except for that that had been given him by those in authority. Still, the disease of failure and doubt was a constant threat to his own strength of will; one he knew could easily consume him if given enough place in his heart and mind.

He caught the blank stare of a small child hoisted onto its mother's back as she busied herself with the task of packing what little they had. It held him briefly in place as he searched for the light that seemed to shine in every child's eyes but found none. Snuffed out by seeing too much that no one in a lifetime should have to witness. He felt despair's cold sickness coming to life within him hungrily feeding on his emotions and trying to gain sway over his heart. Unbidden thoughts raged within his mind gaining strength as his eyes remained locked on the child's empty, blank stare. *You can't beat them. You will never win. You are all doomed. All of these people will die. That child is fodder to feed the belly of a hungry young troll.* He felt his eyes blur as the hopelessness threatened to overwhelm him.

"Why do you wait, Ghar of the Chufa?" Jne asked, touching his arm and suddenly pulling him back from the brink of despair.

He looked at her as if he didn't know her, his thoughts still slightly clouded.

"Thane!" another voiced called drawing their attention. It was Tam pushing her way through the crowd. Thane's look of loss quickly melted into a half smile as he raised his hand in recognition. Jne scowled slightly. "What news?" she asked when she reached them.

Thane glanced back to where the child had been but its mother had already gathered their things and had moved on and disappeared into the crowd. "They move," he finally said, keeping his voice low so that only Tam could hear. "They have left Calandra and are pushing on toward us."

Tam's face darkened. "Will we make it to Calandra in time?"

Thane looked away to where he and Jne had come and slowly nodded. "Yes. The dragons do not come for us but have been unleashed on the others. We will make the city gates, but none of the others will follow us."

Tam's eyes watered at the implications in his words. There was too much death and suffering. Too many were paying for the mistakes and arrogance of the few.

"Where is Jack," he asked before she could control her emotions enough to speak further. She could only point behind her. Thane nodded, understanding her inability to speak and started to move in the direction she had indicated. But Tam grabbed his arm and pulled him in close so that their eyes met. A tear suddenly let loose from her lid and made a track down her dirty face.

"We must speak, you and I, soon, before we reach the city. I will seek you out at the end of the column."

Thane let out a sigh and nodded slightly. He knew what this was about. He had been avoiding it for as long as he could but realized that sooner or later he would have to confront her and lie about his feelings for her. He could not have her no matter what their hearts told them. He had hoped to save her this added grief and even now would flee and not add to her sorrow, but it was time. Better to make the wound a clean swift cut that it might heal than to allow it to fester further. It was for the best. She should not be left to hope for him.

Turning away, he pressed into the crowd followed closely by Tam and Jne whose scowling face was enough to break through the dark infesting the hearts of those around them and move them away at their approach. They quickly found Jack in discussion with Colonel Myles Braxton who had been Haykon's leader when it fell. He also recognized the young Waseeni boy, Teek, who, with his giant bird, had saved his life only days before. He was somewhat surprised to find Domis nowhere in sight.

Domis, a young HuMan, had been a stable boy and sometimes runner for Colonel Braxton in Haykon. Since the city's fall, he seemed never to leave Jack's side finding, he supposed, comfort in the man who had been instrumental in saving his life. Thane had also been a part of his rescue but he didn't blame the boy for avoiding one who claimed to be Tjal-Dihn.

"We should be there by sunset tomorrow," Jack was saying when they finally reached him. Seeing the young Chufa he turned and asked, "What news?"

"They come," he replied without embellishment.

"We should have time," Braxton quickly added as if to pacify the fears of those nearby and listening.

"We have time," Thane confirmed. "They sent the dragon out first to herd back those who were on the road." A thick silence fell over the group at the revelation. Everyone knew who 'those' were and they also knew that herded was the proper word. They were to be used to feed Zadok's army, strengthening it for the attack on Calandra. "We also passed a group of men headed toward Haykon. We attempted to warn them but they refused to even acknowledge us."

"Prissley," Jack spat. "No, you would not have been viewed as worthy to hear his voice." Thane cocked an eye in question but Jack waved him off. "No matter, he of all people deserves what awaits him there."

Thane just nodded. "Though we have time, the sooner we move the better. No one is truly safe with dragons still flying about."

"But we have you, Master Thane," a small voice broke in from behind him. Thane turned and found Domis had joined the group. "You can stop the dragons, can't you Master Thane? You can kill them with your powerful touch."

Thane's expression fell. If only that were true. Yes, he had killed two dragons so far. The first one had almost caused his own death twice; first from the use of his Tane and second when he woke up with amnesia in a Tjal camp and became desperate enough to ask for the Tjal adoption ceremony. Luckily, where his Tane had almost killed him the first time, the second time it saved his life. The other dragon he killed had also been thanks to his Tane but he had been touching it when he killed it. By all rights he should have died from that experience as well.

"It is not that simple friend Domis," he said, the strain heavy in his voice. "One does not just walk up to a dragon and ask to touch it."

"Can they not be pierced by arrows?" Teek asked timidly, still unsure of himself around such men of valor as he saw them.

Thane shook his head. "You might as well try and pierce a blade of steel my young…" but he didn't finish his sentence. "Pierce a blade of steel," he repeated in a half whisper. "That's it!"

"What?" Jack asked, somewhat encouraged by Thane's sudden change in attitude.

"Dax," A voice said, drawing all eyes to Dor who had come up unnoticed and was now standing next to Tam.

Thane nodded. "Dax!"

"What is a dax?" the colonel asked.

"DaxSagn," Thane corrected. "DaxSagn is one of our people."

"Can he kill the dragons from far?" Domis asked.

"No," Thane shook his head. "But he has an arrow that can."

"What fool talk is this?" Jack asked, his demeanor one of irritation but his voice revealing a glimmer of hope. Zadok's army was still larger than they could possibly hold off alone, but it was certain death with his dragons flying around. If they could defeat the dragons, it might just give them the edge they needed to defeat the rest of the army.

"DaxSagn," Dor answered, "or Dax, as we call him, has an arrow that can pierce steel."

"That's impossible," Braxton chided. "You would have to be right on top of the beast to even have a chance at penetrating its skin, and that not likely."

"I agree," Dor continued, "with a normal arrow. But Dax has no normal arrow. His it is rumored comes from the heart of a YeiyeiloBaneesh tree."

"A yeilo what?"

"They were the sacred trees of our people that were destroyed when..." Dor paused for a brief moment before continuing, "...they are no more. Dax has the only known surviving arrow, and it can pierce steel from a distance. Thane and I have seen it."

"Then we must have this arrow," Braxton said.

Thane looked at Jack whose face had suddenly become unreadable. He knew they needed Dax's arrow but he also knew what it would mean to try and get it. Was he ready to return and face his people? A people who never trusted him and who, in the case of some, plotted his death? Asking for their most treasured possession to use in a war to save HuMans was not going to bide well with the Chufa—that is, if they believed him at all. It was an impossible chance, but he also knew that they were without any other viable options. He couldn't count on luck to drop him on top of another dragon again, and without an anchor tree to lend its power, he could not attempt another kill using his QenChe Tane.

All eyes had fallen to him waiting for a response. It was madness, but there were no other options. He felt the weight of the entire HuMan race suddenly pressing down on him. "I'll go," he finally said.

"You know he won't give it up," Dor pressed.

Thane stared at his friend. He knew Dor was right, but he still had to try.

"But how will you get there and back in time?" Jack asked.

He turned to Teek. "Master Teek, do you think your bird friend might offer me a ride once more?"

Teek shuffled nervously under the gaze of all those around. "I don't know," he shrugged. "She does as she pleases mostly."

"Then I will just have to ask her," he smiled slightly.

Braxton chuckled at the notion but was alone in his doubt. All the others knew that there was more to Thane and his abilities than even he possibly knew. "Best ask her for two," Jne interjected.

"Three," Dor and Tam added in unison.

"Now wait," he said turning to his friends. "Even if she can hold that many, there is no reason for you all to go. Dax will either give me the arrow or he won't. Having the rest of you along will not change that, especially you, Jne." Jne's face turned red but Thane kept talking. "Our people would shoot you full of arrows before you could even speak because you are a HuMan."

Jne spat. "Do not place me with the dung of the field, Ghar of the Chufa. Being *Jinghar* does not mean I will be insulted by you."

"What does she mean dung?" Braxton asked, his face clouding over.

Jack placed a hand on his friend's arm. "Let it go."

"It is not that," Thane said. "I do not call you HuMan, but my people will not know the difference. All they will see is a person that is not like them, that fits the description of what they think HuMans are and they will kill you without question.

"It doesn't matter," she argued. "I go where you go. *That* is what *Jinghar* means."

Sighing heavily, he gave up. He knew that it would be easier to talk Zadok into taking his army away than convince her to stay behind. But Dor and Tam were something else entirely. "Fine," he said to Jne and then focused on his two friends. "You two may go but only if you agree to stay there."

"Really?" Tam huffed.

Dor cut her off. "I am not your *Jinghar* or whatever it is Jne is to you. I will come and go as I please with or without your permission. We are friends, Thane, and you need me this time. Maybe you are forgetting what brought us all here in the first place. I'm not so sure that you won't be shot on sight either."

Braxton shot a questioning look at Jack, but his friend just shook his head slightly while Teek and Domis were all eyes and ears enjoying every bit of the exchange.

"I don't plan to just walk into camp and let them shoot me, Dor," he replied rather calmly.

"Really, then I assume you have some sort of plan?" Tam put in.

He shrugged. "Well, no, not yet, but…"

"Then you'll need our help," Dor interjected, cutting him off.

He shook his head and muttered something under his breath. "We still don't know if Teek's bird can even carry all of us."

"Her name's Tchee," Teek suddenly added.

"Right," Thane said. "Tchee."

"Well then," Jne interjected, "you'd better hurry and ask so we can be on our way."

Thane threw up his hands. He couldn't believe this. It was like he was still home and being bullied by PocMar and his friends. He looked to Jack for support, but his friend wisely stayed out of this argument. To him it wasn't important who went on this mission as long as they brought back this arrow they had spoken of and that it really did work as they said. He had to admit that it was a little hard to take in and believe, but in desperate times like they found themselves, all options became viable.

Thane turned to Teek. "Where is your large friend, Tchee?"

Teek rolled his shoulders up to his ears. "I don't know. She comes and goes as she pleases."

"Then in the meantime let us cease our idleness here and help get these people to the city where they can be better cared for," Braxton said.

"You will let me know when she returns then?" Thane asked Teek.

"Yes sir, Master Thane. I will at that and right away."

He smiled. "Thank you, Teek, and please stop calling me Master. Just Thane will do nicely." It bothered him when people made a fuss about him. He was not used to such positive attention and since he started receiving it he decided that he almost preferred the opposite. He didn't want anyone thinking he was more than he was or that he felt like he was better than any other person doing all in their power to protect those in need. It was especially strange hearing such praise from someone like Teek who was, after all, close to his own age.

Their course of action decided, the group began to disperse in different directions. "You will let me know when you plan to leave," Jack said to Thane in a tone that made it hard to decipher as to whether it was a request or a command. Thane just nodded and then turned to make his way through the crowd that, as a whole, was beginning to move east toward the distant city when he was stopped by someone grabbing his arm. It was Tam. She smiled at him and he suddenly found it difficult to breath.

"Can I walk with you a minute and talk?"

He looked for Dor but only caught sight of his back as he walked away and into the crowd. Jne was still at his side, as she always was, and the look on her face would have frozen boiling water. "I really should help with moving the camp," he tried lamely to protest, but Tam would not be deterred. Although she was smiling, he recognized that stubborn look in her eyes that told him that short of death he was not going to change her mind.

Grabbing his arm more firmly, she just moved him away from Jne saying, "You won't mind if I borrow him for a moment." It was not a question and he could see the daggers shooting from Jne's eyes. But, she did not protest and he was led away like a lamb to the slaughter—at least that was how he felt. In all actuality, it was Tam who was to be the sacrificial lamb. He just hoped he had the ability to let her down easily and that the time spent away from him and with Dor would make it easier for her. She deserved to be happy. If he could have just one wish it would be that Tam could live a life of joy and happiness even though he knew that that meant a life without him.

"I really wish you and Dor would reconsider," he said, trying to change the subject he knew was coming before Tam got a chance to start it. "I mean, on the one hand, yes, I would rather you both went back home where it is still safe—for the moment. But, I know that that is not your intention. I appreciate your help, I really do, and all the concern…"

Tam pressed her fingers to his lips to stop his talking. "Thane, we have already gone over that and you know my mind and Dor's as well. We will not be veered from our course and I think you know that. I have more pressing matters to speak with you, matters that affect just you and me."

His stomach tightened. There was no getting around it now. His heart ached for her, for the pain he knew she would feel. But the time for pretending was over. He hoped that she would not hate him for it, but there was nothing he could do. No matter the love he felt for her they shared the same Tane and that eliminated their every being able to be together. It was not something they could ignore. Though he wished it otherwise, he could do nothing to change it.

"Thane, you know that I…"

"Wait," he said holding up a hand to stop her.

"No, Thane," she continued, shaking her head. "Please, let me get this out and then you can speak all that you want."

He stopped and looked away to the river to the west. It was spring and all of the trees were in flower, some with white pedals, and others with red and gold. The grass was getting thick and green and was sprinkled with wildflowers that lent a clean, pleasant scent to the air. It was a beautiful morning. One cherished by those in love as they basked in the light of their affection and what appeared to be nature's blessing on it. He looked to the sky as a cloud suddenly blocked out the sun and he couldn't help but feel that it was all a reflection of his life and love for Tam.

"I love you," she said, but instead of warming him they were like the steel of a knife to his heart. "I have always loved you, Thane," She continued. "Since I can remember I have always felt that you were someone special." She chuckled through the tears that began to form in her eyes. "I know that I had an interesting way of showing it, but I was unsure how you would treat me should you know how I really felt. Anyway, the day that I woke in Haykon and found you sitting there by my bed watching over me was, in a strange way, the best day of my life—and," she added softly, "the worst."

He suddenly felt confused. "Worst?"

She smiled slightly and then wiped at the tears that had begun to fall down her cheek. "Yes, worst. Best because you were there, you were with me, you cared about what happened to me but also worst because you were there and that you cared about me."

Thane's look turned to one of concern. "Are you well, Tam? You make no sense."

"Just let me finish," she huffed, more angry at herself than anything for the way she was not getting across what she so desperately needed to. "Finally, after all the years we've been together I recognized the same love in your eyes as I had always felt in my own heart."

It was too much for him. "Tam, wait."

"No," she said, pounding a fist on his chest. "No, please," she continued, her voice softer as she stood straighter grasping for the courage she needed to continue. "I have always loved you, Thane, but I also have always known that we could never be together."

Her last words hit him hard. He suddenly felt nauseated as his head seemed to spin.

"When I saw that same love in your eyes at first I rejoiced in it. I really think it was what finally got me through those difficult first days and weeks in Haykon after you healed me. But then I realized that I was living a lie and that in the end it would only lead to heartache and pain."

He couldn't believe what he was hearing. All this time he'd been avoiding her for the very same reasons. All along he was afraid to tell her the very same words thinking it was going to be too painful for her to accept and now she was telling them to him; and he was surprised by how much they hurt. He opened his mouth to say something but she cut him off.

"There's one last thing I must tell you and I hope that it will not create a void between us but since Dor and I left the Ardath and came looking for you I have felt a bond begin to develop between us. At first it was something I fought. I didn't want it to happen but the more time we spent together the stronger it grew. And after you cured me of my addiction and Dor has been with me ever since, I think that he feels the same way. I think we love each other, Thane, Dor and me. I've been trying to tell you for a long time now but with everything that has been happening and, I admit, with my fear of how it might hurt you, I have not been able to speak of it to you as I wanted and as you deserve." She reached out and grabbed his hand. "I'm so sorry, Thane. I really am. Can you ever forgive us? Can you ever give us your blessing and be happy for us?"

He looked at her long fingers that seemed to fit in his hand so perfectly. His stomach was a knot and his breath seemed to come with difficulty.

It hurt. It hurt greater than anything he'd ever imagined. He felt anger suddenly building in his heart but he quickly pushed it away. He had no right to feel rage or hatred. These were his two greatest friends. He'd known all along that he could never have her. What she had just said to him was the talk he had been avoiding giving to her. And now he finally realized that his avoidance of the subject was not so much to save her from any added pain but to save him. He had convinced himself that it was all for her, but he now had to admit his cowardice; the pain was his. She did what he could not do; make the cut precisely and cleanly. He only hoped that the healing would come quickly.

Tam's demeanor slowly changed as she let her hand slip from his and her expression became one of concern as he realized that he had not responded to her question. Using all the strength he could muster, he pressed a broad smile onto his face and, to his relief, Tam's expression immediately softened.

"Of course you have my blessing, Tam. What kind of friend would I be not to find joy in the love of my two greatest friends?" What type of friend indeed. He was happy for them but he also knew that there was pain and jealousy mixed in with those feelings that he feared would never completely fade.

His next act, he knew, would be the most difficult to pull off. As with Dor, he hoped he could be convincing enough. "I do love you, Tam, but as a special friend, as a sister. And I am sorry that you misunderstood my feelings for you. With almost losing you to the *dranlok* we were all very concerned and I am sorry if my actions caused you to worry or be pained in the least."

He watched her face closely and almost thought he caught the slightest disappointment but couldn't be sure as a bright smile suddenly filled her countenance. "Oh, Thane," she said, throwing her arms around his neck and pulling him in close. "I am so relieved."

He hugged her back not wanting to ever let go but knowing he could not linger lest she suspect his words did not match the feelings of his heart. Reluctantly pulling away, he smiled down at her, his heart breaking once more. It was almost more than he could bear. "Now that that has been cleared up," he said, straining to keep his eyes and face free from his true feelings, "I must get back to helping move this camp to safety. Give Dor my heartfelt congratulations if I do not see him first."

Tam smiled back at him. "I will, Thane."

Without another word, he marched passed her back to where Jne waited for him, a murderous scowl on her face.

Tam watched him go, following his every movement, before turning her back and brushing away the tear that suddenly blurred her vision.

Chapter Three

All eyes turned to the tent flap as Helgar entered followed by Bardolf and finally Rangor. They were the last called to the council that now met in a makeshift hall hastily raised by joining two small tents together. The quarters were cramped but afforded just enough space for those present. A quadra of guards took their places at the outside corners mostly to keep any of the refugees from listening in. Ranse felt it best that no one 'accidentally' overhear something that might throw the camp into greater panic.

All the participants were seated on what carpets could be acquired giving the meeting a disheveled look that, from appearances only, more resembled a meeting of the local beggars guild than one having representatives from five different races that also included two princes.

Helgar and the two other dwarfs sat where room had been made between Jack and Colonel Braxton. Ranse was standing at the back of the tent while his ever-present bodyguard, Jace, took a commanding post by the tent door. Jne, Thane, Dor, Tam and finally Teek, who sat near Jack, completed the assemblage. Now that all were present, all eyes focused on Ranse waiting for him to reveal why he had called them all there.

The prince took a deep breath as if preparing himself. Looking about the room one final time he finally spoke. "Thank you all for coming tonight. I know this is somewhat unexpected and sudden, but I felt a need for us all to be prepared for what may very well await us when we enter Calandra in the morning."

"A city that be preparing for war I would think," Helgar state flatly.

Ranse looked at the dwarf prince and frowned. "Yes," he continued, "that would be as most would suspect but I am afraid that in this case it is very unlikely. As most of you know, your calls for help while under threat in Haykon went all but unanswered and, as some of you have witnessed, the only response that did come was in the person of Prissley Maggest who was sent to merely negotiate. I don't need to remind any of you what it is we face with the enemy coming behind us, but many of you may not be aware of the enemy before us.

"For quite some time now the ease of life that has surrounded the city of Calandra has had an ill effect in poisoning many a mind into thinking that nothing can ever threaten our existence. Too many years of plenty have created a ruling class that no longer thinks much farther than what is being served at the next meal and who will be serving it to them. Prissley is a prime example of the type of people who rule over us in this dark hour."

"My prince," Braxton spoke, his voice tight, "I fear that you edge very near to words that might be considered treason by some."

Jace moved forward slightly but a quick look from Ranse sent him back. "I understand your concern, Colonel. You are duty bound by your covenant to the king and I respect that loyalty. It is not my intention to start a revolt against our king, or to even suggest such a course of action. My intentions are that we prepare ourselves for what will likely occur in court tomorrow."

"What be ye saying, lad?" Helgar harrumphed, never one for long speeches or much talk. He was a dwarf, and dwarfs acted; they didn't sit around talking pleasantries or bantering words that veiled their true intent. Dwarfs addressed the problem and then attacked it with full strength— generally with battle axes flying. "Let's have it out and quickly. What is it ye *are* trying to say?"

Ranse smiled slightly at Helgar's words. As a member of the court he'd learned the art of speaking using the dual meanings of words to relay information without seeming to relay information. He had been taught the subtleties of speech and how to decipher each little nuance of a person's meaning through not only words, but inflections, body posture and the indistinct pauses between words that could speak more clearly than the words themselves. But, like Helgar, he'd never stomached it much. He also preferred direct speech with clear intent.

"What he means to say," Jack volunteered, "is that we need to plan for the worst. We need to have a plan that we can use if the king's diplomacy fails."

"Thank you, Jack," Ranse said, "but I would change one thing that you said. Not 'if' the king's diplomacy fails, but when."

Braxton stood and Jace's hand dropped closer to the hilt of his sword unnoticed by all save Jne. "My apologies my lord prince," Myles said, "but this is certainly treasonous talk and I cannot be part of it. Nor do I desire to be privy to such arrangements as you would make. My honor will not allow it."

Jack looked up at his friend, the regret obvious in his eyes. Myles returned his look and then continued as if speaking only to Jack. "I am sworn to the king, and unless one can prove that Dagan is not the king and another should rule in his place, I must retreat from these proceedings."

There was a long moment of silence as if the very world had paused for breath. Colonel Braxton's expression was hard as he stared at Jack as if willing him to say something but his old friend just closed his eyes and bowed his head. Braxton's eyes looked like they meant to bore a hole through Jack's skull but his fierce gaze only lasted briefly before changing to one of deep sadness. Turning back to Ranse, he saluted quickly and then hastily left the tent. All eyes followed him as he went and then snapped back to the prince whose face had also dropped. Jace watched his liege as if waiting for some sign of action on his part, but Ranse merely sighed and shook his head.

"Are there any others who feel as the Colonel?" he asked, his voice almost too low to hear.

"We have seen the king's disregard for his people," Jack suddenly spoke. "If it be treason to speak it, then so be it. All who witnessed what happened at Haykon and have ever been to the capitol city know that Calandra will fall even quicker and with a greater slaughter. We are no longer discussing the intricacies of politics or the pros and cons of one man's rule compared to another. We are now in a situation where our very survival, and that of all of our people, is in question."

Teek brought up a hand to his eye, wiping at what may have been a tear. Of all at the council, he knew what Jack meant, his own people having been completely destroyed by a single dragon. He still fought the nightmares brought on by that terrible day.

"And what is this plan?" Jne said, addressing Ranse.

"As Jack said, that Calandra will fall is not a question," he started. "Though it puts on the façade of being a fortress city, it was not built for defense. And with the size of our enemy, it will fall quickly under their weight."

"Where else then, can we go?" Dor asked. "Are there no HuMan keeps strong enough to hold against such a horde?"

"Not in the close proximity but there may be one place that might hold against our enemy's numbers," Ranse paused as he briefly scanned the room, "Bedler's Keep."

"Yes," Jack immediately agreed, pulling at his beard. "But it is quite some distance. And what army will we have to hold it?"

"Where is this keep?" Thane asked.

Ranse turned around and grabbed a parchment that was leaning against the tent wall behind him and then spread it out on the ground for all to see. He pointed to their current position just outside of Calandra. "We are here." Then moving his finger to the southwest he rested it on Bedler's Keep. "And this is the keep."

"Aye," Rangor said, nodding his approval. "We passed it on our way here. It be a mighty place indeed."

"But," Bardolf added, "as friend Jack has said, what army will ye be havin' to protect it and how will ye be supplyin' it? There be near to no one there now."

"We'll have to gather as we go," Ranse replied.

Jack sighed loudly. "With your father's blessing and help we might be able to get the people there with an army and enough supplies to last, but we both know that he will not only refuse to help, but he will stop you from even trying. He's proved that much already."

"Well," Ranse shot, his temper suddenly flashing to the surface, "if you have a grander idea then I would have it!"

Jack bowed his head and Ranse almost instantly regained his composure, silently running through the mental exercises he'd been taught since a child to enable him to mask his feelings while in front of others. It wasn't that he was angry with Jack, or his questions. He was, like everyone in the tent, at the end of his strength. Too many would die, perhaps some or all now sitting around him, before it was all over.

"I have none," Jack admitted. "But the question remains, how will we gather enough strength?"

"Will any of the people in Calandra come with us?" Thane asked, his own doubts arising as to whether they could actually accomplish what was proposed. It was a long distance, and there were so few of them.

Ranse stared hard at the map stretched out before him. He hesitated and then sighed heavily. "Jack is right on that account. The soldiers at Calandra, like the good colonel, will give their lives for the king. They will not join with us."

"We possibly could sway Wess and his lot from Hell's End Station," Jack offered, trying to give some hope where there was none.

Ranse nodded his head. "They had reached the city before I left and were causing any number of problems."

Jack smiled slightly. "There was purpose in sending them away in the first place. That is a group that will willingly snub a finger to the king's loyalty."

"Be they many?" Rangor asked.

Jack and Ranse both shook their heads. "Not so many as needed," Ranse answered, "but it's a start. I think we could get the garrison stationed in Aleron, here to join us as well." he said moving his finger south of Calandra to a mark on the edge of the Underwoods forest. "They are a hardy lot accustomed to fighting the filth that attacks from the Underwoods almost on a daily basis."

Jack nodded his agreement. "You very well might, but it is out of our direct path to Bedler's Keep."

Ranse absently tapped his finger on the map. "We'll have to split up."

"What?" Thane, Jack, and Dor all asked in unison.

"Master Ranse," Thane continued, "we are struggling with uniting a force together as it is. Splitting it will only weaken us."

Ranse smiled. "We won't be splitting the army. Jace and I will go alone. You are right, Thane, we do need to keep to the little strength we have. Also, only one from the royal family can convince the soldiers there that they need to leave their posts. You just leave it to me."

Thane looked at Jack for a brief moment. "It's still not enough," Jack sighed.

"What of the Tjal," Dor shot, "and the dwarfs," he continued, turning his gaze toward Helgar. "Will you stand with us?"

"I was beginnin' to be feelin' unwelcome," Helgar huffed with a gleam in his eyes. "We dwarfs be always ready to join in a good fight when there be orcs wantin' to be killed."

"And what of the Tjal?" Dor asked, redirecting everyone's focus to Jne.

Jne's eyes narrowed dangerously as she met each gaze in defiance and open challenge. "The Tjal have been hated and reviled by you humans since the very beginning," she spat. "Your race is without honor and you further prove that by asking us to spill our blood in your defense when you have treated us as less than dogs."

Thane nervously glanced about the room seeking to read the reactions of those present but all kept their expressions extremely guarded. Though her words were probably true, and he could add some of his own, he also recognized that none of the races would survive unless they all worked together. He suddenly felt as if they were all pressed against the edge of a knife.

"Jne," he said tentatively, trying to calm her and the situation. But she ignored him and continued with her tirade.

"The Tjal do not answer to the calls of humans who think themselves masters of all. I will seek my people again when we reach Bedler's Keep and we will counsel together, but whether or not we decide to cross swords on the side of the humans is our choice. It will be because we decide it is best for the Tjal, not because the humans think to demand our presence."

The room was silent except for the perceptible exhale of relief that seemed to come from all corners. In her own way, Jne had agreed to call for the Tjal to help. Even though she may hate the fact that their coming would directly help and benefit those who had spit upon and ridiculed her people for centuries, she had also been witness to the foe they faced and knew enough of war to recognize the futility of the situation should any one group stand alone and not offer to help.

"It is decided, then," Ranse said breaking the silence. "We will approach the king when we reach Calandra and try to speak reason to his mind. If that should fail, then we will carry on with our current plan."

"And what of the people in Calandra?" Jack asked. "Are they to be left as fodder?"

Ranse shook his head. "We will use the good people of Haykon to quietly spread the word. Whether or not the king decides to give in to reason and quit Calandra matters not at this point. The people will be informed and have a choice. We will need to act immediately upon arrival to gather as many as will come. Our time is short, so as soon as we can supply ourselves we need to be heading away from the city toward Bedler's Keep."

"Once I find Wess, which shouldn't be very difficult," Jack said, "I can get him to help with his men."

"And we will be marchin' back to Thornen Dar within a couple of days to be rousin' the alarm there," Helgar added.

"I'll find Kat and Bren to get their help," Thane said. "We'll need all of the healers they can muster. I don't think they'll have any problems getting them to come."

Just then a loud EEEEERRRRROOOOOCCCCCC echoed in the distance and Teek jumped to his feet and raced for the tent door. "She is back!" he shouted as he bolted out the flap. Thane, Jne, Dor and Tam all rose quickly to follow after him.

"I guess this council is adjourned then," Ranse said with a shrug and a half smile as Thane and the others exited the tent after Teek.

The giant bird's arrival caused no small stir amongst the refugees as some screamed in terror thinking the dragons had returned. A large gap in the crowded area opened up as people tripped over one another to get out of the way, tipping cook pots and crashing into makeshift tents. But as the small Waseeni boy raced up to the bird and threw his arms out against her chest, the crowd seemed to calm slowly. Tchee cooed softly, rubbing the side of her head on top of Teek's as he nuzzled up against her. It was just like seeing a mother with one of her chicks.

After a brief pause, Thane stepped forward, followed by the others. "Teek," he said softly, calling the Waseeni boy away from his giant friend.

"Thane," he smiled. "She's back!"

He smiled back at the boy who was really only a year or two his junior. "Have you asked if she will take us to the Ardath?"

Teek frowned for a moment as if not understanding before he shrugged and looked back to Tchee. "I don't know how. I mean, she seems to know what I want and what I need but it's not as if I can directly communicate with her as I do with you."

Thane nodded his understanding. The others began exiting the tent and moving off into different directions as they went about other duties. Jack came over to stand by Thane. "Will you let me try?" Thane asked, slowly approaching Tchee. Teek nodded and Tchee just merely looked at him with her sharp blue eyes though seemingly unbothered at Thane's advance.

He locked onto those eyes drawing them in as he willed his inner self forward. Almost instantly he found he was staring down at his own body and he could feel Teek stroking the front of his chest.

"*Welcome, earth child.*" The words seemed to form in his mind though they weren't really words at all. It was communication on a different level than that shared by people. It felt like pure emotion yet he could understand the meaning behind it as if it had been spoken with words. It made normal communication between people seem barbaric and base.

"*How do you know me?*" he asked using his own emotions to convey his thoughts in return. He couldn't really say how he did it other than it just felt innate. It was as if they shared the same intellect and the thoughts just naturally formed and communicated.

"*All know the earth child. Your mere existence calls to us.*"

Though he wanted to follow along the current path and ask how he called to them and if there were no others who did the same, the urgency of the situation would not allow it. "*I need your help.*"

"*It is all for the earth child to ask.*"

"*I need you to take my friends and me to our home in the Ardath forest beyond the Shadow Mountains.*"

"*I know the place you seek, but I cannot do it. It would be unnatural.*"

Unnatural? What did she mean by that? How was her giving them a ride unnatural? "*Why is it so?*" he asked.

"*I have chosen. Once one is chosen, no other may take his place.*"

Though the words themselves did not answer his question directly, he knew she was speaking about Teek. She had chosen him and would therefore not carry another. *"But you carried me once before,"* he pressed.

"It was my duty. You were in danger."

"But we are all in danger now. My friends and I must get to the Ardath for the protection of all."

"I am sorry, earth child, but it is not possible in this situation for me to carry you."

Thane was getting desperate. He could feel it in his emotions as they began to strengthen and grow darker. *"Is there no way?"*

Tchee paused and he could see through her eyes as she regarded him as if searching for something hidden. *"There may be an alternative but I make no promise."*

He was about to respond but suddenly felt himself jolted back into his own mind and body as if he'd been pushed by some unknown force. His eyes refocused on Tchee just in time to see her spread her massive wings and leap into the air and then wing her way southward.

Chapter Four

Dor found Kat late in the afternoon the following day. He'd been watching with interest the growing mass that was Calandra as it continued to expand to his vision with every step he took. He had volunteered to find the healers and reveal their plan should the HuMan king continue to reject good council and judgment. They would need all the healers they could gather to leave with them should it come to that. Tam had wanted to come with him, but knowing Kat's aversion to her, he thought it best she stay with Thane and Jne.

Kat was just finishing up with wrapping a child's arm when he approached. He noticed her quick scan of his immediate area as if she were looking for someone else before her face broke into a warm smile. "Dor," she cried, "It warms me to see you—alone."

He blushed at the obvious show of affection. Though he knew that Kat was aware of his feelings for Tam, the healer still displayed her unabashed feelings for him whenever they were together. It made him uncomfortable which seemed to only please Kat that much more.

"And you, Kat," he answered without directly looking at her. "We need to talk. Where is Bren?"

Her demeanor changed instantly to one of ice. "And what is it that requires him more than just me?" she snorted.

He raised his hands in defense. "It is not like that, Kat, I would just rather say this once to you both then have to seek him out on my own and repeat myself."

She glared at him briefly as if trying to decide the validity of what he'd said and then just shrugged and pointed behind her. "He's this way. Come, I'll take you to him."

Pushing through the throng of refugees that slowly pressed on toward the capitol city in a slow moving mass, they veered slightly to the right, darting between the ragged and weary people of Haykon. Shuffling along in silence, for an extended length of time, Dor was becoming convinced that Kat was just leading him about. But finally he caught a glimpse of the tell-tale brown robes, worn by all healers, draped around a person bent over in the back of a cart that was being pulled along by a woman and her daughter. Bren jumped from the cart and walked toward the woman just as they approached.

"Your husband's fever has broken," he said to the woman whose face clearly showed her relief and gratitude. "He is still weak and will need to rest more but as soon as he is up you should feed him as much as you can get into his belly to give him back his strength."

Dor could see the tears of joy slipping down the woman's cheeks as she thanked the healer profusely. Bren just nodded and turned away addressing the approaching pair. "What news Master Dor?" he said, clearly pleased to see the young Chufa. "And what of Master Thane, will he keep our meeting tonight? I am anxious to know whether or not I have the gift of the wind."

Dor smiled slightly while his own face paled. He remembered all too well his experience with Bren when the healer tried to teach him to pull fire from a piece of wood. He'd never felt so wrong in his life. Though Bren had pushed again and again, insisting that he could learn the gifts from other Tane, Dor wanted nothing of it. In his mind it wasn't natural. Nor, as his reaction had proven, was it to his body.

"If Thane promises something," he finally said, "then you can count on it. My errand deals with something of greater import." Pulling the two healers aside where others would not hear, he quickly went over the previous day's meeting and the decision that had been reached.

"It is a long journey, Master Dor," Bren said. "But we see the wisdom in it. There are many healers in Calandra and many more that can be gathered quickly from other towns. We will assemble all we can and give what aid we are able."

Dor bowed his head slightly in acceptance. "Your help will prove of great worth I am certain."

Bren grinned. "Especially if Thane and I are successful tonight."

Dor didn't respond. Instead he merely turned into the crowd and forced his way against the current of people back toward Thane and Tam. He wanted nothing to do with the healer's plans to "expand" his gifts. As he went he thought he could hear Kat's voice rising above the noise accusing Bren of chasing him off. He sighed. Not for the last time he longed for the innocent days of the past that were filled with nothing more than mundane activities mixed with the occasional bout of mischief. Even PocMar and his gang seemed appealing at times. What he wouldn't give to have those times again.

*   *   *

Thane and Jne rode up just as the last rays of the sun were bathing the plains with their glow and casting a revealing light on the outer edges of the great city of Calandra. Jack turned in his saddle, waiting for his report as Thane eyed the massive sprawl of brick and wood buildings that surrounded the city proper.

"And what is the news, my friend," Jack had to ask, pulling Thane back to those who now crowded him to get his report. He'd been out again on the winds to check on the progress of Zadok's army but seeing Calandra up close after watching its form ever growing at their approach had captured his attention.

Finally looking down as Jack's voice broke his concentration, he blinked. "They have not moved. The sacrifice of those behind may not have been in vain, though they did not choose it. It would appear we have possibly a week to move as many as feasible out of the city on our race to Bedler's Keep."

Jack smiled though the pain he felt at those lost was still evident in his visage. "A tiny ray of light in the face of such hopelessness," he said softly.

"Not enough time though for us," Dor said. "Without the help of Teek's flying friend, it will take us that long, if not more just to reach the Ardath. We may be too late to help at all."

Teek looked at the three Chufa and then bowed his head slightly. "I am sorry, Dor," he said meekly, "but I have no control over what Tchee will or will not do. I would gladly go for you if you thought I could retrieve the thing you seek."

Dor shook his head. Tam smiled at the young Waseeni who, though just a couple of years her junior, seemed so innocent and naïve. "We do not blame you, Teek," she said, trying to reassure him. "Nor do we blame, Tchee. You both have been a tremendous asset to us all. I am sure that what she has in mind will help us greatly."

"Whether that is true or not," Thane added, "we cannot wait much longer for her return. We need to be on our way whether the king will side with us or not."

"We will have to camp on the outskirts of the city tonight," Jack said, "but come sunup tomorrow morning he will have to accept our presence in court and then we will know who our friends, and our enemies, really are."

"Aye," said Helgar, "but it be no matter to us what his mind may be," he said indicating himself and the dwarfs that marched with him. "We will be making our way west before the morning sun back to Thornen Dar. We have done what we could be doin' to git ye here and the purpose of our comin' be no longer of concern since the fight be on us already. Now we must be preparin' our people to lend an axe or two to the battle."

"Our thanks to you Master dwarf and to your people for what they have done to help us and what they will yet do," Jack voiced for all present. "We will bid you safe journey with our thanks and will look to your coming at Bedler's Keep."

Bardolf smiled, a bright twinkle in his eye. "Ye can be countin' on it."

"Aye," all the dwarfs present voiced their agreement.

"Ye will, of course, be watchin' after me friend here, Teek, now won't ya?" Bardolf asked, ruffling the Waseeni boy's hair.

"You can count on that, Master Bardolf," Jack said winking at Teek, "like he was my own."

Teek blushed at the attention. Part of him wanted to leave with the dwarfs. Bardolf and Helgar had become like fathers to him and he still wanted to work their mines to appease his people. But he knew that Jack and his friends still needed Tchee's help. He couldn't leave until she came back. And after all, he would have no trouble catching up to them should he want or need to later.

Domis smiled at the exchange. He and Teek had become fast friends, both being orphans, and both falling under Jack's care since they left Haykon. He was not anxious to see his friend gone so soon.

*   *   *

Thane hailed the two healers as they approached the campfire. With confirmation that Zadok's army was still a good distance away and since they were right at the doors of Calandra, it was decided that cook fires would be allowed. Knowing what had happened to Dor when he'd tried to learn the QenChe Tane Thane jokingly asked his friend if he'd like to light the fire. His reply was a launched rock that passed extremely close to Thane's ear. Thane chuckled at Dor's response. "I guess that means no."

Dor just harrumphed at Thane's apparent amusement at his expense but Tam placed a calming hand on his arm that brought a smile to his face and a poorly hid frown to Thane's. It was still difficult for him to see them together but he knew he'd have to do better at masking his pain if they were to maintain the friendship that was more important to him then practically anything else.

He jumped when he felt Jne's hand rest tenderly on his arm but she recoiled immediately in response to his reaction. He turned to look at her and thought he saw some of the same pain he felt but masked over by the burning look she gave him as she pointed out the two approaching healers. He held her gaze for a long moment, her eyes boring into his as if daring him to say something. Looking down at her slender hand, now balled into a tight fist, he felt his own hand lift and then tentatively reach for hers.

"Thane," Bren called, pulling him, and his hand, back.

Jne quickly rose and walked out into the camp disappearing into the darkness. He sighed as he watched her go and then reluctantly turned his attention to the healer. He wished Bren had not been so punctual in their meeting but he couldn't blame him too harshly. He too was anxious to see what exactly he could teach the healer regarding his Tane. If they were successful, it could mean a light of hope against their enemies.

"Welcome, Bren," he finally said, directing him and Kat to sit where Jne had just been.

"I am sorry, Master Thane," Bren said before sitting, "if I have offended Mistress Jne in anyway."

Thane laughed. "Oh no my friend, you would know if you'd offended her. That is you would come to know it as you left this life for the one beyond."

Bren swallowed hard and nodded, absently bringing his hand up to his neck. "I understand," he whispered.

"Do not fear, Bren. It is something between Jne and me that I am finding that I need to deal with more quickly than I had supposed. Now, let us get on with why you are here."

Bren smiled and nodded his assent. Kat seemed to be ignoring the whole exchange, her eyes boring into Tam's turned head as she whispered something to Dor. Dor suddenly nodded and then started to rise. "I think we will take our leave then and leave you two to your…" he paused as if searching for the right word, "…work."

Thane quickly stood. "Wait," he pleaded with his friend. "I know how you feel about this but I really wish you would stay. This may be extremely important to us all and I might need your help."

Dor's face paled noticeably. He had met death multiple times and had stared it straight in the face and almost dared it to take him but such situations held no discomfort for him like the time he'd tried to use the powers of another Tane. This was something that did not sit right with him.

He would gladly face ten wolgs without so much as a knife than try to use any Tane other than his own.

"I won't do it," he finally said. "I won't try to learn another Tane and there is nothing you can say that will get me to change my mind."

Thane smiled. "I don't ask that of you, and I never would. It seems most likely that you, or Tam for that matter, are unable to use any Tane other than your own. I can't explain it, but I believe it has something to do with the purity of your blood in that direction. You are MarGua and nothing else."

Dor nodded enthusiastically. "I agree, but what then could you need me for?"

"I need you to help test a theory I have and then figure out how to pass what we may learn onto others."

Bren chuckled. "There is nothing really to figure, Master Thane. We have been teaching the ways of multiple Tane for years. I know what it will take for you to teach me the TehChao Tane."

Thane shook his head. "I'm not going to teach you the TehChao tonight, Bren," he said. "I'm going to teach you how to draw out water."

While the others present drew in deep breaths of surprise, Bren laughed nervously while shaking his head. "Impossible. Drawing water is not a power of any of the Tane. How can I learn something that cannot be done?"

Thane gave him a hard, serious look. "But it can be done, my friend. And if I can teach you how it will be of great benefit to us all." Turning to Dor, he added, "As well as you my friend."

Dor looked surprised. "Me?"

Thane nodded. "Yes. Whereas you are unable, like Bren or Kat, to learn another Tane, pulling water from an object is a power reserved for the MarGua."

"But it's impossible," he started to say and then realized who he was talking to. Thane had pulled the water from the dragon using the MarGua Tane. It was that power that had saved the lives of hundreds and, very probably, his life as well. Could it really be done? That was a poor question since he knew that it could be—he'd seen it. But could he do it?

"Then I want to learn to ride the winds as you do," Tam suddenly said, the excitement obvious in her voice. All eyes jerked to rest upon her.

"Tam!" Dor said incredulously.

"What? If you can learn to pull water, then it is only fair that Thane teach me to ride the winds."

"But we don't know that he can teach me," Dor pressed, though he really didn't understand why he was arguing with her about it. He of all people knew that Tam was stubborn to the core and that when she set her mind to something it was easier to hold back the tide than deny her what she was after.

Her face suddenly became red. "That does not mean that I cannot learn," she spat and then turned to Thane. "Will you teach me?"

Thane smiled at Dor, suddenly feeling relief that it was his good friend she had chosen and not him. Bowing slightly to her, he said, "As always, I will teach you what I can, but not tonight. Tonight we concentrate on the power of the MarGua" His comment was not lost on her, her mind following back through the memories of the past when she'd blackmailed him to teach her how to use a bow and a knife. It was ironic that his teaching her was partly why they were all there together now instead of dried bones on a desolate mountain.

"Fine," she said, the smile returning to her face. "But soon."

Thane smiled and quickly reached for a leather water skin resting against the rock on which he'd been seated. He tossed it to Dor and then motioned for Bren to come closer. "Now, I don't know whether this can be done or not but the fact that Kat and Bren have been able to learn multiple Tane and the fact that I, though having all five, can perform what would seem extraordinary things with my Tane, leads me to believe that the powers I have are found in all the Tane but lie dormant or their skills forgotten. I believe we can change that. Dor, I want you to pull the water out of the bag."

His friend smiled. "That's easy." Opening the top of the skin he took a long drink before replacing the top and giving Thane a knowing look. "You were right, I can do it."

Thane shook his head but couldn't help smiling back. "Very good, Dor. Now, since you seemed to have mastered the top, let's move onto something more challenging. Place your hand on the side of the bag."

Dor complied, his smile still evident, though he doubted Thane's reasoning. Thane was special. He had a special gift. There were no stories told of others manifesting his power other than the one the Chufa called traitor, who they now understood to be anything but. Still, there was something inside him that hoped his friend was right and that he could do more with his gift that would help in the war. Sensing poison and holding ones breath under water for extended periods was all well and good but thus far, they really hadn't made much of a contribution to fighting the enemy.

Bren edged closer, intent on everything that Thane said while keenly watching what Dor did.

"Now," Thane continued, "clear your mind of everything and

concentrate solely on the water in the bag. Sense its presence. Make contact with it. Let it touch your senses and then call it to you. Pull it from the bag."

While the others watched, almost leaning forward with anticipation, Dor closed his eyes and let out a big breath. Placing his hand on the bag he tried to make contact with the liquid inside. He could smell it. He could sense its make-up and relative purity. That it was safe to drink was certain, but he knew that he needed more, a closer connection, if he were to do as Thane had asked. He needed to make contact, but how? He concentrated harder, willing the water to make itself known, to answer his call and break free from its prison.

He suddenly felt the anxiety of those watching him like a great weight upon his mind as if demanding he succeed. Drawing on that pressure he tried to focus it into his hand willing the water to connect with him, willing himself to connect with it and pull it from the bag.

Long minutes passed and Dor's body began to shake slightly. *Come to me*, he willed. *Answer my call and break free.* Over and over again he chanted the words in his mind like a mantra as he tried to make a connection but all he felt was his own energy beginning to wane as if the water were pulling him in instead of him pulling it out. Doubt began strangling his will as time continued to slip along and the reality of failure crept into his mind, gaining strength with each passing moment. It was no use. He was not like Thane. He did not have command of the elements as his friend did. He would fail. He had failed.

Pulling his hand from the bag, he opened his eyes and shook his head. "It's no use," he said, wiping what must have been sweat from his hand. "I do not have the power you possess my friend."

Thane grinned. "Why are you wiping your hand off then?" he asked, motioning to the hand that had been on the bag.

Dor sighed. "It's just sweat."

"Really?" Thane asked, obviously not convinced. "I think it is more than that. Did you make contact with the water? Could you feel it in the bag? Could you sense its makeup? Its elements?"

Dor nodded slowly. "Of course. It's water. It's the thing with which I feel most comfortable."

"Exactly!" Thane replied, his enthusiasm obvious. "I think you made contact, and what you find on your hand, that you now wipe off, is water from the bag. I think you were more successful than you realize."

Dor stopped and stared at his hand. Some moisture still remained on the inside of his fingers but he could not tell whether it was really water or just sweat. What if Thane was right and he really had connected? But if he, in fact, had, he was unaware of it. How would that be helpful? He couldn't very well climb onto the back of a dragon and hope for the best without knowing what true contact was or felt like. "But I didn't feel anything. If there was contact and I did indeed pull some water out, I don't know how it was done. Nothing felt different or out of the ordinary."

Thane's eyebrows curled in thought. "That may be so. I did feel a definite connection when I pulled that water from the dragon. So much so, in fact, that I could more easily do it again should the need arise, now that I understand what to reach for."

Dor nodded his agreement. "Right, so where does that leave me and my feeble attempt?"

Thane smiled. "I would say that leaves you with a lot more practice ahead of you. Practice until you feel the connection and can call all of the water from the bag instead of a few drops only."

Dor wanted to protest, but the fact that Thane still held to the belief that he'd actually succeeded, that the moisture on his hand was actually water and not just sweat, gave him a sudden boost of confidence. Maybe he was right. Maybe, with more practice, he could make the connection and recognize it for what it was. The idea of complete success sent a thrill through him. Such a boost in the powers of his Tane would indeed make him useful. If Thane was right and he could do it, it would change the whole Chufa race and even possibly the war. Though he knew that that was a stretch, the glory of it still filled him with the desire to continue and try.

Reaching for the bag, he once again closed his eyes, this time using some of the concentration exercises DaxSagn had taught them when first learning to fire a bow. Again he reached for the water, willing his hand to connect with the liquid waiting just on the other side of the thin leather.

Turning to Bren, Thane open his mouth to give the healer his own instructions but found he had already retrieved his own water bag and was in the process of trying to pull water from it. Thane placed a hand on his shoulder. "I think it best we start smaller with you," he said. "First you must learn about the Tane itself and see if you have any skill with it."

Kat moved forward. "I would learn too," she stated flatly as if daring anyone to deny her. Were all women this stubborn?

Thane just nodded his assent. "Of course. The more that can learn, the better it will be for all of us. In fact, once either or both of you acquire the skills, I would expect you to teach it to all the healers you can."

Both quickly nodded in agreement.

"Now," he continued, "the MarGua Tane."

Into the night they discussed what it meant to be MarGua and the powers that came with it while Dor continued to fight the water skin with a tenacity that surprised them all. He was determined to succeed. No matter that he did not progress any further than his first attempt, he continued to feel after the water and struggled to bring it under his will. By the time Bren and Kat left the camp for their own, both could smell moisture on the wind and accurately choose between two liquids which was safe to drink. Thane was amazed at their ability to pick up the subtleties that were the MarGua so quickly. At this rate, he wondered if both would not be pulling water from skins before Dor could, though he hoped not. Such a defeat might dishearten Dor enough to convince him to stop trying.

Chapter Five

Jack exited his tent leaving Teek and Domis still curled up on the floor fast asleep. Since he had taken them in, neither had spent much time away from him and both insisted, though at his objection, that they should work as his servants to pay for his kindness and help. So far that consisted of them running errands on his behalf. Once they tried to prepare him a meal but he put a quick stop to that. Not even Erl would have sniffed at the concoction they'd put together.

Thinking of his long absent wolg friend, he scanned the horizon in every direction to see if he couldn't catch the slightest glimpse of movement but all was still. He didn't worry about Erl's safety, knowing his large friend was safer than any of the rest of them, but he did miss having him around.

Picking his way through the encampment he found Thane and Jne at the head of the refugee camp taking in the grand city in the pre-dawn light. The people from Haykon would have to stay where they were currently camped until the king was made aware of their presence and accommodations secured for them. Movement to his right revealed the approach of Colonel Braxton closely followed by Prince Ranse and his bodyguard Jace. Jack was surprised to find the prince still in his traveling garb having thought he would be in full royal regalia for a meeting with his father but apparently he still felt it necessary to keep his identity shielded.

Dor and Tam quickly materialized from his left and all converged on the spot where Thane and Jne stood. Dor looked drained. He'd tried a good part of the night to pull the water from the bag but never got any further than a wet hand. It was progress though and he was determined to make the connection. He knew Bren and Kat had been more successful in what they were learning but he also knew that calling water through a sold object was many grades higher than smelling water on the wind. Most non ArVen could do that when a storm was close enough.

Tam had not stayed very long, deciding instead to get what sleep most of the others had forgone. Thane had promised he would teach her later and she didn't doubt that. She also knew that though another set of eyes in the air might be helpful, Thane was more concerned about fighting right now and how best to use their gifts to their advantage. If he could get them to pull water from their foes, they would have one more tool to help tip the overwhelming advantage Zadok had.

All remained silent, exchanging mere nods of greeting as they quickly fell in line behind Ranse and Jace who would lead the way to the palace and the king's court. A sudden call shattered the silence and all heads turned to see Teek and Domis running up behind them calling out for them to wait. Everyone turned questioning looks to Jack who glared back. "What?" he snarled. "I didn't invite them."

"Master Jack," Domis called, "You didn't wake us."

"For good reason," he snapped. "What do you both think you are doing out here making such a ruckus? Do you mean to wake the whole camp?"

The two boys looked at each other somewhat shocked and then put their hands to their mouths as they looked around at the people behind them, some currently stirring in their blankets. "Sorry," They whispered in unison.

"We thought you were leaving without us," Domis added.

"I was," Jack retorted. "You were not invited."

"But Master Jack," Domis continued, "isn't it necessary for one representing Teek's people to be present? After all, this is a war that affects us all."

Jack glared at the Waseeni boy but then quickly softened his features. In his frustration he wanted to point out that Teek was no longer the representative of a people but merely himself but knew such a blow would be worse than a sword stroke to the young lad. "Possibly," he finally harrumphed, "but that does not explain your presence."

Domis looked surprised that Jack had even asked him to justify himself at being there. "Why Master Jack," he said, the incredulity obvious in his voice, "one of your station should not be without a servant when addressing the king. It would not look proper."

"My station?" he roared, causing grunts from many in the near proximity who were still trying to get some sleep before the sun rose.

Oblivious now to the volume of his own voice, he was preparing to unleash a barrage on the young boy when the prince appeared at his elbow and whispered, "Is there a problem, Jack?"

He looked at the prince and then back at the two boys who were giving him their most innocent smiles. He sighed heavily. "No, my Lord," he seethed. "We are ready."

Ranse smiled, knowing all too well the dilemma Jack faced. "Then let us be on our way," the prince said lightly.

Jack glared at Domis and Teek and held up a finger of warning. They knew they had gotten away with something enormous but they also knew not to press their luck any further. They would be as quiet as mice in a cheese shop if they knew what was good for them, and they did.

Calandra, though touted as the grandest city, was something of a disappointment as they first approached. Though the city proper was all that it claimed, and certainly more to those, like Thane, who hailed from simple circumstances, the outreaches of the city had grown into a type of slum area where the poorest, and possibly the roughest sort resided. The homes, if they could be called such, were mere shacks and hollows held up with whatever could be scavenged. And because they did not approach the city from an actual road, they had to pick their way through those dwellings like walking through a giant maze. More than once, Ranse had to turn them around and retrace their steps when they came to a abode that had been placed right in their path.

They didn't run into many people as most were still in their hovels escaping the harsh realities of their world in the blessed dreams of the night. On the occasion a person did appear, most merely turned about and disappeared again into their shelter or scurried away as if in fear.

They stayed as far from the center of the path as possible as that seemed the designated spot for refuse and human waste. Steam drifted into the air from where the debris had been cast creating a pungent fog that ran through the streets like a vaporous wraith ready to catch the unwary. The smell, at times was almost too much to bear as they moved along as fast as they were able. No one spoke as each contemplated what was likely to happen to these people outside the walls of the city. Thane realized with heavy heart that the people of Haykon, who they had been able to save and bring this far, would likely be forced to remain where they were and expected carve out what life they could with the other poor who lived like outcasts from the city proper. He tried not to think about what that meant when Zadok's army reached the area.

Finally reaching the north road, their pace quickened as they approached the city's northern gate. The city wall was made from rough rock that at its greatest height was possibly twice as tall as Thane and stretched out to either side for as far as he could see. An archway supported a double gate made of plank wood that would probably only cause a slight pause to an invading army. He could hear Jne's snort of derision as they neared. It didn't take a great general to realize that this was not a fortress.

Two guards were posted at the open gates but neither said a word as the group approached and then passed silently into the city. The mud of the previous road was now replaced by rough cobblestones that had been haphazardly placed into the dirt and packed down over time to create a rough surface that was only slightly better than the dirt road. The buildings were also an improvement, however slight, from those that were left outside. Rough stone structures marked, like the road, a step up in class and income from those forced to live outside the city gates.

Though the street remained straight, a web of pathways and small avenues fingered out on either side into a maze of stone structures that mimicked the disorder of the outside city in its seeming chaotic creation. Most of the buildings were one story in size although an occasional anomaly existed in a second story as if to proclaim its inhabitants were that much above the rest of the people with whom they were forced to share space.

A few people came in and out of the buildings, beginning what would be another backbreaking day as they struggled to feed themselves and their families. No one talked to the group as they passed, in fact, most scampered away at their approach like beaten dogs accustomed to the sting of the master's boot. Those they did see were dressed similar to that of their buildings; rough clothes made from canvas that were put together to be as hardy as possible with obvious signs of constant repair. The clothing lacked any color other than gray and dirty gray and seemed just sufficient to protect the wearer from the outside elements.

An occasional doorstep displayed the body of a sunken figure sleeping off whatever was the drink of choice the night before. The companions watched as one such figure was rudely awakened when the door he was propped against opened up, dropping his head to the ground with a thud eliciting a slight moan from the drunkard's lips. But it was the bucket of water that followed that roused the man to sputters and curses as he sluggishly extracted himself from the doorstep while swinging wildly for anyone close enough to feel his wrath.

Jack stopped and watched the man with the bucket easily duck away from a wild punch before placing his boot on the vagrant's rear and pushing him out into the street where he landed in a clump at Jack's feet.

"Wess?" The man moaned slightly and then kicked out a foot trying to connect with Jack's leg. Jack caught the foot easily with his own boot and then kicked back hitting the man's thigh and educing from him another groan. Marching over to the shop keeper, he asked to borrow the man's bucket and then filled it in a nearby barrel before dumping it on the pitiful creature still sprawled out in the road. The man gasped and, with effort, pushed himself into a sitting position as he tried to open his eyes and focus on his attacker.

"Show yerself so I can kill ya'," the man slurred, still trying to force his vision to clear enough to distinguish between the blurry shapes that seemed to dance about his head taunting him.

"Wess, you old flea bag, it's Jack." Jack stood over him now, still keeping clear of any fists that might suddenly lash out but stooped down so the man could get a good look at his face.

"Jack?" The man sounded confused. "Did I cheat you in cards?"

Jack laughed. "As a matter of fact, yes you did."

The man smiled. "Then you must be a friend," he slurred, gripping the cobblestones in an effort to steady himself.

Jack smiled but returned to the water barrel before dumping the bucket on the man's head again.

"All right, all right," the man said, batting at something only he could see.

Jack squatted down beside him again, this time grabbing the man's shoulder and shaking him gently. "Wess, what has happened to you?"

Wess opened his eyes slightly and stared at him for a long moment. "Jack?"

Jack gave an impatient sigh. "Yes, you dolt, it's Jack. What are you doing down here sleeping in a doorway?"

Wess tried to spit in disgust but only managed to drop it on his chin. "That rat king, that's what I'm doing down here. Takes away my post and then releases every last one of us to fend for ourselves."

"The whole company?" Jack asked, the shock obvious in his voice. "But why?"

Wess started to shake his head but quickly stopped, realizing it threatened his ability to keep himself upright. "Don't know. Somethin' 'bout not needed us anymore now that the trolls were gone."

Jack's face was quite red by now, using all of his strength to hold back the anger that boiled within him.

Wess suddenly laughed. "I don't think the king realized what he was doing when he called all of us back from the frontiers and then let the company loose on the city. Crime rate has jumped considerably, I bet."

Jack grabbed Wess by the shirt and pulled him close. The stench of ale on him was suffocating but Jack didn't seem to notice. "Listen to me, Wess, and listen carefully. Do you think you could find your men?"

"What for?" Wess protested. "I say that Calandra deserves what it gets by them."

"I agree," he growled, "but can you find them?"

Wess shrugged, his head bobbing slightly from side to side. "I guess, that is, at least those that haven't found their way to the dungeon."

"Good," Jack said, pulling Wess to his feet and holding him steady. "Now listen to me, and listen straight. You have to remember what I am telling you and do exactly what I say."

"What's this all about?" Wess slurred, the annoyance at being bothered growing stronger in his tone.

"Just shut up and listen," he said, shaking him. "You need to gather all the men you can from your company and get out of Calandra as quickly as possible. Move them southwest toward Bedler's Keep and we'll catch up to you there when we can."

Wess seemed to sober some as he stared at Jack in obvious confusion. "Bedler's Keep, why in Seless' name for?"

"You know those trolls the king is convinced have gone for good?"

Wess nodded his head slowly.

"Well, they're about to come knocking on Calandra's gate with a host larger than you or I could ever have imagined existed. Haykon has already fallen to them and now they march on us here."

Wess' eyes opened wide despite the pain it caused. "Are you certain?"

Jack spat. "Barely got out of Haykon alive myself as they overran the city. They're coming, and Calandra will fall within hours."

Wess staggered back from his grip and then fought to maintain his balance. Lifting his hand he saluted, clearly struggling to keep from collapsing back into the street. "I'll gather everyone that I can, Jack, I promise."

"Just do it quickly. Try not to spread alarm but get as many people as you can to start leaving the city. We're on our way now to see if we can't convince the king to get everyone out, but our hope is faint that he'll listen"

"And what of my men in the dungeons?"

"We'll take care of that," Ranse said, eliciting a strange look from Wess who clearly had no idea in whose presence he found himself.

"Don't fail me on this, Wess," Jack said. "Get yourself something to eat and then get your men, and anyone else who'll listen to reason, and get out."

Wess nodded, staggering as he did so but able to keep from completely falling over.

Jack glared at him for one last moment and then turned and started walking up the street, followed by the others. No one spoke but Thane couldn't help but notice the smile playing across Jne's lips. He wanted to ask her what she found so amusing but decided it best to just keep his mouth shut and follow the others in silence.

"We should have just left him here to his fate," Dor hissed, just loud enough for Tam and Thane's ears. Tam looked at him quizzically, the hatred glaring and hot in his eyes.

"What is the matter?" she asked him, but he just shook her off, not offering a reply, and pressed ahead catching up to Jack and whispering something into the old man's ear.

Tam stopped for a moment and stared after him in confusion before picking up her pace to catch Thane and Jne. "What is wrong with him?" she huffed at Thane.

Thane sighed, wondering how much he should reveal about Dor's capture by the HuMans. It was not something he wanted to burden her with, especially since they were right in the middle of the HuMan's seat of power.

"After he had escaped from the trolls, Dor was captured by the HuMans and held in a cell. He would have been brought here when Wess and his men left Hell's End Station, but we were able to get him free."

Tam was shocked. She'd never known that Thane and Dor had found one another before, always figuring that they had all been reunited at the same time when Thane found her and saved her life. She opened her mouth as if to say something else but then shut it, apparently thinking better of it.

They continued up the road in silence until all caught sight of another wall and gate. This wall was made of white brick and was approximately the same height as the outer rock wall. True to the other wall, this one's thickness was no more than two feet and again was not designed to repel an attack. The gate seemed a bit sturdier though still made of wood planks and left open on rusty hinges that appeared to never have been used to close the gate. Again, two guards were posted but as before neither challenged the visitors or stopped them to ask their business.

As before, as they passed through the gates, the buildings changed as did the road. The road they now walked on was of polished cobblestone that seemed to have purpose in how and where it was placed creating a smoother and easier surface to walk upon. A trough had been carved out in the center allowing a free flow of waste that was directed in its path rather than with the previous two areas where it seemed to run wherever the road took it. The buildings were also made of brick and were all two stories in height. Small shops seemed the norm for the first story while strings of line running over their heads, most covered in laundry, revealed the upstairs as living quarters. As the day was growing older, more people were found on the streets, running about their business, which for most meant opening their shops and preparing for the work day.

Though not as disorderly as the previous district, there were still a myriad of side streets and alleyways that broke off from the main road and spindled through the rest of the environs. They did pass one other main road that crossed their path going to the left and right and seemed to follow the curve of the city in a great circle.

The inhabitants still wore clothing that was obviously meant for hard work, but a few more colors and different fabrics were seen among the populace that crossed the streets and moved in and out of the buildings. Some even wore shoes, though most appeared too big or well worn. Thane was starting to get an idea as to how the city worked and what he could expect as they drew closer to the center where he was certain they would find the king.

As he'd thought, another wall and gate suddenly appeared in the distance. The wall was of cut stone blocks that were fit together and mortared in precision. This time the height was half as tall as the previous wall and was at least four feet thick. One of the thick beamed, iron studded gates was closed forcing any who entered to pass through one side where four guards carefully scrutinized any who approached. This time they were not allowed to pass freely as before.

A guard dressed plainly in snug leather pants and a cotton tunic with a hammer emblazoned on the front, held up a gloved hand and called the group to halt. The other three gathered behind him, their hands resting on the hilts of their swords that hung sheathed at their waists.

"What is your business?" the guard called out with a self important sneer.

Jne's eyes narrowed slightly but a smile played across her lips and Thane knew she had already picked apart every weakness each of the soldiers had and how she could exploit them to her advantage. Had it been just the two of them, he didn't doubt that all four would be dead by now with Jne holding two of the swords while he held the other's she'd have passed to him.

Advisedly, Ranse made sure that no one brought any weapons with them knowing that to do so would only slow their presently hampered progress even more. Even Jace was without his sword though Thane had a very strong feeling that multiple weapons could still be found upon his person expertly hidden and waiting to be called forth at his command.

Ranse didn't say a word but merely pulled a medallion out from under his shirt and flashed it to the guard who immediately placed a hand to his heart and then moved aside as he and the other guards bowed. Thane tried to get a glimpse at what was on the medallion but was blocked by Jack. He did notice Teek's eyes suddenly grow larger as he grasped at something hidden under his own shirt.

The street, like the wall, changed as they passed under the archway and was now made of large cut stones that had been placed just so to create a smooth surface worthy of any carriage providing a bump-free ride through the city. Noticeably missing was the trough down the middle of the lane that carried the day's waste. Instead, Thane noticed small grates on either side of the street that spoke of an underground sewage system.

The buildings were made from a similar cut stone as that of the wall and the street and rose up to three, and sometimes four, stories high. The fronts were also crisscrossed with wood planks mortared into the stone and each story stuck further into the street covering the road in shade. As in the previous section, the lower levels were for business while the stories above held more merchandise and housing. Pubs and inns were found quite frequently and a larger mixture of people and classes seemed to mingle together along the road. It was obvious who was of the higher class as they were carted around in coaches or chairs on wheels that were pulled about by servants. The streets were laid out in a more uniform fashion here, crisscrossed with large avenues at many intersections leading to other parts of the city in such a standardized fashion as to make it appear rather easy to find ones way around with the proper guide or directions.

Though it was still early, the bustle on the streets had increased significantly. It was obvious that this was where the upper end shops and merchants were and that those from the higher class condescended to do their business with them. Although many sent servants to do their dealing there were still a good number of people, women especially, who jaunted about with their entourage of helpers picking through shops and flaunting their wealth. The merchants wore innumerable types of clothing to match the seeming countless goods they hocked on the streets or in their storefronts. Women with too much face paint, large satin dresses that flared out at the bottom and large wigs of all sorts of sizes, shapes, and colors bustled about like peacocks trying to outdo one another in their snooty gaudiness.

The group didn't have much difficulty pressing through the crowd as most looked down their noses at them like so much trash blowing through their streets. The women pulled scented handkerchiefs from pockets placing them with a look of disgust to their nostrils as the companions passed by. Jne's smile only broadened finding the whole scene pathetically humorous. It quickly became obvious to Thane that these people had never seen a Tjal-Dihn before and would not recognize one if they were skewered by one's sword. There was not the same respect, awe, or fear that typically followed the Tjal whenever encountered. To the self important upper class of Calandra, they were all just mere bugs—filthy distractions that were to be quickly shooed away. If they only knew what awaited them. No amount of perfume sprayed on a cloth would extinguish the awful scent that would soon be at their gates.

Thane almost laughed at the looks on Teek's and Domis' faces. Domis had lived in Haykon and was no stranger to city life but nothing in his experiences could compare to this. His familiarity was more akin to that part of the city they had just recently left. And Teek, well this was all new to him. Thane suddenly realized that this was all very new to him as well, but he was familiar with the type of people that flocked about. He had seen the same in his own village. Those who thought themselves above everyone else who tried, in his case, to kill that which may be different or threaten what they felt their station should be. It was a sad comedy indeed.

He sighed audibly when they finally reached another wall and gate. This time the wall was built of smooth mortar covering six feet thick large cut stone blocks with a cap of polished wood running along the very top. The height was not as grand as the previous wall but was reduced to approximately twice Thane's height. He reasoned that the upper class that most likely lived behind these walls were not so afraid that the merchants, the people with whom they were so free with their money, were apt to attempt to break in. The two gates, both extremely ornate and polished but lacking any real strength, were both closed with two guards posted in small cylindrical rooms on either side. They were dressed similarly to the previous guards but with more pomp and ornamentation hanging from their helmets and shoulders. The thought of peacocks returned again to Thane's mind as he took in the ridiculous looking plumes jutting from their head pieces.

As the group approached they were stopped but this time the guards had spears leveled as if they faced a real threat. "And what, may I ask," the first guard spat, "are the likes of you doing in the Merchant's Quarter?"

Ranse stepped forward once again and without so much as a single word revealed the medallion he wore to the same end as that of the previous gate. In quick order the group was ushered through the entry but this time a guard of four, who were stationed just inside the walls, was dispatched to escort them. Thane couldn't be sure whether it was really for their benefit or to satisfy the inhabitants.

As with the walls and streets of the previous areas, the street changed to a smooth, hard surface that looked to have been poured, leveled and then cured leaving it completely smooth and white. The street also opened up to twice its original size.

Thane couldn't keep back the gasp that escaped his lips at the buildings and foliage that greeted them. The buildings were not pressed together as with the other areas but were set far apart with spacious lawns, gardens, flowers of every sort and pools with intricate fountain displays. Though one who preferred the natural beauties found in nature, what greeted him here was nothing less then breathtaking. The buildings were all exquisitely white with rounded blue and green tops that capped most of the attached structures. The walls were smooth, like the street, and each house was grander than the next as they made their way up the road. He figured that even in the upper class there must be class distinctions that grew the closer one lived to the king's quarters. Trees lent their shade along the wide street with benches scattered about to rest oneself, though it appeared that only the servants walked. There were very few people out, and those who were, rested lazily in a servant pulled chair or carriage. It was then that Thane noticed the complete lack of horses. Any who rode in a vehicle were pulled by servants.

Though decadent to the extreme, he had to admit that the architecture and landscaping was exquisite in its design and presentation. Something so magnificent just waiting to be burned and pillaged by an army of hatred and malice. He suddenly felt extremely sad and tired. He didn't approve of how these people lived while so many suffered in squalor just three gates beyond, but he still felt sad that it would all be destroyed in as few as seven days.

To his surprise, it took very little time to reach the final wall and gate. Most of Calandra's population lived just outside and within the first two walls. Its wealthy class was extremely small in comparison. This time the wall was quite large reaching well above thirty feet and made from the purest marble. The seams in the blocks were so tight as to make them almost completely invisible. The two gates were quite large but were not solid in their design rendering the walls completely useless in their protection. These gates, though made of iron, were merely ornate bars of metal twisted every which way in all sorts of patterns while allowing any to see through to the other side. As a defensive position it was useless. They were a mere mockery of status to those on the outside who, though able see through to the other side, would not be allowed to enter—unless by a tiny bit of force.

Only one guard patrolled the gates keeping himself just inside. He was dressed, if at all possible, even more elaborately than their escort. He wore a large metal helmet with a horsetail plume that draped down his back over a fine red silk cloak. His tunic was white satin with a blue sash across his midsection while his pants were a deep azure and appeared to be velvet and were tucked neatly into knee high black leather boots. The sword he wore at his waist was covered in gold ornaments about the hilt and then laced through the sheath that appeared to be polished ivory. His hair was a dark brown growing long out the back and matched the color of a long mustache that grew almost straight out to either side.

This time Thane could hear Jne's laugh of disgust at one so obviously a mere showpiece without the slightest skill with which to back himself. The honor guard moved forward announcing the presence of the prince. The king's guardsman did not move to open the gate though but merely sneered at the roughly dressed group with a turned up nose and an expression that clearly showed his disgust.

"I will need more proof than your word," he spat, but whether addressing the other guard or the prince himself, Thane could not tell.

Ranse stepped forward without the slightest show of annoyance and for the final time produced the medallion chained around his neck. The guard called for it through the gate forcing the prince to press himself against the bars as the guard grabbed it for his personal examination. After long moments of turning it first in one direction and then another, the guard finally let it drop allowing the prince to resume his previous stance. Pausing, he eyed the prince up and down again before finally moving to unlock the gate and allow them to enter. Though he was now in the presence of one of the royal family he didn't show any sort of courtesy or solute as they passed through the gate.

"I will call an escort for you," he said, not even attempting to mask his annoyance at being put out to do so.

"That will not be necessary," was all Ranse said while motioning the group forward, his medallion left to hang prominently against the front of his tunic. Thane now understood what it truly meant to be the youngest of three royal brothers and the last to have claim to the throne. But Ranse didn't seem bothered by it. In fact, Thane could almost sense a feeling of relief in the prince at having so much freedom from such ridiculous ceremony and pomp.

True to the previous sections of the city, the road changed with the wall to one of great marble slabs perfectly placed to give the allusion of one single piece of stone as the road ran straight on to Calandra's castle. The area surrounding the road was wooded but not like the thick forests that Thane was used to. These trees seemed too uniform in their location as if planted there with purpose. Great lawns, shrubs and flowers, small streams and grand fountains were visible from all around as they proceeded up the road. Large statues of white marble lined either side of the street and continued along the avenue. On closer inspection it became obvious that they were all carvings of the same person in different poses or actions. Thane figured they must be likenesses of the present king. Jne merely harrumphed in derision.

It was all excessive to a fault yet extremely beautiful at the same time. Occasionally, Jack let out a grunt as if in disgust reminding Thane why they were there and what was being sacrificed so that the king could live in such opulence. It was a stark contrast to the outskirts of the city and would, in a mere week be left in ruins.

As they continued toward the castle Thane caught site of a large mansion tucked away in the trees to his right and then another a little further up on the left. "Who are those for?" Domis asked.

Ranse didn't turn around but answered with a clear tint of disdain in his voice. "My brothers and I do not live in the castle proper but have estates of our own where we reside."

"Is one of those yours?" Teek asked.

Ranse shook his head but didn't offer up anymore information so the subject was not forced.

It was then that the trees opened up for a full view of the main castle. It was enormous, like six of the mansions they'd just seen connected together with a myriad of towers jutting up from all different locations. Since they were approaching from the side, the full grandeur of the front was not visible but what they were able to see was beyond anything any, save Jack, and obviously Ranse and Jace, would have ever imagined. Walkways split off in every direction leading to more fountains and pools and private gardens with another splattering of statues proudly displayed on large stone blocks.

The castle itself had a white exterior with a light blue-gray roof and was six stories tall except for the towers, some rising up to at least twice that height. Some of the towers contained bridges or walkways to connect them with outside causeways and balconies that led to rooftop gardens and tucked away private areas. The whole structure suddenly gave Thane the feeling that Calandra's king was trapped in a giant maze.

Ranse led the group up a small flight of stairs to one of the side doors. Though not a main entrance the door was made of thick wood beams belted with iron and was tucked away in a dome shaped alcove where a guard stood out of plain view. The guard looked to move to intercept them but upon seeing Ranse's medallion merely stood at his post as if they were not even there. Ranse reached for the large ornate handle. Thane thought for sure he would need assistance pulling open the door but was surprised when it swung out with little effort at all.

"How will we find that king in such a large place?" Dor asked as they entered Calandra's castle.

Pausing only briefly, Ranse spoke over his shoulder answering, "The king already knows we are here and will wait for us in the throne room. That is where he meets all who come for an audience. It is where he feels most powerful and in control. Do not expect a warm welcome."

The prince led them on, past a small foyer and into a maze of rooms and hallways of differing sizes and lengths that confused even Jne as to which direction they were taking at any given time. Only Jack and Thane, and, of course, Ranse and Jace seemed unaffected by the seeming web-like route in which the prince led them as he pressed forward toward the throne room and their ultimate goal. Through the power of the TehChao Tane, Thane would be able to retrace their steps exactly if they needed to retreat and exit the massive palace, but Jack's seeming comfort with their location was a mystery. It might have been the grim and determined look that had clouded his face since seeing Wess in the city that masked the true wonder that everyone else seemed to display. But for one whose life had been relegated to the open ranges of the Shadow Mountains, his demeanor seemed uncharacteristically comfortable in the confines of Calandra's seat of power.

Every room, every hallway was spacious and grand to an extreme. The ceilings reached up to an extended height almost outreaching the light given off by the occasional window or the myriad of candles lined along the walls. The furnishings were extravagant down to the tiniest latch that appeared gilded in the purest gold. Plush rugs and the finest crafted furnishings filled in the spaces down the long hallways and through the many different rooms through which they passed. At first glance, the chairs might have been thought a resting place for anyone required to traverse the great expanse through the castle, but on closer examination it was clear that the furniture was not meant for comfort, or even use, but as a sign of wealth and power—of opulence and excess.

No one barred their way as they continued their trek deep into the bowels of the palace. Thane thought he caught a glimpse of a servant girl quickly ducking through a door as they approached but saw no sign of her when they passed the room into which he thought he saw her escape. It appeared as if they were completely alone to the point that it became eerie.

Prince Ranse suddenly stopped at a small, nondescript door just to the left of the hall down which they had been striding tucked back in a small alcove that would have been easily overlooked by any not searching for it. Pausing, he looked at the companions that gathered about him expectantly.

"As I said before, do not expect a warm greeting. To the king, it is likely we are viewed as the enemy in all of this, and certainly, any friend of mine is immediately mistrusted. We will do our best to talk reason to him, but I fear he will not hear us."

No one offered a response. Jack looked like steal incarnate, his jaw locked, his teeth grinding audibly as he tried, without success, to control his anger and his breathing. Teek and Domis stood with wide eyes, anxious and nervous at the same moment realizing they were about to be in the presence of the king. The three Chufa seemed resolute, though Dor seemed to waver between resolve and trepidation. Colonel Braxton looked uncomfortable and though standing still, seemed to pace back and forth like a caged animal. Even Jace seemed to exude an inkling of nervous energy that only magnified the feelings the others were experiencing. Only Jne gave off an air of confidence that vacillated toward the edge of contempt.

Ranse opened the door revealing a cavernous hall that swallowed the group in its girth as they entered. A large domed ceiling constructed in a star burst of steal and glass radiated from the center and out to all sides allowing the sun's rays to filter in and illuminate the entire area in soft light. A circle of massive pillars outlined the room creating a hallway of sorts that circumvented the inner court which was completely open. The floor was highly polished and decorated with scenes of war and conquest. To the far left was a grand stairway of marble leading up in a large half circle to the dais that held the king's throne. Surprisingly, the throne was not large at all but instead afforded those forced to look up at it full view of the king making him the focal point with nothing to distract attention away.

The king wore silks of the finest make in a shimmering blue with a golden sash draped across his shoulder. He was a man of middle age who was not overly handsome and would most likely be described as plain. A large powdered quaff protruded from his head like a helmet and his face was covered in white powder with bright red painted on his cheeks and lips.

Though seated on the throne as a demonstration of his power and authority, it was the tall man next to him that dominated the room. Dressed in plain brown robes with the cowl pull up, covering his features, the man was ominous in his simplicity of dress, towering over the king, who, should he stand, would not have reached the other's shoulder.

Halfway up the stairs, and to either side, were two other chairs that were occupied as well by two men who could only be Ranse's older brothers. They too wore the opulent clothing made fashionable by their father and king as well as the powdered wigs and painted faces that made them almost look like the women who filled the bottom steps of the stairway and who seemed to be pressing each other for advantage trying to capture the eye of either the king or one of his sons. It was as Ranse's party entered the room that two women had been dismissed from either side of each prince and sent back with slight squabbles to the coop, as it were, of cooing women below.

Ranse led the companions across the expansive floor to the base of the stairs where the women, holding their noses in disgust, skirted away as if the prince and his friends carried the plague and would infect them all by mere proximity. Reaching the bottom stair, they spread to either side of the prince and followed his lead as he bowed and touched one knee to the floor. All remained in this position for what seemed an excessive amount of time before the king snorted in disgust as if he'd been presented with maggot filled bread and then commanded them to rise.

It was as Teek raised his head and stood with the others that the short, wiry form of a Waseeni boy came from around the back of the throne to stand next to the king, opposite the man in the brown robes. Teek gasped in shock at seeing one of his own still alive though obviously hurt, sporting a bandage that wrapped his left leg from the ankle to the knee. How was it possible that one of his people had survived the attack on their home and then beat him to Calandra? The impossibility of it was quickly overrun by the excitement and joy that welled up in him that he was not the only one of his race still alive. If this young Waseeni had survived, then it was certainly possible, even probable that there were others too who had escaped the fiery death that wiped out his people and his home.

"I'm surprised to see you here," the king spoke, his voice dripping with disgust, his glare first searing into Colonel Braxton, who immediately looked down, before resting on his youngest son. "Especially in the face of your disobedience to my wishes and the fact that you sully my home with the likes of these," he finished motioning toward the others.

"My lord," Ranse answered, "you must hear me out."

The king shot to his feet, his face red with anger. "You dare command me, your king and your father, in my own court and household!"

Ranse bowed his head as Jace almost imperceptivity moved his hand towards his belt. It was then that Thane noticed there were no guards in the room. Though unrehearsed in the rules of HuMan royalty, he found it odd that their extreme ruler would not have a guard posted for his protection. Even the battle hardened dwarf prince, Helgar, had a company of guards to defend him. "My lord," Ranse tried again, "I do not intend to command you at all but only to alert you to the dangers…"

The king waved his hand and sat once again. "I know of the perceived dangers you speak of." The other princes both snickered as if their brother were a fool for the courts enjoyment. "I have already sent an emissary to treat with Lord Bedler and his friends and have received word that a mutually beneficial agreement has been reached. They come to the city as we speak as a sign of friendship where they will bow to me and swear their allegiance."

No one could believe what they were hearing though Thane recognized the appeals that Bedler or Zadok had used to almost draw him in as well. "But, my lord," Ranse continued trying, "what of Haykon and its annihilation? What of the people that were butchered at this Lord Bedler's command?"

The king stifled a yawn with one hand. "A simple misunderstanding," he replied, looking at his finger nails. "Had there been a competent leader," he suddenly spat, his mood vacillating erratically, as he shot a withering look at Colonel Braxton, "Haykon would still stand instead of its refuse clogging the outskirts of my city with their filth!" The king sat back and let out a sigh once again seeming in control of himself. "But," his voice was steady, "what is done is done. A sacrifice for the greater good. Their deaths will prove the catalyst to a better life for us all."

Neither Dor nor Jack could stand to listen to anymore of the king's insanity and apathy for his own as both moved as if intending to scramble up the stairs. Thane grabbed Dor's arm holding him back and flashing a warning look. Jack, though more restrained, did take a step forward mounting two steps before finally realizing where he was and stopping.

"Dagan!" Jack shouted, his anger taking over completely. "You pompous piece of royal dung. You are not fit to rule this people. You never have been. You have allowed your indecent, amoral, decadence to cloud your mind with what pleasures you while your kingdom is being systematically torn down around you!"

King Dagan's face was red with rage that someone should speak to him in such a way, but it took him a moment to find his voice as the shock had completely overwhelmed him. Rising from his throne, he descended a couple of steps toward Jack as if in an open threat of physical harm.

"How dare you speak to the king in such a manner! I will have your head as a toy for my hounds for such insolence! You forget yourself, man."

"No," Jack raged, moving up the steps himself now as if eager to clasp his flexing hands around the king's neck. Ranse's brothers recoiled in obvious fear as the women suddenly bolted for the sides of the hall screaming in terror. Colonel Braxton, still sworn to protect his king, grabbed Jack's arm before he got too far up the steps but that didn't stop the raging mountain man from continuing his verbal barrage. "You forget yourself! You are no longer fit to rule this people in carelessness and self indulgence. You are no longer worthy of such a responsibility or station. You must be removed."

King Dagan retreated at Jack's lunge and now stood behind his throne as if keeping it between him and Jack would protect him. Neither the man in brown robes nor the Waseeni boy moved but merely watched and listened in amusement as if witnessing the squabbling of two squirrels fighting over a nut. "And who do you think will remove me?" he hissed. "What army do you own that you can bring to bear against me and those loyal to their king?" he laughed.

Jack paused for a moment, the anger suddenly giving way to an inward struggle that made him appear as if struck physically ill by the king's words. The sudden change in his demeanor seemed to give the king courage and he moved to the front of the throne once more.

"You see," the king spat. "You are nothing, and you will die for your impudent words to one so much higher and greater than yourself!"

Jack's face still revealed the struggle that was obviously tormenting him as he stood dumb before the ranting king. Thane moved up the stairs beside his friend, followed closely by Jne, and placed a hand on Jack's shoulder. Jack turned to look at him and when their eyes met, the struggle suddenly seemed to dissipate into a decided victor. Turning back to the king, Jack reached into his shirt and pulled out a medallion that hung from a necklace around his neck. Teek recognized it immediately and reached for the one Twee had given him thinking that Jack must have taken it when he slept, but his was still tucked securely away in the pouch hidden in his loin cloth. It was identical to his.

"I have this," Jack said finally, holding up the medallion. "I have the mark of the kings of old passed down from generation to generation as I received it from my father just as he had from his father. And in the face of your incompetence and ineptitude I, once again, declare myself the king and ruler of these lands reclaiming my birthright to do so as the lost king returning! I am Lord Kenden, rightful heir to the throne."

Chapter Six

All eyes focused on Jack as the room suddenly fell into hushed silence. Even the chattering sounds from the women stopped as everyone seemed to take a deep breath. Dagan's eyes were riveted to the amulet in Jack's hand as it swung slightly from side to side, his face suddenly draining in color to pale. The brown robed figure turned and stared at the Waseeni boy who returned his questioning gaze as if communicating their own wonder without words. Thane and Dor traded glances between each other and Tam with a mix of disbelief and wonder while Domis and Teek beamed with pride at the privilege of being attached to someone whose importance had just exploded in size. Ranse looked at his father and then back at Jack and the medallion he held, recognizing the symbol but uncertain whether to believe what Jack had just claimed. Jne seemed unaffected by the revelation and merely watched with a slight grin, waiting to see what would happen next, clearly hoping it would include a fight.

Braxton released his hold on Jack's arm and took a step back, a strange look of relief and joy mixed in his countenance as he bent his knee and suddenly knelt before his old friend. "Upon my life…" he started.

Dagan took a step toward them. "What are you doing?" he said almost in a whisper.

"…I again pledge my service, my land…"

"Stop what you are doing," Dagan squealed. "He is not the king. He's a fraud."

"…my posterity, and my sword, to uphold and protect your name and person…"

Dagan's protests suddenly became a rage. "Stop what you are doing! Stop it this instant! He is not the king! I am the king! I am the one!"

"…though it require my very life to lay down in your defense…"

"STOP!"

"…I will give it and count myself blessed in the process. I am your man today and forever." The colonel finished his oath and then stood, a broad smile filling his face. "Welcome back, my Lord Kenden."

At the speaking of that name there was an audible gasp in the room. "It can't be," Dagan breathed. "Kenden died with his wife and child when the trolls attacked them."

Jack leveled his gaze on the once king. "Not so, Dagan. Only my wife was killed. My son was captured and I have searched for him these many years. I left the crown for good that day and if it weren't for your complete inability to think of anyone else but yourself, I would have remained as I was. But you forced me out, and I will not easily forgive you for it."

Dagan's face suddenly became twisted in hate and rage. "You're supposed to be dead! I am king because you died with your son. I am the rightful king, I…" Dagan never finished his thought but instead suddenly fell in a crumpled heap down the steps where he landed face up, his death mask eternally carved into a stupor of incomprehension.

Everything seemed to happen at once as the brown cloaked figure dropped the slightly beating heart he'd ripped from Dagan's chest and then shot with incredible speed toward Jack, his clawed fingers intent on repeating their gruesome work. But Colonel Braxton, having seen him take Dagan from behind, was already at Jack's side, pushing him away as the robed figure bore down on them. Jack tripped on the stairs and went down as Braxton took the claws directly into his own chest. Only the chain mail he wore beneath his tunic saved his life though the force of the attacked sent him flying.

Jace pulled a dagger from his boot while Jne and Thane jumped on the brown robbed assailant struggling to hold him down. Thane wrapped an arm around his throat in an attempt to subdue him and felt an almost instant connection between himself and the man. But he was no man. Just as understanding was forming itself in his mind, Thane and Jne were catapulted back with more force than ten men could have mustered. But it was too late. Thane knew the truth.

He landed hard on the marble floor knocking the wind from his lungs and temporarily stealing his voice with it. Amazingly, Jne landed on her feet, as if part feline and crouched in defense, though the look on her face betrayed the amazement she felt at having been so easily dislodged.

Jack tried to regain his feet as Tam and Dor rushed to help Thane. Meanwhile, Jace pulled another dagger that had been hidden on his person and tossed it to Ranse. Dagan's other sons sat in their chairs, unable to move as their screams mixed with those coming from the gaggle of women who were now running about pell-mell as if unable to form the complete thought that would direct them to one of the exiting doors.

Jace let fly his dagger, its force enough to have easily penetrated the man's robes and pierce his heart but to his amazement, the blade merely bounced off and fell with a clang to the floor.

Teek and Domis were quickly at Jack's side, pulling him to his feet and trying to get him to one of the exits when the brown robed figure rose to his full height and then continued to grow in size. Thane watched from where he had landed, his brain knowing what was going to happen but his voice still unable to communicate it as he struggled to refill his lungs with oxygen. The others watched in horror as the brown robed figure grew larger, the fabric of his clothing expanding around his body, as if another skin, before hardening into small sections. No longer was a man standing before them but a scaled creature that continued to expand in size and bulk.

It was then that Thane was finally able to work his diaphragm enough to shout to the others, "Get out! It's a dragon!"

Teek looked to the Waseeni boy still watching from the dais and called out to him. "Hurry! Come with us, now!"

The boy looked at the growing, brown figure, his eyes locked on its transforming shape with a look that could almost be described as envy before he suddenly leaped down the stairs toward Teek and the others as they ran for the pillars and the door beyond. The dragon was now at full size, its terrible girth filling much of the room as it roared a terrible sound that shattered the glass domed ceiling and rained deadly shards down upon those still in the center of the room. Dagan's oldest son's screams were cut short as a large piece of glass sliced his neck, cutting his vocal cords, and almost completely severing his head. His brother escaped immediate death, receiving a slight gash on his arm but was not spared as the brown dragon bore down on him. He opened his mouth to scream but the dragon fear gripped his heart, stealing his voice and releasing his bowels. The prince was frozen like a bird caught in the hypnotic gaze of a great serpent waiting to be eaten. But it didn't eat him, instead it released its terrible breath in a stream of liquid decay that hit the prince directly in the chest and almost instantly decomposed him into a mass of rotted flesh that dropped into a rancid pile.

Turning quickly, the dragon expelled another load of liquid breath at the fleeing companions just missing Jne as she ducked behind the nearest pillar. The rock immediately began to age and then started crumbling away, unable to hold against the dragon's exhalation. The deteriorated pillar, no longer able to sustain its top heavy weight, dropped under its own mass and then toppled to the side where it cracked the pillar next to it before crashing to the ground creating a huge divot in the marble floor.

Not looking back, Jne jumped for the open door where Thane stood calling for her, the others having already raced through and down the hallway. The dragon's roar filled the great hall and was quickly followed by another stream of decaying breath that shot through the open door where Thane and Jne had just been and sprayed against the opposite wall where it immediately decayed the stone revealing the room beyond.

Thane feared the dragon would use its breath to continue to rot away the walls in an attempt to capture its escaping quarry or bring the whole castle down around them in a heap but after the last discharge of corrosive breath, the dragon seemed to stop. As they raced further down the hall and around the many corners and through the countless rooms, the rumblings from the dragon ceased. Thane didn't stop to wonder why, though he felt that it still didn't bode well for them. Instead, he concentrated his efforts on catching the others, hoping they had followed the same route out as they had used coming in. Using the power of the TehChao Tane he knew he could at least get them to the same door they used on entry.

Making a final turn, he discovered the door from which they had entered, and to his relief, saw the others there catching their breath, waiting for them. "What now?" Ranse asked, directing his question to Jack.

"The dragon does not seem to be following," Thane offered, "though I can't be certain. It's too big to walk through the hallways but that is not to say it hasn't returned to its HuMan form."

"We are compromised," Jack added, "that is for certain."

"But whether it follows as man or beast," Braxton inserted, "we need to sound the alarm and get the people out of the city."

"But what if it attacks while we are in the open?" Dor asked.

"Then better to die fighting and with honor," Jne said.

"I agree with Jne," Tam added, "but with what can one fight such a thing? Only Jace seems to have any weapons, and a couple of daggers will not help." Jne smiled at the Chufa woman as if suddenly gaining a greater level of respect for her.

"Well, we can't stay here and argue the issue," Jack said. "We need to act now and start moving people out of the city. Whether the dragon attacks or not, Bedler's army certainly will, no matter what Dagan thought." Jack looked at Ranse with his last comment to gauge the once prince's reaction but saw nothing there but determination.

"Wess' men!" Ranse suddenly added. "I had forgotten them. We need to get them out."

Jack paused for a moment to think. This was unraveling faster than he'd hoped though with Dagan dead they might at least still have a chance at getting most of the people, including what army was left, out of the city. "All right," he finally said. "You and Jace go to the dungeons and release Wess' men and anyone else you find down there. See if you can't gather supplies and weaponry as you go, especially long bows and quivers, and meet us at the west gate. Spread the word as you go and keep your sight to the skies. The rest of us will take to the streets from here and see what we might do to rouse the rest of the city. It won't be easy to convince people to go so a visit by that dragon may not be a bad thing after all."

"But where are we going?" the young Waseeni boy asked.

Jack regarded him for a moment surprised at his mixture of emotions. Though happy that Teek was no longer alone, there was something that gnawed at him about the boy that he couldn't quite wrap his mind around. He had, after all, been at Dagan's side in the throne room, a strange position for someone so young and who didn't fall under the king's rule. "What is your name?"

"Tryg," the boy answered, his tone sounded almost challenging.

"Well, Tryg," Jack said, forcing a smile, "We will make our stand at Bedler's Keep."

Tryg looked as if he might say more, but Jack quickly cut him off. "Now let's move. It will take all the time we have just to get the women and children out of the city."

Jack moved as if to open the door and Ranse and Jace were turning back to the castle's hallways when Jne stopped them. "Wait. You must save those who can fight first."

Jack gave her a stern look. "What?"

"You must alert and gather all that can fight first. You cannot waste time on those too young, too old, or too weak. We cannot waste supplies and time coddling the helpless or we all suffer and perish for it."

Thane was shocked by Jne's words, as were most of the others, but then their logic suddenly pierced him. It was a cruel thought indeed, but the time to act had almost passed them and sacrifices would be necessary if they had any hope of survival. Jack seemed to come to the same conclusion at the same moment, but he could tell the taste was bitter indeed for his old friend to stomach.

"She is right," Jack whispered. "We must first gather our army."

Jne nodded, her demeanor not revealing any sorrow or regret with what she'd said. She was a warrior, and warriors were well accustomed to the tragedies and terrors of war. It did not mean she relished the idea of innocents being slaughtered; she was not so calloused as that. But she understood that some things were necessary when it involved assuring the lives of the greater number of people—in this case, possibly multiple races—no matter how horrid the costs.

"But we will deny no one the chance at life," Jack added. "All who are willing will be allowed to come and we fight to the end to protect them."

Jne just nodded, as did all the others, though their faces reflected the horror of the situation.

Ranse turned to go, motioning to Jace as he did so, but the large bodyguard stopped and turned back to Jne. Reaching into his boot, the weapons master produced another long blade that he tossed to the Tjal woman. "You might need this," he said, and then smiled.

Jne deftly caught the blade by the hilt and smiled back, nodding her appreciation as Jace turned and followed after the once prince. Thane watched the whole exchange and suddenly felt a slight pain in his chest that quickly turned into anxiety. It surprised him and he instantly recognized the feeling as being the same he'd felt when Dor and Tam were together. Jne looked at him quizzically but he quickly brushed past her as Jack called all to prepare to leave.

"We don't know what we will face when we go through this door, but when we reach the outside, immediately fan out and sprint for any cover available. Once we know we are clear, we will then make our way back to the city." Everyone nodded, steeling themselves for what lay ahead. Jack did not wait long before pushing open the door and leading them out.

The guard stationed in the alcove was slightly alarmed to see them suddenly dashing out of the castle at a dead run but all were passed him before he could even raise a call of inquiry. A large roar from above, like an exploding cannon, heightened his surprise which turned swiftly to terror as a great shadow filled the courtyard followed by the dragon's massive body as it dropped from the sky in quick pursuit. True to Jack's instructions, everyone scattered as they exited the palace, which more than likely saved their lives as the dragon paused as if uncertain who it should take down first. Roaring in anger it released its decaying breath at the first group it saw as they ducked behind an oversized statue of King Dagan slaying a troll. Teek, Domis, and Tryg dropped behind the base just as the liquid completely wasted away the king from the knees up. The overspray splattered the ground creating large divots in the marble walkway and came dangerously close to Tryg's wounded leg.

Tryg jumped up immediately, cursing the dragon as it passed while promising retribution. Teek grabbed the boy's arm and pulled him down, his face flushed. "What are you doing?"

"Come on," Domis said, before Tryg could answer. "We can make it to those trees before it returns." Not waiting for the other two to answer, he shot out from their hiding place quickly followed by Teek and Tryg who shouted another curse to the skies.

The dragon twisted, raising itself into the air and then banked for another pass but by this time everyone was secreted in various locations out of direct sight making an aerial assault impractical. After swinging around for another pass the dragon dropped its colossal body into the courtyard and let out a deafening roar of challenge. For a brief moment, all was still as no one dared move and give away their position. Thane watched from his hiding place behind another of the many statues of the dead king as the dragon moved its great body away from him directly to the spot where Colonel Braxton lay beneath a wide bench by a large fountain. He knew that if the dragon continued on its current route, it would easily catch sight of him. Closing his eyes Thane reached for the wind and found it immediately answered his call. Gathering it in strength above him, he twisted it into a rushing tornado that sucked at the grass beside him threatening to lift him from the ground with its increasing strength.

The howls from the air currents caught the dragon's attention and jerking its head back it immediately caught sight of Thane who was concentrating too hard on what he was doing to notice. Thane continued to gather more force oblivious to the imminent danger now approaching. Jne, crouched nearby, reacted instantly by darting from her place of hiding and swinging her blade in a wide arc landing it hard against the dragon's flank. The dragon roared, but more in anger than pain since the blade was like a reed against a piece of steel sliding without effect to the side. Jne jumped back, barely escaping being crushed by the dragon's rear leg. But now she was exposed. The dragon whipped its head around and opened its jaws, its head pulling back to release its deadly breath. Jne stood frozen, not from fear but from a certain knowledge that her time had finally come. She faced it with courage and honor, knowing she was about to lose her life to a foe worthy enough to take it.

Bringing its head forward, the dragon released its breath just as Thane's twisted winds connected with the side of its head sending it hurtling against the castle. Its putrid breath jet passed Jne, its force blowing her hair back. Seeing that her opportunity at a worthy death had passed, Jne quickly sprinted to the tree line surrounding the courtyard while Thane did the same.

Somewhat dazed, the dragon bellowed in anger and then spread its wings, lifting its great mass from the courtyard to once again direct its attack from the skies. By now all had made it to the trees and were tracking the dragon's movements as it lifted high above the castle and then swung out wide, dropping down to attack from the east. This time, it did not search out its prey, but instead leveled itself over the tree line, raining down a storm of decay that covered the first row of trees where everyone hid. None of the liquid made it through the foliage but as the trees quickly deteriorated, huge branches and great limbs showered down from above covering the ground in composted vegetation.

In an effort to escape one such falling branch, Jack was forced back into the courtyard where he tripped on a molding branch and fell hard onto the marble pavers just as the dragon banked for another run. Trying to regain his feet, Jack watched the dragon press forward with remarkable speed, bearing down on him with talons outstretched prepared to tear him from the ground. Jack dove to the side just as three large forms rocketed over the castle and right into the dragon sending it crashing into the tree tops where it floundered before falling to the ground in front of Teek, Domis and Tryg. Tryg again jumped at the dragon, cursing it before grabbed from behind by Domis and Teek who pulled him back behind a tree.

Though uncertain as to what brought the dragon down, Thane understood that this was possibly the only chance he would get to dispatch it using his Tane. Determined in his resolve, he raced headlong toward the giant serpent using his skills as a Chufa to make his passing more silent then a gentle wind. The dragon, though obviously stunned and possibly hurt, was able to regain its footing and was attempting to spread its great wings so it could escape the ground just as Thane reached its tail. Reaching out his hand, he pressed it against one of the brown scales and endeavored to concentrate his mind enough to connect with the fluid running through the great beast's veins. Unaware of Thane's presence, the dragon continued its attempt to clear itself enough to gain sufficient uplift to raise its girth from the forest floor.

Reaching deep, Thane searched for the door that would unlock the dragon's physiology to his will and answer his call for its fluids. A tremendous gust of wind pressed against his face causing him to lose concentration as the dragon began to beat its massive wings. Time was running out. If the dragon took to the skies again his opportunity would flee with it. Struggling to settle his mind, he pressed, delving for the connection, willing it to come to him as it had once before.

The dragon's tail was now lifting as its wings were finally able to create the force needed to free it from the confines of the earth. Thane's hand rose with it clutching the edge of the scale as if he would allow himself to be lifted skyward attached to the dragon's tail. His arm was fully stretched now and he knew that in mere seconds he would lose touch. And then, it was there. The door opened to him, the connection was made. He felt the water that flooded the dragon's body and knew it would answer his call. Smiling with satisfaction he began to form his will and send it out to be obeyed when, to his dismay, the connection was suddenly cut off, the door slammed shut. The dragon's tail slipped from his fingertips as it broke through the trees, once again rising into the sky.

Thane sank to the ground, a tear falling from his eye. He was there. He had been connected. A mere second longer and the dragon would have been his. His opportunity had passed and with it the very real possibility of hundreds, even thousands, of lost lives. A thunderous cry from overhead shook him from his misery as three large shadows passed over his position. Could it be more dragons? He jumped to his feet forcing with effort the ghosts that tried to haunt his failed attempt. The thought of more dragons loose made his stomach turn. They could not fight a foe in such numbers. Even if they could get the arrow from TaqSagn, it would mean very little against such a threat as five dragons.

Thane hurried ahead, thinking to still lend a hand to save his friends when a thunderous cry broke out above the dragon as it rose up over the trees. He paused, uncertain, but watched as Teek suddenly broke from cover to search the sky. He new that sound well, but where there had previously been only one, now there were three.

EEEEERRRRROOOCCCC! Three giant birds attacked with vicious precision as the dragon continued to labor against its colossal size and weight to free itself from the trees and escape the barrage of beaks and talons that continually pounded it overhead. The rocs worked in unison as if firmly planted in each other's minds, knowing what each would do and working it to their advantage. The dragon tried to take them down with its decaying breath but the rocs were too quick and agile to be caught in an open position.

Darting in and out of the trees and keeping to the rear and above the dragon, they were able to harass it until it finally turned northward pumping its powerful wings as fast as it could to get away. The three large birds followed after until the dragon cleared the city before turning back to the castle and settling into the courtyard where the nine companions now gathered and hurriedly checked each other for wounds.

Teek ran up to Tchee as she set down near a statue of Dagan posing with a sword. Chirping happily, she bobbed her head back and forth, singing like a child that had just done something particularly well and was awaiting the praise it was due. Teek wrapped his arms around her and nuzzled his head into the soft feathers on her chest. "Tchee!" he cried, his voice muffled against her. Pulling back he pointed to Tryg. "Look, this is my new friend, Tryg. I am not the only one to survive." The emotion Teek felt was obvious, but was overshadowed by Tchee's sudden change in demeanor. Gone was the happy chirping, replaced by a low grumble in her throat. Tryg stepped back, the concern on his face obvious. Teek regarded his large friend with shock. "It's all right, Tchee. He's our friend. He's one of us."

Tchee was not so easily convinced though with her feathers laid back and the rumblings in her chest continuing. Tryg's demeanor also changed to one that was almost raptor like as he glared at the bird, almost challenging it but, at the same moment, taking two steps backward. All eyes wandered back and forth between the two, shocked into silence by the exchange.

Finally, Thane stepped forward, sending one last sidelong glance at Tryg. Smiling, he patted Teek on the shoulder. "It would appear that your friend has kept her word," he said, looking up at Tchee who watched him with her deep blue eyes. Thane wasted no time, turning his own gaze toward her and willing himself forward and quickly making contact. Almost immediately he found himself staring back at his body, his mind filled with the roc's thoughts and concerns. He found himself glancing once again at Tryg with feelings of distrust and danger. He wanted to discover why her reaction was so harsh toward the boy but his own press for time weighed heavy bringing their thoughts back to the issue at hand. *You are welcome, friend Tchee*, he thought, though not with words but something more pure in its communication.

I come with others who have agreed to carry you to your destination. It is against our ways to offer love where it is not returned but the sacrifice is needed.

Thane tried to grasp the significance of what she had just communicated but was uncertain he fully understood it. *What do you mean by offering love?*

Tchee let out a mournful sound that Thane felt came from his own throat. It was something so heartrending in its resonance that all present suddenly felt enveloped in sorrow and pain. *These are life given. They are beholden to one another. To carry you will destroy their bond to never again be rewelded. They will be lost to each other and to my kind.*

Thane almost pulled back from the connection. Suddenly he understood what had been offered with a keenness that threatened to rend his heart at the mere thought of it. The rocs with Tchee were mates and would lose their bond forever by giving flight to him and his friends. Neither would they ever be able to return to their own kind. He didn't understand the reasons completely, but he knew that it was true and that what was being offered him was of the greatest sacrifice. He pulled back, letting go the connection between them and once again in his own body, felt the crushing weight of what he would be taking away from these innocent creatures by his need to return with speed to his homeland. Tears fell unchecked down his face as his friends stared unknowing at him. "We cannot do this," he whispered.

Jne stepped forward. "We must, Thane. We need the arrow your people hold."

He shook his head. "There has to be another way."

"Unless you have the power to carry us with speed over the mountains," Jne pressed, "then there is no other way."

He turned away. "No. You don't understand. You don't understand the cost, the sacrifice that will be made to do this." Turning to her, he gripped her arm. "We don't even know that he will give us the arrow."

Jne's face was hard and unyielding. "You dishonor me anew," she said, her voice low and steady. "I do know what is required. I fully understand the sacrifice. I am well learned in the ways of the roc. These two are life partners. They are joined, and by offering flight to us, they break the bond forever never to reforge it in this life or the one beyond."

Tam gasped audibly at Jne's explanation bringing her hand to her mouth while the others looked to the two giant birds standing resolutely by. Thane's eyes widened slightly. "You know, and you would still ask me to do this?"

Jne's eyes hardened briefly but then suddenly softened, her shoulders drooping slightly. Gone was the Tjal warrior he was so accustomed to when he needed to borrow strength. Gone was the rough exterior that deflected emotion. Gone was the proud woman that had only moments before stood with her face gladly looking to death with a smile of welcome. Left was the beautiful woman that had stayed by him. Left was a person who cared deeply for the lives of others ignoring what cost it might require at her own hands. Left was an open heart that warmed his own with the honesty that made Jne what she was to the core of her being.

"I know what it is to love. I know the sorrow and pain of a desired heart that may never receive in return what it offers constantly." She looked deep into Thane's eyes and he couldn't help the feeling that she was a part of him. "I know the anguish that comes with letting go the only one that makes you feel complete inside."

Thane suddenly felt that he and Jne were the only ones left in the courtyard. Her words held him for a long moment, warming him while at the same time filling him with grief matching that which he'd felt while connected with Tchee. It was at that moment that he realized that she had laid herself bare before him. Stripped away were all the walls of protection most people carried to keep themselves from being hurt and now Jne was offering it all to him, allowing him to see her as she truly was, with all the insecurities and uncertainty and she was giving it to him to do as he pleased. It was like a volcano of ice erupting out of her and filling him with its promises of warmth while chilling him to the core.

And then he understood. He'd grown up knowing disappointment and hurt coming from those who should have loved him or been his friend but now he finally comprehended what it was to give. What it meant to strip oneself of all false pretense and offer up what was left to another without thought or care as to how it would be accepted or handled. It was love in its purest form and nothing could destroy it. The sacrifice in its offering was what made it infinite. To hold it back in even the slightest degree was what weakened it and made it of less worth; what starved it and withered it to the roots. And to deny the offering, to cheapen the sacrifice by turning away when it was offered so freely, was to blaspheme it and desecrate its purity.

He held Jne's gaze for a moment longer before turning to stare at the two large birds standing silently and proud behind him and for the first time he saw beauty. For the first time he truly understood honor.

"We go."

Chapter Seven

Jne pressed her face against Thane's back; her arms wrapped like securely tied rope around his stomach becoming a noose that threatened to choke off his breathing. She dared not look down or even open her eyes for fear that the ground might see her and snatch her back like a jealous lover. Though at such altitudes the wind was certainly cold, her constant shiver was not a result of the air temperature but instead revealed her perceived shame at the terror that gripped her while soaring at such heights. Never would Thane have thought there existed such a thing that would cause the Tjal woman to manifest the slightest inkling of fear but, apparently, flying was it. His first reaction was amusement with a slight desire to rib her for what he identified as an exhilarating experience. But the image of her in Calandra standing before him completely open and exposed quickly reminded him of the total trust she had exhibited and he realized that he would never tease her when it came to her sense of honor.

Thane, on the other hand, felt more alive and free than he ever had. His ArVen Tane was filling him with utter exhilaration to the point that he felt he never wanted to touch the ground again. His hands lay slack against the roc's body that had freed them from the confines of the earth and brought him to a point of such total communion with the ArVen that it bordered on worship. Never before had he given himself over so completely to one Tane allowing it to fill his body and senses so fully. He felt a sudden connection to it that all at once exhilarated him yet filled him with fear that he would be consumed by it to the point of losing his identity, his body becoming an integral part of the air surrounding them. It was pure and raw power wholly at his bidding to command as he wished to the degree that he knew it had no capacity to deny even his slightest whim. He was the master of the air.

Tam was also experiencing a sacred moment as she too communed with the ArVen, though not in the slightest bit equal to what Thane enjoyed. She could feel the faintest pull as if invited to be free of the roc and merely fly on her own. The wind caressed her senses and seemed to be calling for her to join it offering up promises of complete freedom and an uninhibited life.

Dor had agreed to let her sit in front, knowing full well before they even elevated the slightest distance from the ground that this was not going to be an experience he would cherish. He too held tightly to Tam though, unlike Jne, he was still able to appreciate the beautiful vistas offered to one soaring so high above the ground.

Once Thane had given the word of acceptance to the roc's offered sacrifice, they wasted no time in mounting the giant birds. It was a sad and sacred moment as the life-given rocs relinquished their hold to one another, giving all in sacrifice to carry them. At the last moment they turned their sharp eyes onto each other and let out a mournful cry that reduced all present to bitter tears.

Jack agreed that he and those remaining would gather as many as would come and start heading west toward their ultimate goal of Bedler's Keep. Thane, and those with him, would catch up as soon as their mission was complete whether that meant success at retrieving the arrow or not.

He tried not to think too much about what it would be like to return to his people after having been beaten mercilessly and left to die at the hands of trolls. He wondered about his father. Would he be happy his son was still alive or would he turn his back in disgust. He had not thought much about his home since being left on the Shadow Mountains, blocking out, he supposed, the painful life that had been his up until that time. It was ironic to the extreme that he finally found acceptance and love from one whose race had almost annihilated his own many centuries past. Jack had been more a father to him in the relatively short amount of time he'd known him than his own father had been his whole life. Though he had come to embrace who he was, no longer ashamed of the powers he possessed, the darkness of his past still clouded over him stealing the exhilaration he'd been feeling while communing with the ArVen. Doubts began slicing through his confidence like water freezing in the cracks of boulders that eventually expand to the point of breaking them into pieces. Still, he would give almost anything to have even the smallest relationship with his father.

He thought of the jealousy he'd felt toward Dor and the love and respect he shared with his own father and suddenly Thane worried for his friends. His return could not be any worse than when he'd been exiled, short of losing his life, which he now felt confident would not happen. Dor and Tam, on the other hand, had left behind loving and secure homes to come after him and now they were returning to what would most likely be joyous reunions to real homes full of happiness and family that wanted them. He suddenly felt conflicted. In the face of all they confronted west of the Shadow Mountains, would they not rather stay with their families? Tam had chosen Dor and now, in the presence of the kinpa, they could be joined and be a family of their own. Though he would miss them terribly, they had lives waiting for them in the Ardath. They would be welcomed home and wanted. They had a responsibility to the Chufa race. Against the great host of evil that threatened, two Chufa would most likely not change the tide of the war. It was the arrow that would make a difference, not Dor or Tam. And even then, the arrow would not provide the power to eliminate the massive army now bowing to Zadok's bidding. If they failed and Zadok's minions won the conflict, it would not matter where their lives were ended. At least, should they stay in the Ardath, they would know happiness for a time. He knew he would not be able to convince them otherwise, but he hoped that once they were back home, with their families around them, that they would finally decide to stay. He, on the other hand, knew already in his heart that his return would be ill accepted. Only his mother would show any joy at seeing him, and he hated knowing that it would probably cause her more pain to see him again than if he'd just never returned. He wanted her to know he was safe though, to know that he loved her and that he was fighting to protect her. And no matter if they never saw each other again, she could be proud, and know in her heart, that her son had given all so that those who hated him most might be safe. He had chosen the correct course no matter what others thought.

Even with the added speed and ease that flying offered, they still figured it would take the better part of three days to finally reach their destination. Then at least one day, if not more, to try and convince DaxSagn to give up his most prized possession before turning back toward Calandra. By that time, Zadok's army would most likely be in the process of stripping the city of its remaining life and wealth. He only hoped the trip would be worth it. A part of him felt guilty for leaving Calandra at such a crucial time but as Jne had pointed out earlier, there were no easy choices in war, only those that were of most benefit to the greatest numbers. War was not for the weak or faint of heart.

As the sun reached its zenith, the birds slowed and then circled lazily before descending to the ground. Thane knew they must be tired and need something to eat, as did he and his companions. As the ground reached up for them, he tensed, bracing himself for a rough landing but was surprised to find the giant bird set down gently onto the soil. It took a moment to peel Jne's arms away from his waist and convince her that they were indeed on the ground and that she could open her eyes. When she finally did, she almost tripped in her efforts to set her feet firmly on solid ground. She glared at the three Chufa as if daring any of them to say something about her fear of flying but at once relaxed when she realized no one was even looking at her, each happy to be free of their mounts so they could stretch their legs and search their packs for something to eat.

Before leaving Calandra, they thought it best to return to camp and retrieve their packs and weapons. The two rocs descending on the crowded refugee camp caused no small stir as many thought the dragons had returned. The relief they felt was short lived though as the call went out for everyone to pack up again and start for the western gates where they would meet up with Jack and the others. Thane quickly spoke with Bren and Kat apprising them of the situation and urging them to retrieve all healers from the city. A number of the refugees had refused to leave, placing their trust, as it were, on Calandra to protect them. No amount of pleading or arguing would dissuade them so they were finally left to their fate as they willed it.

Tam shouted a protest as the rocs suddenly leapt into the air and took flight, leaving the four of them behind. "They're leaving us!" she cried, reaching a hand skyward as if to pull them back to earth.

"Do not worry," Thane soothed, as they all watched the magnificent birds turning south before racing away. "They go to feed and replenish their strength. They will return soon enough."

"They can take all the time they like," Dor complained while trying to rub feeling back into his legs. Jne just nodded while Thane and Tam shared a smile.

Everyone busied themselves with pulling from their packs what they wanted for the midday meal and then sat in the late spring grass that was plentiful in the area and spread across the many small knolls and mounds that rippled the landscape. Little patches of wild flowers lent color to the area and the slightest buzzing sound was heard as honey bees hungrily supped on the flower's nectar. An occasional tree or shrub sprung up haphazardly, breaking up the terrain with chaotic splendor and lending the slightest patches of shade against the day that was warming up quite nicely, giving a sense of peace and security that contrasted greatly with the terrible circumstances that threatened.

"Do you think they've changed much?" Tam suddenly asked.

"Who?" Dor mumbled while shoving another piece of cheese into his mouth.

Tam smiled. "Our families, of course."

Dor smiled at her. He had not really given it much thought, his mind having given so much effort to keeping his body on the roc's back and his breakfast in his stomach. "I don't know. It seems like an entirely different life though we really haven't been gone all that long, have we?"

Thane watched the exchange in silence, not offering any of his own thoughts while Jne watched him with a flat stare that revealed nothing as to what she might be thinking.

"I can't wait to see the wonder in their faces at our return," Tam said, the excitement obvious in her voice.

"We'll need to be cautious," Thane abruptly offered.

"Why?" Tam asked, regarding him for a moment her expression changing from one of surprise to one of painful understanding.

"We are not the same children that left the Ardath forest in the months past," he continued. "Look at how you are dressed," he said, pointing out the Tjal garb they had all adopted to cover their true lineage. "And Dor's head," he added, referring to the slow growing hair that had still not reached the back of Dor's neck. "No longer flow the black hairs of the Chufa down his back, a leftover result of his rescuing you." He now turned his green eyes on Tam. "And you," he breathed, "you still demonstrate the physical degradation of one addicted to *dranlok*. You have yet to regain all the weight you lost. Though you do your best to hide it, you are still not back to your full strength." Thane shook his head. "We are not the children they remember," he continued, his gaze now set on the distant horizon. "And there is one among us who will be seen as an enemy," he finished, though whether he meant Jne or himself, none could tell.

Dor and Tam looked at their friend, the immediate shock of his words slowly turning to understanding. He was right. They were different and to carelessly saunter into the village without the least bit of preparation may find them all pin-cushioned with arrows.

"Our clothes are easy to change," Dor proffered, "and Tam's thin frame might be expected of one suddenly appearing out of the mountains. And though my hair may cause a stir, I don't think it would be enough to have me banished." Dor said the last word and then immediately wished he hadn't. Looking to his friend, he waited to see his response, already preparing to apologize.

But Thane smiled sardonically. "You are right. Nothing so minor would be cause to beat you and leave you for dead."

Dor sighed. "Thane, I'm sorry. I didn't mean…"

Thane waved him off shaking his head and giving him a genuine smile this time. "Don't Dor. It is not your fault what has happened to me and I should not burden you with my own bitterness. You have always been the greatest friend to me."

"You are right, though," Tam added. "We do need some sort of plan for getting into the village without taking an arrow to the chest."

Jne watched the exchange in silence, unable to offer an opinion not knowing the culture or background of the people with whom they were dealing.

"And what of Jne?" Dor asked, and all could see her tense as if watching the hackles of a wild animal rising in warning. "We cannot take her into the village with us. That will certainly start a fight."

"I go with Thane," she stated flatly, though the embers in her eyes betrayed her growing anger.

Thane ignored the exchange, instead addressing the problem at hand. "With all of the trolls gone from the Shadow Mountains, the patrols may have grown careless in their vigilance which could give us the opportunity to slip past them, but then what? As soon as we reach the village the alarm will still be given and we may risk losing one of us to a stray arrow."

"We could go to my parent's hut," Dor offered. "Once inside, we would be safe. My father could then bring DaxSagn to us without alerting anyone else."

Thane's brow creased as he thought upon what Dor had offered. "It might work," he finally said, "but we will need to be certain that your father and mother do not inadvertently raise an alarm."

"What do you mean by that?" Tam asked.

Thane stared at her for a long moment giving her the uncomfortable feeling that he was judging her, as if trying to decide if she could cope with his reply. She glared defiantly back as if challenging him with her resolve to see the mission through. "They'll have to be held and gagged."

Tam brought her hand to her mouth. "You can't mean that," she protested, her determination crumbling instantly.

"I agree with Tam," Jne stated. "To bind ones enemy and not allow him to fight is a great dishonor to self."

Thane sighed. "It does not break with honor," he argued. "They are not our enemy, and it is necessary to keep all safe from unnecessary harm. There is no other way to follow such a plan and get us all in the village safely."

Jne made to dispute his logic but Dor cut her off. "I'll go in alone."

"Dor," Thane protested, but his friend continued over him.

"You three can hide in the forest, close to the mountains while I go to my parent's hut. No one need know I have come save them. I know the patrol routes and how to slip past them; you know that, Thane. We've been slipping past the patrols almost since we could walk."

"And how do you think they will react when you suddenly walk into their hut?"

"It does not matter," Dor replied. "Once they see that I have returned I can follow through with the rest of the plan."

"It's too risky," Tam added. "With your hair cut like it is, they may not recognize you quick enough. There could be trouble. It would be better for me to go."

Thane opened his mouth to say something but Tam snapped at him, her anger rising quickly. "Do not try to tell me it is too dangerous and that I should not go. You both know that I am right!"

Thane gave Dor a quizzical look before turning back to her. "I was not going to fight you, Tam. I was going to agree with you. You, of all of us, are the most likely to cause the least amount of upheaval, at least in any negative way. And we can easily get you past any patrols. It should be you."

Both Dor and Tam stared at him with open mouths, neither willing to accept what they had just heard.

"Then we are decided," Jne suddenly announced, as if to halt any further argument.

The conversation turned away from their plans and instead skipped down the corridors of memories shared by the three Chufa and the years they grew up together in the Ardath. It was a welcome departure from the hard truths that overshadowed them and the uncertainty of the outcome of their mission. Soon, Dor and Thane had them all laughing out loud at the pranks and trouble they had found as children. Even Jne found humor in their childhood high jinks.

Though the dark mood that had permeated the group was lifted for a brief period, when the rocs returned to reclaim their charges Jne and Dor both eyed the birds with a certain amount of distaste. Jne especially glared at them as if finding fault in their very existence, hating that their desperation at having to use the rocs was tarnishing her honor. Tam and Thane happily regained their seats, anxious for their renewed communion with the ArVen. Thane wondered what situations would give him the same feeling with his other Tane.

Night was beginning to blanket the land when the rocs descended on the foremost roots of the Dedrik Forest. Both Thane and Dor had quick flashes of memory from their first visit here and both shared a quick nod of understanding. Without a word to the others, Thane searched out a spot by himself where he could sit and concentrate on the surrounding area. Calming his mind he pressed all thoughts into the inner niches of his mind and then willed his senses forward and out. He suddenly become aware of every minute aspect that made the forest the living, breathing creature it was. Penetrating deeper he found nothing that felt odd or ill at ease. The forest seemed to sing in joyful greeting inviting him to enter its confines and rejoice with it in intimate unity. It called out to him beckoning him down its paths, begging him to delve deeper toward its heart where peace and solitude were found and promised. He basked in the forest's touch and caress. It remembered him.

Reluctantly, he retracted himself and turned his attention outward from the trees and past his friends to the surrounding plains. He sensed every movement, from the smallest beetle digging in the dirt, to the mouse shivering in fright as it desperately tried to hide from the searching eyes of a nearby snake, to his extraordinarily disruptive friends who crashed about as they set up camp. He caught the secretive glances shared between Dor and Tam as they traded stares when each felt the other was not looking. He felt the warmth and bond that beat in their hearts as if in unison, washing over him with the obvious love they shared for one another. And he could feel the steel covered velvet that was Jne.

There was no other way to describe her. She was battle and honor hardened like the toughest and sharpest metal, yet, she could not completely hide the tenderness that was also such a part of her. He had seen it before they left Calandra and now he allowed himself to explore it even deeper. A part of him balked at what he was doing, feeling shame for invading her most private parts hidden behind the walls she had so carefully constructed to protect herself, but he soothed his conscience with the fact that she had just recently shared those places with him. He turned his gaze on her as his senses delved past the steel to the soft core that was Jne. She suddenly turned to look at him as if sensing him there. He immediately pulled back as if he'd been caught doing something wrong but then felt her pulling him closer again. Though he really didn't think she shared the same abilities he was using, something in her called to him, welcoming him, inviting him to explore every hidden corridor, every nuance, every substance that made her who and what she was. Thane suddenly felt encompassed about by warmth and belonging that refreshed him like sipping from the purest pool of new spring water. And then she shared with him one of her rarest smiles and, though still at a distance, he felt his breath catch as it washed over him, the beat of her heart suddenly matching that of his own and a rush of emotions cascaded over him like the plucking of a warm, tender wind. He felt whole.

Reluctantly, he gently pulled away, fearful that if he did not, all sense of duty and resolve to their mission would be siphoned away in the sudden rush of emotion filling him. Left to himself he suddenly felt empty—like part of him was missing. Jne held her smile for a brief moment longer before letting it go back behind the steel that protected it.

Though Thane had scouted the area and found no threat, out of habit, they still took turns keeping watch through the night. The rocs left again, most likely to find a perching place, while the four friends bedded down by the fire they agreed was safe enough to light. The following day still found Dor and Jne reluctant to mount the giant birds though Jne did chance a peek or two at the scenery such heights afforded and found the fear that had seized her lessoning its hold, but just slightly. Thane and Tam still gloried in every moment such altitude gave them with the ArVen, feeling for the first time that the Tane was a living power, an entity that was to be cherished more than controlled.

By day's end, even Thane and Tam felt a sense of gratitude when they finally descended on the deserted fortress of Hell's End Station. Though Dor still fought the rising mixture of loathing and dread at returning to the place where he'd been caged, he also felt relieved to once again put tired legs on solid ground. Rubbing life back into their limbs no one made an attempt to open the closed gates that were once the border protection between the outlying area and the troll infested Shadow Mountains. There was nothing within the fortress gates that any cared to seek out or investigate. None of the Chufa spoke much, all deeply involved in their own thoughts as the knowledge that the next evening would find them over the Shadow Mountains and back home weighed on each to a different degree.

Thane, of course most dreaded the idea of returning though he was anxious to see his mother once more and assure her that he was well. Dor and Tam, on the other hand, both fought mixtures of joy and uncertainty. Though they had not been away from home very long, the reality of what they had faced and what still lay ahead made them restless. Yet, to be home among family was something that pulled at them unceasingly.

Jne took the first watch moving just out of the immediate light cast by the small fire. The three Chufa curled up in blankets welcoming the fire's warmth to beat back some of the cool night air that was somewhat unseasonable in its chill. Few stars were visible as dark clouds blew in overhead though Thane and Tam assured them that there would be no rain this night. Soon a rumbling sound like distant thunder was heard that drew Jne's gaze skyward until she realized the sound was coming from Dor who wasted no time in falling deep into slumber.Tam also found the pathway to sleep an easy one to follow but Thane was not so fortunate. He couldn't settle the racing thoughts that bombarded his mind as he contemplated his return to the Ardath and the people who mistrusted and even hated him. A feeling of dread and ill constantly pressed itself against his thoughts to the point that he was beginning to doubt the wisdom in what they were trying to accomplish. He fought back with the conviction that they had to try. Though it was slight that Dax's arrow would cause a turning point in the war, and even slighter that the Chufa protector would part with the prized artifact, it was still important enough to give it all their effort. And though he did not want to entertain such thoughts, it could be the last time any of them saw their home again; certainly that was the case for him. He knew his return would not be met with favor.

He finally gave in to the obvious and rose from his bedroll. Quickly finding Jne with his night eyes he went to her and demanded she sleep while he took the first watch. But typical of the Tjal-Dihn women, she resisted him. "I am not ready for sleep," she said dryly, "nor will I surrender my responsibility so quickly. Why do you so suddenly desire the watch?" she asked as he sat down beside her.

"Sleep flees from me even as I attempt to overtake it," he sighed. "I will not find rest this night."

Jne nodded her understanding. "It is like the ferment that overtakes the warrior just before battle."

Thane absorbed her words, at first wanting to reject them, but finally realizing, as was archetypical, that what she spoke was truth. That was exactly what he was feeling. It was as if he was preparing for battle, but these were his people. Though he had never been accepted by his own he felt that he should at least feel the smallest bit of joy, or even melancholy, at the prospect of returning home. Instead, he was tensing for war.

"Do not berate yourself for what you are feeling," Jne suddenly offered as if reading his thoughts. "You *are* going into battle. And though you may not draw weapons in this fight, it is nonetheless full combat."

He stared at her, letting her words fill him, comforting his doubts. "You amaze me."

She started at his words as if he'd caught her unaware.

He ignored her reaction, though it certainly struck him as out of place. "Everything before you is certain. There is no middle position or indecision. How do you do it?"

Jne, having regained her composure, stared at him as she once had when he first fell into her company and she felt he was being childish. "I am Tjal, as are you, though you refuse to completely embrace your heritage. Until you let go of everything that is not Thane, you will never see clearly and will always suffer doubt. That is true honor. I have seen it in you but you still test it. You cloud your vision with hesitation. You are no longer Chufa. You may not even truly be Tjal." Jne's head and voice seemed to drop slightly with her last words but her voice quickly regained its strength as she continued. "You are a race unto yourself, Thane. And as such, you are the only one to decide what it truly means to be Thane, what it is your race will embrace. Only then will you see straight and no longer know uncertainty in what you do."

His eyes traced the contours of her face as his heart and mind embraced her words finding comfort and strength in their telling. The idea that he was not Chufa was something that felt foreign but at the same moment seemed to ring with truth. His birthright was Chufa but when he thought of what the Chufa had become and what they now had devolved to he realized that what Jne revealed was truer than anything else. He was not one of them. He had always begrudged the idea but now looking at them from the outside, he realized that he did not want to be as they now were. His people were fallen. They no longer embraced what it truly meant to be Chufa, what it was to be honorable and true. The nobility of their race had been snuffed out and he no longer felt at home with them.

For the first time he felt gratitude toward PocMar for leaving him in the mountains to die. It was his act that had freed him from the bounds that had been placed on him since birth. Suddenly he felt the last pieces filling in the broken life he'd been leading. Embracing forgiveness and letting go of his anger, his hatred and doubt, he finally felt whole and free. And as Jne had promised, his vision became clear. And though his physical appearance and gifts named him Chufa, his clothing and weapons placed him as Tjal, and his purpose named him HuMan, he was none—yet he was all. He was Thane.

The following day found them high above the Shadow Mountains as their mounts carried them ever closer to the Ardath and the Chufa. The nervous excitement was obvious in Tam and Dor, though Dor tried his best to hide it. Thane was happy that his friends were going home. If it were up to him he would leave them there to enjoy each other and their families until the end but he no longer felt he could make such a decision for them. He may try to convince them of reason but in the end he knew they would make their own choice and he feared that it was with him that they would decide to place their lives.

His course was clear. No longer did he fear or doubt what he was doing and why. It was as if a mist had been burned away by the bright, purifying rays of a noonday sun. He felt Jne's chin resting on his shoulder as she peered ahead, no longer cowering behind his back, though her grip was still the noose of the previous days.

The clouds grew thicker and darker, gathering en masse as the wind increased and raged as if trying to forbid them to reach their goal. Thane and Tam caught the scent that told them rain was not only imminent but that a great storm was quickly developing and would overtake them before they reached the Ardath. The sun was completely blotted out, casting a dark shadow upon the rough mountains that separated the Chufa from the rest of the world. The rocs still pressed forward but were buffeted now by the winds that continued to gather and press against them.

Thane felt a rush of power with the coming storm that filled his every fiber calling him to relinquish his hold on the physical world and be free with the air, partaking of its power, becoming one with its strength of force. He resisted the urge to throw his spirit into the thunderous storm, though barely, the desire to release himself almost completely overwhelming him.

"Is there nothing you can do?" Jne yelled in his ear as the rocs shot upward in an attempt to rise above the winds.

He reached tentatively to the winds calling out to them to abate but pulled back almost immediately from the attempt. It was wrong. It felt intrusive and unnatural. He had commanded the winds many times and at the moment felt more powerful than ever before in what he could make them do, but to call them back from the innate processes that governed the planet felt...immoral. He could not do it. He would not do it. To do so would be nothing less than to throw himself in with the likes of Zadok and his evil manipulations of the world's natural functions.

"No!" was his only reply as the rocs continued to reach for the storm's zenith. A web of light crackled through the air followed almost immediately by the pounding sounds of thunder just as the first drops of rain began to batter them.

Quickly, the giant birds changed their strategy and suddenly the four companions were dipped into an incredible dive as rain pelted against their backs while lightning lit up the darkened sky. Jne's face was once again pressed hard against his back and he felt his breath squeezed from his chest as her grip tightened around his waist. They would be forced to fight the elements on the ground.

The mountain peaks loomed closer as the rocs shot toward them, the wind threatening to dislodge their passengers as it whirled about in an angry barrage that menaced the birds ability to remain level. Even with their immense size, the birds were no match for the powerful wind that battered them on every side. They needed to land quickly or risk not only their own lives, but those who clung tenuously to their backs. Sweeping past a large peek, the birds swung out of their dive as they approached the jagged mountain surface. There was nowhere soft to land. The best they could hope for was a shelf-like indention where they could drop in without too much difficulty and hopefully stop their momentum once their talons touched earth.

Thane's roc suddenly banked left and he caught sight of an area that would have to do. Following its lead, the other roc fell in behind as they plunged toward a small level patch that was protected on one side by a few ragged looking trees and on the other by a large rock wall that rose up to a straight, narrow peak. The roc swooped lower, its wings teetering against the wind barely able to keep its flight straight as it rode the current while approaching the ground. Flapping back its wings at the last moment, it tried to ease the landing and pulled back to a stop but was caught by an overpowering gust that knocked it forward sending it hard into the ground. Thane and Jne were sent flying over its head and onto the mountain rock where they landed with a thud, both sliding forward at a dangerous speed toward the rock wall. The roc let out a terrible cry of pain as it twisted to the side, its right wing extended in a horrid fashion where it had been slammed into the mountain. Thane and Jne both hit the wall hard, stealing their breath and leaving them in a heap.

Chapter Eight

Dayne set down the small box in the center of the busy square and then nervously looked around. He'd been issued this command only an hour before and had been sent out, with the rest of his company, with boxes and a charge to see their duty completed. They had rolled dice for location and he had been one of the losers. Originally he'd thought it better than those who were unlucky enough to have to knock the doors of every mansion in the next level, but he now realized that those soldiers were unlikely to encounter anyone at home since all of their inhabitants were more than likely out shopping—where he was—in the upper merchant quarters of the city. The sweet smells wafting past him from the bakery across the street weren't helping the churning in his stomach as he stepped up onto his box.

The contempt that flashed from the eyes of those passing by was obvious. Since he was part of the king's army none would actually force him out but it was evident from the stares that he was only endured at the lowest and most base level. A bug on one's sleeve was given more leave than what would be proffered him. He found no favor here, and with what he was about to announce, he knew the degree of tolerance currently stomached would be strained to the utmost.

"Fine citizens of Calandra," he squeaked, straining to control the quiver in his voice. He was about to continue but realized that no one was paying him any mind as the city's elite passed by on every side. A large woman with too much make up and a hideously large wig bumped him with her flared skirt knocking him from his box and then cursed him for having dared stand in a spot that she desired to occupy. She even tried to kick his box away but the circumference of her skirts made it impossible for her to get close enough and only resulted in the hoop of her skirt pushing the box along the street.

Dayne quickly retrieved his pedestal and thought of leaving the high nosed upper class to their fate but realized he had to at least warn them of the peril that approached. Even though he knew it was futile, he would fulfill his duty. Slamming the box down again, he took a deep breath to calm himself while letting his anger build as best he could to give him the courage to proceed. Placing his index fingers inside his mouth he blew out a loud, high pitched whistled that stopped everyone in the area almost instantly. Most of the women and many of the men placed hands to hearts and lips as if they had just been struck and suddenly he felt the heated glares of everyone in the square focusing on him as if willing he be incinerated where he stood. He tried his best to glare back, but quickly felt his resolve waning in the face of such an enemy. Steel he would face happily, but this type of warfare was foreign and seemingly more lethal than any he'd experienced before. Pushing away the sudden desire to run, he took another breath to steady himself grasping in vain for the last wisps of anger he could muster.

"Fine citizens of Calandra," he began again, no longer worried about the quiver in his voice, just wanting to get his message out and then be gone. "By order of the king, Calandra is ordered emptied by sundown this evening."

There was an ominous moment of silence like the last exhaling breath before death claims its victim and then a sudden uproar filled the square. He was surprised to find the din was not from screams of terror or concern, but rather high peels of laughter. He looked around at the city's upper crust incredulous at their reaction. "A great army approaches," he tried to yell above the noise, but no one seemed to be listening. "You don't understand," he continued in vain, "everyone is leaving. There will not be anyone left to protect you! We must make for a safer haven! You will all die if you stay!"

The last sentence touched enough in the crowd that now some of their faces turned to him with the slightest stroke of worry lining their eyes. Maybe he would be able to talk sense to them after all.

"My friends," a shrill voice suddenly raised above the crowd. Dayne looked to his left spotting the woman who was speaking and felt a chill pass through him. Madam Maggest. There was no hope for them now. "Do not worry yourselves by this…" she paused long enough to shoot the soldier her strongest look of repugnance and condescension, "…servant's ill spoken words. There is no danger. My Prissley is in negotiations with the enemy as we speak drawing up terms for their peaceful surrender. Throw some day old bread at them and a promise of annuities and all will be as it always has. King Dagan has assured me personally that we have no reason to concern ourselves." With her final words she shot Dayne a withering look as if challenging him to dare say anything more.

Knowing that all was lost, Dayne, to the amazement of all, found enough courage to respond. "King Dagan is dead." The response he received from his revelation, though, was not anything at all what he expected.

Madam Maggest merely cocked an eyebrow and he couldn't be certain, but he thought he caught the slightest curl of a smile cross her face. The crowd was hushed by the news but no one seemed the slightest distraught as hands quickly rose to covered whispering lips as the upper class in the square began to chatter about what this meant for them politically. No longer was the imminent threat of an approaching army commanding their attention, but rather how each could use the king's demise to maneuver themselves to a higher station.

"And who sits in his stead now?" she asked, her voice not questioning, but commanding an answer.

"His majesty, Lord Kendun, has returned." Dayne felt sick by what he was witnessing and almost felt relief that none of these people would be leaving the city. Deciding his duty had been fulfilled, he stepped off his box, not bothering to take it with him, and overheard Madam Maggest's shrill voice, in what she obviously thought were hushed tones, "Jack Kendun was easy enough to get rid of the first time. It shouldn't be any more difficult to be rid of him again."

✳   ✳   ✳

"Master Helgar," a voice whispered in the dark as rough hands gently shook the dwarf prince's shoulder.

Helgar's eyes shot open, his hand instinctively reaching for the large battle axe resting beside him. "What be the problem?" he hissed, gripping the axe handle in ready.

"The dragon returns," the voice replied barely loud enough for Helgar to capture the words and their meaning. Since turning west from the outskirts of Calandra the group of dwarf warriors remained vigilant to the skies expecting at any moment for a dragon to drop down on them. No longer did they camp at night in the open by the road but would instead travel miles out of their way to find a stand of trees to bed down under. This night they were nestled tightly in a grove of ash trees that offered thick cover from above and enough trunks to cover their location from the road.

"Where?" Helgar asked gruffly, the battle rage starting to boil within him.

Placing a finger to his lips for quiet, the watch guard motioned with his head for Helgar to follow. Making certain to keep well out of sight from the road the two dwarfs quietly passed from tree to tree using the trunks to hide their movement. Finally, they reached the outskirts of the grove, their backs pressed against the same trunk. "South of the road," the guard whispered softly, "and farther to the west."

Helgar nodded in understanding and slowly moved to the side where he could just see past the tree. The night was dark, the moon just barely making its way into the sky, though the light it offered was minimal being only a day past new. Helgar's eyes strained to focus on what the guard had reported but as he swept the area he was not able to lock in on anything. Normally he would have chastised the dwarf for having a lively imagination, but the King's Guard were no babes new to the world. These were the dwarf's most elite fighters and though they had faced a dragon's wrath previously and understood the fierceness of their enemy, it was still not enough to make them jump at shadows in the night.

Helgar continued to scan the area willing his eyes to draw in more light by which to see when suddenly something large and dark moved farther south and to the west of the area he'd been searching. His eyes locked on it, understanding the girth of such a creature could only equal that of one of the dragons they had faced earlier. He watched it as it raised its serpentine head and then suddenly leaped into the air, spreading its wings and pumping them furiously as it rose from the ground. He followed its flight, moving slowly around the tree to track it until it was too far from sight for him to make out any longer. Turning to the guard he motioned him back toward the camp. "Wake the others!"

The dwarfs maintained a forced watch through the rest of the night in case the dragon had actually discovered them and decided to return, but it never rematerialized. When dawn finally lit the sky, Helgar lead them from the tree cover and investigated the area where the dragon had been spotted. The locale was easy to find with the grass pushed back where its large girth had pressed it. A closer search revealed some blood splattering and a small patch of wool.

"Looks like it found itself a mutton meal," Bardolf proclaimed. If the wool wasn't enough to confirm his thoughts, a distant bleating was suddenly heard carried on the wind coming far to the south of their location.

"By what ye be seein' yesternight," Rangor added, "I'd be sayin' it came from back to the west and be joined with its kin betwixt Haykon and Calandra by now."

Helgar nodded in agreement, his eyes rising to look in the direction of his home to the southwest. "Aye. And I suddenly be feelin' the need to be returnin' more quickly to Thornen Dar."

For the next two days the dwarfs continued at a quickened pace along the road headed toward their mountain home. No longer did they pass the night in slumber but instead took short breaks for food and quick naps before once again taking to the road at a rapid walk or half run. Though still extremely vigilant, no signs of dragons appeared either above or on the ground to the point that the threat of another engagement seemed to be slipping away. Not much was said between them as a fog of foreboding seemed to settle over the group pressing them on even faster as if tragedy threatened to catch them unaware.

On the third night, Helgar pulled them off into a stand of trees not fifty feet from the road for a moment of greatly needed rest. He informed them they had half an hour before setting himself down at the edge of the grove to keep watch. Bardolf offered him a piece of jerked meat and then leaned against a tree just opposite his prince and friend. "I know ye don't be wantin' to hear it, but…"

"Then don't be sayin' it," Helgar snapped.

"…but ye be needin' yer rest too."

"I'll rest when we be back in our home preparin' fer war," he snorted in reply.

"Aye," Bardolf nodded. "It be a grand thought indeed to be splittin' orc and goblin skulls again."

Helgar didn't reply, his thoughts guarded and his mind obviously occupied elsewhere. Bardolf regarded his friend for a moment and then suddenly went perfectly still. "Movement!"

Helgar nodded, seeing the dark form at the same time as it shuffled along the road moving toward Calandra. "What do ye be makin' of it?" he whispered.

Bardolf suddenly left the tree line, trotting toward the form that seemed to struggle to keeps its feet. "Dwarf!" he called back.

The elite guard was at Helgar's back almost instantly as all rushed the figure that was now aware of their presence and had stopped to face them in a defensive stance, his axe held ready.

"Hold friend," Rangor called out as he sprinted passed Helgar who snorted in disapproval. "Ye be in the presence of yer prince."

The figure immediately dropped his axe and dropped to his knees. "Lord Helgar?"

Just then the group converged on the lone dwarf who was obviously wounded and short on energy from a lack of food and water. A skin was passed to him but he brushed it aside, his wide eyes seeking out the prince. "Lord Helgar," he repeated when he wasn't able to pick his liege from the crowd.

Helgar stepped forward. "I be here lad, but what be this nonsense of calling me Lord?"

"My Lord, Helgar," the dwarf said reaching a bloody hand out and taking hold of Helgar's arm. "It be yer father, the king. He be dead!"

"No," Helgar gasped, the full weight of his father's loss and the responsibility it instantly placed on his own shoulders pressing heavily upon him.

"How?" Rangor barked, his own emotions a mixture of anger that the Home Guard did not protect their charge and regret that he was not standing by his king when he fell.

The injured dwarf's eyes got large, a look of terror and incredulity washing over them as he remembered. "Ye'll be thinkin' me daft, but I swear on me axe that what I be tellin' you be true. We were attacked right in the heart of Thornen Dar by a large snake-like creature with great wings."

"Dragon!" Helgar spat. "Do they be formin' from the very rock itself now that they be poppin' up all over the country?"

"If that be the name of such creatures, then aye, it were a dragon," the dwarf answered.

Helgar's stony face turned even harder. "I need only be knowin' one thing about my Da's death. Was it in battle?"

"Aye, my Lord," the dwarf answered. "It were glorious."

Helgar nodded and turned away. No one followed him, understanding his need to be alone at the moment though Rangor motioned with his head for one of his men to keep track of the new king.

"And what of the others?" Bardolf asked. "Be the dragon defeated? And where be the survivors?"

"When it were obvious that none could harm the beast with our axes we took to the deepest tunnels where the mass of the beast no longer could be followin'. We lost many a fine lad in the battle but there still be pockets of others in the bowels of the mountains. I were sent to find King Helgar with another lad but he disappeared not three night past. Have ye not been seein' him?"

Bardolf look away from the dwarf. "Nay, but we seen yer dragon three night past." No one said it, but all knew what Bardolf was thinking.

⋆　　　⋆　　　⋆

"Are these all the horses then?" Jack asked the soldier standing at his elbow.

"Yes, my Lord," the man answered crisply. It hadn't taken long for the news to spread that King Dagan was no longer and that one of the first line of kings had returned. Though most of the men had no memory of Jack and when he first ruled so many years ago, most took the news without the least amount of resistance. It appeared that the previous king was not well loved by those not of the so-called elite class.

Jack had called for the royal coffers to be pilfered of all their wealth and for any owning horses not agreeing to leave the city to be paid twice the horse's worth so that all the animals could be gathered in assisting the massive exodus. Any not agreeing to sell were privately dispatched and the horse then confiscated. It sounded a harsh and murderous command at first, but those not willing to leave would have met a much worse demise at the hands of the enemy. Plus, all the animals were needed to aid the living to escape. Jack had made it clear that no one in the city was to be mistreated but that those staying behind should be considered dead anyway.

Hundreds of horses had been lined up and quickly assessed to see where they would be of the greatest worth and then shuttled off to their assigned duties. The strongest would be used to pull carts of supplies and those people too young, too old, or too unhealthy to match the quick pace that would be required. The remaining horses would be used to carry women and children. All able-bodied men were required to walk. The people were also categorized and shuffled along to different areas according to their health and ability to handle a sword. The armory had also been emptied and all who had them were required to bring any and all weapons with them. Jack had noticed that many of the outlying farmers walked about with their pitchforks and scythes bearing them as their weapons of choice just like many a smithy he'd spotted deftly hefting their hammers. Swords were not the only weapons that could kill.

The groups had been split into companies of tens, fifties, hundreds, and thousands with each group having a commander who was in charge of and spoke for the group. These groups were then surrounded by the cavalry with the regular soldiers and guards to the rear to cover the retreat from the city.

Jack knew they had a day or maybe two at the best to distance his people from the city before Zadok arrived. Though gruesome to contemplate, the elite, all of whom refused to leave, and some from the other classes who still put their trust in Prissley Maggest and his ilk, would be the fodder that stalled and bogged down Zadok's horde as they ransacked the city killing all in their path. In a sick sense, it was those who were staying behind, and unknowingly sacrificing themselves for the rest who were not so clouded by greed to leave, that would turn out being the unlikely heroes. Their eventual sacrifice would give the others a chance to get away—as long as the dragons stayed close to their master.

Jack found himself suddenly scanning the skyline as if expecting to discover the masses of dragons winging toward them. "Good," he said to the soldier while absently pulling at his beard. "Make sure that everyone of them has a rider or is pulling a wagon. I want us leaving by sunset tonight." The soldier saluted smartly and was turning to leave when Jack suddenly called him back. "Oh, and one final thing. Spread the word to the leaders and have them inform everyone that once we leave there will be a single wolg that will be joining the camp."

"Sir?"

He turned to the young man who was obviously perplexed by such a statement. Wolg's were known as natural allies to trolls after all. "He answers to the name Erl," he said, and then his demeanor became hard and intense so that there could be no misunderstanding between them. "No one is to harm him or in any way hassle him. He is not an enemy but one of the greatest allies we have. Do you understand?"

The soldier quickly saluted again. "Yes, sir!"

"Good. Now make sure everyone else understands because if the tiniest thing should befall him, I will be coming after you. Am I clear?"

"Yes, sir!" the soldier answered, the slight quiver in his voice unmistakable.

"Good. Dismissed." The soldier hurried off through the crowds immediately grabbing one of the group leaders to pass the word about the king's strange pet. Jack could not hold back the smile as the man's head turned toward him flashing a look of incredulity. "We've been apart long enough, my friend," he sighed and then turned away catching sight of Ranse and Jace as they approached.

He had been expecting this confrontation ever since he finally revealed his identity in the king's court, but the press of the moment and the almost impossible feat of evacuating a whole city had pushed all other matters far from their thoughts. Now he would finally determine the emotions and mind of the once Prince Ranse. He felt fairly certain that Ranse was not the type to seek office or begrudge a loss in station that he never really held anyway, but Jack had been king long enough and, as a child, been witness first hand to what the hanging carrot of power and authority can do to someone thought beyond such temptations.

"My Lord," Ranse said while saluting and bowing submissively. There was no mockery or spite in his voice or his motions but Jack was still on guard for the slightest hint of resentment.

Smiling faintly, Jack stretched out his bear size hands and grabbed Ranse by the shoulders. Jace flinched slightly at the contact, but did not change his position or reach for his sword. It was obviously an adjustment for him as well. No longer was he the bodyguard to the prince but instead a comrade at arms. "Please, Ranse, call me Jack. I have been too long from the formalities of the royal court to get used to such manners any longer. Plus, I am too old to change now."

Ranse smiled and nodded. "I understand how you feel."

Jack eyed him for a moment, searching his face, still seeking for the slightest sign that would tip him off to any angst toward what had happened to his father or the hunger for a return to position. But all he found was the sincerity of a true heart and the fervor of one who loved his home and country. Still, he had to be absolutely positive. And that is what motivated his next words. "I am sorry for your father and brothers. The last thing I wished for them was their demise."

Ranse looked down for a moment while nodding his head. "Thank you," he finally said, bringing his head up and looking him straight in the eye. "My family was corrupt and broken and, I suppose, they received what they deserved. Had my father acted properly from the start, he would still be alive and our people safe. But, sadly, that is not what will be remembered in the annals of history."

Though Jack didn't want to come right out and ask, he needed to know without doubt and suddenly the words were just falling from his lips. "And what of your sudden loss of power?"

Ranse smiled wearily and slowly shook his head. "As the youngest son, I never really had any. But if you're wondering where I stand concerning your return to the throne I hope you will know my sincerity when I say I am relieved. Now, after all of this is over, I will finally be able to live the life that I choose not one cluttered by formality or duty. You have my pity."

Jack studied his eyes and demeanor for a moment and then smiled sadly. "Thank you. Now you know partly why I disappeared all of those years ago; and also why I was forced to return now."

Ranse smiled, nodding his understanding. Power in the right hands was never something sought after but rather accepted and endured. Those who yearned for it would never be suited for it and would eventually be destroyed by it. "Actually, the main purpose for our coming was to offer you something that is rightfully yours." Ranse looked sadly at Jace who just stared straight ahead.

As if on cue, the large weapons master suddenly bent to one knee, and with a quick and fluid motion drew his sword and placed it on the ground at Jack's feet. "I offer you my sword and my life in defense of your person from any who would seek you harm."

Caught by surprise, Jack looked down at Jace and then looked back at Ranse who just nodded in confirmation. Jack cleared his throat, not certain at first how to respond. "Yes, right, well…" he stammered and then paused. Finally he took a deep breath and stood straight trying to muster an air of authority. "I accept your offer Jace but direct you to remain with Ranse in his service until such time as I feel the need of your arm."

Jace looked up hesitantly, not knowing how to take what his new king had said until Ranse laughed and then spoke. "Well, I guess, old friend, that you are still not rid of me after all. It will be a strain to keep you around but I suppose I cannot counter the command from my king." Ranse nudged Jace with his boot and the large man finally retrieved his sword and slowly stood. "We will serve wherever needed, my Lord," Ranse offered and then both bowed their heads.

Jack nodded back. "I suspect you will."

Chapter Nine

Gorbrak's massive form dropped from the night sky mere yards from the farthest reaches of Zadok's army. His sudden appearance caused quite a stir in those closest to him as he immediately pulled himself inward and resumed his human form; a shape in which he'd spent a majority of his time of late. It had not been difficult to infiltrate Dagan's inner circle of trusted allies as his dragon-fear could also be manipulated to create a sense of total trust in the weak minded. Dagan had been easier than he had anticipated.

Walking through the camp, he had no trouble sniffing out Zadok's presence while a pathway instantly opened for him by those tripping over each other and themselves to keep out of his immediate reach. Though the creatures that made up Zadok's army were typically offensive to his advanced palate, he wasn't beyond killing for the mere enjoyment of wrenching the life out of one of their inferior forms.

He knew Zadok was going to be furious by the news he had to deliver, but he also recognized that all was not lost and that most things had not changed. True, he was no longer in the king's court where he was expected to be at Zadok's arrival, but things had happened that were beyond his control.

Quickly finding Zadok's tent, he entered to find him in deep conversation with his sister, Krengor, also in her human form and Resdin who never seemed to leave his side. Zadok's head turned with a snap, his eyes hot with rage. "What are you doing here!" he shouted.

Gorbrak bowed, though only as far as absolutely required and no more. Zadok was his creator, for which he owed gratitude, but it was only the sorcerer's magic that kept him from ripping out the man's black heart.

Someday he would find a way to nullify his master's power over them and then he would free himself and his siblings from his commands. "There has been an unforeseen change," he answered smoothly.

"There are no changes," Zadok shouted in reply, "unless I make them!"

Resdin sneered at him, obviously enjoying the exchange. It used to bother him that such an insignificant pest would dare mock him. Resdin was like a fly that could not be killed or pushed away. But he quickly discovered that the best way to get back at him, short of eating him outright, was to just ignore him. Like a favorite child, Resdin couldn't stand to be ignored by anyone.

"The king is dead," he said flatly, as if bored by the whole interchange. Though Resdin could be disregarded, he knew he had to still take care with how he dealt with his master. Zadok's power was too great to battle, but that didn't mean he couldn't push the limits a bit. "He has been replaced by another who has claimed the throne."

Zadok composed himself with this new information. "And who is it that now sits in authority?"

"Some lowly human named Kendun."

Zadok suddenly laughed out loud. "So, Kendun returns after all these years." Then becoming serious he asked, "Does he have another heir?"

Gorbrak shrugged. "He came with others but none that appeared to be his pup."

"And where is he now?"

"Don't know," he answered honestly, but just as quickly changed to a lie. "I felt it important to bring you the news so I left right away." He was not about to confess that he'd been chased off by mere birds.

Zadok stared at him as if judging his words. Gorbrak held his gaze, knowing to turn away would reveal his lie. "And what of Wargon?"

"He stayed back to keep an eye on things."

*　　　　*　　　　*

The massive army took up residence in the slums just outside Calandra's first gate, as Prissley and his small entourage escorted Zadok and Resdin, and their three hooded advisors, right up the main street toward the upper level. The gates that had been guarded just days before were now open allowing access to the different levels in the city without the slightest challenge. Prissley seemed faintly agitated by the fact that the streets were completely empty as all those who foolishly chose to stay behind were now hiding in their homes in terror as the realization of their folly had fully revealed itself.

It was just after they reached the second gate that Zadok's army started to follow, pouring into the city proper. They spread out through all the side streets, filling each level as they went, until they were all within the city walls. Zadok's magic was barely able to maintain control over the bloodlust now pumping through their veins, anxious for the killing spree they craved and had been promised.

Prissley seemed totally unaware that the closer he got to the city center the closer he was coming to his demise. All he could think of, for the moment, was that his family would finally sit on Calandra's throne where they would be able to glut themselves on the backs of the people they ruled. Zadok, on the other hand, was becoming agitated. Where were all the people? He had fully expected some sort of trap from Kendun but the time to spring such a stratagem had already passed. The army's bloodlust that was constantly beating against his inner will was beginning to find its way into his own psyche to the point that he felt himself wanting nothing more than to feel someone's blood wash over his hands.

Glancing at Resdin he calmed himself in the euphoric irony that had recently unfolded. Gorbrak's lack of control had actually played more into his twisted will than he could have thought imaginable making this moment all the sweeter. Yet, it bothered him that nothing had yet occurred. They were almost to the inner city and his army would soon be positioned throughout its streets. Though victory had always been his, the glory of the moment was quickly being swallowed up in its relative ease.

A lone woman suddenly approached them followed by her attendants; one holding a bundle of peacock feathers over her head to shade her from the sun while the other carried the train of her bulbous dress so as not to allow it to be defiled by touching the ground. Zadok forced his most charming smile. *Where are you Kendun?*

"My I present," Prissley said, in his annoying nasal tone, "my mother, her Ladyship, Madam Putressa Maggest."

Zadok flourished his best bow taking her outstretched gloved hand and pressing his lips to it. "Madam Maggest," he said, smiling broadly, "it is indeed a tremendous honor to finally make your acquaintance. Your beauty surpasses even that I had imagined when Prissley described you to me."

Putressa blushed, waving a fan she produced as if from nowhere, to cool her flushed face. "You do me too great a tribute, your Lordship. It is I who am honored by your arrival." Over anxious, Madam Maggest suddenly cut right to the business at hand. "I assume Prissley has laid out the groundwork for a mutually successful agreement between us?"

Zadok almost laughed. Prissley had indeed laid the groundwork but to the finality of that work they were yet unaware. "Pardon me if I should sound rude, your Ladyship," he spoke smoothly, "but where might be the king, that the matters at hand might be discussed by those having the proper authority?"

Putressa flushed for a brief moment, obviously offended but then quickly smiled. "Of course, you are right, but let me assure you that all of the authority of Calandra is here present. The previous king has abdicated, of sorts, while the next claimant to the throne has turned tail and scurried from the city leaving my family as the rightful heirs to the throne."

"What!" Zadok raged. Prissley and his mother jumped at his breach in protocol, both bringing over-jeweled hands to their mouths, their entourages stepping back in fear. Zadok was suddenly right in Putressa's face. "What do you mean he left the city? Where is everyone else!" he demanded.

Madam Maggest felt herself almost at a loss for words. "He…well that is…"

Zadok nodded to one of his hooded servants whose hand suddenly reached out and caught Prissley by the neck. Prissley froze, the terror thick in his eyes that seemed to bulge from their sockets. "I asked you a question, woman," Zadok hissed.

A puddle suddenly formed underneath Putressa's dress as she fought to gain the air necessary to answer. "M-most h-h-have gone," she stuttered, barely above a whisper.

"Where?"

"I, I d-don't know exactly. Th-th-they've left the c-c-city." Suddenly gaining her breath she pleaded. "Please, my Lord, there are still enough of us here to work out a satisfactory agreement. I'm sure we can accommodate you."

Zadok flashed his most charming smile. Putressa seemed to relax some though her eyes still darted back and forth between Prissley, who was obviously struggling to breathe, and Zadok. "Yes, my dear," Zadok answered, "you will provide us with all we need—and more."

Madam Maggest tried to scream but her throat was already squeezed shut.

✶   ✶   ✶

Tryg watched with obvious concern as Tchee circled above the camp in the early morning light. Since he joined up with them, Tchee had not let him out of her sight. He loathed the winged creature but knew he could not let his hatred for her get the best of him. He needed to stay with the group and there was nothing, at this point, that he was willing do to invite a dismissal.

The tent flap opened behind him and Jack emerged stretching and still trying to rub the sleep from his eyes. He could hear Domis and Teek stirring within. "Good morning," Jack offered, throwing him a poorly veiled look of suspicion as he passed. Tryg merely nodded, grateful the newfound king did not stop to wait for an answer. Waiting until the king's back had almost disappeared from sight he checked the air once more, taking in Tchee's position before stepping forward to follow Jack.

"Hey Tryg," Domis' voice emerged from the tent, "where do you think you're going?"

He sighed, stealing his resolve before turning to face the head that had popped from the tent. "I have things to do," he spat, trying to control the hatred that suddenly flared and leaked into his voice.

Domis' eyes narrowed slightly. "I agree. But they aren't in that direction. We need to get the tent packed and today would be a good day for you to start helping."

Tryg waved him off. "I didn't sleep in it. It's not my problem." Then turning, he stormed off in the direction Jack had gone.

"He'd just get in the way," Teek's voice offered from the belly of the tent drawing Domis back in.

"Were all of your people like that?" Domis asked while helping Teek pack up their bedding.

Domis and Teek had made a spot for Tryg in the tent they were sharing with Jack but the boy had refused, claiming he preferred to remain outside. At one point during their first night, Domis awoke to find Tryg standing over Jack. When he called out to him to find out what he was doing, he seemed startled and turned himself back out of doors without the slightest word of explanation. He was beginning to make Domis very uncomfortable.

"Who knows what he has been through?" Teek answered tying one of the bedrolls together.

"Exactly," Domis replied. "No one knows because he refuses to tell us anything."

Teek looked away. "It's not always easy to deal with loss. People handle it in different ways."

Domis sighed. He and Teek had spoken rather freely about the loss of each of their parents and had found that it helped them both to heal, as well as bonded them as friends. He knew that Teek's tragedy was still fresh in his mind and that for Tryg it must be even a greater shock still. Though Teek did not remember the boy from home, he had told them that he had been on an Appeasing Journey and hadn't heard about the demise of their people until Teek told him. Even then, his reaction seemed less than interested. It was as if Teek were merely showing him how to tie a knot he already knew how to fasten.

"I don't mean to make light of the tragedy you both face or the way he chooses to work through it. It's just…I don't know. My hair seems to stand on end whenever he's around. He's not like you."

Teek smiled. "I think I understand what you are saying."

Domis cheered. "You do?"

"Yes," Teek said, nodding. "And you don't need to worry about it. Just because Tryg and I are both Waseeni and you are not, doesn't mean our friendship will change at all."

Domis shook his head in disbelief. "That's not it, Teek!"

Teek just smiled back. "We're best friends, Domis. And that's not going to change."

Domis just let it go at that. He did have to admit that at first he had been worried he would be left out when Tryg first showed up. But he was already beyond that. It was something else. He didn't trust Tryg, and he was fairly certain it had nothing to do with his friendship with Teek.

*   *   *

Jack moved quickly away from the camp, anxious to be out in the grasslands alone. He'd been too long around people and just needed a few moments of his own to clear his thoughts and listen to the quiet without having to be constantly interrupted by someone needing one thing or another. He'd forgotten how demanding it had been to be king.

It was only the second day since they left Calandra but the excitement of the adventure had quickly fallen away for most. To move such a large group of people was difficult at best. Few fully understood the reason they were leaving which meant most complained almost incessantly. After the first night, a large group of the merchant class was determined to return to the city. It wasn't until they were told they would forfeit all their goods and animals and have to walk back without supplies that they finally agreed to stay. And though he knew their tongues would be poison to many of the others, he was not willing to give their lives up so easily; even when they cared less for themselves than he.

He was close to a mile off before he stopped to take in his surroundings.

Typical of the area, small patches of trees in various sizes sprang up from the grasslands and dotted the countryside as if at war with the grasses to see which would rule over the landscape. A slight breeze brushed his hair blowing out of the west as the sun was quickly drying the remaining dew that clung tenaciously to the prairie. The land smelled clean and it invigorated his old bones to commune with it alone. Since his authority and royalty was still not well known among even the army, he was still relatively free to move about as he pleased. That, of course, would change once circumstances improved and he was officially recognized. Moments like this would be mere memories of the past once he sat on the throne. He wanted nothing to do with a bodyguard or any of the other pomp that was visited upon the royal household that left him as free as he was—for the moment.

He looked toward the mountains in the northeast just barely visible from this distance and thought about Thane. He'd become accustomed to having the Chufa boy around and wondered how he faired. He knew he would be safe under Jne's protection and that of his friends, Dor and Tam, but he couldn't completely be rid of the worry that constantly beat itself into his thoughts. Turning back toward the camp he thought he caught the slightest glimpse of someone approaching but was blinded by the rising sun as it suddenly broke over the distant horizon. Shielding his eyes as best he could, he tried to focus on the area where he was almost certain he'd spotted someone but it was to no avail. Whomever, or whatever, he saw was gone.

Turning back north, away from the sun, he sighed and dropped his hand just in time to meet the dirt with his face as a great weight suddenly toppled him to the ground. Reacting almost by instinct, he didn't resist the force but moved with it using the momentum of his attacker to throw it off and then regain his feet in a crouch. But before he had a chance to react, the large form was back on top of him, pinning him to the ground where it viciously attacked, slobbering all over his face as its large tongue licked him in delight. Jack started laughing, trying to push the huge hairy beast off his chest.

"Enough, Erl!" he cried helplessly as his long missed companion continued his soggy assault. "I have missed you too, old friend," he gasped, reaching up and scratching behind the wolg's ears while trying futilely to avoid his lapping tongue. "But it won't do for you to drown me in slobber!"

With another heave, Erl finally moved away long enough for Jack to roll over and regain his feet. Erl whined, his whole body gyrating with the constant wag of his tale. Jack knelt in front of his formidable companion, embracing him around the neck while rubbing his ears.

*   *   *

"It's good to have you back, my Lord," Myles said while saluting his approaching king, his eyes darting to the wolg at his side that casually kept pace with him. "I see you have found your friend," he added, pulling at his horse's reins to hold him in control. Word had gone out about the king's strange choice in companions but that did not mean anyone was comfortable with the idea of having a wolg walking around the camp. The refugees seemed less apprehensive about it since almost none of them had ever seen a wolg before, let alone knew that all but Erl were fierce enemies. Still, his size alone, kept any from getting very close. Jack had to smile. He'd not wanted a bodyguard but it appeared he had one after all.

It was just two hours past midday and the large mass of bodies was relatively quiet now as they marched along the road spread out to either side for close to a quarter of a mile. Colonel Braxton had been too busy with the business involving his troops and their role in the escape to seek out the king himself. Few could meet the relief he'd felt when Jack finally revealed himself in Dagan's court. It was his honor and sense of duty that had kept him from doing anything that would go against his sworn king, even when he knew the true king was present. Until Jack remade his claim to the throne, he'd been duty bound to Dagan and would have still remained in the court at that moment, waiting for certain death with his liege, if Jack had not come forward. But it was not that that relieved him so. His life would have been offered without regret. No, his relief came from the realization that their people might finally have a chance against the enemy.

"I told you, Myles," Jack said gruffly as he pulled his mount up next to the colonel's to walk beside him, "Call me Jack."

Colonel Braxton smiled. "You've been away from court too long, old friend. The title is your right and the mere mention of it gives you greater authority in the eyes of the people. No one will follow Jack. But all will pick up and trail after their liege, the king."

Jack frowned but nodded his head. "I suppose you are right," he conceded, looking around at the faces closest to them but none looked back at him with anymore recognition than they would have given to any of the many common soldiers milling about. The only looks that were passed around belonged to Erl alone. "But, I don't think any of them know me."

Myles made to disagree but noticed the blank stares. "They are happy to have you, nonetheless," he replied, "even if they are not aware of it as of yet."

Jack harrumphed. "Where's Wess?"

Myles nodded toward his right shoulder. Turning, Jack caught sight of him carefully picking his way though the crowd of people leading his horse so as not to accidentally step on anyone. Reaching the other two, he quickly took his seat in the saddle, saluting to Jack as he did so and nodding a warm welcome to Myles. "Looks like we're all back together again," he said, smiling contentedly and then looking at Erl added, "plus one."

"Well," Jack returned, taking stock of the man who at their last meeting was crawling about in the gutter, "at least this time I recognize you."

Wess smiled and bowed his head. "A circumstance in which I would still be in if not for the mercy of your grace."

Jack bristled at the formality but didn't say anything more about it. "And your men?"

"All accounted for, thanks to your friend and his large body guard. Didn't take much explaining I hear, once the guard had a sword at his throat and the royal seal swinging in his face."

"Good," Jack said. "We'll need every last one before this is over."

A horn suddenly blew at the head of the line as a ripple of fear seemed to race through the crowd as they suddenly turned and started running back to Calandra. The three men halted their mounts and looked westward where a large, dark form quickly materialized in the distant sky. Erl growled low in his throat.

"Dragon!" Jack shouted, turning around to look down the road. About a quarter of a mile back, a large grove of trees stood as sentinels on a rising knoll just to the north. Grabbing Myles' arm he pointed to the trees. "Get these people under cover!" he barked and then turned to Wess. "Follow me!" Kicking his horse into a hard gallop, Jack raced toward the approaching dragon.

By this time, the dragon fear had spread throughout the mass of refugees that suddenly trampled over each other while running in all directions feeling a desperate need to escape. Those crushed in the initial panic would never know why their lives had unexpectedly been snuffed out.

Jack tried to press his horse forward calling for archers as he did so, but his progress was slowed by the mass of people cutting in front of him as he tried to make ground toward the dragon. He watched in horror as the great form suddenly dipped for what could only be an attack on the refugees still bunched together on the road, the dragon fear paralyzing them where they stood. Jack caught sight of a ragged line of archers gathering just to his left pulling back their bows and preparing to fire. "Hold!" he called out to them knowing their arrows were useless and that when they ricocheted from the dragon they might take out some of the people huddled together below. He felt helpless as he watched. The only one who had ever brought a dragon down was somewhere in the Shadow Mountains.

Suddenly a white blur caught his attention as it shot passed him on the right bringing a surge of hope to his heart. The giant bird shot up in a direct course to overtake the dragon. In the press of the moment, Jack had forgotten about Teek's large ally. He knew the bird would not be able to do much damage to their foe but he'd seen Tchee use her smaller body and quick maneuvering to harass and chase a dragon away before.

Tchee came at the dragon from the side, aiming for its wing but struck its chest instead. Seeing the great bird approach it had suddenly veered to protect itself and then reached out a claw, as Tchee struck, and grabbed the bird's leg. Jack gasped as for a brief moment it appeared the dragon had Tchee and would certainly take her life but her beak shot out at its exposed wing. In an instant, she was free once again, quickly extricating herself from the dragon's clasp. The dragon cried in frustration and anger but nonetheless turned away southward toward the Underwoods Forest and flew away.

Chapter Ten

"Turn back!" Dor screamed at the roc above the din of the raging storm. "Turn back, I can't see them anymore!"

The roc let out a tremendous scream in reply as it continued to fly away from their companions, now left on the mountainside possibly injured or worse. They had seen what had happen to the bird Thane and Jne had ridden as it was slammed to the ground by the powerful winds that continued to berate them. The roc Dor and Tam rode had let out a terrible screech at seeing its companion dashed against the rocks before it turned upward, overshooting the shelf and continuing east away from their friends. Dor tried, without success, to get the giant bird to go back, worried his friends, who he'd seen catapulted toward the solid wall of rock, were also injured. But their mount either did not understand his desperate cries or it was ignoring him as it descended over another peak before dropping into a mountain meadow where they landed somewhat roughly, but intact.

Dor kicked at the birds sides trying, like a horse, to get it to move again, but it's wings remained firmly tucked against its sides, a low rumble of warning vibrating through its chest that Dor felt rather than heard. Tam grabbed his leg, also feeling the bird's discontent at Dor's treatment. "We have to get this thing to take us back," he cried to her his voice barely audible above the storm.

"I know," she replied, "but it's obvious we're not going right now. I'm just as worried as you are, but we can't get to them safely in this weather. You saw what happened to Thane and Jne."

"I did. That's why we need to go back. They might be hurt. From the way their bird hit the mountain, I wouldn't be surprised if it were dead. We need to go back."

Tam laid her head back against Dor's shoulder. "I know," she said softly in his ear, the emotion breaking in her voice, "but there's nothing we can do right now. What help will we be if we kill ourselves? We need to find shelter and wait out the storm."

Dor took a deep breath, the smell of her hair almost intoxicating. She was right, and though he wanted it to be otherwise, he knew the choice was not theirs to make. Without the roc they would not be able to reach their friends, let alone find them in this weather. He nodded his head and then reluctantly let go of her as they both slid off the giant bird's back. As soon as they touched the ground the roc's large wing reached outward and engulfed them pulling them close in a cocoon of protection against the raging storm. At first they resisted, uncertain of the bird's intentions, but it quickly became evident they were being treated as if they were its young. It was warm and dry nestled among the bird's downy feathers while the storm raged just beyond its protective wing.

∗   ∗   ∗

Thane slowly opened his eyes and blinked to try and bring them into focus. Jne was leaning over him, her voice a distant echo as she cradled his head. He could see her lips moving but the sound was lost in the storm bearing down on them and the one now raging in his skull. The top of his head was throbbing but other than a few scratches, he didn't think he was hurt. He concentrated on the pain which seemed to focus his mind and Jne's voice that suddenly rang in his ears at full volume.

"Thane, can you hear me?" she yelled. "Do you know who I am?"

Suddenly regaining his full senses, he nodded slowly and then gingerly sat up. "I'm fine," he shouted against the wind, which didn't help the pain that crashed like waves against his skull. "Are you hurt?"

Jne shook her head though he could see a small trickle of blood flowing down her left arm. Seeing that he noticed, she eyed him, almost daring him to make reference to such a minor injury but he just smiled and nodded. "Where are the others," he asked, searching the small precipice, his eyes landing on the large bird. At first it appeared it had died on impact, its head resting on the wet rock, its eyes closed. Seeing it, he shot to his feet, forcing back the nauseated feeling that rose in his throat.

Jne followed him, pressing her body close to his for support and warmth. "I don't know, what happened to the others. Before we hit, they were close behind us."

Thane didn't reply as he bent down and tried to discover if there was any life left in the roc. The blowing wind ruffled its feathers making it difficult to determine if it was breathing or not. Its right wing was obviously broken by the way it was extended out to the side. Timidly placing a hand on the bird's head, its exposed eye suddenly opened and a gurgling rumbled in its chest.

Thane let out a slight sigh. "It's still alive," he breathed, but looking at the broken wing he realized that there was no hope to save its life. A bird without flight, even one as large and powerful as a roc, would not be able to feed itself or defend itself for long. It was lost. Thane sat back on his heals and looked up at Jne. "We can't save it."

"You must tell it," Jne said flatly, as if speaking to a bird was the most natural thing. Of course, for Thane, it was but he didn't see the point. Rocs were extremely intelligent. It would know there was no hope for it. Telling it so seemed almost profane. He resisted.

"I think it already knows."

"Of course it does," she said with that tone she used as if addressing a child. "You must tell it so you will know if it desires us to ease its passing. Even an enemy is not left to suffer if he begs for a quick end."

He held her gaze for a moment. She seemed so simple in what she held to that he thought he understood her but then she always surprised and amazed him. Finally, he just nodded and then turned his focus on the roc's open, blinking eye. In a rush he suddenly felt himself become a part of the bird, the pain in his right wing was almost unbearable. It was hard to fight through it to form the thoughts necessary to communicate. *Why do you wait, Earth Child? Why do you make me suffer this pain? Have I not given all to you? Then why do you treat me so poorly?*

Thane was suddenly so overcome by the roc's thoughts and feelings that he was disgusted by who he was and almost lost his connection. *I wanted to ask permission first*, he finally sent back his reply. *I didn't know if you would want me to.*

A sense of confusion and incredulity washed over his senses and he found himself questioning his own answer as foolishness. There was only one thing he needed to know. *Would you like me to do it or my companion?* The question was simple. Either one of them could easily complete the task, but then why did he suddenly feel a wash of confusion?

Of what do you speak? The female is no Earth Child. Only you can heal me.

Thane let go of the contact with a snap that sent him back a step. "Heal you!?" Jne opened her mouth to speak but already he was diving back into the bird's psyche. *Heal you? I can't heal you.*

You are Earth Child. You can heal me. All you need do is make it happen.

He was suddenly feeling desperate. He was preparing to pull his sword and quickly end the bird's life while all along it was thinking he was stalling in healing it. But how was he to do it? This was not like the elements that seemed to answer to his call with the slightest bit of concentration. The roc was talking about putting bone, vessel and tissue back into their proper place and order and then mending them there. Where would he start? Which Tane did he need to call forth? And how did the roc know he could heal it when he'd had no inclination to even try?

Thane broke contact and looked at Jne. "It wants me to heal it."

Her facial expression did not show the slightest surprise but she did question him. "Can you do that?"

Thane shook his head. "I don't know. The bird thinks I can but I wouldn't even know where to start." He rubbed his right shoulder as if the memory of the pain he'd felt while connected with the bird lingered into his own body. "I know the wing is broken." He shrugged. "I even know where, but I just don't know how to proceed."

"You must decide," Jne pressed.

"Decide what?"

"Either you heal it or we must end its life. There are no other options."

He nodded. Jne's statement was obvious but he still didn't know how to go about it. He made contact again. The pain was so intense now that he saw himself gasp as he peered through the roc's eyes. *I will attempt to heal you. I have an idea but you must trust me and endure additional pain.*

I trust you came the reply and once again he was back in his own mind, the echoed pain still quite real in his own shoulder. "I need your knife," he motioned to Jne.

"So you will kill it?" she asked while passing him her dagger.

"No," came the quick reply as he took the blade and approached the bird. Reaching out, he slowly and gently moved his hand over the wing. It was easy to locate the break right at the shoulder where a sickly lump pressed outward against the skin and feathers. Looking down at the roc he took a deep breath and then brought the dagger up and pressed it against the lump, quickly slashing open the skin and exposing the bone that now protruded out. The roc screamed an awful cry but amazingly remained still save for a shiver that shook repeatedly through its body. Sweat was mingling with the rain that continued to pelt them as he passed the blade back to Jne giving her a quick glance before turning his full attention to the broken bone.

This was where he was the most uncertain as how to proceed. This would also be the most painful part. He just hoped that the roc would be able to control itself from snapping him in half with its powerful beak. He took a deep breath and then reached out with both hands. He had to realign the bones together. The roc let out a slight whine and then rumbled in its chest as Thane's hands reached into the fresh wound. The muscles were pulling the bone past the break while the other end was now protruding through the wound. Grasping them with each hand, he turned and called out to Jne. "When I say, pull the wing towards you. We need to get the two parts back together." Jne just nodded, grabbing the wing with both hands and then digging her feet into the rock as best she could to get footing. He looked down at the roc, its eye pressed tightly shut and then glanced back at Jne who nodded her readiness. The blood from the roc's wound was mingling with the rain making Thane's grip on the bones slick but there was no helping it. Concentrating on what he had to do, he called out above the thunderous wind, "One, two, pull!"

Jne jerked back on the wing, fighting the muscles that spasmed and pulled against her. The roc let out an awful cry and moved involuntarily almost knocking Thane to the ground as he worked to position the bones back in their natural place.

"Harder!" he shouted as Jne pulled, making progress but not quickly enough to alleviate Thane's fear that the bird would soon lose tolerance and lash out at them. Jne grunted and pulled with renewed effort slowly overcoming the pull by the bird's muscles. "That's it," he called out, "almost there," as the bone inched back and then suddenly popped back into position.

The roc's body went limp, its muscles relaxing now that the break was returned to its natural position. But now what? Thane was able to hold the bones together, but any movement from the roc would just throw them out of position again. He had to mend the bone, but how?

Holding the broken bones tightly together he concentrated his mind on the break hoping that something would awaken in him to mend it. The bird said all he had to do was make it so, but he had no experience with such a thing to know how to proceed. Which Tane did he need to call forth to heal bone? He could sense the five within him waiting for him to call upon them to do his bidding but which of the Tane had the power to mend it. Shutting out the wind and rain that continued its barrage upon the mountain, he sank deep within himself eliminating all distraction save the pieces of bone that now became a part of his own body, connected to him through his hands. He delved deeper into the pores and marrow seeking a connection that would allow him to fuse them as one again.

Then an idea entered his thoughts. It seemed so simple, but he had nothing else to draw upon. Taking a deep breath, he began to sing the song of growing used when the Chufa planted. He started off soft but then his voice grew louder. Suddenly he could feel his TehChao Tane awakening within him, its power flowing down his arms and out through his hands that gripped the bone. He feared it wouldn't have the effect he desired but he continued the song anyway. It was the only Tane he knew of that encouraged growth and it had awaken within him at his call. The bone in his hands began to warm and then suddenly he could feel both sides reaching toward each other and then intertwining and solidifying, bringing the pieces back together and mending them into one. It was quick, without extravagance, but complete. He slowly let go, the crack no longer visible as if the bone had never been broken.

Not wasting anytime to admire his work, he quickly brought the knife to his hand and cut it allowing his blood to flow into the roc's wound and mingle with its blood to eliminate any possible infections. Then pressing the sides of the wound together, he used his QenChe Tane to cauterize and heal it. No longer did the large bird struggle, its breathing slowing to normal. Then, with the slightest hesitation, it stood up and tentatively stretch out it wings. Had Thane and Jne just happened upon the roc they would not have been able to tell that just moments before it had been writhing in pain with a broken wing.

Thane smiled slightly and shook his head in amazement. "I did it," he said, his surprise registering in his voice.

Jne looked at him, a slight glint of something in her eye that he couldn't immediately decipher and then she flashed him that magnificent smile that so rarely surfaced. "I knew you could."

He held her gaze for a long moment until she surprisingly looked away, the slightest touch of red coloring her cheeks. He didn't think he would ever fully understand this woman that was so rigid and uncompromising yet, at times, seemed, for the briefest moments, a little child just barely weaned from her mother's lap.

A screech from the roc brought their attention back as they watched it bounce on its feet and then bob its head, the cooing sounds coming from its throat just audible over the wind. Thane smiled at its celebration at being healed, happy that it had the faith in him to make him try to heal it. Turning to Thane it locked on his eyes and drew him in. *Thanks be to you for healing me. I am Azaforte. My once mate is Debipena. The giving of names is a sign of respect and honor. You are named Irmante, or friend.*

Touched, Thane responded as he thought proper. *I am Thane of the Five Tane. You have given all for us. We owe you so much more.*

We give willingly without expectation of anything in return. The choice was always ours to make. Our sacrifice, though great, is only a small part of what others have already given and will eventually give in the end. Others will yet make the last great sacrifice to save us all.

Thane broke contact but instead of feeling the joy he had originally felt at healing Azaforte, he suddenly felt dark and cold, like a part of him was dying. He looked at the roc for a moment longer trying to understand why he suddenly felt so alone. A warm hand touched his arm startling him. He turned to see Jne, her face seeming slightly pale in the dim light.

"We must find the others," she said softly, her hand lingering on his arm before she almost reluctantly pulled it away.

He blinked, and then just nodded. Forcing a smile, he pointed to the roc, "This is Azaforte."

Chapter Eleven

"Try again," Dor encouraged.

Tam gave him an exasperated look but said nothing. Instead she closed her eyes and tried to make contact with the raging wind that whisked her hair about stinging her face as it cracked like a whip against her skin with the changing gusts. It had only been short moments after they where encased in a cocoon of roc feathers that Dor had suggested she try to ride the winds like Thane and attempt to find and make contact with their friends. At first she was hesitant, unsure of herself or the possible dangers inherent with riding the winds, but necessity and fear for Thane and Jne's safety had won out and she now found herself facing the angry elements as she tried to throw her spirit into the air currents. She actually felt grateful for the strong winds as she could almost feel her ArVen Tane stirring within her, begging for release.

Dor watched with anticipation feeling completely useless as Tam's eyes were pressed shut, the concentration she was exerting marring her face. She thought back to the thrill she'd felt while flying on the roc and how the wind had called to her in such a way that made her want to just completely lose herself in its force and power. She tried to clear her mind of any other thought or sense other than the air currents flowing past. She tried to reach out to them but felt as if a door still remained locked mocking her efforts.

Something was holding her back, she could feel it. It wasn't the wind. It seemed to call to her like a distant echo barely noticeable above the multiple sensations that bombarded her senses. She was the one creating the wall, she knew it, but she wasn't sure what she was doing to keep it there, not allowing her to just let go and travel along the air's currents.

She tried again to clear her mind of the thoughts that seemed to race unbidden down its many corridors, disrupting her ability to touch the wind with her soul and release herself from her body. She could feel her heart pounding hard and fast against her chest, the rhythm of it sounding loudly in her ears. The wind whispered to her, caressing her skin, inviting her to let go and follow. She wanted to listen, she wanted to obey the quiet voice, but still she remained earthbound, her soul locked tightly within her solid frame.

The wind slapped her as if mocking her for choosing to remain stuck to the ground. She suddenly felt ashamed as if she were denying her Tane, as if she were denying the person she was. A tear slowly slid down her cheek and opening her eyes there was Dor, patiently watching and waiting.

"Did you do it?" he asked excitedly.

Tam's expression dropped as she shook her head. "I can't let go," she said, the tears coming more quickly now. "It's right there but I can't seem to reach out and touch it."

To both their surprise, Dor's arms suddenly wrapped around her and pulled her close. She could feel the slight shiver in his body, but whether from the cold or the nervous excitement that came from being so close she couldn't tell. She felt warmed by his touch, letting go with a sigh the anger and frustration she'd felt only moments before.

"You're trying too hard," he whispered into her ear. "You can't force it. You just need to allow it to happen."

She looked up at him, her voice more stinging than she'd wanted it to be. "That is so easy for you to say when it's not you who has to perform." She immediately regretted her rebuke as Dor's arms slipped away leaving them separated again.

"I don't chide you," he said, his voice remaining surprisingly soft. "I only meant to encourage. I know what it is like to try and fail. Every night, since Thane challenged me to use my Tane and pull water from a bag, I have spent hours trying to force the water to obey my command. It's not until watching you now that I understand why I fail. The Tane are not to be forced or commanded. It is us who need to bend to their will. Only then comes the ability to direct that will where we want it to go. For once, Tam, stop trying to control everything and let yourself go."

His words stung and her natural reaction was to lash out, but she knew by the tone he used and the way he was looking at her that he hadn't said it as a challenge or a rebuke, but with concern, and even—love. She bit back the anger that had flared and instead reached out and drew him in, hugging him close. No words were exchanged but when she finally let him go she felt calm and serene.

Sitting down, she leaned back against the roc that had remained in the same spot since they landed; it appeared to be sleeping, though how it managed in such a storm was beyond her understanding. Closing her eyes, she let herself sink back against the downy feathers and freed her mind to wander releasing, as she did so, all the stress and pressure she'd felt. She didn't think about wind or trying to force contact, she just let herself feel it as it ripped past her as if in a rage. The power she felt in it was intoxicating and she wanted to embrace it but she forced herself to do no more than be aware of its existence. She could feel it calling her now and something within her cried out for release; it was her Tane. It struggled to be unconstrained and answer the wind's bidding.

Tam hesitated for a moment, a sudden fear rising in her that she fought hard to suppress knowing that it would extinguish the spark that had started to grow. And then, she let go. Let go of herself, let go of who she was, gave herself over to the control of her Tane and the fierce energy that was the wind.

All at once she felt herself gliding, flowing along with the greatest sense of freedom and joy that she had ever felt in her life. Up and down she floated, racing along a river of air that carried her farther and farther away. She hesitated in opening her eyes, afraid that the sensations would turn out to be tricks of the mind. She suddenly laughed at the thrill feeling an unspeakable amount of elation and independence. Nothing held her. Nothing bound her to its will. She was nothing and everything all at once.

Slowly, she opened her eyes not quite knowing what to expect. She gasped involuntarily. She'd done it. She was free from her body and racing over the wondrous peaks and lush valleys that made up the Shadow Mountains. For a place of such extreme danger it was intensely beautiful to behold from high in the air. For the moment she completely lost herself in the power and liberty the winds offered, letting them carry her along at their whim to wherever they deemed to go. Never in her life had she felt so alive. It was an ecstasy that defied description.

She watched the mountains slip away below and suddenly found herself carried over the Dedrik forest past Hell's End Station. She felt herself picking up speed now as she was dropped low to rush over the plains back toward Calandra. Her heart sank as wisps of smoke snaked through the air over the capital city, obviously overrun by Zadok's army.

"And who are you?" a sinister voice suddenly spoke.

Tam gasped as an evil face seemed to appear out of nowhere directly in front of her. Though the wind continued to carry her along, the face remained as if locked in with her movements. The air suddenly felt strange;

oily was the only thing she could think of to describe it. She felt like she needed to bathe. The face cackled malevolently, sending a shiver through her body. Though she'd not felt the sensation of temperature with the wind, she suddenly felt cold.

"Whhh…at do you waaa..nt?" she finally managed. "Who are you?"

The face laughed. "It does not matter, my sweet," it said smoothly but without emotion. "You will not live to remember it."

Tam's eyes widened in terror as she suddenly felt the air around her begin to dissipate. She knew from Thane that to lose all the wind in such a state was to lose her life. "Wait!" she cried in desperation, her voice pleading. "Don't. Please, don't do this."

The face merely laughed, the evil stench of its form sickening her. "Don't worry my dear," it sneered. "This will only hurt, a lot."

She became desperate as the strands of wind holding her up and keeping her alive suddenly began to unravel more quickly. She tried to call out to them but she didn't know how to make them stronger. One by one they simply let go and faded away. One by one the strands of her life were snuffed out by the evil form bent on her destruction. One by one the pain she was suddenly feeling increased as parts of her seemed to fade with the currents the wicked figure destroyed. She struggled in desperation but it was no use. The wind would not come to her rescue and there were very few strands left keeping her connected to life.

The pain was almost more than she could handle and she suddenly found herself yearning that the last wisps of current would be torn away so she would no longer have to suffer so. She whimpered and then let out a terrible scream.

"Tam!"

Her eyes snapped opened and she found Dor, Thane and Jne standing over her with bright smiles on their faces. The storm still raged but she didn't seem to notice as she let out a terrible cry before falling into Dor's arms.

Dor looked up at Thane, a concerned look on his face. "What is wrong with her?"

Thane knelt down by his friends while Jne merely watched, her expression unreadable. "Tam," he said gently, placing a supportive hand on her back. "What ails you? You are safe."

She looked up at him, her sobs coming in waves almost to match the storm. "It was killing me," she said, gasping between sobs.

"What was killing you?" Dor asked in confusion.

She rested her head on his shoulder, the sobs still coming uncontrollably.

"It was awful. I was riding the winds on my way to look for Thane and Jne."

Thane suddenly grasped her arm. "You rode the winds?" he asked excitedly. "You actually left your body and rode the wind currents?"

She only nodded. "But there was this face."

Thane's expression instantly turned dark. "A face?"

"Yes," she said, finally gaining some control over her tears. "It was evil and it laughed at me as it unraveled the wind and tried to kill me."

"Zadok!" Thane cursed. "But how did he find you?"

She shook her head. "I don't know. How is it that he can ride the winds like you and me? Is he a Chufa?"

Thane shook his head. "Once, maybe, and even then I'm not so certain. He uses sorcery to force his will on nature."

"I was almost lost," she cried. "How is it that I am not dead?"

Dor's face suddenly looked ashen. "I called your name and you just opened your eyes. Thane and Jne found us. I thought that you had fallen asleep, so I was waking you to tell you that you didn't have to try to connect to the winds anymore." He gave Thane a questioning look.

Thane shook his head. "I don't understand how it works exactly. All I know is that when we leave our bodies they remain in some type of trance-like state and to disturb that immediately returns us to our bodies."

Dor swallowed hard, the knowledge that Tam had almost been killed striking him like nothing else had before. He suddenly felt weak.

"There was something else," Tam said, finally gaining some control over her emotions. "I saw Calandra. It is taken."

Thane just nodded. All of them knew that the city would fall. And though he was concerned for Tam, the danger to her had past and was quickly being devoured by his excitement at what she'd accomplished. With the revelation that came with Kat's and Bren's ability to use multiple Tane he had hoped that not only could he teach others to go beyond their own Tane, a complete failure when Dor tried, but also to use the powers their existing Tane offered. Now he had proof that others could wield the same powers as he. His people had fallen into mediocrity because they lost the ability, or will, to use what the Tane offered. If he could just get them to listen to him when they reached the Ardath, the Chufa could rise as a great people once again. Not to rule or press authority over others, but to become the beautiful race he knew they must have been during Gelfin's time.

Gripping Tam's shoulder, he motioned toward the rocs sitting close to each other huddled in against the storm. "Are you able to ride again?"

She nodded her head.

"Good. We need to keep moving. Time is no longer the luxury it once was. If Calandra is taken, as you say, then we probably only have a few days before Zadok's evil satiates itself on the lives of their victims and they begin to move on after the others. We need to get the arrow and return before then so we can fight against the dragons."

Tam and Dor only nodded in agreement, Dor helping her to her feet. Thane turned to Jne who was suddenly smiling at him. It captured him how beautiful that smile was when she shared it with him. Not wanting it to end, though confused why she had chosen to gift him with it, he smiled back but then raised an eyebrow in question. Jne moved past him toward their mount and merely said, "Your honor makes you extremely attractive."

Thane turned and watched her pass, his face flushed by her words. Though he didn't quite understand what she meant, her brazen declaration made it suddenly difficult for him to concentrate on anything but her.

"Let us be gone," she announced from atop the roc, "and test the honor and heart of the Chufa people."

Thane had the rocs fly to the north of the Chufa village where they were able to find a clearing large enough for the two giant birds to land without notice from the local population. It was probably an hour's hike to reach the outskirts of the place the Chufa called home, but it was better to remain unseen for as long as possible. To have landed right in the town would have caused a great stir and possibly the loss of life as those on guard duty might think themselves under attack and unleash a volley of arrows into them. As it was, Thane was not very certain as to the welcome they would receive. The last time he'd been in the Chufa village he'd been beaten and left for dead.

Holding a finger to his lips for quiet, he led the group through the trees toward his former home. A shower of emotion rained down on him with every step they took closer to the home that never really was his. The painful memories of hate and mistrust washed over him like an avalanche that chilled him from the inside out. His mother was the only one he really had any desire to see again. She had always shown him the love that he so craved from others, like his father, who offered nothing but abhorrence. He wanted his mother to know that he was well. He knew he could not stay, and probably would never be able to return again, but at least he wanted her to know that he lived and that he loved and cherished her. He felt a small tear run down his cheek and was grateful for the waning sun and his leading position so that no one would see it. He wasn't ashamed of his emotion he just did not want to share it with anyone else at that moment.

He could almost sense the energy and excitement Dor and Tam felt at returning home. For them, the Ardath had fond memories of loving families and a safe haven. Both had experience such horrible things since leaving that he felt that this time he might be successful in convincing them to stay. It had been easy to deny him while they were in the wilds of the HuMan world, but now that they were back in the forest, taking in its scents, hearing its sounds and feeling the trees around them, he was fairly certain he and Jne might be the only ones leaving.

Holding up his hand for them to stop, he scanned the forest ahead. There was a small thicket on the right, a perfect place for a trap. Though he had no reason to believe that anyone knew of their presence, they were close enough to the village now to meet up with those picked to stand guard. Closing his eyes, he sent his senses outward becoming one with the forest and everything it held. He could hear his companion's hearts beating, feel the heavy emotions exchanged between Dor and Tam and was somewhat surprised by the little emotion he felt because of it. Their love had been difficult to deal with in the beginning as he tried to stifle his own emotional bond to Tam but now he felt truly happy for the only friends he'd ever known as a child.

Pausing with Jne, he inhaled the almost intoxicating scent of her hair. He wanted to linger close to her, to delve deeper into the feelings he knew would be easy for him to decipher but he felt it would be too invasive and wrong to do so; a violation of the one for whom his feelings had continually grown stronger. Turning from his companions he inspected the thicket but then quickly turned away from it, concentrating instead on the sudden rhythm of two extra heartbeats. They approached from the east and would soon be upon them. He knew if he stretched himself farther he would be able to gather more information about who drew near but to do so risked their being discovered. They had to act.

Motioning to the others, he led them to the very thicket that, moments before, posed a threat. Now it was they who would be in position for a trap. Watching from their concealed location they waited until Dor wondered if Thane had misinterpreted his misgivings. He was about to voice such an opinion when his eyes suddenly caught movement. Three figures appeared out of the trees in the faded light of dusk. Dor's eyes narrowed, recognizing immediately the arrogant swagger of the one in the lead. Glancing at Thane he could tell that his friend also recognized the person who had been responsible for his near death on the mountainside. It was PocMar.

A wicked grin suddenly spread across Thane's face and Dor half expected him to rush from their hiding place with both swords drawn and finish off the coward where he stood. He would be justified in doing so and even were he brought before the Kinpa and examined, they could not have condemned him. PocMar's actions had been cowardly and he deserved nothing less than death at the hand of the person he'd offended.

Thane looked at him and then motioned his head back. Dor followed his gaze and rested his eyes on a ripening patch of Shue berries. A boyish grin suddenly formed on his lips while an impish sparkle flashed in his dark eyes. Without a word, both gathered up a handful of the deep red berries while PocMar and his two companions drew closer. Their mannerisms, along with their noisy passage, revealed that they were not on alert or suspicious of anything out of the ordinary. With all of the trolls gone from the mountains, it was evident that the lack of raids had made the guards slack in their vigilance.

Jne's expression made it obvious she could not decipher what the two meant to do while Tam's face was that of a mother about to discipline her two unruly boys. "And what exactly do you two plan to do with those?" she asked in a demanding whisper.

Thane glared at her, bringing his finger up and motioning for her to stay quiet. PocMar and his companions were still approaching unaware of their plight. Tam's fists were firmly planted at her waste in defiance while Jne's face revealed her complete perplexity at the situation. Thane showed Dor his fingers as they counted down from five. Dor stifled a laugh as he nodded, preparing for the assault. Thane's fingers showed three, two, one. Both stood unleashing a barrage of berries raining dark red terror upon their victims. PocMar was their main target and he took the brunt of the hits before realizing what was happening.

"We're under attack," he suddenly yelled and raced through the trees scurrying back toward the village leaving his companions behind who readied their bows but who had not moved from where they stood. One of them, who'd taken a stray berry to the chest, wiped the area with his finger bringing the mashed berry flesh to his lips. He smiled slightly but then aimed his arrow at the thicket. "Who's there? Come out!"

Jne reached for her sword, but Tam placed a hand on her arm and shook her head. Thane and Dor were both in tears trying to hold back the laughter that wanted to roll off their lips like thunder. A few snickers escaped, instantly revealing their position. It was then that Tam took matters into her own hands.

"You and Thane stay here," she whispered to Jne who merely nodded. "Don't shoot!" she called out to the guards and then unceremoniously grabbed Dor by the ear and pulled him along behind her as she withdrew from their hiding place. "We are Chufa."

Dor smarted from her hold on his earlobe but at the same time could not hold back the laughter now that they were caught and were not trying to stay hidden. Thane, still hidden in the brush, placed a hand over his mouth trying desperately to not give himself and Jne up. He knew that to do so would cause no small stir, especially since Jne would be seen as HuMan. She glared at him now as if understanding the jeopardy in which he and Dor had placed them and without warning reached up and flicked his ear hard with her finger. All laughter quickly faded as he gave her a questioning look while trying to rub away the sting.

"Name yourselves," the guard commanded, lowering his bow but keeping it nocked. The other guard did the same while taking up a better defensive stance close to the trunk of the nearest tree.

"TamVen," Tam returned, "and DorMar," she finished, giving Dor a rough tug on his ear before letting it go.

"What mischief is this?!" the man by the tree interjected, his gruff voice breaking with emotion. "TamVen and DorMar are no more."

Tam's breath caught in her chest while Dor stood in stunned silence. They had been so occupied with watching PocMar that none of them took real notice of the other two guards. Tam stepped closer, the changing dim light of dusk making it difficult to see as neither their day nor night vision was at full capacity. "Paeh?" she called, tears suddenly streaming down her dirty face.

The man at the tree rushed forward. "Daughter?"

Chapter Twelve

Helgar pressed them to almost complete exhaustion not allowing more than an hour's rest a day for food and to regain what little strength they could. They were all anxious about their kin and the safety of Thornen Dar but even the elite guards were beginning to tire. The one who'd brought the message was left behind and told to follow as he could for they would not wait for him to recover knowing that to do so would only slow the rest. It was a near constant march since word came of the attack and the king's demise and though they all wished for home they would not be able to continue like this much longer. Luckily, the mountains that marked their abode continued to rise in the distance tapping some unknown reserves that strengthened them and pushed them onward.

Now, even more than before, Rangor was determined to protect his prince. With the king dead and Helgar the only living heir, it was all the more imperative he be protected and kept from harm. Until he was crowned king in the Great Hall, Thornen Dar was without a ruler. The sooner Helgar was coronated the better for the dwarf kingdom.

Bedler's Keep rose up like a beacon in the distance calling them forward, encouraging them to press on, telling them that Thornen Dar was only a day and a half farther. The dark castle was a mere half a day away to where they could just about smell the hard rock of their mountain home. Bardolf considered the keep for a moment realizing that their lives and those of all the good races would be determined there. It was dark and foreboding where it rose from the valley floor, a fortress almost impenetrable by an army alone. But Zadok had no simple army. How would it hold against an army back by sorcery and dragons?

"We be restin' fer one hour," Helgar grumbled, "then we be marchin' until we be reachin' our gates. Git what sleep be at yer eyes now fer ye won't be gettin' none 'til then."

There were no protests as the guard simply dropped where they were, not willing to waste precious sleep time on arguing. They were too hardened and loyal to complain anyway. They would have marched straight on the whole way had their lord asked it of them. All were willing to die for their liege, whether that be in battle or marching toward it there was no difference to them. Helgar barely had the words out of his mouth before loud snores could be heard coming from every quarter.

Bardolf approached his friend who had slipped beyond anyone's grasp since he'd heard of the loss of his father. "Ye be needin' sleep more then the rest o' us," he stated simply. "I'll be keepin' watch this hour." It was a statement; there was no inflection in his voice to suggest otherwise.

Helgar growled. "Do ye be supposin' to command yer lord?" he spat.

Bardolf ignored the rough edge of his friend's voice. "If need be," he answered flatly. "I'll not be arguin' 'bout it neither. Ye can throw whatever royal fit ye be cookin' up in that stone skull o' yers but I won't be backin' away from it. Now stop wastin' the hour and git yerself to sleep!"

Helgar's face was a mask of rage. How dare he talk so insolently to him? He was the rightful king and none dare speak to the king in such tones or countermand him. Helgar rested his hand on the dagger at his side as if he might pull it and bury it deep into Bardolf's chest, but his friend still remained solid where he stood, his expression tired but resolute. "I won't be coddled," Helgar hissed.

"Good," Bardolf replied. "And I won't be coddlin' ye neither. But neither will I be bullied by me friend who not be himself at the moment. Ye need to be restin' so as ye can be leadin' us proper when we be reachin' Thornen Dar. If the beast still be within the mountain we'll be needin' a king that can keep his feet, and his wits about him."

Helgar took in his words and seemed to chew on them for a moment as if seeing how they tasted in his mouth. Finally, he spit but didn't put up anymore resistance. Turning away he planted himself on a soft piece of grass and almost instantly fell asleep.

It was dusk when the ragged group of dwarves finally reached the heavy doors that marked the entrance to their ancestral home. It had been a hard climb over treacherous rocks and precipices to reach the hidden entrance. No one who did not know exactly where they were going could have found the entry to Thornen Dar, yet alone gained access through the solid stone doors that were hidden to view to the untrained eye. The entrance was of thick rock cut right out of the mountain and fitted so exactly as to leave the entryway invisible; a mere mountain face without sign of being anything else. But all took in a deep breath of awe as they gained the top of the outcropping that was the porch, as it were, to their kingdom. The doors had been blown outward with such force as to unhinge one of them, leaving it face down on the ground before them.

"A dragon indeed," Helgar hissed, pulling his axe from its resting place on his back. "Prepare yerselves lads," he continued. "We be huntin' serpent."

"To the square!" Rangor commanded the guard as they snapped to formation around Helgar.

The new king made to protest but backed down quickly, realizing he would have to fight them all to get his way. He was the king. And though he hated the idea of being left out of a fight, he knew it was no use in trying to change their minds. These lads had been trained since they were nigh off their mother's breast to protect the king with their lives—whether the king liked it or not. He knew they would follow Rangor's orders over his own and there was no time to argue with their captain right now.

The entranceway opened up into a large circular cave-like area that was rough cut all around, making the need for a barred entrance seem ludicrous. Nothing appeared grand or out of the ordinary except for the twenty offshoot tunnels that left the area going in all directions. The dwarfs didn't even pause to determine which entrance they should pursue but instead moved quickly, with axes ready toward the seventh one on the right. All the other tunnels lead their followers through a myriad of pathways that eventually led to nowhere keeping the dwarf stronghold a secret from any outsiders who stumble upon the entrance.

The corridor quickly closed in, only allowing passage in a single file line. Two of the dwarf guards took the lead allowing Helgar the third place in line. He knew Rangor would not be happy about it, especially since he was forced almost to the rear, but Helgar had elbowed out the dwarf just behind him for the spot and he knew no one would argue now that they were inside and on high alert.

Through multiple twists and turns they pressed on until greeted by five more options. Again, without hesitation they moved to the tunnel just to the left and continued on as the floor gradually sloped downward. Five more small foyers offering multiple tunnel options were passed before they finally reached a large set of thick oak doors that had also been blown out from the inside. Though heavily damaged, the doors still hung precariously to at least one of the hinges though threatening to breakaway from the sheer weight at any moment. Passing through the entrance the dwarfs spread out into their protective square, each peering into the semi darkness in all directions, as they entered Thornen Dar.

"And what be this?" Rangor spoke softly while running a hand over the interior side of one of the doors. "It be wet and the wood turned sodden."

Helgar inspected the door for himself. "The whole of the area be damp," Bardolf said, wiping a bead of sweat from his forehead. "Even the air be dank and pressin' in, almost like that that be infestin' the Underwoods."

"Aye," Helgar nodded, trying to dry his hand on his damp shirt. "It be stinkin' of a foul evil."

The dwarfs spread out quickly as they entered the great city, their axes at the ready should anything still remain to attack. The air was fouled from the great number of dead that lay scattered about leaving the impression that the city had been caught by surprise. Men, women and children were mixed in the gruesome fray that pulled at the hearts of even these battled hardened dwarfs.

Helgar squatted down by a woman still holding her young daughter. With a hand covering his nose he inspected the bodies. "Look at their skin," he breathed. They were waxen looking but with large pieces of skin peeling away from the muscle. And they were wet. No one spoke for long moments, each looking at the bodies closest to where they stood, trying to understand what had happened to their kin. Rangor finally commanded the guard to search for survivors while he and Bardolf remained with Helgar.

The once beautiful city that puffed up the dwarf people with pride lay in shattered ruins in all directions. Ornately carved buildings that had once awed the passerby with their artistry and grandeur were now cracked or ruptured into rubble, leaving piles of stone and mortar. The beautiful trees and garden spots that had made the inner cave of Thornen Dar the rival of any aboveground park were torn up or withered while the falls that fed the city was no longer running. And yet, the air was uncommonly hot and wet causing the dwarf's clothes to dampen and stick uncomfortably to their skin.

Their search was superficial, sticking to the main thoroughfare that led up to the king's palace. With such small numbers they couldn't venture far or risk being separated should they face an assault. If it was, in fact, a dragon that attacked their beloved city, as appeared evident from the damage, they needed to stay together to have even the slightest chance.

"Remember lads," Helgar offered as they inched toward his father's home, "dragons may be harder than diamonds at their scales but we know that they be soft underneath and bleed just like anything else." He was referring to their encounter on the journey to Calandra when he was almost taken away in the clutches of a dragon's talons that had caught him up. It bled well enough then when he'd gotten his axe blade under its scales at the leg. Another of their companions had not been so lucky.

Helgar was anxious to reach the palace and search out his father, but Rangor reined him in, not willing to risk caution for speed. They had to be deliberate and thorough. Though the report was that the king had fallen, Helgar still held on to a sliver of hope that his father and king had somehow escaped the attack. The guard that remained should have been sufficient to at least get him back away from the battle.

After an hour of slinking about from one pile of rubble to another, they finally approached what had once been the pride of the city—Thornen Dar's grand palace. Though it had faired better than many of the buildings in the city, there were still plenty of marks of battle and damage to the outside. Helgar, Bardolf and Rangor stopped just at the entrance waiting for the rest of the guard to return. Helgar was anxious to get inside and search but Rangor was able to hold him off, at least for the moment.

"Let the guard be regrouping first," Rangor insisted. "Then we be at an advantage to more quickly be findin' yer father."

Helgar huffed but recognized the intelligence of Rangor's plan. It would just slow them down to go about unorganized and risk researching rooms already looked at or miss others thought to have been searched. Still, it made him want to crawl out of his own skin with anxiety to have to wait. At this point, he would have welcomed a dragon attack just because it would have given him something on which to vent his anger and frustrations.

"I've found somethin'" a voice called out to their right.

Everybody quickly converged on the spot. Not far from the steps leading to the palace, next to an overturned cart, one of the dwarf guards was on his knees peering through a small gap created by a large piece of rubble supporting a back corner. "Help me," shouted Bardolf as he gripped a side and prepared to turn the cart back over. Three others assisted, easily lifting it onto its side. A tiny form instantly scurried back away from the group trying to find escape but quickly found he was surrounded. Pressing his back against the cart he looked like he might try to claw his way over it. "Easy their, laddie," Bardolf called out, shouldering his weapon and offering opened hands of peace. "Ain't none of us here goin' to be hurtin' ya now. Ye be safe."

It was a young dwarf boy, his bright red hair, not quite long enough yet to be braided, was knotted and dirty. His clothes were torn and ragged, and it looked like his left arm had been burned. His deep blue eyes darted about for a moment as if he still might try to run before finally settling them on Bardolf who slowly inched forward.

"We have to be hidin'," the boy suddenly hissed. "It cannot be killed" The boy's eyes seemed to go out of focus and widened as if he were looking through Bardolf to something terrifying. "It comes with the burning fog. No weapon can harm it."

All were silent for a brief moment, the boy going quiet save for slight mumblings that were barely audible but nonsensical. "Where be the others?" Bardolf asked, drawing the boy's attention and focus back to him.

"Deep," he whispered. "Deep as can be gotten, those that got out. But they will be diein' jist as soon as it be findin' 'em. There be no place it not be findin' with its burning fog."

"And what of the king, boy," Helgar interjected. The boy's eyes shot about as if suddenly seeing the others for the first time, his body tensing. "Answer me, boy," Helgar insisted.

The boy's eyes glazed slightly. "The king be livin' in the palace, of course," he whispered, "with all his guard about him."

Helgar's face flashed a glimmer of joy and hope that was quickly overrun by doubt. "In the palace, ye say?"

The boy looked at him blankly and then slowly came to his feet. "I'll lead ye there." No one moved, all looking to Helgar who regarded the boy as if trying to decide the truthfulness of his claim. Finally, nodding his head, he motioned to the guard to let the boy pass. He wanted to believe that there was truth in the boy's statement but what he saw around him told him otherwise. The boy paused for a moment as a corridor was open between the rough, weapon clad guards. Looking at Helgar, he smiled slightly, a devious glint in his eyes as he finally moved forward. Helgar watched him pass. Pausing just beyond Helgar's reach, the boy looked back at him his eyes suddenly filled will wild terror.

"Run or die!" the boy suddenly shouted and bolted, just slipping past Helgar's grip as he reached out to halt the boy's escape. The guard instantly took up the chase but Helgar called them back.

"Let'im be," he said with a sigh. "None be knowin' the horror that boy been seein'. Let 'im be off." All eyes turned and regarded the prince, waiting for his instructions. "I be knowin' as good as any where me Da would be in the palace."

Bardolf approached his friend and stopped briefly at his side. "Then let's be to it," he said softly only able to guess at what his prince, and probably his new king, was thinking and feeling under his rough exterior. Though tough as the mountains that bred them, dwarfs were also big hearted, willing to make the ultimate sacrifice for those they loved or respected.

The palace was almost unrecognizable inside. The once pinnacle of dwarf craftsmanship and ingenuity had been reduced, in many areas, to piles of rubble and dust. Dead guards and house staff left a gruesome trail of blood and gore laid out in such a manner as to direct any who entered toward the location where it must have all begun. Helgar's heart sank and the light of hope he'd kept shelter suddenly waned to near extinction as the pathway of carnage led the group toward the great hall where sat the ancestral throne. The once great and ominous room looked small now with the mounds of rock and statuary strewn about in a pattern of chaos. The air was thick with moisture and difficult to breath.

Though the guard remained ever ready and vigilant, as was their duty, Helgar walked almost aimlessly toward the throne where, against hope, he knew he would find his father. Climbing over one of the great troll statues that once lent ominous trepidation to the hall, Helgar finally caught site of his father seated on the throne. For a brief moment his breath caught as his father's posture seemed to suggest relaxed repose but almost as instantly, the pile of dead guards that surrounded him and the cracked look of his skin were indefatigable proofs of his father's end. The skin on all the dead around the throne mimicked that of those they had seen in the city. It was like the fissures left in an empty lake bed that had been flogged by an unrelenting sun until it fractured the surface into a spider web of caked ridges.

Helgar made to approach the thrown, and his father, but a firm hand suddenly caught his arm holding him in place. He turned a scathing look on the one who dared disrupt his thoughts and motion only to be met by the moistened eyes of his elite guard's leader. "Let us be turnin' our backs on this place of dread," pleaded Rangor, "and not be rememberin' our king in such a state."

Helgar's fierce, rage-filled eyes held Rangor's for a brief moment before he turned back to his father, yanking his arm free as he did so, intent on approaching the throne to pay proper respect.

"Please," Rangor whispered, the emotion escaping through his voice.

Helgar stopped short. Whether it was the word itself or the emotion that coated it, he could not tell, but something touched him as he looked about at the guard who had been charged to protect his father and who would now protect him. He could see the sense of loss in their eyes at having been absent when their king had needed them most. He could see the desire they held in their hearts to be among the many dead surrounding the throne instead of among the living who were mere witnesses of the unthinkable. It was his father, Helgar told himself. He had the right to mourn as he would. But the darkness that seemed to enshroud the guard and the obvious pain they felt at seeing their charge dead softened the battle hardened dwarf to the point of heartbreak.

Taking a deep breath, he forced one last look at his father before turning back to Rangor. "We must be findin' all that yet be alive who can be holdin' an axe. We be goin' to war."

Chapter Thirteen

Tam let the warmth of family wash over her as she sat by the fire wrapped in her mother's arms. It had almost been too overwhelming for her when they came upon her father out on patrol earlier that day. Since then it had been a storm of activity as word spread quickly that she and Dor had returned. Questions about where they had been and how they survived had pressed upon them from all sides as family after family had come to their hut to see for themselves if the rumors were true. Finally, BekSagn, her father, had to close off their home to anymore visitors, except Dor and his family, until they'd gotten the answers they had yet to receive and understand about their children's sudden disappearance. All had given them up for captured and killed by the trolls that infested the mountains and who had so often raided their village and killed their people. Bek had been on one of the very patrols that were sent out to protect against such attacks when he'd found her.

Tam gave her mother a squeeze with her arm letting the stress and pain of the past months wash away in the comfort of her embrace. Now that she was home, it was almost as if the trials she had faced hadn't even happened. It all seemed to melt away in the warmth of home. The only thing that stood as a reminder of where she'd been and what she'd faced was the story Dor was telling their parents at that moment. They had agreed that until they could talk to DaxSagn and get his arrow that it would be best to stick to a story that didn't involve invasions or HuMans. They needed that arrow and couldn't risk the repercussions that would likely follow should they tell the whole truth at once.

Dor glanced at her as he laid out the narrative they had agreed upon, some of which was actually true. He even made up that they used his hair to start fires to keep warm to explain how short it was. That had caused no small stir of hero worship by Tam's family and beaming pride from his own. Had they really known why it had been cut the hero worship quite possibly would have moved up to god status.

"But if you were trapped in that cave for so long, how is it you were able to survive without starving?" All stared at QalSagn, Dor's mother, who had voiced the question that all had wondered but which none were willing, or desirous, to ask. One could only imagine the horror of the situation. Luckily, of sorts, Tam still had not completely regained all her weight back from her addiction to *dranlok* lending credence to their claim of being lost and trapped in the mountains this whole time. It also gave cover to the fact that Dor had put on a little extra weight.

Dor fidgeted for a moment as if uncomfortable with the question. Tam watched him knowing that his discomfort was not a show to go along with his answer but because they had not thought to discuss that part. She knew he was squirming because he was trying to come up with a plausible answer. She held her breath. They needed for them to believe their story. If their families had doubts then surely others would not believe either. Though she wanted to shout out to everyone the dangers they were facing, they had to stick to the plan or risk losing their opportunity to make a difference. Dor glanced at Tam and she caught the brief glint that flashed in his eyes. He had something.

"I…I'd rather not talk about it," he stammered, "if you don't mind. Let's just say that we did what we had to."

Tam's head suddenly felt light and she realized that she was still holding her breath. But she didn't let it out until their parents all joined in with only words of encouragement and sympathy. "We understand," her father said. "Of course," Dor's father, TaqSagn, offered. "You poor children," his mother gushed, while PanChao, Tam's' mother gasped and just squeezed her tighter. Tam smiled back at Dor who masked his own mischievous look behind a down-turned mouth and a shake of his head in acceptance of their pity.

"It doesn't matter," Pan finally added, the emotion breaking into her voice. "What is of most import is that you have returned, never to leave again."

Tam stiffened at the announcement, her eyes quickly filling with tears as her mother's words slapped her across the face. *Never to leave again.* She sighed, fighting back the emotion that luckily everyone took as happy acceptance and joy at being back in her family's hut. Dor looked at her knowingly wanting to reach out and embrace her but holding back since no one was yet aware of their growing relationship. The joy of the evening was suddenly gone and both young Chufa were left feeling empty.

All remained silent for long moments deep within the recesses of their own thoughts when loud laughter outside broke through the rigid walls. "That's right!" Qal exclaimed. "Tonight is the FasiUm." All eyes suddenly fell on Dor and Tam whose faces both flushed. Once a year, at the end of the spring moon, the Chufa all gathered together at a great celebration where those males who were of age were put on display for the females of age to choose, if they so desired, who would be their life mate. It was generally encompassed in a great feast and dancing and no real ceremony was involved save for the simple act of an eligible girl taking who she desired for her mate by the hand. If the young man accepted the match he need merely keep hold, if not, then he could release his grip at any time and the girl was free to pick another. Should the couple agree to the match then each was then considered espoused with a ceremony finalizing the union during the first spring moon the following year.

"Of course," Pan offered, "no one would expect either of you to go after all you have been through. There is always next year."

"Right," Taq said in support, "and the Kinpa will be early with the sun to visit with you both. A good night's rest is probably what you need most right now."

Dor stole a glance at Tam but was unable to determine her thoughts as she had half buried her face against her mother's arm. He knew they were all waiting for an answer but he wasn't quite sure what to say. If he seemed eager to go without Tam leading out he was afraid she might think he was hoping another would choose him. Although, should he decline, Tam might think him not interested in her choosing him. Both were just barely of age so no one would think twice if neither entered but that didn't matter to him. Why wasn't Tam responding? He could feel the sweat forming on his forehead as the time seemed to tick away into a gulf of silence. But Tam still remained like a mountain face, treacherous and immovable. Suddenly the thought came to him that maybe, now that they were home, she was no longer interested in him. Maybe their relationship had been built on the excitement and fear of the moment and now that that had passed she had other ideas. The sweat was now starting to roll down his face and his heart felt like it was stuck in an avalanche of rock.

His mother noticed his reaction turning a concerned look in his direction. "Are you well, son?" she asked.

Almost on top of her, Tam suddenly sat up and said, "Yes, I want to go."

Dor almost fell over. Waving his mother off who had risen to catch him, a bundle of worry for the boy she had thought dead only hours before, he let out a heavy sigh of relief only able to nod his head to the original question and to his mother. "I'll go too," he finally squeaked.

*   *   *

Passing silently in a wide arc around the village, Thane marked the patrols that had been set should the trolls make a raid. He could tell by their careless manor that there hadn't been the normal raids in quite some time. He smiled sardonically to himself knowing all too well why that was. None had even the slightest notion that he had been close, although he hadn't gotten too near their immediate vicinity to discover each individual person.

Darting through the forests he felt a moment of peace as he ran. Though his mind was set on what needed to be accomplished, it was invigorating to once again take in the smells and feelings of his forest home. He'd not realized how much he had missed it until he'd returned. Seeing something to his left, he abruptly stopped, his breathing controlled though his heart suddenly quickened its pace. Frozen in place, as if becoming one of the towering trees surrounding him, a tear unexpectedly trailed down his cheek. A flood of emotions crashed over him making him feel woozy as he sorted through the mixture of anger, loneliness, love, shame and a hundred other feelings that marked his life growing up in the hut now facing him in the dark. He chastised himself for not thinking of coming here the first thing after their return. Besides the obvious urgency in their mission, there really was only one person he wanted to see—his mother.

He found himself taking a step forward as if he would merely walk up to the door and walk in but with great effort forced himself to hold fast. Those days were long past since his father had sent him from the hut. His mind battled over the possibility that his mother might be in there this very instant and how easy it would be to just sneak in to see her, to hold her close one last time and let her know that he was alive. He took another step forward but stopped when a loud cry from the direction of the council fire broke through the night air. He looked past the hut in the direction of the noise and blinked. Of course, she would be there as well. A feeling of complete isolation quickly took hold of him and the one tear turned into many.

Running quickly through the trees, he dared not looked back at the home that had housed so much love yet a tremendous amount of pain. He would come back, he told himself. He would see his mother before he left, no matter what the sacrifice or cost. His tears were making it difficult to see and more than once he almost threw himself into the trunk of a tree. Finally he slowed, whipping his eyes and forcing away the feelings that continued to beat him mercilessly.

A shadow in the dark caught his attention and for a brief moment he felt his hand reaching for one of the two swords that were strapped securely to his back. Taking in his immediate surroundings he quickly realized that he had returned to where he'd begun and that the shadow was Jne, poorly hidden behind some brush. He chirped the sound of a cricket as he approached having made the mistake once before of coming up on her in silence and almost taking her blade into his chest for it. He could see her head snap around a blade instantly pulled from its hiding place somewhere on her body. Knowing she lacked the night vision he possessed, he whispered to her as he drew near so she would know it was him and avoid the problems that might arise should she forget his signal.

Returning her blade to its hiding pace, he could see her visibly relax as he closed the final distance between them. Though he knew she could not see as well in the dark, she surprised him when she almost instantly asked, "Are you well?"

He shrugged off the question. "Just strange to be back, I guess." When she didn't respond he found himself blurting out, "How long must you remain *jinghar*?"

She gave him a puzzled look that quickly dissolved into the stone face she always wore when there was something unpleasant that had to be done. A long moment passed into uncomfortable silence and he was beginning to think that she would just not answer when finally her eyes took on a challenging fire as if steeling herself for what might occur next. "My debt to you was paid that day I saved your life from the orc."

Thane was incredulous. "But then why...?" He let his question tale off without being voiced. She had stayed with him all this time acting as if she were still beholden to him but for what purpose? Suddenly the answer was so obvious that he felt the fool for not having seen before. The moment came back when she'd seemed a different person when the birds had first come and she'd seemed emotionally naked before him. The day she'd promised him a *svaj* and Jack had made such a huge deal about it. All the other tiny moments and smiles she'd given him without the slightest return on his part. She loved him. He suspected it for some time but had been afraid to believe it or broach the subject lest she become angry and deny what he suddenly realized was something that he'd been hoping for deep within. He wanted to reach out with his senses to confirm what he already knew was true but understood that to do so would be a gross breach of decency and trust.

She eyed him closely but could not make out his facial features in the dark to see what he felt inside. Part of her was grateful for that darkness so Thane would not see the embarrassment and pain splayed across her own face. She wanted to say more but felt there was no reason now. He would either both accept her explanation and allow her to stay or send her away to her ultimate shame.

As if on its own volition, Thane's hand suddenly reached out and took hers into his own. It was warm and calloused baring the marks of one who lived by the sword. Jne soaked it in, a thrill she'd never experienced before racing through her body as she allowed herself to be swept away by a cascade of new emotions and feelings. She opened her mouth to speak, her hand tightening its grip on his when suddenly he broke contact. She gasped from the pain of lost touch but her ache was quickly extinguished by his words.

"Someone approaches."

Jne immediately reached for her sword but Thane's hand shot out and caught it, an amazing feat in and of itself. Leaning close to her ear he whispered. "Stay right here." Her immediate reaction was one of disdain at being told what she should do as if she were a mere damsel needing the protection of a man. But she surprised herself when she remained still and didn't argue. And though the feeling of his breath and the closeness of his lips had suddenly made her feel dizzy, she trusted him with her life.

Thane rushed away without the slightest rustle as he navigated the forest floor in complete silence. She watched him, her face still flushed as he suddenly ducked behind a tree and disappeared. Whether he was just beyond on the other side or rushing headlong into the night, she could not tell. Remaining still so as not to give away her position, she strained to see or hear any sign of an intruder. Long minutes passed without so much as a whisper against the night when suddenly, the passing of a shadowed figure caught her eye as it moved cat-like toward her position not too far distant from where Thane had left the area. She instantly felt exposed, knowing all too well that should it be one of Thane's people, she would be easily spotted in mere moments. Still, she remained frozen, knowing that to move now would certainly give away her position. No, the closer her opponent got, the worse it would be for him and the better chance she would have at dispatching him before the alarm could be called.

The form drew nearer and then abruptly halted. Jne knew she'd been marked but still had the discipline to keep still on the off chance that something else had grabbed the intruder's attention. She strained to see who or what it was but the shape was still too far off for her to make out. Where was Thane? Then, with the fluidity of water, it moved, reaching for something at its back that it then pointed toward her. All she heard was the slight twang of a bowstring as its arrow was released towards her.

*   *   *

Dor moved slowly with the rhythm of the dance and the other young men positioned on either side of him. The circle surrounding the fire was not large as the number of eligible male participants was never more than just a few. Since Chufa women did not reproduce very quickly, the whole Chufa nation had struggled to increase its numbers since almost being completely wiped out over a thousand years before. Luckily, their life cycle was extended as compared to other groups but the regular raids on their village from the trolls in the mountains had offset any progression in population increases.

Still uncertain of Tam's intentions, he'd joined the dance just in case she decided to make their budding relationship more permanent and official. At the same time, he feared she might misinterpret his actions as trying to force her into something for which she wasn't ready or even worse, a desire to find someone else. The sweat was dripping off his chin now more from the anxiety of the moment than the heat of the flames. He kept a keen eye locked on the crowd as he slowly made his turns around the fire as he tried to catch even a quick glimpse of Tam. He'd been at it with the others for close to an hour now and still had not seen her even once. What if she had changed her mind? There was no shame in being left not chosen during the FasiUm, especially at his relatively young age, but though he wasn't certain himself that he wanted to make such a commitment at this point in his life, he still felt a little unsure about what Tam wanted or if she really even had the same intensity of feelings for him that he'd developed for her.

A cheer went up from the crowd as one of the older boys in the group had been chosen by a girl who had just come of age. Though he seemed a bit surprised at who had taken his hand, he seemed pleased with the match and did not let go. As the dance made one more turn around the fire ring, the couple broke away to the congratulatory words and back slaps of friends and relatives. It would now be left to the parents to determine the price to be paid by the boy's parents as an endowment to the couple and to the girl's family.

Dor's heart leaped briefly when he thought he'd caught sight of Tam but then thudded like a fallen rock when it turned out to be someone else. Another cheer broke from the noisy crowd as yet another match was made and agreed upon. Dor was suddenly feeling somewhat foolish and thought of leaving the dance all together. He was still young after all, as his parents had reminded him. More importantly, he didn't know what was going to happen in their lives or if they would even be back the following spring to complete the ceremony. Maybe he had rushed into this a little too quickly. His face fell. *Tam must think me a fool*, he thought as another of his companions was chosen to the exultation of the crowd. Just he and one other remained. He loved Tam, he knew that and the fact that she had not chosen him this year did not change his feelings for her in the least. It was just too soon, he could see that now.

Completing one more circuit around the fire he finally decided to drop out. Nodding to the other dancer, he turned on his heel and had taken one step toward the crowd when an immediate hush fell over the gathering. His eyes widened slightly at the sight before him, his mind racing, when a hand suddenly slipped into his and a soft voice spoke into his ear. "And where do you think you are getting off to?"

*   *   *

Jne dropped to the ground feeling the arrow pass over her shoulder knowing it would have embedded itself straight through her heart had she remained erect. Rolling to the side, she pulled a dagger and made ready her attack when suddenly another shadow sprang out the tree next to the intruder and wrestled it to the ground. Not waiting to see who the winner might be, she rushed to the spot where the bodies continued to grapple and find Thane with his dagger suddenly pressed hard against the attacker's neck.

"Stop fighting," he said, "or I'll slit your throat." The shadowy form suddenly went limp all resistance ended. Thane turned quickly to Jne and whispered, "J'enst!"

She hesitated at his command for her to hide. Her natural reaction was one of anger but the inflection in his voice seemed almost as if he were pleading with her.

"J'enst," he repeated, adding, "J'omane'bak'silfaj."

Immediately, she slipped back behind the tree where he had been hiding and then moved as quietly as she could away and then behind another trunk.

"Who are you?" the person under Thane demanded. "What is that language you speak?"

"I ask the questions," he hissed, pressing the blade a little harder against his opponent's neck.

"I am DaxSagn," the person said, his voice strong and without the slightest hint of fear.

Thane's grip suddenly went slack. "Dax?"

Another roar could be heard from the village revelers as Dax got to his knees and then turned toward Thane. There was a moment of anger at seeing that he'd been attacked by one of his own people but that instantly turned to shock when he saw who it was. "By the Mother's blood and all that lives, I don't believe it. Thane?"

Thane smiled and nodded.

"But how?" Dax asked, his surprise still not abated. "We thought you dead."

Thane's eyes narrowed. "Yes," he breathed, "I am certain that some would have hoped that true. But I have not the time to explain about that right now."

"Wait," Dax raised his hand for silence. Looking back to where Jne had been, he could see that the body he thought should have been there in a heap of death had disappeared. "Where is it?" Turning back to Thane, he asked, "Did you see it?"

"See what?" he asked, knowing by where Dax had looked, exactly who he was talking about. "I saw nothing."

"But it was there," Dax insisted, pointing his finger to Jne's ill gotten hiding place. "I shot it."

That's why you have that crack on your head, he thought. Whether by his attack on Dax or Jne's quick reaction, or both, he didn't know how the arrow had missed but he knew that Jne was lucky to still be alive. "I saw nothing," he lied. "But, as I said, we have no time for this. I must have a favor of you or all might be lost."

Dax touched his head where Thane had initially hit him, the grimace on his face confirming a solid connection from the hilt of Thane's dagger. Still searching the place with his night vision, Dax was not so easily convinced that he'd not seen something. "What is this you speak of? There have not been any troll attacks since…" he paused, "well, actually, since you've been gone." Now his attention was fully back on Thane. "Isn't that strange," he commented, though Thane could not tell if he was being accusatory or simply stating an anomaly.

"Listen," Thane insisted, his knife unconsciously rising with his voice. "I told you. I don't have time for this. I need a favor of you and how you answer may determine the lives of all Chufa and more."

"What are you blabbering about, boy?" Dax hissed angrily, his eyes flashing at being threatening by his dagger once more.

"I need your arrow," Thane blurted out. It was not how he and his friends had planned it, but since they were together and he'd been discovered, he saw no need for pleasant manipulations.

"My arrow?" Dax asked incredulously. He knew which arrow Thane meant without asking. There was no other arrow he had that Thane, or any other Chufa for that matter, couldn't just as easily make on their own. Thane was after the arrow that could penetrate steel. "Well, if that's all your after," he said, "then the answer is, no."

Thane sighed, rubbing a hand through his hair. "I can't explain right now. All I can tell you is that if I don't get that arrow, we will all certainly perish."

Dax regarded him for a long moment. Though hated by most, he always thought highly of Thane and his abilities. Never had he known him to be negligent in his duties or to speak anything but the truth. But this was too much. To simply show up after so long and ask for the Chufa's most prized possession without the slightest explanation was just too far beyond sensible.

"Please," Thane pled, his need fused in his voice and posturing.

Dax sighed, shaking his head. "I can't. Not without more information as to why and what threatens us. But I will consider it after I hear the whole story and receive the consent of the council."

"Not the Kinpa," Thane insisted. "I will tell you all you want to know, even though there is no time, but please leave the Kinpa out." He still wasn't convinced, that although it was PocMar and his friends who had beaten him and left him for dead, that the Kinpa were not complicit as well.

"I'm sorry, Thane, but something of this magnitude requires the voice of the council as well."

He thought for a moment of just taking the arrow from him. He still had his knife out and if he called to Jne they could easily overpower him and simply take the arrow for their own. Yet, for some reason, he felt he could not do it and still use it the way he intended. Whether the arrow was in some way attached to Dax to call forth its power or whether just his honest heart telling him to do so would be wrong, he couldn't steal it. Finally, he dropped his head in defeat. "I will go with you to the Kinpa."

Dax just nodded. Both regained their feet and then started silently down the path toward the center of the village passing where Jne had originally hidden. Thane caught Dax searching the area as they walked by, the signs that someone had recently been there obvious to the trained eye.

*   *   *

Dor tore his eyes from Thane who had suddenly appeared out of the darkness. The village had grown eerily quiet as all focused their sights on his friend, their faces filled with amazement, while some were mixed with the clear look of terror. Looking down at his hand he barely registered the fact that it was encased by another more slender than his, yet just as strong. Following the arm past the shoulder he finally met the eyes of the person who was picking him as her own. His mind reeled for a moment, suddenly feeling light and disoriented.

"Well?" a familiar voice intoned. "Have you nothing to say?"

"Tam," he finally breathed but was instantly cut off.

Chapter Fourteen

From the silence, a loud ripple of noise suddenly rumbled through the crowd like the clap of thunder that follows a quiet lightning flash. Somewhere a woman screamed and all eyes were now focused on Dax and Thane who had appeared like apparitions from the darkened woods. While Dax lifted his hands for quiet and calm, Thane seemed unaffected by the people's reaction. Scanning the faces of those he once knew and trusted, he suddenly found himself with the feeling of being in a foreign land with people he didn't know. What shocked him even more though, was the complete lack of desire he felt in his heart to become reacquainted with them. None of them had ever really accepted him or treated him with more than annoyed tolerance other than Dor, Tam and his mother. His eyes quickly scanned the crowd seeking her out, wanting more than anything else at that moment for her to know that he still lived and loved her, but his search ended in vain. She was nowhere to be seen.

"Calm yourselves, people," Dax called out as the Kinpa moved through the crowd toward the disruptive pair.

Thane's eyes narrowed as they approached, his once awed reverence of the Chufa elders now reduced to bitter contempt. No longer did he see the wisdom and strength that, in his mind, had represented the Kinpa office. All he saw were five old men who were hungry for power more than they were for the greater good of a collapsing civilization. He was surprised to find himself thinking that the extinction of his race might not be as horrible as he once thought. All ideas of a noble Chufa people had quickly disappeared. They had destroyed themselves far more than the HuMans ever could have. This was their last chance to find any redemption and possibly reverse the spiral they'd been falling down for so many years.

The Kinpa surrounded him in a half circle, the crowd now at his back. They were puffed-up in their pride trying to intimidate him with their presence and self aggrandizing importance. But Thane was not impressed and didn't move in the least. Surprised at his lack of reaction and understanding that he no longer feared them in the slightest, two of the Kinpa took an involuntary step back while the others shuffled their feet nervously. FelTehPa forced an uneasy smile. "So, Thane, we see you have returned."

Ignoring him, Thane suddenly stepped forward, brushing past the Kinpa so that he was free of the crowd and could be seen and heard by all. Seeing the Kinpa closest to him jump as he did so was not lost on him. He would not speak directly to the Kinpa but would, instead, address the whole Chufa nation. He was surprised by the sudden rage and disgust he was feeling.

"I have come," he started, his voice rising to be certain none would have trouble hearing, "to ask for something that will ultimately save all of your lives."

Dor and Tam were dumbfounded by their friend's sudden boldness and majesty in addressing their people. Thane had always been one to keep mostly to himself while growing up, for obvious reasons. But now, he was truly a man and a leader with the confidence and mere physical presence to call forth respect, if not reverence.

Thane briefly waited for the crowd to settle down again following the rumbled reaction to his words. It was then that he caught sight of his father whose face had quickly become a beacon of rage. Thane's eyes did not falter though as he stared at the man who should have been his greatest support, but who, for reasons of selfish arrogance, had been indirectly responsible for all of the pain and suffering for which he had been forced to endure as a child. The feelings of hope and love that had once pulsed through his heart were no longer a boulder to weigh him down. All he saw now was an aging man who was worthy of no more nobler sentiments beyond mere pity.

"We are all in the gravest of danger and the choices we make from this moment on will decide whether we are severed asunder on the blade of fate over which we hover, or escape to something greater than ourselves."

Many eyes looked about in confusion and fear at such bold language coming from one so young and ill accepted. "Your absence has muddled your senses," someone shouted. "Since you left we have passed the worse time of year without a single raid, let alone sighting, from the trolls."

Shouts of agreement rang out as the mob suddenly gained control over their initial fear, replaced now with the ill gotten courage found in numbers.

"That's right," Thane countered, "you haven't. And that is why I am here. The reason you have been left alone is because the trolls have left these mountains and gathered together with other beasts that your darkest nightmares would not dare to conjure. And once they have conquered the lands that stretch out beyond the Shadow Mountains they will turn their faces back here and when they do it will only take mere moments to completely destroy you all."

A hush fell upon the crowd save for a few young children who were suddenly reduced to tears in their mother's arms. "There is but one thing that might turn back such a horrible swarm of evil and it is for that that I have returned."

"He wants my arrow," Dax exclaimed. The crowd erupted in angry shouts and threats at the foolish boy who would impishly call for the Chufa's greatest weapon to carry off into unknown lands where it would be squandered and most likely lost leaving them helpless against the raids that would certainly come again. Thane stood motionless, watching and waiting as the mob-like crowd continued their tirade. He was not interested in stroking their childish beliefs or ignorant superstitions. Neither did he have the proper time needed to win them over. He already knew that none but those that were with him were willing to listen to reason when it came from his lips. He watched his father who joined in with the shouting while darting his eyes about to make certain none were connecting him to his son. It was then suddenly clear to Thane that his father's real quandary was the shameful secret that he was a coward. He could not stand alone, instead placing all his self worth on the backs and minds of those with whom he lived. He had no core of self-esteem or understanding.

BinChePa, gaining courage by the people's outrage, stepped forward and raised his hands for quiet. With a deprecating look, he confronted Thane, but still kept some distance from him. "If what you say is truth, then what is one arrow against so many? Surely it would not be more than the death of one combatant."

Thane eyed the Kinpa his anger and disgust still fresh and bitter in his mouth but at the same time, he knew he was lost. He could, and would, explain the dragons that were the true threat, but he already knew that none would believe him. "What you say, I do not deny." At those words a collective gasp and rumble passed through the crowd at their incredulity that he would make such an admission. "But," he yelled above the din, "it is not for the trolls that I make such a request." Once again, quiet fell upon his listeners as they waited to hear what he would say. "It is for another creature, far larger and more terrible, that I call for Dax's arrow. A creature that freezes its victims with fear as it drops from the sky and devours them in a single bite."

No one made a sound but instead all eyes turned to the Kinpa to see what he would say to such a horrific assertion. Thane's claims were incredible at the least but none had ever ventured over the mountains before and returned alive to speak of what they saw. BinChePa quickly ascertained the mood of the people and knew that they waited for his word to make up their minds for them. A bead of nervous sweat formed on his forehead calling attention to, any close enough to see, his fear that Thane was telling the truth. He understood that to lose the crowd in the least now would likely turn them enough to Thane's favor that they might call for him to take the arrow just in case what he spoke were true. He had to say something quick as his silence would only bode in favor for Thane. A smile suddenly creased his lips and he bent himself over holding his stomach while letting out a loud guffaw. There was a slight pause as those around watched him and then a sudden roar of laughter erupted from all.

Dor was furious by such a disgusting display of abusive power and ignorance. No longer did he feel he could stand by and watch. He stepped forward, pulling Tam with him as he clung to her hand. "He speaks the truth!" he screamed as loud as he could and then did so again as the people started to calm down. With Dor's movement forward, Thane suddenly became aware of the obvious sign that declared his friends espoused to one another. Tam eyed him expectantly afraid of what it might do to him but was relieved by a slight nod and smile that acknowledged the match though his eyes seemed to remain neutral.

"I have seen the things of which he speaks," Dor cried. "He speaks truthfully. We would not be here otherwise," he finished more quietly, knowing that his words would wound his family and Tam's but also knowing in his heart it was true. The only reason they had come was to get the arrow. In a horrifically ironic sense, it was thanks to the dragons that he was now holding onto his promised bride matching his feelings of hopelessness against their foes with equal rays of joy for the recognition of his love for Tam. "Only the arrow can bring down the foes of which Thane speaks. And only then do we stand a chance against the gathered army."

"Even if what you say is true," BinChePa retorted, his tone one of disbelief and contempt that a mere child would dare challenge him, "then how are we to defend against such a host as you claim is gathered?"

"It is not you who will fight this battle," Thane shot back, "but..." he paused. He knew that to mention the HuMans would only worsen his case further. "Others will fight for you and for themselves."

BinChePa turned to the crowd. "Enough of these childish games," he called out. "We have heard enough from this troubled boy who has obviously suffered mentally from his long stay in the mountains. I say we deny his request immediately and return to the celebration."

At the very outskirts of the village circle a lone figure nocked an arrow and pulled back the string of his bow resting it along his cheek as he took aim at Thane's heart. His breathing slowed as he settled into his target knowing that he had but one shot to be rid of the freakish Chufa boy that put himself above others because of his mutation at having all five Tane. It was such an easy shot, one that would never be fingered back at him and one, he knew, that really would never be questioned because all would welcome it gladly. Holding his last breath he steadied his arm one last time as he prepared to release his hold on the string.

Suddenly, his aim was made unsteady as the cold, sharp edge of a large steal blade slid threateningly under his chin and rested against the soft skin at his throat. He froze as a hand reached out pushing his bow and arrow down toward the ground where he let them drop without the slightest resistance.

"All if favor," BinChePa shouted to immediate roars of agreement as the crowd, once again, took up its cheers against Thane. Thane looked at Dor, who was livid at what was taking place. His anger had slipped into a rage greater than any he'd ever experienced in his life and it was only Tam's hold on his hand that kept him from rushing forward and throttling BinChePa.

It was then that the sudden cheers began turning into cries and shouts of alarm. Thane followed the pointing fingers and terror stricken looks to his left where he saw Jne coming toward him, a Chufa male, her prisoner, out in front. It was PocMar. A great pandemonium was beginning to erupt that could swiftly turn into a hysteria that would threaten innocent lives. Thane quickly moved forward, waving his hands and yelling to get the people's attention and calm them down. Already some of the men had rushed away to their huts to retrieve their weapons and he knew if he didn't rapidly get control that this night might well turn into a massacre.

Jne seemed unconcerned as she directed PocMar to the council fire area by Thane. The fact that she was not Chufa and was obviously from the other side of the mountains had many calling out that the HuMans had returned and that they were all doomed to destruction. Many angry words were directed at Thane labeling him as a traitor for bringing such a monster into their village. Jne watched curiously at the way his people were acting and immediately determined that Thane was truly not one of them. She had expected so much more from a race that had produced someone of his quality.

"Please," he called out. "There is no reason to fear! There is no reason to fear!" The crowd seemed either unable to hear him or unwilling to listen. Cries of "traitor" and "kill them all" erupted from all ends as women and children were pushed toward the back, some rushing into the forests while men were already taking positions with their bows ready should the need present itself. Thane looked at the Kinpa, who were the first to call for protection from the nearest persons wielding a weapon, offering a look of pleading for them to gain control of the crowds. This one act of humility on his part seemed all they needed to return their feelings of import and superiority. Now they had him back in their control where they wanted him. His previous power over the crowd was ended and though they still feared the power they suspected he held, they knew that all would give their lives to save that of a Kinpa.

FelTehPa was the first to act, moving about the crowd and calling for calm. The people were slow to even yield to the Kinpa's commands but finally, as the men returned with their weapons, they began to settle into an uneasy silence.

"And how do you explain yourself?" DanGuaPa demanded, "bringing an outsider, a HuMan killer into our village!" Cries from some of the women were heard at the mention of a HuMan while others seemed almost curious since most considered the story of such a fierce and bloodthirsty people apocryphal.

"I am no HuMan," Jne called out to the surprise of all. Most thought that she was no more than slightly above an animal, yet she spoke the Chufa language.

"She is one who will fight for you," Thane cried, taking advantage of the sudden change in attitude, although slight. "And there are others like her over the mountains that will do the same who have no interest in the Chufa other than to be left to live peacefully while allowing you the same."

"These are lies!" BinChePa screamed. "Now that they know where we live, they will come here and destroy us like their ancestors tried before." Pointing at Thane, he continued. "And just like the nameless one of the past, it is a Chufa who has betrayed us!"

Thane could see that things were deteriorating quickly. He suddenly regretted not following the plan though his choices had been limited when Dax took aim at Jne.

"I have not betrayed you," he insisted, still trying to talk reason so that he might do his all to defend them even though they did not deserve it. "I am here to help protect you, as is Jne," he said pointing to the Tjal woman who still held to a mask of neutral expression.

"To bring danger to this people as you have is betrayal," FelTehPah called out.

"Is it betrayal to seek the life of one of your own?" Jne asked, drawing all eyes to her.

No one answered. All were still in awe at the presence of one who was not of their race. Most believed themselves and the trolls the only living things and that there was nothing but a void beyond the mountains.

"This one," Jne continued, pointing at PocMar, "was about to shoot at one of your own while hidden in the woods."

Suddenly, PocMar became the focus of attention, though he tried to remain hidden behind Jne. All knew of whom she spoke when she'd said "one of your own." Thane shrugged off the information but Dor was not about to let this go unanswered.

Reluctantly, he released his hold on Tam's hand and moved forward in front of Thane and Jne waving his hands and calling for everyone's attention. "This man is a coward!" he shouted pointing toward PocMar. With his position so close to Thane, many thought it was to him that he directed his insult which caused many in the crowd to call for quiet. Finally they would see the end of the one who the Kinpa had whispered was like the traitor of old. And this act of bringing a dangerous outsider into their midst had sealed the rumor for many of them. Now it would be the one who had given his friendship naively that would pay him for his treachery.

"This man is a coward!" Dor shouted again, but this time he grabbed PocMar by the arm and pulled him out in full view. The village fell instantly silent at the accusation that was no longer directed in their minds to the one who deserved it, but one whom, many, if they honestly considered it, would have agreed but under the circumstances found themselves swayed into PocMar's defense.

Tam stepped forward, as if to stop Dor's angry tirade but it was already too late. She knew all too well what this meant for Dor and PocMar and her heart was wrenched with the fear that somehow Dor would not come out triumphant. To call one coward in the Chufa culture was to openly challenge that person to a battle to the death. No Chufa would allow himself to be called such without fighting to prove his accuser wrong. Dor was challenging his boyhood enemy now and one of them would not survive the evening.

"What is your claim?" one of the Kinpa insisted, calling Dor to present his reasoning behind the charge.

Turning to stare at PocMar as he spoke, his face was a cool rage as he spat the words. "To attack a Chufa in such a secretive and craven manner is the truest definition of the word coward."

"This woman lies," PocMar insisted. "No true Chufa would accept her word over mine." Thane reached out a hand to hold Jne from reacting to PocMar's disparaging comment. But surprisingly, she did not seem concerned with what he'd said. To her, one that is without reason is never taken for his word or held responsible for their foolish acts. "No matter though," PocMar continued. "You will pay for your lying tongue once and for all!" he screamed at Dor. "DaxSagn will not save you this time!"

Dor smiled at his opponent. "Choose," he said calmly. According to Chufa law, the person who had been challenged was given the option to choose which ever weapon he deemed to his advantage thus assuring that a false claim would never be made. Death was near placing over Dor the calm assurance that always came when it approached. Whether it came for him or PocMar, it was close now and Dor urged it ever nearer.

"Daggers!" PocMar spat, his voice confident, his rage still boiling. His anger actually wasn't directed at being called a coward so much as it was that he had failed in his desire to finally have Thane dead. He'd thought he had accomplished that goal before, and nothing would have made him happier than to have Thane in Dor's place, but alas, one at a time. Thane would still be dead this night as well after he finished off his only friend.

Dor's smile grew larger at his choice. "Are you certain you don't want to pick something else?" he offered.

PocMar paused, a glimmer of uncertainty flashing across his face. Then it was gone, replaced by his ever present rage. "Of course, I am certain. You bluff at your skill DorMar. But even if you don't, you cannot have improved more that me since you've been gone—chasing after your friend, was it?"

Dor smiled at the remark unwilling, and possibly unable, to allow himself to lose the calm that surrounded him in a shroud like death's embrace. Pulling the dagger that sat securely sheathed at his waist, he waited for PocMar to draw his weapon.

Reaching behind him, PocMar pulled free a blade he'd won when one of his followers had taken down a troll that he took credit for. Knowing PocMar was better with a knife, the one who had earned it had not spoken up for fear that he would end up dying by that same blade in a similar challenge as PocMar faced now. "You just keep your friend," he sneered, referring to Jne, "out of this."

"Don't worry," Dor answered, unable to control his own tongue, "I won't let her harm you."

PocMar's face distorted into a furious rage as he lunged forward, an obvious break in the etiquette of the challenge as he had not first asked Dor if he were ready. Dor easily sidestepped the lunge leaving PocMar completely exposed. He could have slit his throat with a quick cut and ended it right then, but he was not ready to see his opponent die. No, he must be seen for the coward he truly was.

Recognizing his vulnerable position and the mistake he had made, PocMar ran forward to clear himself from Dor's cut that never came. Though he immediately took confidence that Dor had missed a grand opportunity, Dor's smile said otherwise. Coming more cautiously this time, PocMar advanced on his opponent as he slashed across the chest and then quickly reversed his momentum with an uppercut swing designed to bury the dagger under the chin and up into the skull. Dor, though, was not fooled and easily turned his blows away and, with an incredible display of ability, effortlessly deflected each assault as PocMar continued to unleash his arsenal of attacks but to no avail. Many opportunities had arisen when Dor might have used an attack himself to at least injure his opponent, but as of yet he merely parried against PocMar's constant barrage.

Sweat was beginning to pour off of PocMar as his frustration continued to build, as well as his apprehension as to his ability to beat Dor. Dor, on the other hand, still remained encased in the calm of death that watched eagerly, waiting to feed on the one who failed. After deflecting another attempt at his throat, Dor smiled as PocMar backed away pretending to prepare for another attack, but Dor knew, as did all watching, that it was really to catch his breath. Dor had him and he knew it. PocMar would have also known it but for his arrogance. The crowd watched in relative silence though whispers could be heard among the clanging of metal. Jne seemed bored by the display while Tam and Thane, though concerned for their friend, were beginning to feel more confident.

PocMar waited. Jeering at his opponent, his breathing was labored and becoming forced. The sweat on his arms was now dripping over his hand making his grip less certain. Dor stood waiting, almost in a completely upright position as if unconcerned that he might not be able to react quick enough to another attack. It was then that PocMar finally started to realize that he was beaten and that his life was completely given into Dor's hands. Once Dor decided it was ended, his life would be over. Suddenly, his eyes started darting about as if looking for a way to escape but the crowd was at his back pressing in as they watched. The only way was forward past Dor or back to the woods past the foreigner that had caught him with the bow. Making his decision, he flipped his blade over catching it by the blade and then threw it at Dor with all his strength. Clearly against the rules of dueling, Dor was caught off guard by PocMar's aerial assault and let out a gasp of pain and surprise as the blade embedded itself into his right shoulder.

All stood frozen. Tam made an unconscious move toward him but Thane caught her arm. To interfere in a duel would forfeit the life of the participant as well as your own. Dor dropped his blade and then staggered forward. PocMar watched him approach uncertain as to whether he should attempt to flee or if he still might have a chance to win. Stopping within arm's length, Dor held his opponent with his glare while he reached up and, with a slight twinge, pulled the dagger free. "I believe this is yours," he said.

PocMar's expression revealed the fear he was feeling though he tried his hardest to hide it. Looking at the blade, he moved as if he would take it when Dor's other hand shot forward, catching him by the throat while raising the blade and pressing its blood-soaked edge against his neck. Through the pain, he suddenly felt his rage break through the calm that always seemed to wrap him in a cocoon of nothingness when death approached. He flexed his grip on PocMar's throat squeezing a little bit tighter making it more difficult for PocMar to take in air. PocMar's eyes were globes of terror now as he waited for the final cut that would end his life and declare him a coward and Dor the victor.

His shoulder throbbed now with the beating of his heart as his rage seemed to increase with the pounding rhythm. Everything else around him seemed to fade into nothingness leaving only him and PocMar who he could feel was trembling with anticipation of the killing stroke. Dor concentrated on the pain to increase his rage willing him to ignore the blade and rip PocMar's throat out with his bare hands instead. He could feel PocMar's pulse increasing rapidly as his artery throbbed against his hand that gripped it. Dor concentrated on the feel of PocMar's blood flow as it raced through his neck trying to feed his brain and keep him alive through the increased pressure Dor was applying. And then suddenly, he felt it. The water that mixed with PocMar's blood; he could feel it as if they were connected. After the countless hours of practice and failure, the connection seemed to come of itself revealing its secrets and offering its power to him if he so desired to take it. He felt himself smiling. It was so simple, and now he knew how. All he had to do was call for it to come out and he knew that it would obey his bidding. He could reduce PocMar to a husk.

His eyes widened at the realization leading PocMar to believe that the moment had come making him suddenly go slack and dropped to the ground breaking Dor's connection as he fell into a heap into the dirt. Dor stared at him, his rage unexpectedly swallowed in the joy of his discovery and leaving him with a feeling of pity for the young Chufa boy that had always been a coward, and who would forever remain so.

He let PocMar's dagger fall to the ground, where it landed next to him, and then turned back to retrieve his own. "It is finished," he spoke, to everyone's amazement. "Let him live with the shame he has heaped on others for most of his life. Let him live with the knowledge that he will always remain a coward." He paused. "But should we meet again," he hissed, but then didn't finish his sentence.

Chapter Fifteen

Tam ran to Dor and checked his shoulder, which was now bleeding rather profusely. Looking to Thane she was about to ask for his help but already he was placing his hand over the wound and calling forth the QenChe Tane to cauterize it. No one approached PocMar who still lie in the dirt unconscious and unaware of his good fortune at still being alive, though he would regret it in the years to come as his cowardice would haunt his every breath.

Thane nodded to Dor accepting his thanks and then stepped forward once more to address the crowd. "Now is the time to break free of the mire of hate and superstition that envelopes the Chufa existence. Now is the time to once again regain the noble majesty that once was our heritage and indeed our inheritance. Give me the arrow that will turn the tide back to the favor of those who fight for your very existence and live in the assurance that as you take breath every day it is thanks to the noble within you that refused to be shackled by the doubts and ignorance of the aged who would keep you chained in fear." The Kinpa scowled at him for his last comment recognizing all too well his reference to them.

An eerie silence fell over the people as they digested his words. More than a few were stirred by the emotion and conviction with which he spoke. Slowly, voices could be heard rumbling as neighbor spoke to neighbor in whispered tones as to whether they should believe the young outcast who suddenly returned in company with one not of their race. All their lives they had been taught by the Kinpa that nothing but horror and death existed on the opposite side of the mountains that protected them. Now, one who lived there was in their midst and it seemed, on the surface, that what they had been told was true. Yet, it was not easy to disregard the beauty and nobility that seemed to encase the strange woman in spite of the aura of danger and lethality that surrounded her as well.

The Kinpa scanned the crowd easily recognizing in the faces of many those that they had been swayed by Thane's words and were in favor of passing the most prized Chufa possession on to him to do with as he pleased. They could not let victory fall to defeat so suddenly.

LorVenPa, who had remained silent through most of the debate, stood forth with his hands raised to call attention to himself. "The Chufa have always been, and continue to be," he looked at Thane, "a noble and grand people. It was not we who waged war in the times of old with the HuMan's but they who attacked us in innocence. We were exiled and almost left to ruin as our ancestors struggle to make their way through the troll infested Shadow Mountains to our present home where we live in peace. Peace is all we have ever sought and it is peace that we continue to desire now. The fact that we hold such a weapon as the arrow that DaxSagn so ably carries and wields is so that peace might be maintained against those who would take it away." Again his eyes turned accusingly toward Thane. "It is due to warmongers and wrongdoers that we are forced to live sheltered as we are or else be annihilated by those bent on evil intent."

Motioning toward his fellow Kinpa, he continued. "We are mere servants to the people, chosen to guide in matters concerning your welfare and protection. But it is you, the people who have the voice that truly determines all matters and it is to that voice that I offer this one caution. Already one of our own has betrayed us," he didn't turn his gaze toward Thane this time but the statement was left for the people to decide on whether he referred to Thane or the ancient nameless one. "Our meager existence has been thanks to the powers of the arrow that has been the salvation of our people countless times. Keep that in your hearts as you ponder the question as to its fate. Keep that in your hearts as you decide what your thoughts will be this very night as you lie down with your little ones to sleep as to whether you feel that you have done the right thing to protect them. There is no turning back from such a choice. It is up to you to decide whether you will embrace peace and life, or the war of foreigners and death."

Thane watched as the Kinpa turned a sickening grin toward him before returning to his previous place in the crowd. All were silent, the sounds of the night and the crackle of the center fire the only thing to be heard when a slight rumble suddenly began in the center of the crowd and then quickly spread out in all directions as the cry began to be raised, "Keep the arrow! Keep the arrow!"

LorVenPa smiled in triumph at Thane as the other Kinpa gathered together to discuss what should be done now that he'd returned. All the frustrations that he'd been holding in check suddenly erupted to the surface as he shouted above the din of the crowd, "You will lament this day! When the hordes crest the mountains in a swarm of death and you are left standing impotent with no one left to protect you, you will remember this day when a fallen people dug themselves even deeper into the filth in which you presently mire about! And as you watch as your children are devoured and your wives are turned to slaves, you will remember this day and weep!"

The crowd suddenly turned silent again, many losing the color in their faces as they turned toward the Kinpa as if begging them to denounce such language. But Thane did not wait to see what would be done. He had given all he could for his people, and yet he knew he would give so much more. He knew that he would still pay the ultimate price for their protection but no longer did he do it for them directly, but only because it was the right thing to do. No longer did he hold hope in his heart that he one day might return and live with the Chufa in peace. No, he would turn his back on the Ardath Forest and the people who called it home and never again return.

Passing Jne, she fell into step behind him as he headed for the woods. He had one more thing that he must do before they departed and he saw no reason to delay. He wanted to be away from there as quickly as possible.

Tam looked up at Dor, the tears welling over her eyelids at all that had happened. The joy she had felt with the FasiUm had been beaten down by the sorrow and hurt that came from Dor's duel and now her people's inability to see beyond themselves.

Dor looked back at her, the concern in his eyes evident though their meaning was lost on her. She thought they spoke of her being left behind and a touch of anger forced its way through the sorrow.

"I will not stay!" she insisted. "I will not sit here safe from harm while you and Thane throw your lives away trying to save people who are not intelligent enough to save themselves!"

Dor smiled at her outburst and shook his head. "I would not think of it." She was caught off guard by his words. "Why would I want to embrace death alone without you by my side as my companion? I have not come through so much to take the final journey alone."

She smiled at him, the sudden warmth of her choice returning, as she finally felt that she was seen as an equal and not as the young child that once tormented him. "We must prepare to go so as not to miss Thane," she replied, a sudden sense of urgency filling her voice. Though she'd gained Dor's respect and support, she wasn't too certain that Thane felt the same way, especially now that she and Dor were espoused to be made one.

Taking her hand back into his, Dor moved them forward toward where their parents had been standing. "Let us bid our farewells quickly," he said, navigating through the crowd that was now dispersing as many had lost the will or desire to celebrate any longer. Usually, the FasiUm ceremony went deep into the night, often times ending well after the rising of the sun, but too much had occurred for the spirit of celebration to reinstill itself into the hearts of the revelers.

Finding their parents huddle together and talking of the night's activities, Dor and Tam approached just as his father said, "I always felt sorry for Thane, but now he has gone too far. It will be best if he left, for all of us."

"How can you say that?" Dor demanded, surprising them as he and Tam materialized out of the crowd. "He has nothing but all of our lives at heart. I know of what he speaks and it is truth. I have seen the hordes that run wild bent on nothing but death and destruction."

"Maybe that is so," Tam's father offered, defending his friend's statement, "but that is what comes to those who live by war and hate. Eventually, they are overrun by those of the same mind but with greater might."

"So they've had it coming to them, is what you are saying," Tam interjected.

"They are horrible people who do horrible things," her mother answered. "It is justice after what they did to our people. They are only harvesting what they have sewn."

Tam was disgusted by her parent's comments. "You have never even met a one of them and you are passing judgment as if you had first hand knowledge of their minds and hearts. Thousands have died already and thousands more will yet be slaughtered fighting to protect their families and their homes. They will die, though they don't know it, protecting you."

"What Thane said is true," Dor interjected. "The trolls have gathered and fight together. They are a vast number that none here would ever fathom and they will come back, should they turn victors, and annihilate you all."

"You don't know that," Dor's father insisted, his voice tinted with anger at his son's threatening words and tone.

"But I do, Father," he returned, his own words heating with his ire. "I did not tell you all about our time away because I didn't want to worry you, but both Tam and I were prisoners to the trolls. They have tunnels and caves dug all throughout the mountains and their numbers far surpass our own. It is only through their own hatred toward all things, including themselves, that they never joined up to battle against us as one. If they remain united and conquer those on the other side, you will be next."

"Wait," Tam's mother interjected. "Don't you mean, we?"

Tam and Dor looked at each other and then Dor turned back to their parents. "We are not staying."

"What is this talk?" TaqSagn demanded while their mothers gasped in disbelief, tears instantly coming to their eyes. "You have a wife now to think about. How is it that you, if what you say is true, are so carelessly willing to drag her off to her doom in the company of HuMans?"

"He drags me nowhere," Tam huffed. "I go willingly. I would go even if he decided to stay, in fact." She earned a quick look of surprise from Dor but she didn't stop to even acknowledge it. "You don't know what those things are capable of," she insisted, her eyes quickly filling with tears. But she refused to lose herself over to the emotions of the past. Bracing herself, she forced her them back and continued boldly. "I will not sit here and wait to see whether or not they will eventually be coming for us. I will not sit by idly while others fight for me, risking their lives so that I might live without fear. I choose to fight, and fight I will until the last breath escapes me and my spirit is set free by the fires of the SaiEeDu."

"Please," her mother begged, "don't do this. Don't throw your lives away when they are just starting."

"It is this people that throw their lives away," Dor insisted, not cushioning his words in the least. "You had the chance to stand with us in this fight, but instead you denied us the one thing that could have made a difference, the one thing that would have given a greater assurance of our safe return. Think of that after we are gone, when you wonder if you will ever again see us in this life." Grabbing Tam's hand, he turned away from their parents and they both disappeared into the crowd as their parents called after them, their mothers reduced to sobs.

"You didn't have to speak so harshly to them," Tam said, though her voice held no accusing tone.

"I did," he rebuffed. "I could not stand it any longer to be lectured by them and feel the love and respect I have always held for my parents chipped away by their careless words. We will return to them again some day. I feel that to be the truth, but that doesn't mean I will want to come back to stay. It is different here now. Maybe it is I who am different." He stopped and held both of her hands looking deep into her eyes. "I will not hold you to your choice if you hold any doubts."

Tam was suddenly flabbergasted. "Though I am not totally certain that I want to spend my life in hiding in the HuMan world, never think that I wouldn't do so in the enemy's own lair itself if it meant being with you. I have made my choice, DorMar, and it will take more than this war, more than death itself to break that bond."

*   *   *

Thane and Jne sat motionless as they waited, keeping their own council in silence. It had been easy to sneak in since with Jne's appearance, all of the night patrols had been called in should there be a sudden HuMan invasion and all their forces were needed.

The bile of the evening's events still soured Thane's mouth as he replayed it over and over in his mind trying to discover something he had done wrong or something else he should have done to win over his people. But he knew it was senseless. What he had said about them was more than the truth and he, most of all, could see it clearly.

Jne had said nothing, remaining, as always, his quiet strength in the storms that seemed to twist about him wherever he went. He looked at her in the dark knowing that without his night vision she would not be able to see him. She seemed unaffected by all that had occurred as if seeing a village of Chufa and the strange activities that made up their culture was the most natural thing. He was constantly amazed by the inner calm and self awareness that seemed to cover her like a coating of armor. He thought of Dor and Tam and their recent espousal and was surprised to find that he wasn't jealous in the least. He pictured Tam in his mind, the one he had secretly held a light for his whole life and it now seemed the most natural thing to place Dor next to her. He tried picturing himself with her instead, but it felt wrong. Not only as a match, but his heart no longer seemed to cling to the idea or yearn that it be so. Now when he thought of being with someone it was Jne that filled his thoughts. He stared at her. What sort of life awaited them when this was all over?

Suddenly, the sound of cracking leaves invaded his thoughts and announced the arrival of the person he'd been waiting for. He didn't pull a weapon, certain there would not be any physical violence, though his blood ran hot with disdain. The covering over the hut was pulled back and a man stepped through the threshold.

"What are you doing here?" the man almost immediately asked, easily seeing them with his night vision. "And why have you brought that thing with you?"

Thane shot Jne a quick glance, having warned her beforehand that their host would not be a gracious one and that she should take nothing he said as a personal insult but instead as the ramblings of a broken man. Jne had only nodded. Though he couldn't be certain about what she thought, he was content in knowing he had no fear when it came to her word—be that spoken or merely gestured.

"Where is she?" Thane shot back, not relishing time spent with his father but knowing it was necessary after he'd shown up to his family hut, looking for his mother, but finding it empty. "Did you send her out?" he spat.

DelVen glanced at Jne briefly as if trying to determine her motives but she remained completely still where she stood. "She's dead," he finally answered, the words falling out with disdain. "Died not long after you left."

Thane stared at his father for a long moment as if trying to determine if what he spoke was true.

"If you don't believe me," DelVen offered as if sensing his doubts, "then you are welcome to hide out like a thief in someone else's home and ask them."

"Then she is finally free of you," he answered, his face and voice expressing no emotion other than contempt for his father. The announcement that his precious mother was dead was like an arrows barb to his heart, but he would show no emotion in front of his father.

"I should have killed you when you were first born," DelVen suddenly spat with venom.

Thane sniffed and then smiled shaking his head slightly in disbelief at the sad creature standing before him. "You are welcome to try now," he offered.

DelVen paused as if he might consider it but quickly set the challenge aside, revealing once more his cowardice. "If we are done here then get out."

"Gladly," Thane answered. "And know this," he added as he stepped past, Jne already out of the hut, "we will never lay eyes on each other again, for if we do, it will be the last time you see anything."

DelVen opened his mouth as if to say something in retort, but Thane and Jne were already gone.

*   *   *

"Hold," Dor called causing both Thane and Jne to reach for their swords before recognizing him and Tam as they approached. Dor had feared that they would not be able to find their friends before they left but took a chance that they may have returned to where the birds had dropped them in the slight chance that their carriers might still be about. They were alone. It appeared that Thane and Jne were weighing their options before taking to the mountains and going at it on foot.

"We hoped you would be here," Tam called out. "Is there no sign of the birds?"

"Why are you two here?" Thane asked, his question sounding more accusatory than he meant it to be.

"We are here to go back with you, of course," Dor countered.

Thane sighed. "I am sorry. I did not mean for it to sound that way, I just figured that now that you two are espoused that you would opt for the safety of home."

"And you think that it is safer here than out there?" Tam huffed, pointing toward the mountains. "Do you think us as low as those who call themselves our people?"

Thane was taken aback by the venom suddenly dripping from Tam's voice. "I meant no offense," he stammered. "I only thought…"

She cut him off. "No, you didn't think and that has been your problem since you were a child."

He looked to Jne for help but she merely smiled as if she found some great humor in the exchange. Looking to Dor, all he got was a blank stare back and he knew that, once again, he was all alone. "I'm sorry," he finally offered. "Yes, I would do all I could to get you both to stay, but I see that to do so would only incur your greater wrath."

Tam huffed. "Then you had better clear all such thoughts from your head, Thane of the Five Tane!"

At that, he also smiled. For the first time in his life, his true full name did not cause him to cringe in contempt or embarrassment. "I am glad," he offered, "to see that you are finally back in form and to the person you once were."

Tam smiled. "Just don't forget with whom you are speaking."

"And what will we do now that we have failed?" Jne asked, pulling them all back to the reality of the situation.

"First we have to get away from here," Dor said. "I have no desire to stay any longer than is necessary."

Thane looked at his friend, sadness filling his eyes. He had reason to never want to return but it troubled him to see that same sentiment in his friend. "I hope that someday that desire will change," he said to no one in particular.

"And what of you?" Tam asked.

He looked at the ground, steeling his emotions, still not wanting to think of his mother and the pain he knew she must have passed through when he disappeared. "I will never return," he said.

"And what of your mother?" Tam continued to press.

He raised his head and locked his eyes on hers. "She is no more. And so passes my reason to ever return."

Tam placed a hand on her mouth. "Oh, Thane," she began, but he turned away and cut her off.

"I might be able to find and contact the birds," he said, "by using the ArVen Tane, though I am uncertain as to whether I will be able to communicate with them should I find them."

"That reminds me," Dor interjected. "Thane, I touched the water!"

He gave his friend a quizzical look. "That moment," Dor continued, "when I had PocMar by the throat. I touched his water. I felt it coursing through his veins and filling his skin. I touched it and I knew that should I have so desired, I could have called it all right out of him."

Thane smiled but his joy seemed to be more calculated. "That is good news indeed, my friend," he said. "If we can just teach the Healers to do the same, we will have a mighty weapon indeed against our enemies."

Dor looked at him as if he'd never considered that that was why Thane had tried to get him to learn but, to his surprise, the idea didn't bother him. Thane was right. "And should we ever get close enough to a dragon…" Dor let his thought trail off. Thane had already killed one of the great serpents by calling the water out of it.

"Maybe our trip has not been a total failure after all," Jne finished as the two rocs suddenly appeared setting down next to them.

Chapter Sixteen

Jack shot up from his bed reaching for his throat as the trailing mists of a nightmare melted away in the early morning dawn. He had not slept well that night, his mind filled with terrible dreams that seemed to chase him into the recesses of darkness terrorizing him with their horror. He pulled back his hand expecting to see it wet with blood as if he'd taken a cut to his jugular but it was dry and empty. Touching his throat again, he tried to remember what it was that had haunted him so but all memory of his evening of terror had passed.

The feeling of dread stuck with him as he swung his feet around and began to dress. Erl looked up briefly from his comfortable spot beneath the brazier but quickly dropped his head back down falling almost instantly back into quiet slumber. Jack regarded him jealously for a moment and then stood up, passing through the inner tent door to the outer area where Domis and Teek slept comfortably. He eyed the empty bed that had been made for Tryg but ignored it knowing that the young Waseeni boy never had once slept there, claiming he preferred the openness of the great night sky.

Passing through yet another opening he entered the relatively large room that was for greeting and discussing court matters. A guard snapped smartly to attention as he entered. Another "benefit" of being king was the constant pestering of having a guard at your back and a number of others close by should someone try to attack the royal body. Jack harrumphed but waved to the young man politely knowing he was only doing the duty for which he'd been charged. It had been such a long time since he had been in court that he'd forgotten about all of the formality and precautions made on his behalf.

Finally outside, two more guards offered a quick solute but this time he ignored them as he walked out into the camp. He needed to clear his head. So much had suddenly fallen upon him as the king that he barely had a moment to breathe. The guards stationed in front of the tent broke away and followed after him. Though they kept a decent distance he was still very aware of them. He had received quite the reprimand from the captain of the house guard the day he'd gone off out into the plains area alone. Since then it was a minimum of two guards at all times.

He wasn't sure what he was looking for or even why he felt the need to be out in the camp. It was still too early for most of the people to be awake and taking care of the morning meals and chores before the long trek onward toward Bedler's Keep. They were still some days away and still not as far from Calandra as he would like, but moving such a large camp of people was snail slow in the best of conditions. They did all that they could to hurry them along but the immediate danger they were in had yet to settle into their minds. Most had fled the city merely because they had been order to, not because they understood the dread of an approaching army that few could even comprehend in their most frightful night terrors.

He paused, sending a greeting to an older man who was just returning with some firewood for his morning cook fire. It wouldn't be long now until the horns were blown to awaken the camp and once again get them moving. Suddenly, a voice cried out bringing him back around to find Domis, Teek and a young courier rushing through the maze of carts and gear to catch him. "Milord," Domis cried again, "milord, there is news!"

Jack waited patiently for the three to approach, sighing to himself that once again the day's business would be piling in; every little thing an emergency in the mind of someone. He wondered what it would be this time; a lost pig? Another merchant angry that a peasant had the gall to bed down in a spot that was nicer than the place where his grand tent had to be erected? Or possibly another call to return to the city or demands that better facilities be erected for those with a gentler constitution to relieve themselves. The list was never ending.

"Milord," the courier spoke after bowing in a grand manner. "Your immediate attention is requested on the eastern side of the camp about a quarter of a mile back."

Jack pulled at his beard. "What is the problem?" he asked, his voice steady though a slight coloring of frustration dyed his words.

"Trouble," the courier said, seeming rather anxious to be on their way. "I was not told exactly what the trouble is, your highness, but only that you were needed posthaste." Again he bowed and then threw out his arm in gesture for the king to move ahead in the direction indicated.

Jack sighed, audibly this time, and then directed the courier forward. "Lead the way," he said.

The courier bowed once more and then rushed off into the camp. "Quickly, milord," he called over his shoulder.

Luckily, they reached the area to where he'd been summoned before the morning horn or the pandemonium that accompanied the waking camp would have made it almost impossible for them to reach their destination before midmorning. A large contingency of guards were gathered about two huge tents, merchant's tents by the looks of them, keeping all curious onlookers away. Jack absentmindedly reached for his throat as he approached, the slight whisper of his early morning dream suddenly calling back to his memory. Wess was there to greet him.

"Your highness," he said, bowing gracefully.

Though Jack hated the formality, Ranse had convinced him that it was necessary for the comfort of the people. They needed someone to worship and follow no matter, like in the previous king's case, how ruthless and terrible the person might be. It gave them a sense of belonging to something that mattered. Something that was bigger than themselves that made them feel taken care of and protected. At first he had resisted, but he recognized the wisdom in what Ranse had said and decided that for the time being it was necessary to go along with it. After all, he could manage it until the war was past. Then he would either be dead or he could merely disappear into the mountains again to live out the rest of his life searching for his lost son.

"What is the problem, Wess?" he asked, almost impatiently.

Wess gave him a grave look and motioned him toward one of the tents. "You had better come and see for yourself, milord," he said quietly.

Jack's look turned to one of slight surprise and sudden concern to see one of his oldest and most battle hardened friends act in such a strange manner. Again, his hand reached for his throat, but this time he caught himself and grabbed at his beard instead.

Moving to the first tent's entrance, Domis and Teek followed right behind as if they would follow him in but Wess held them up. "Best you boys wait out here for now." With Jack's eyebrow raised in a questioning look, Wess added, "It's a little crowded for so many."

Jack regarded the tent that was of a size that easily was twice that of his own. Space was not a problem, but he didn't say anything to contradict his commander. "We'll be out soon," he said to the two boys who didn't seem happy or convinced but who took up positions near the entrance so as to be right there when he returned.

Jack passed through the tent flap, Wess right behind him and the only other person to enter. Immediately he was struck with the smell of death and the sound of flies that were already buzzing about the carrion was that was giving off the smell. He held his nose while letting his eyes adjust to the dim morning light that passed through the fabric in an eerie reddish hue. It was then that he noticed and remembered that the tent was not made of red material but of yellow to make it easy to see from the outside and also assist in lighting the inside with the filtered sunlight. He looked at the tent walls, trying to decipher what the dim light would not reveal.

"It's blood," Wess said, guessing his confusion. "It's been sprayed all over the tent walls."

Jack's reply was of shocked horror. "But how and with what?"

Wess pointed to his left and there Jack finally made out the body of one victim and then another. Small and large mounds were spread out throughout the room making up at least six dead. "There are more in the other chambers and the same in the tent next to us."

Jack approached the closest body but then quickly turned away. He was no amateur to death and the horrors of what evil men could do to their fellows, but never had he seen anything so grim as what greeted him here. It was as if the whole chest and stomach cavities had been scooped out and removed. "Who or what did this?" he breathed.

Wess shook his head. "Nobody knows. Nobody heard or saw anything."

Jack turned in shock at his reply. "Not even a scream? Surely there must have been some fight or noise from such a slaughter."

Again, Wess shook his head. "Nothing. We've asked all those in the immediate area and all claim to have slept without waking, though many spoke of terrible nightmares."

Jack's hand went to his throat. "Who found them?"

"A young boy, possibly a relative, approached one of the night guards early this morning. He's in deep shock and mostly just stares off into the distance. The most we could figure out when we could get him to speak was that he had fallen asleep in the tent of one of his friends and had woken early to get back to his family and this is what he found."

"Has anyone else seen this or talked to the boy?"

"No," Wess replied. "We have him quarantined and none others but the guard he approached and I have been in here."

"Good," Jack said, running a hand through his hair. "Let's keep it that way. Any idea as to what did this?"

"Looks like wolg work but there is no way so many could have gotten into the camp without being spotted. Also, no prints."

Jack nodded, his mind racing for the answer though staying away from the thought he most feared and figured most likely.

"What are your orders?" Wess asked, interrupting his thoughts.

He considered for a moment. It would be obvious to those in the immediate area that something was amiss when the merchant families failed to dismantle their tents when it was time to leave. But removing the bodies in front of everyone would be even worse and they certainly could not lose a day by staying camped until nightfall when the work could be accomplished under cover of night.

"We will leave a small detachment of guards to keep the people clear as the camp prepares to leave and then when all have passed we will set it to fire. I don't want word of this spreading. We don't need panic overtaking the camp now. Though it may hurry them along a bit faster, most likely it will just send them all running pell-mell throughout the countryside in a mass of terror."

A horn suddenly called out in the distance followed quickly by others as the camp was called to awaken. "I will stay behind as well in case there is any trouble."

Wess gave him a curious look. "We can handle this, Jack. There is no need for you to stay behind."

He smiled slightly, thankful for the informal use of his first name while they were alone. "Now that the horns have sounded the likelihood of me getting back to my tent will be next to impossible. Plus, I want to talk to the boy who found this. Where is he now?"

"In a tent not far from here. Shall I bring him to you?"

"No," he countered, "He doesn't need to be traumatized more by the sight of these tents again."

Lifting the flap, Wess escorted the king back into the fresh air that was more than welcome even with the mixture of the myriad of cook fires sprouting up and spitting out their smoke and grease fumes. Domis and Teek eyed him expectantly, waiting to see if they would try to make the trip back to their own tent and the hot breakfast that was sure to be awaiting them. Turning to the closest guard, Jack motioned to the two boys. "Make sure these two get something to eat," he said to their chagrin. Although they were grateful for the coming meal, they did not relish having to wait to clean up their own camp and prepare for the daily move. The guard saluted and then quickly disappeared into the chaos of the camp. "It can't be helped," he said to the boys who didn't answer but appeared moody about it all the same. "And where is Tryg?"

Teek shrugged. "Haven't seen him for a day or so," Domis answered for them. "He does this. Leaves mostly when there is work to be done and then doesn't return for long stretches."

Jack stared at him blankly, his hand absently rubbing his neck. "When Tchee returns," he finally said, "I want you two up and checking on the enemy's progress."

Both boys smiled at that. Not only were they finally being trusted with something more important than making sure their area of the tent was cleaned up and their faces were washed, but they welcomed anything that broke up the doldrums of the constant march that seemed to never bring them closer to their destination.

Jack spent the next hour with the young boy who had stumbled upon the gory remains of his family and their servants. He tried all that he could to get more from the boy but it was obvious that his mind had shut down and that the once innocent child had retreated into an area where such things were never seen or even thought of. For the time, Jack knew that it was the best for the boy to remain locked inside of himself.

"Find a family to care for him," he finally instructed Wess who'd sat in with him during his attempt to reach the boy. "The friend's family he'd been with, if you can find them, would probably be the best choice."

The camp was up and starting to move forward when they finally left the tent where the boy had been kept. Though a slow moving march, it wasn't all that easy to keep people from trampling the tents where the dead bodies still lie decomposing. Luckily the air was still brisk enough that the stench was kept down. The flies though were becoming a greater problem as they swarmed in extreme numbers around the tent and in the immediate vicinity. The guards were forced farther and farther away from the area making it that much more difficult in turning the refugees to either side. It wasn't until midday that the end of the camp finally split around the tents that were now deluged with flies and giving off a nauseating stench.

Jack told them to wait still another hour, until the camp stragglers were finally close to a mile away before ordering the tents to be torched. Since it was impossible to get close enough now to ignite them with torches, archers were used with a volley of fire arrows to set the tombs ablaze. The fabric quickly ignited sending up clouds of flies and smoke as the remains were finally given some sort of dignity in burning that they'd been denied in burial. Jack watched the dark column of smoke rising in the air, a beacon to any nearby enemies and a mark of triumph for the perpetrators of the murders. It could not be helped though. In war it was often the least detrimental of two bad choices that was offered and had to be decided upon.

"Your highness," Domis' voice suddenly broke through Jack's dark thoughts. "Your highness, something approaches."

Jack followed his pointing finger that marked the two dots in the western sky that approached the small group. At first glimpse he was about to call the alarm but something held him fast as the shapes grew larger and clearer to his view. His immediate reaction had been dragons, but now he could tell that there size was nothing close to the monstrous serpents that had rained death down upon them from the skies. No, these were birds.

"They've returned!" Teek suddenly cried out and instantly all knew of whom he spoke.

All watched as the birds drew closer and then circled twice before making their final approach and setting down near the small crowd. Thane was the first to drop off of the great bird and was making his way toward Jack before any of the others had yet set foot on the ground.

"We have failed," he said darkly. "We were unable to retrieve the arrow. They are a fallen people," he spat vehemently.

Jack sighed but did not speak. Hope was quickly draining away as their situation continued to worsen.

"Begging your pardon, sir," Teek asked, "but what good is one arrow against so many?"

Thane looked at the Waseeni boy who in age was no more than a cycle or two younger than himself though the rapid maturing process inherent in the Chufa made Thane appear many years his senior. "It is a special arrow that has the ability to pierce through metal and thus, in all probability, the hide of a dragon. We cannot take down such beasts with what we have now."

Dor, Tam and Jne finally approached, Dor and Jne appearing somewhat nauseated from the ride.

"Can we not just forge another one like it?" Domis asked innocently. "With more than one dragon, we will need more than one arrow anyway won't we?"

"One does not just forge such arrows," Dor stated flatly.

"Then from where did it come?" Teek asked the obvious question.

Thane looked around at the eyes that were now locked on him expectantly as they waited to hear the answer. He hesitated, his knowledge almost as limited as there own concerning the arrow save for the small amount of Chufa lore that may or may not hold any truth. "It is said that they come from the heart of the YeiyeiloBaneesh tree."

"Which our people destroyed over a thousand years ago," Jack finished. "It is ironic that such a thing that our ancestors did would be the vehicle to bring about our utter destruction."

"What were they like?" Domis asked continuing the questioning. Everyone seemed to move in closer as they waited for his answer. Even the guards found themselves taking some cautious steps forward so as to be certain to catch every word.

Thane shook his head. "None know any longer. That knowledge has been lost to time." He suddenly took on a far away look as if seeing them in his mind. "But it is said that they were glorious, that they radiated light and peace. Nothing exists that could ever be compared to them." Focusing again on the gathered crowd, his expression fell. "We will never know them again."

All remained in silence, a pall of dark sadness overtaking each. "And what of the fire?" Thane asked, pointing to the remains of the tents that smoldered in ashen piles, wisps of smoke still rising with the wind and drifting away to the north. "They were an easy and welcome beacon to finding you but would also be the same for our enemy."

Jack's face was grave. "It was necessary." Motioning to Dor, Tam and Jne as well he said, "Come and we will counsel together."

Moving off away from the others Jack spoke in hushed tones so that his voice would not carry. "We were attacked in the night."

"Attacked?" Thane asked, somewhat surprised that the enemy was not still upon them.

"Two merchant families were slaughtered in their sleep but by what no one knows. None heard a sound and there were no tracks to reveal the enemy. The victims were gutted, there innards gone," Jack paused. "I suspect that they were eaten."

"A dragon?" Jne asked.

Jack nodded his head. "That is what I suspect. I don't know how anything else could have come into camp without being seen and then cause such a slaughter without so much as a whisper."

"But dragons are so enormous," Tam said. "How would one fit in a tent? Even a merchant sized one?"

"They can take HuMan form," Thane answered.

"Which means there might be one in the camp among us," Dor said putting voice to what everyone else was thinking but were not willing to speak as if to do so would turn it into reality.

"And how do we defend against such a threat?" Tam asked.

"We can't," Thane said bluntly.

"If there is such a creature among us," Jne offered, "and this is the first that it has attacked, then it could be possible that it did so only because of hunger. It may not do so again for some days."

"There is sense to your words," Jack said. "And we can hope that they prove true. In the meantime we need to do all we can to flush it out, though I don't know how one would accomplish such a thing. Right now what is of most import is to keep it quiet and among only ourselves and possibly a few others. Should such information reach the ears of the general camp it would only lead to chaos and a scattering of the people."

"Like sheep," Jne said.

"I've got it!" Teek suddenly yelled as he ran toward them. "I've got it! The trees! The trees! I know where they are!"

"What are you talking about boy?" Jack rumbled.

"I know where we can find some of those special trees!" he said excitedly.

"Impossible," Thane said, "they were all destroyed."

"No," Teek countered. "I don't think so. I remembered a story that old father Twee once told me, the one for whom I left my home to make an appeasing journey."

"Yes," Jack said absently reaching for the royal symbol that now hung from his neck. "I remember him well."

"Right," Teek continued. "He told me that once he had to pass through the Underwoods on an important mission for the king and that as they were deep within the forest they were attacked. All were killed but he was able to escape. It was then that he stumbled upon a small grove of trees like none he'd ever encountered before. They were off the path somewhere to the east, I think." Teek's face became serious as he tried to remember but then shook his head. "Anyway, he said that they cared for him and that they were just as Master Thane has described."

"Could it really be?" Tam asked, caught up in the growing excitement that was suddenly running through them all. "Could there really be some of them left after all these years?"

Thane shook his head. "I don't know. I guess it could be possible."

"Even if they are," Jne asked with a sudden slap of reality, "how will we find them, and if you do, how will you extract the arrows from them?"

Thane pointed to the two Rocs that preened themselves in the distance. "We will search from the skies. Once we've located them, then we can see about getting the arrows."

"I hate to be the one to douse the fires of excitement," Jack said, "but even if you do spot them from the air, the Underwoods forest is too thick and tangled to be able to land there and then retreat again."

"Then it is of no hope," Tam said, the sadness dripping from her voice. "Even if we searched from the ground, the forest is too great to ever discover a few trees at best."

"No," Teek pressed, the excitement suddenly rising in his voice. "No,

I remember where he found them. I remember where he left the road and found them!"

"Where?" Thane and Jack asked in unison.

"It was just past a great thicket of blackberry bushes. Just beyond that and to the east, I'm certain of it."

"That forest is probably full of such bushes," Jne said flatly.

"No," Teek still insisted. "No, I remember he spoke of it as something unusual. He did not mention any others either. And when he came out of the woods he was just east of Willow Wood."

All suddenly fell silent, lost in their own thoughts of this new revelation and what it might possibly mean for their side. It was a long shot, everyone knew it, but it was also the only chance they had left.

"We must go," Thane finally said.

"I agree," added Dor. "There is no other option left to us."

"The Aleron road is days from here," Jack said, "it will be some trek to get there, find the trees and then return to us at Bedler's Keep."

"We can use the birds," Tam offered. "They can get us there quickly and then wait for our return to carry us the rest of the way to the keep."

"You speak as if you would go," Thane said.

"We will," Dor said before Tam could open her mouth. "Who better suited to find and unlock the mysteries of the YeiyeiloBaneesh than us?"

Thane nodded his agreement, no longer feeling the need or ability to try and convince his friends to do other than they pleased. They knew the risks as well as he, both having suffered more than he had. It was only proper, as Dor said, for them to go together.

"Then we fly again," Jne said, her voice revealing her distaste of the idea.

"And we will go with you," Teek offered, including Domis in his assertion. "I am the one who knows best the story," he added quickly before anyone could counter him. "Plus, I tire of walking."

"And Domis?" Jack asked, an eyebrow raised.

"I know it second best," Domis replied with a smile.

Thane regarded to the two young friends and was reminded of himself and Dor in more innocent days. He wanted to deny them, knowing the dangers they faced were great and unknown but he also remembered the fire that once blazed in his belly to be out and doing; to be part of something grander than himself. Jack looked at him as if waiting for him to deny the request but was surprised when he finally said, "We leave at first light, be ready."

Chapter Seventeen

Thane stared at the flames that licked the air, feeding on the oxygen that gave them life. His mind had been racing since Teek's revelation about the existence of the sacred trees that had been the life blood of the Chufa and would possibly be the salvation of all good races. He tried to keep his excitement in check, knowing that what they were planning to do was a desperate gamble at best, but one they could not afford to let pass. Though Teek acted confident that he could lead them to their destination, they still were dealing with secondhand information that might well have been the confused imaginings of an eccentric old mind. He wished he could speak once more with Gelfin and find out what secrets he knew about the matter.

Jne sat down next to him and offered him food from her plate. Though he was not hungry, he had learned long before that to reject an offering of food from a Tjal was more insulting than spitting in one's face. Taking a large piece of roasted pork, he took to it immediately; not because he enjoyed it, but to show respect to its giver. He didn't even like pork. Jne smiled, content with his enthusiasm and the honor he showed her. Her rarely seen smile alone was enough for him to choke down just about anything she offered.

Quickly finishing he turned to her and took a deep breath but she cut him off before he could let any words fall from his lips. "You will ask something of me that I will not like," she said flatly. It was not even a question but a statement of complete confidence in her assumption.

He sighed and turned back to the fire. "Is it that obvious?"

Jne swallowed a piece of carrot and nodded. "You have become quiet and your sense of resolve and confidence wanes in your visage. It is not a very attractive look for you or any man."

At first he wasn't certain how to respond to such a comment but decided it was best to just present his opinion and have it over quickly. "I think you need to go back to your people and seek their help." When she didn't respond, he continued. "Though I would have you with me, whether I and the others succeed or fail we will still need all the swords we can muster. The Tjal are the greatest swordsmen having none to equal their skill. We will need them," he paused and then corrected himself, "we will need our people if we hope to win this war."

There was a long pause and he was beginning to think that she had not heard him. As he waited, he realized that he meant what he had said. The Tjal were his people now. No longer did he have the slightest desire to return and live with the Chufa as they were at that time. They were without honor or integrity. It was with the Tjal that he would make his home when all of this was over; with Jne.

"You honor me," she suddenly whispered, the emotion escaping into her voice as she fought to contain it, "in requesting that I complete such a task. I too have thought of this but was not sure how you would react at my requesting to leave."

"Why? You said you are no longer *Jinghar*," he responded and then immediately regretted his words as he saw how they stung her. He still hadn't gotten used to the fact that she stayed because she wanted to and not because she was duty bound. He was not used to such loyalty even though Dor and Tam had always given it. And he knew that it was not the same type of loyalty that kept her at his side. Before she could answer he quickly added, "I have dishonored you. Please forgive me or mete the punishment equal to my thoughtless words. I know why you remain with me. I desire your company for the same purpose."

He waited, expecting the harsh words or physical pain he knew he deserved but suddenly Jne's arms were around his neck and her lips were pressed against his cheek. "My honor is intact," she finally said, releasing him. "I will depart immediately." And without another word she was swallowed up in the night.

Thane suddenly felt both hot and cold. His body missed the parts where she had held him while his cheeks burned, the feeling of her lips still lingering in the spot where she had kissed him. The few others around the small fire kept their eyes straining on their plates of food or into the fire not daring to make a comment or interrupt the silence that had fallen. But had anyone spoken he would not have heard it. His eyes could not focus and his head spun to the point that he knew that to try and rise would be folly as he very likely would land in the fire pit itself. He wanted to chase after her so as to see her one last time in case she was serious about leaving that moment, but he still didn't feel confident that his legs would hold him should he try to stand.

"Are you well?" a voiced asked him that sounded strangely familiar. He could make out the form of a person to his left, but his mind still refused to focus on anything other than Jne and the too quickly fleeting feeling her lips had left on his cheek. Were he able, he would have halted time and relished in that moment for eternity.

"Thane," the voice interrupted again and then a hand was on his shoulder chasing away all signs of the moment from his mind and body. "You appear flushed. Are you ill?"

He turned his head, wanting to lash out angrily at whoever was crass enough to steal away such a cherished moment and was met by a pair of concerned dark eyes. It was Bren, one of the many healers that now canvassed the camp applying their healing arts to those in need. Kat was also with him smiling slightly as if she held onto a secret that she wished to spread to any who would listen. He had called for them, but not for healing. His intentions were just the opposite of those that brought relief to the sick or injured. He wanted them for war.

"Come," he said as he rose to his feet. "Let us speak in more private quarters."

Silently, the healers fell in behind him as he lead them a short distance to the privacy of his tent. Entering, he quickly called fire to the candle resting on a small box by the door. The tent was small, lacking any other furniture save for a small canvas bag and a mat on the floor for sleeping. He had never gotten used to sleeping in the raised soft beds of the HuMans. Moving to the center of the small room, he sat and motioned for his guests to do the same. When they were settled he spoke directly to his reason for calling them. "How comes your progress with pulling out water?" he asked.

Bren shrugged, looking at Kat as he did so. "We have yet to meet any real success though we continue to work at it as often as time will allow."

Thane frowned. That was not the answer he had hoped for.

"It is strange," Kat added. "Never has a skill been so difficult for any of us to learn and master. Even those whose first strength is the MarGua have been unsuccessful."

Thane perked up some at her words. "So you have been teaching others then?"

Bren nodded. "Yes, but there seems to be some vital piece of information missing. It's as if we were blocked from touching the water."

He shook his head. "I have no other help to give. It is more of a feeling sense than it is a thought process. Other than what I have shown you already, I have nothing else to offer. I guess it will just take more time."

Kat and Bren nodded. "And that is something that we don't seem to have in much abundance," Kat said with a sigh.

Thane nodded his agreement and then suddenly noticed that Jne's belonging were gone. His heart seemed to slow in its beat; she had already left.

*   *   *

"I can't believe he said yes!" Domis cried with excitement.

Teek smiled. "How could he not? I have the information he needs to be successful."

Domis frowned at his friend's words. "Are you certain you know where we are going and how to get there?"

Teek shrugged. "As certain as anybody," he said.

Domis' frown deepened. "You don't sound very certain."

"Listen," Teek said putting the final shine to a pair of Jack's boots. "I remember perfectly the story that old man Twee told me. As long as he told the story straight, then I should be able to get us pretty close to the right location."

Domis bit at his lower lip. "I suddenly don't feel so excited about this adventure any longer."

"Don't worry," Teek insisted. "We'll be with Thane. He's got magic that he can probably use to find his own way without us. You saw how his eyes lit up when I told him the story. This is grand and we are going to be part of it." Though his appetite for adventure had decreased greatly since the loss of his family and their people, Teek was becoming ever more depressed by the mundane existence they had been leading as King Jack's stewards. Even Domis had made mention that he was tired of walking all day and that though he didn't relish the fact that they were at war, he never thought it would be so boring. Now they had the opportunity to take part with those who were shaping history and the excitement of it was like adrenaline to their systems.

"Come. I have to check that the enemy has not left the city yet," Teek offered. "Maybe Tchee will let you ride with us this time."

Domis hesitated. "She doesn't ever let me ride her," he protested.

Teek didn't give in. "Well, maybe she will today."

*   *   *

The three friends met, as agreed, at Thane's tent. None had slept well that night as their minds were constantly revolving around the possibility that after over a thousand years they may be the first Chufa to regain the sacred trees that were their ancestry. Tam stifled back a yawn and then adjusted her pack higher onto her back for comfort. Thane hefted his own bag and then with a quick word led them through the camp toward Jack's tents. They were not the easiest to spot, being positioned well in the middle and lacking any outward sign that would indicate that they were anything other than regular tents as used by many in the company. Though Wess and Ranse had insisted on using formality when addressing and acting around Jack, they all knew that in times of war it was only commonsensical to keep the king's position a mystery to the enemy. Especially now after they had been so blatantly attacked.

They found Jack questioning the guards stationed outside his tent, his ire evident by the look on his face and the slight tremor evident in the guard's stances. Domis was at his side looking rather pale like he might be sick if he had not been already.

"And you are certain he did not return?" Jack demanded.

"Yes, milord, I am certain," the guard answered quickly trying to maintain his composure. "I have been at this post this whole night and none have come or gone since I got here."

"What is going on?" Thane asked.

Jack pulled at his beard. "He's gone," he snapped back. "Left in the afternoon yesterday to check on Zadok's army and hasn't been seen since."

"Teek?" Tam asked, the concern obvious in her voice.

"It's my fault, Master Thane," Domis suddenly interjected, his lower lip quivering as he fought to hold back the tears. "He said he needed to check the enemy's progress one last time before we left. He asked me to go but I said no because she never lets me ride anyway and I didn't feel like watching from the ground. I should have gone with him. Do you think he's hurt?"

Thane took it all in and felt bad that his concern was not really on whether the Waseeni boy was well or not but on the fact that his only hope in finding the lost YeiyeiloBaneesh trees was now missing. "Are you certain he was only going to ride the roc?" he shot at the boy.

Domis nodded.

"He didn't say anything else about going somewhere different?"

Domis shook his head, his control over his emotions quickly waning. "Do you think he's dead like that merchant family?" Domis asked to the surprise of all present.

Jack was beside himself. "How do you know about that?" he demanded.

Tam stepped forward and placed an arm around Domis' shoulder while giving Jack a fiery glare. "Don't worry," she soothed. "I'm sure he's just fine. I'm sure he just lost track of time and will be arriving anytime now."

"Has there been a search?" Thane asked.

"As good as can be had in such a crowd," Jack answered, recoiling some from Tam's glower. "I sent Erl out early to search for him, but he has yet to return. If he can be tracked, then Erl will find him."

Thane scratched his head; his thoughts no longer on the stable boy turned royal steward or the missing Waseeni. They hadn't the time to sit and wait for a careless boy who went and got himself lost the night before the most important task of his life. But without Teek, how were they to find the correct path to the trees? A shadow passed over their heads drawing all eyes to the skies as the two rocs circled high above waiting for their passengers to clear the camp so they could finally be on their way. Thane turned his attention back onto Domis. "You said last night that you knew the way second only to Teek. Is that true?"

Domis hesitated. Originally he'd only made the comment so that he would be included but now that the success or failure of the mission might rest completely on him he wasn't so sure he still wanted to hold to such a claim. Without thinking, he slowly nodded his head. "Yes, I suppose. I've heard him tell it some few times."

"Good enough," Thane decided. "We can wait for Teek no longer." Looking at Jack he continued. "We must be away so as to return as quickly as possible or we will be of no help to you and the army. Zadok's forces will certainly be leaving within the next day or two which leaves us very little time."

"I agree," Jack said still pulling his beard.

"Good. If Teek does get here soon, send him after us. As agreed, we will get supplies in Aleron and then start into the forest. If he does not reach us before hand then he should return to you. From what I have heard of the Underwoods he should not go in there alone. We will make our search and then return as quickly as possible to you at Bedler's Keep."

Jack nodded and then smiled sadly. "We have come a long way in such a short time we two."

Thane smiled back, the love he felt for this man equal to that he would have happily given to a worthy and deserving father. Absently he looked to his side where Jne had always been and a feeling of deep sorrow and loss quickly swept over him to not find her there.

"You have forgotten one thing, Master Thane."

All eyes turned to see Prince Ranse and his constant companion, Jace, approaching them. "We need the men stationed at Aleron."

Thane bowed slightly in greeting but countered the once prince's argument. "I haven't time to try and convince the people there that a Tjal-Dihn warrior is on a mission from the king to pull them away from their posts."

Ranse smiled. "You will not need to. I and Jace will be coming with you."

"Impossible," Jack countered. "They take the sky road on the backs of the giant birds," he said, pointing to the winging creatures overhead.

Ranse did not look up, but instead stared at Thane. "We will go with them." Then, turning back to Jack he included, "with your permission, my liege. We need those men and like Thane has so aptly accounted, they will not answer to his call. That is why I have volunteered myself to go in his place."

Jack considered the offer. It was true what all of them had said. And though he appreciated Ranse's candor and experience when dealing with the daily responsibilities with court matters, it was essential to gather as many to them as could carry arms. "Can they carry you all?" Jack asked.

Thane shrugged. "I can't say but it would appear that we will find out very quickly."

Jack nodded, his hand still held fast to his gray beard. "Apparently we will."

Chapter Eighteen

The wind pressed against him with increasing force and Teek could not help the scream of excitement that dribbled from his lips. No longer was he taken by the sickness that had made his rides with Tchee almost unbearable. Replacing the nauseated stomach was now one that thrilled at the altitude, speed, and maneuvering that was the giant bird. Gone too was the depressing boredom of camp that had been chipping away at the wall of emotions that he'd been building to keep back the emptiness that was still his burden to carry at the loss of his family. Tryg had not been the lifting spirit he'd originally thought he would be. The knowledge that he was not the only Waseeni still in existence was a sort of comfort in some sense, but Tryg's lack of any social skills in the least made him almost more of a burden than a relief. Luckily he had found a good friend in Domis and wished now that he were there with him enjoying the ride.

Tchee dipped left and then rose with a current of air as she sought for greater altitude so they could spy out Zadok's army without getting too close to Calandra or becoming an obvious target for his pet dragons. Though Tchee's size made her much quicker and agile in flying, they still did not relish an encounter with the death breathing serpents. Trying to concentrate on his duty and purpose for being in the air, Teek scanned the area between the capital and the fleeing refugees. The long swath they had cut in their escape from the great city was clear but still remained empty of any pursuit. He shuttered to think of what had kept the enemy within Calandra for such a long period of time while their ultimate quarry inched farther away.

✶   ✶   ✶

Quickly pulling his sword from his opponent's chest cavity, he splattered the dead man's blood on the approaching guard just before burying it into his chest. Three others came at him from the side but the blood lust that fueled his strength was just beginning to rage as he quickly dispatched the first and then attacked the remaining two. It was obvious from the start that though they outnumbered him, neither had a chance except to run if they desired to extend their lives a few moments more. He did give them credit for at least making an effort to protect their employer to the end as she cowered in the corner, her gasps at the violence making him even hungrier for the death that came at the end of his blade. Though the floor was slick from all of the freely spilt blood, he was an expert at such play and could not be counted on to falter in his movements or his steps. Feigning such a mistake drew the other two in for what they assumed would be his demise but both were surprised to find themselves slashed to the ground awash in their own gore.

Scanning the room for any others who thought to play, Resdin finally found himself alone with the Dona of the house, her husband having fled the residence earlier to find his death on the slow roasting spit of a troll somewhere.

"Well, my dear," he smiled wickedly while wiping the blood from his blade in the hair of the still breathing guard that lie at his feet anxiously awaiting death's reprieve. "Alone at last."

Sheathing his sword, he approached the woman who put on her best airs of defiance though her trembling lip gave her away to panic. "How dare you, sir," she snapped. Resdin found himself somewhat impressed that her voice at least held firm without quivering. "You will pay for such audacity."

"Actually," he sneered, grabbing a handful of her hair and pulling her head back, "I figured I would be rewarded." Leaning close, he forced a kiss to her lips and though she struggled to extricate herself from such a vile murderer, he was too strong for her. Finally pulling away, Resdin gave her his most evil grin. "Now tell the truth," he slithered. "That was better than you thought it would be."

The woman, whose face was now wet with tears, spat in Resdin's face hoping it would earn her a quick death. Resdin's hand cocked but was stayed by a soft voice calling his name from the doorway.

"Resdin. That is not how you were taught to treat a woman."

Dragging his shirtsleeve across his face, he turned and bowed slightly to the old man that glided across the marble floor, careful to avoid the puddles of blood without seeming to even notice them. "My lord," Resdin offered.

Zadok sighed as he surveyed the carnage. "With such a fine home as this, you would think they could afford decent servants to clean up the messes. What is the report?" he demanded, his voice taking on an icy tone.

Resdin looked at the woman and whispered, "We will continue our discussion later, my love," before releasing her and turning his full attention back to Zadok. "It would appear that they flee for the stronghold that is Bedler's Keep."

Zadok laughed, his chilling cackles echoing through the large hall. "What irony, my son, that this should end where it began so many centuries ago. I cherish the taste of it in my mouth."

"But the keep will pose a greater defense," Resdin offered.

"That it will," Zadok smiled. "But you forget I have the memory of the place. Its secrets were given up to me long ago and I have not let them slip away. And what is it to me that more trolls should find their deaths as we assail it to take it? The promise of even greater treasure will be more than enough to keep them under foot until I am through with them." His voice took on a tone of mocking grandeur. "Have I not already given them the spoils of Haykon and now the grand capital of Calandra? Their natural lusts for blood and death will press them on to the very gates of hell before they even recognize the leash by which they are held. It will not be so difficult as you might fear."

Resdin watched the woman in the corner of his eye slowly and deliberately move toward the closest guard who still begged for elusive death to finally take him. "But would it not be grander to rob them of their safe haven and cut them down with the very gates in sight?"

"That is your problem," Zadok snapped. "You are too much like the foul creatures at my command; always anxious for the next quick death found at the end of a blade." His voice soothed to a near whisper. "You must learn the intoxicating delicacy to be had in taking in each delicious course, each nuance of pain and suffering that comes from the long, slow, calculated sapping of another's hope as you move to end his life. The sheer ecstasy and rapture as you slowly draw it out, devouring every last portion as it drips from your victim."

Resdin felt a cold shiver running up his neck as he listened to Zadok's words, suddenly feeling revolted by them even in the face of such butchery as littered the floor. Even he was not so sick as that. Yes, he enjoyed the powerful rush that came from holding the power of another's life and then taking it from him, but even he would not go so far as Zadok suggested. His words placed him in lower degeneracy than even the goblins or trolls.

"And what of the dragons?" Resdin asked, knowing all too well that the leviathans were not so easily controlled as the rest of the army. "They grow tired of the wait."

Zadok smiled a wicked grin that seemed to draw the heat from the room. "Yes. I think that perhaps the time has finally arrived to introduce ourselves to the rest of the people, don't you think?"

Even Resdin felt a slight tremor at the lust for death that dripped from his Lord's voice. "As you say, milord," he answered with another bow.

"We move as soon as this rabble is convinced that they have had their fill," Zadok suddenly stated and then turned without further comment and exited the room.

Resdin watched him leave and then turned back to the woman who now held the guard's sword in her hand. Resdin grinned. "Decided to play have we?" he chuckled wickedly.

She turned, almost startled by his voice, the resolute mixture of defiance and fear gone from her face. Now all he saw was the chilling, blank stare of the dead. Turning the sword point to her breast, and without hesitation, she fell upon it and added her life to those taken by Resdin, robbing him of his foul intent.

Without the slightest look of pity, he stared blankly at the woman and then turned for the door after his master.

*   *   *

It wasn't until Tchee had passed the sprawling camp below that Teek realized she wasn't stopping. The sun was waning quickly in the west, making its final farewells as night grew in strength on the horizon and the roc carried forth toward the mountains. "Tchee," he screamed above the rush of the wind. "Tchee, you've passed it. We are going past the camp."

But the giant bird seemed not to hear, her wings' steady beat continued as they flew further away from the others. "Tchee!" Teek called out, this time patting her back to try and get her attention. But she ignored him still, save for a loud screech of annoyance at his pounding hand. Teek looked back at the fading camp as its mass slowly grew smaller in the distance. "But I have to be there in the morning," he said, mostly to himself, a small tear building in his eye. "I will miss helping the others if we don't return." This time his banging was more desperate but Tchee seemed either not to feel it or not to care about his desperation. "Please," he finally said, halting his barrage. "Please."

Tchee belted out a loud roar but her course remained straight and true. Teek leaned forward and rested his head in the down feathers against her neck knowing he had no choice as to their destination. He comforted himself in the fact that he trusted the large bird with his life. Never before had she ever done anything to harm him or allowed harm to come to him. Maybe wherever it was she was taking them would still permit time for them to be back to the camp in the morning.

He watched as the miles seemed to rush away in the blur that was the ground below until night quickly overtook their flight, bathing him in darkness of sight and mood. He now knew in his heart that wherever it was that Tchee was taking them would not allow him to return to Thane and the others by morning. The guilt of failing them washed over him like an icy tide that bathed him in tears. How would they find the trees without him? He felt a sudden flash of hot anger toward Tchee for stealing him away and the thought came to just leap from her back to his doom. He could then be with his family again, he told himself, building his courage with his rising anger that would give him the strength to follow through with it. His rage carried him to point of gloating at the pain that Tchee would surely feel for causing his death. She would be sorry for robbing him and the others of such an important trek as that of finding the old trees that seemed so important. He let his thoughts dwell on how satisfied he would feel at her sorrow as payment for the pain she was causing him now but soon the bitter taste of his revenge lost its appeal as he knew he would not do something so foolish as take his own life just to try and make a bird sad over it. Though he was certain she loved him, maybe it would make her happier to have him gone. Then she would not be tied to him as she was.

He sighed heavily as if clearing his mind of the poison that had been clouding his thoughts. Tchee had been nothing but helpful thus far, and he couldn't fathom her being anything else in what she was taking him to do right then. Her timing was just not what he felt was the most efficient or advantageous. Pressing his body as far into the soft, warm feathers as he could, He was finally able to fight off the annoying rumblings of an empty stomach and drift off to sleep.

It was morning when he was awakened by the loud roar that was Tchee's mighty call. The air was chilled in the early dawn as the sun was again reaching for the skies above. He was surprised that he had slept the whole night and was even more shocked to find they were flying over what could only be the Dorian Mountains. Was she taking him back to his empty home in the Teague swamplands? Was this her way of trying to protect him? Though he knew that the war would likely claim his life, he didn't want to return to the swamps. There was nothing but sorrow for him there now.

Looking in all directions he was surprised that all he could see were mountains. They were flying lower now so his vision of the world was not so broad yet he knew he would be able to see the edges of the Underwoods if she were flying him home. But if not home then where?

Tchee suddenly banked left avoiding an extremely high peak before circling back to the right as they passed as if she sought the far side. Making a long, lazy arch, she swept around and then dropped quickly into what appeared to be a naturally forming bowl protected on all sides by large, jagged peaks. Teek was overcome by the beauty of the place realizing that he was most likely the first person to ever set eyes there.

As Tchee dropped further in he got a better view of the forest of trees that clung to the area fed by the multiple streams and falls that dripped from the ice capped peaks and fed a large lake toward the center. Deeper in he could see the carpeted meadows dotted with a burst of color from the hundreds of different types of plants and flowers that were almost too much for him to take in at once.

Passing low across the lake, he could see large bodies racing through the water just below the surface but far enough down that he wasn't able to clearly make out what they were. He assumed fish, but some of the shapes seemed too long or too large to be any type of fish he'd ever seen or heard about in the most generous of storytelling. He felt Tchee dip slightly and then heard the gentle splash of her talons touch the water before pulling up again just as the lake ended into one of the large meadows that dotted the area.

Slowing quickly, Tchee flapped her wings and settled them down into the soft grass whereupon, dropping from her back, Teek discovered a fish that she dropped from her right foot. He was about to thank her and ask why and where they were going when her wings suddenly stretched out again and quickly lifted her skyward.

At first, he didn't worry much, figuring that she was certainly going to return to the lake for a catch of her own, but she didn't turn back around, but instead flew straight on and then lifted up to the nearest peak and disappeared beyond his sight leaving him all to himself. Though somewhat surprised, he still didn't worry. Many times he'd been left as she had gone about her own business and always she returned again to claim him.

Looking around he quickly determined to have his proffered meal in a way he liked instead of the raw flesh that Tchee seemed to think was good enough. Lifting the dead fish by the tail he carried it to a small grouping of trees to his left where he found plenty of cast off limbs and branches with which to start a small fire. In no time he had his breakfast roasting over warm flames that licked at the fish's skin as if attempting to taste it. Finding some nuts and a shrubbery filled with delicious violet berries, Teek sat down by the fire and turned his fish slowly as it cooked, the disappointment of missing the trek into the Underwoods somewhat lessoned as he looked forward to a delicious breakfast.

After devouring his meal, he quickly put out the fire and cleaned up the area expecting Tchee to return any moment and whisk him away again. Deciding he was thirsty, he made the short walk to the lake and dipped his hands in the frigid water to clean them and then scooped up a handful of water. It was sweet and refreshing leaving him feeling revived and satisfied. His natural inclination was to explore the area. He wanted to see more of its splendor but feared to leave should Tchee return and not find him. Sighing heavily, he forced himself to sit down and wait. Pulling at the blades of grass by his leg, he quickly became bored. His mind was left to wonder and soon entered those dark areas where he still felt angry over being torn away from everyone and the responsibility and opportunity he'd been given at finally being able to help. He felt so small in the grandeur of the war that had enveloped him even though he had done nothing to warrant its rage.

Lying on his back, he let the sun's rays warm his body though his mind was still dark and agitated. He wondered what Thane's reaction would be when they found him missing. He figured it wouldn't be good and felt suddenly ashamed. Thane had gain hero status in his eyes and someone he felt he wanted to emulate. He seemed to naturally command attention and respect as if possessing tremendous power that waited his order for release. Yet, he seemed approachable at the same time. And though their interactions had been few and brief, Teek felt a certain fondness and loyalty toward him. He sighed. Now he would be thought of as unworthy; a mere child that cannot be trusted to follow through with his duty or promises. But that was, in fact, what he was, his mind reminded him. He was a child, not even old enough to be on an appeasing journey.

He felt the tears welling up and then suddenly cascading over the rims of his lower lids and down his cheeks. He was too small and insignificant for all of this. He should be dead with his family instead of alive and alone and involved in such grand moments of history. And how would he be remembered? If they did win and songs were sung or stories told, his would be the name that was either forgotten or marked as the person who didn't so up at all.

Curling up with his knees close to his chest, he let out all of the pain and sorrow that he'd been holding back for such a long time. Without resisting, he let the utter emptiness and loss of his family take hold of him and he mourned for them, welcoming the convulsions that wrung through his body as the tears soaked his arm. He let the loneliness enshroud him and fill his thoughts with the desire to simply cease to exist, his memory wiped away from the minds of the few who had known him. He lay in that state for what seemed to be hours in torment and agony until sleep finally eased him away from his pain.

A sudden air gust brought him abruptly to consciousness just in time to roll away from the sharp beak that darted for his midsection. Jumping to his feet, Teek ran a short distance and then turned to meet his attacker who had hopped after him and was once again bearing down on him in an attempt to peck out his innards. Stepping to the right, he escaped the full brunt of the assault but was clipped on the side and sent sprawling into the grass. The sun disappeared as black wings spread, darkening the sky over him, the outstretched talons reaching for him as the giant bird dropped down on him. There was no time for escape. He would be pierced through and eaten in an instant, his previous wish for death coming true.

There was a sudden flash of white, and Teek was certain he'd moved into the next world where his mother and the rest of his ancestors were sure to be waiting for him. He was somewhat surprised, and grateful, at how painless the crossover had been, having believed that there would at least be some discomfort at being eaten alive. But his thoughts of a quiet passing were quickly interrupted by the sounds of screeches and cries that suddenly invaded his serene death. Sitting up he was surprised to see Tchee and another giant bird locked in a battle of beaks, wings and talons. It was then he realized that the white he'd seen was not death but was actually Tchee assailing his attacker and saving his life.

Both birds pulled away from each other and backed off a step each eyeing the other as if looking for a mistake or weakness so as to make another attack. The air was filled with their raged squawking. Though Teek could not see any blood there were plenty of loose feathers on the ground and floating in the air to leave out any doubt about the seriousness of their intent. Loading his blowgun, he prepared to assist in the fight should the opportunity present itself. He knew it was not likely, with the way the two bobbed, hopped and moved about, but nonetheless it didn't hurt to be prepared.

Tchee settled into a low guttural sound that rumbled in her throat as a warning while the other bird let out another bellowing scream. Though Teek could not understand their exchange, he was certain they were communicating.

Why do you stop me from killing that sub species? He desecrates the sacred lands by being here. You know the law, Ice Feather. You will be outcast for this.

I also know the law of life giving, Night Shadow, which puts him under my protection and care. He is part of me now and as such under the law.

You defile yourself as do those who follow your ways.

They make their own choices for the better good of all not the selfishness that poisons your thoughts.

Foolishness! It is I who flies straight and with the wind not counter to it and crooked as you do.

We shall see, Tchee communicated back, the rumble in her throat still sounding a warning. *When the others touch talon to the ground we will get the decision of all.*

A loud cry brought all eyes heavenward followed, is if in answer, by other cries as more rocs suddenly appeared and began landing in the once peaceful meadow. Teek was amazed that so many of the birds existed and that he had never seen any until Tchee. They all looked majestic and noble in their grace of flight and in the manner with which they held themselves when earthbound. Their eyes, as multihued as the many different colored feathers that adorned them, were sharp and intelligent leaving no question as to the higher mental functions that must be occurring within their sleek heads. Many dipped those heads slightly to Teek as they landed, a warm feeling of kindness and respect reflecting off their eyes, while others seemed to scream at him as did the large black roc that had earlier tried to take his life.

The tension that existed between the two groups suddenly felt palpable in the air around them. Teek felt himself tensing as he waited to see what would happen.

Close to twenty of the magnificent birds filled the clearing and seemed to separate into their decided factions either with Tchee or the black bird. Teek noticed that only five others seemed to side with his friend.

The threat is a real one not only to man but to all of us, Tchee started right in without any preliminary pleasantries. *We must fight with them for our own safety and survival.*

Ice Feather has been twisted by the constant weight she now carries on her back like a slave, the black roc countered lowering his head and screeching toward Teek. *She desecrates the sacred mountain by bringing it with her and now expects us to risk our own survival to protect the ones that have threatened our extinction all along.* Those siding with him suddenly began to cry and screech as if in agreement, many casting threatening glares at Teek who stayed very close to Tchee but remained completely still. He had no idea what was happening, lost in the clucks and rumbles that emitted from the birds as if they spoke to each other, but he understood the danger to his safety should there come another attack.

Night Shadow speaks true, Tchee interrupted the cacophony of sounds and brought all attention back to her. *The land creatures have always hunted us without mercy or care and many have died because of it. I lost my life's mate to such an attack.*

Then why, of all of us, would you sue now for us to risk our lives for them? One of Night Shadow's followers asked. *You of all here have the greatest cause to wish the land creatures dead.*

You are right, Dark Talon, but I have also seen the good that is had in many of them. But not just that. I fear that if we fail to stand with them now, the enemy that attacks will kill them all and then the hunt will turn back on us. You have not seen or engaged with the enemy's winged serpents as I have. Though we are lighter and quicker on the wing, they are more deadly than any flying talon from the earth creatures.

We know, Night Shadow chided, *you spoke of their deadly scream the first time you called. The time, I might add, that you destroyed Strong Wing and Bright Feather's life bond.*

That was their own choice, Tchee screamed, startling Teek, his hand absentmindedly clenching his blow gun. *They made the sacrifice because they know the cost of roosting and waiting. I tell you all now, if we fail to act and help we will not survive much longer than the ground walkers.*

Bold words from one who has bonded herself to one of them, Night Shadow countered, and the addressed the others. *What you do with your own life is not my concern. If you decide to throw it away with Ice Feather then a swift wind for you to your death. Your loss will only ultimately strengthen the flock by not passing on your weakness. I will not cast myself upon the ground for my enemies and I will no longer answer your calls to meet again.* Without another word, Night Shadow suddenly took to the air followed quickly by the others who had sided with him, the wind they created almost pushed Teek back while whipping through his sun bleached locks.

We are still with you, Ice Feather, one of those that remained cooed to Tchee. *We see the wisdom in what you say and know that it is the right thing even under the circumstances.*

Tchee bobbed her head and stretched her wings. *May the winds always find you Snow Tail, but I fear we may not be enough without the others.* Turning her gaze on Teek, Tchee lowered her wing, calling him to mount so they could depart. Looking at the birds that remained, Teek quickly scrambled up onto her back and prepared himself for flight. As they rose into the air, he waved back to the other birds who seemed pleased by his gesture as they cooed and bobbed their heads before taking to the air themselves.

Climbing quickly in altitude, Tchee wasted no time cresting the mountain peaks surrounding the meadow and lake now far below and then banking northeast back toward the camp of Calandra refugees. Though uncertain as to what had occurred or his part in it, Teek was glad to be returning to his other friends. Maybe Thane had decided to wait for his return still giving him the opportunity to participate in the war as more than a mere spectator. The thought sent a chill of excitement racing through him and he couldn't help the scream of exhilaration that escaped his lips. The sorrow he'd felt only a day before was quickly turning into anger at the injustice of situations flinging him about where they would. He wanted to act instead of suffer the consequences of being acted upon. No longer was he willing to sit in the back and let others decide his destiny for him. He could fight, and no one would keep him from doing so.

It was then, in the midst of his growing determination, that a dark shadow briefly enveloped them, blocking out the sunlight for a quick moment drawing his attention skyward just in time to avoid the talons that dropped down behind him, their terrible claws digging deep into Tchee's back. Tchee let out a horrific scream of pain and anger as Teek suddenly felt his building courage sapped away in an instant as he faced the black roc now clutching Tchee's back. In an instant, a sharp beak was dropping down on him forcing him to the side where he tumbled toward Tchee's fluttering right wing. She cried out in pain as the black roc's beak sliced into her back just below the neck where Teek had just been.

Grabbing her wing as he fell, Teek caught himself but was now being tossed about as Tchee tried desperately to stay in the air. They were losing altitude fast as the black roc pecked at Tchee again. Teek knew she couldn't fight back for fear of throwing him off, but to do nothing would invite her own death. Without thinking, he grabbed at the feathers on Tchee's back and pulled himself back up to just under the black bird that was not paying attention to him as it continued its barrage on Tchee. The wind created by its flapping wings almost pushed Teek back off again but ducking behind as the wing rose, he scrambled just behind the black one's talons and then reversed his motion as the wing was coming back down giving him the opportunity he'd been looking for.

Tchee cried out in pain again as Teek scurried up the black roc's wing and then onto his back where he unsheathed his dagger. Tchee's attacker made a final assault on her with his vicious beak, unaware of his new passenger, until Teek dug the dagger into his back as hard as he could.

The black roc shrieked, his talons instantly releasing their grip on Tchee and letting her go as Teek's dagger came down again hard digging deep into the bird's flesh. Moving up as he did so, Teek was at the bird's neck when it turned sharply trying to dislodge him, but Teek had anticipated this having his legs wrapped tightly around the rocs neck. In a frenzy of anger he again dug his dagger in, this time planting it into the bird's neck as much for the kill as to keep him from falling off and plummeting to his death. It was at that moment that Tchee, now recovered somewhat, dropped onto the black roc's back, her own talons latching onto the area where moments before she had been held. The black roc flapped his wings desperately as Teek continued without mercy to plunge his dagger in again and again all about his neck.

No longer was Tchee's hold one of attack but instead was now used to try and keep the dying bird from dropping too quickly as it was starting to plummet toward the jagged mountainside below. But she was weakening as well, her injuries enough to threaten her own survival. She screamed at and even brushed Teek with her beak but he was beyond hearing or feeling anything. The only thing that mattered now was his dagger and the bird that had attacked them and how many times he could plunge his blade into its flesh.

The fight was now completely gone from the dark roc, his death looming as he plunged toward the ground, his great wings barely moving, an involuntary action that occurred innately to try and keep him from hitting the ground with force. Teek paid no mind to the rising mountainside that threatened him as well as once more his dagger sank deep, cutting through feather and flesh and opening another gap for blood to escape.

Teek raised his hand for another stab but was suddenly pitched forward, the air forced from his lungs as he hit hard the back of the black bird's head and then tumbled over onto a rocky outcropping. Not immediately feeling any pain, he rolled over and tried to stand, his dagger at the ready, the anger and battle rage still hot in the blood that pumped so loudly in his skull. Taking a step forward, his vision suddenly blurred and then darkened as the ground rose up and punched him hard in the face.

Chapter Nineteen

The cock called out again as if in anger that Bram had not answered his first call. Groaning into his warm covers, Bram rolled onto his side and forced his eyelids to open just wide enough to take in the blurry surroundings of his small shanty. The cock didn't even belong to him, but had been his town crier at first light ever since he moved into the dirty shack he now called home. Having argued with his father one time too many, Bram was now on his own and the freedom he enjoyed was well worth the price he paid to keep it. Working the early mornings on the docks was difficult work that paid very little. And though half of his wage went to paying rent on the hovel that contained the small cot and molding hay mattress, it was worth every bit to be his own man. He had lucked out that one of his four uncles took pity on him and gave him a job. The other three wouldn't even talk to him after they got word from his father. Luckily, his Uncle Andro was not on speaking terms with his father either and so the job was as much to help Bram as it was to get back at his brother. If not for his Uncle Andro, Bram would have been forced to eek out his living on the streets as so many others like him who had been turned out of their homes.

The cock cried out a third time and Bram finally sat up, pulling his legs around and setting his bare feet on the cold dirt floor. Though he wanted to stay in bed and give more time for his head to clear from the previous night's revelry, he couldn't risk being late to the dock. His uncle's charity only extended so far. Pulling on his only shirt, he ran his hands through his hair and then opened the door into the cool morning air. Since he'd spent his last bit of money on ale the night before, he would have to steal breakfast from one of the cart drivers headed for the open air market near the town center. A quick reach under a cart's canvas in the dim dawn light always produced something to fill his belly. And in the bustle of everyone trying to get on to work, it was almost too easy to do it without being noticed by anyone.

Turning left and then quickly right again, Bram made his way through the maze of shacks that filled this area of town to almost overflowing. It wouldn't be for another quarter mile or so before his feet left the dirt and touched down on the hard, cold cobblestone that was found in the city proper. Though most large cities were protected by walls that marked the borders with the surrounding country, Tigford's walls had been razed centuries before in some war that none remembered and few cared about enough to even pass on. And without walls to contain it, Tigford had simply grown outward like a rich man's waistline.

Bram finally put his feet to the stone streets and started keeping watch for a passing cart and his breakfast. Though the sun was still trying to climb over the Dorian Mountains to the east, the city was a bustle with people trying to get to the daily drudgery that would hopefully earn them enough to fill their bellies that night. Though the streets had widened, now that he had reached the city proper, that only meant they were filled with more people.

Seeing a cart he knew was carrying fruit from the orchards at Walwyn Grove, he almost jumped up in excitement. No one had fruit like the growers from Walwyn. Though most of it went out from the private ports that surrounded the Grove, some was carted into the city especially for Tigford's upper classes. Bram would be one of those lucky rich today.

Pressing forward in the wave of passersby, he reached the cart and positioned himself right behind the guard that watched the cart for people just like him. With the slightest hesitation, he reached up under the canvas and caught hold of an apple that was almost as large as his hand. It was too easy! But in the process of pulling out his meal, his hand froze as a large shadow passed over the crowd pulling everyone up short in an instant. His heartbeat almost instantly increased as he felt a strange terror spread over him as it rushed through the crowd filling everyone with a sudden sense of doom. Turning his eyes skyward, he tried, with the rest of those that crowded around him, to discover what it was that had caused such a shadow and was filling them all with such terror. Not seeing anything, he brought his head down meeting the eyes of the guard who was now staring at him with his hand in the cart. Both stood frozen for a brief moment in time until the guard finally started to react and reached out for him. But at the same moment, the whole body of townsfolk jump and began pushing each other to try and find some escape from the terror that had settle like a cloud over the city.

Someone smashed into the guard's side giving Bram just the instant he needed to pull free his meal and dart into the melee of horrified people. Twice he was nearly knocked to the ground and once tripped on the body of someone who had fallen and had long since stopped struggling to rise again. Another deafening cry rolled through the throng and sent them all into a greater frenzy of fear and desperation to escape.

Bram tried to force his way through the crowd so he could make it to the docks but he was buffeted on every side. Many an elbow or fist connected with his stomach and ribs as people fought one another trying to force their way in every conceivable direction. He was close to the main street that would lead him down to the docks, the thick salty air suddenly more abundant and fresh even in the mass of compacted bodies, but he couldn't seem to push hard enough to lurch the throng in the direction he wanted.

Suddenly finding himself next to a tree, he quickly climbed its trunk. A hand reached up and caught hold of his ankle trying to pull him back but a swift kick to the face quickly freed him. Shimmying up the limbs, he found one that reached a balcony on the second floor of the shop below and threw himself over the railing. Not wasting time with the woman who screamed at his intrusion, he jumped onto the rail and then hoisted himself up and onto the roof. Climbing to its pinnacle he paused to catch his breath but was frozen in place with horror when he glanced over to where the docks had once been. It was as if the whole area had simply been melted away. There was no other way to describe it. Great pieces of ships and their masts were just gone as were many of the buildings that once surrounded the water.

His eyes scanned the area that was in total chaos as people ran in every direction trying to escape the nightmare that had fallen on the port city. He saw some that were knelt down next to puddles of dark liquid crying over them. One person leaned forward into one and seemed to melt away as he watched horrified. A loud screech from above suddenly chilled him as if the hand of death itself had embraced his slight frame. Turning with a shudder he saw what it was that had caused the shadow in the street below and what must be the cause of such destruction and chaos. A great, dark, serpent-like creature flew toward him, midnight colored liquid rushing from its mouth as it sprayed the buildings and people. Anything the fluid touched seemed to merely disappear.

Bram wanted to run away but he was unable to move his limbs. Fear gripped him like a fish caught in his uncle's nets; there was no escaping his approaching doom. The creature opened its great jaws and spewed its watery death washing over Bram and melting him to nothing save for his right arm that dropped to the melting shop roof, still clutching the stolen apple.

*   *   *

"It's dusk boy. Time to be away," Egan called out to his son who was stacking another large log into the cart. Brandt nodded in agreement but bent down and retrieved one more piece which he tossed on top of the others. It was dangerous work to gather wood as they did from the edges of the Underwoods forest. None dared venture into the menacing woods deeper than necessary to cut or gather the naturally discarded timber. Many a life was lost by those careless enough to be drawn in deeper than a few yards. Nothing but evil was found in the Underwoods.

It was a strange livelihood for ones who lived in the port town of Gildor where shipping and fishing were the main occupations, but people still needed to stay warm and most were happy to share their daily catch or vegetables from their garden with ones brave enough—or dumb enough—to gather wood from such a dangerous place. But Egan knew these woods as well as anyone and better than most. He had helped his father before him and was now training his only son as he'd been trained.

"This should carry us for the rest of the week," he said with a smile to his boy as he climbed onto the wagon. "You did good today, son." Grabbing the reins he passed them over to Brandt whose face lit up at the prospect of driving the cart home. Their horse was an old mare that was not long for the stew pots and probably couldn't go any faster than a slow walk if she were trailed by a pack of wolves, but she was still strong enough to pull the log filled cart and had herself spent her life in and around the woods enough to know when real trouble was near.

Taking the reins, Brandt gave them a gentle snap and the cart lurched forward. Egan gave out instructions on keeping the mare on the trail but there really wasn't any need for any since she probably could have walked the road back to their home in complete darkness. They trekked along the south side of the forest heading southwest until a quarter mile down they could catch the lane that ran directly south into town and home. As long as they were clear of the forest's edge by nightfall, they were relatively safe. Most of the dreaded creatures that lived in the Underwoods were nocturnal, though even in the day the forest was to be watched cautiously.

Egan checked the suns position and the long shadows that were forming and decided it would be best to move the mare on a little quicker. "Snap her again, Brandt," he commanded. "I'm hungry for your mother's cooking."

Brandt just nodded, lifting the reins slightly and then snapping them down on the mare's back. Making a noise in protest, the old mare pressed forward a little faster though it would have been difficult to tell much of a difference in speed. Distant calls could be heard deep in the wood now as the forest was coming to life at night's beginning. Egan's hand rested on the axe handle leaning against his leg though he showed no outward sign of alarm or worry. Just up ahead was the turn toward town and the road that would distance them from the Underwoods. Egan breathed a sigh of relief having worried they had left too late when the mare suddenly stopped.

"Give her another whip," Egan directed, his eyes darting to the right to scan the tree line for any signs of danger. Brandt whipped her back repeatedly but still she would not move. Grabbing the reins from his son, Egan snapped them hard on the old horse's hide and she jolted forward but stopped immediately, her body suddenly shaking. It was then that Egan felt the cold grip his heart.

"Papa," Brandt called out, his face white with sudden terror, his eyes large and round.

Grabbing his axe, Egan stepped down from the wagon using all of his will power to resist throwing down his weapon and racing headlong for town. Never in his life had he felt the terror that now reached into his throat and threatened to cut off his breath. His eyes strained, searching the wood for whatever it was that shaking him so. Tears started falling down his face as he could feel his doom was set and there was nothing he could do to stop it.

It was then that a large shadow passed them overhead, and Egan threw himself to the ground, his own scream swallowed in that of the giant creature that was swooping down upon the town in a fury. Egan pulled himself up to the side of the wagon and watched with his son in stunned silence as fire shot repeatedly from the creature's mouth and devoured the town and its people. All night they remained in shocked quiet neither able to speak or move as they witnessed Gildor burn, the muffled cries of it citizens filling the cool night air.

*   *   *

Rem walked along next to his horse letting it rest the last few miles before reaching Waterford and home. He'd been away for three weeks, two of that in travel alone, and he missed his family desperately. It had not been all in vain though as his pack horse was full of goods for which he'd been able to trade the week he'd spent in Clear Water. Normally he would have made the trip the month before, but a late spring had put off his semi-annual trip until now. In the fall he would do it all over again. He didn't enjoy being away from home for such long periods but the income he received from it would almost feed his family for the year. Six total weeks away was definitely worth such returns.

This trip was especially fruitful and he smiled thinking how his little ones would react when he pulled out the presents he'd bought for them. A cornhusk doll for Kaely, a carved horse for Mallory, and a play sword for Teryn would make him their hero for months to come. He chuckled at the thought, finding himself suddenly whistling one of the catchy tunes he'd heard coming out of the tavern he'd camped by on the outskirts of town. With the money he'd made he certainly could have enjoyed better accommodations but he preferred to use the extra he'd save to buy the dress he was bringing home for his wife, Annie.

His step got quicker at the thought of his sweetheart. They had practically grown up together and had decided to marry almost as soon as they could talk. Although no one would have expected them to keep such a promise as was made when so young, everyone could see as they grew how well they complimented each other. So it was no shock when they finally did wed. Many commenting that they either thought they already were or that it was about time.

Rem crested a small hill and paused for a brief moment rising on the tips of his toes as he tried to catch the slightest glimpse of home. If the light was just right he knew he'd be able to see the few houses that were built right at the water's edge, but the sun was low in the sky to the west affording him no such view. He sighed and pressed on. It was only a slight drop and then another climb before he would be standing on the last rise and the short descent into town. There he would be able to see the whole town and feel the salty breeze press against his face; something he had loved since boyhood. Though he wasn't a sailor, it was the sea for Rem. And had it not been for his extreme nausea when even in the calmest waters he would have taken to one of the ships in Waterford's harbor and sailed as far as the eye could see on the horizon.

Clicking his tongue, he urged his mount and packhorse down the gentle slope and forward toward home. It was now less than a mile to go and his stomach growled slightly at the thought of Annie's cooking. His meager rations and the small game he was able to get on the trail had gotten old the first week out. Besides the arms of his wife and children wrapped tightly around him, it was a home cooked meal he was craving the most right then.

Reaching the last rise he felt a strange sensation in the pit of his stomach that made his breath catch as it seemed to spread through his body quickly throwing him into a panic. He couldn't tell from where it came but he suddenly knew that all was not well. He'd heard of the premonitions some women received that typically boded evil, but he'd never believed them true or heard of a man feeling the same. He'd always given it over to superstition and dramatic hindsight, but he couldn't shake the feeling that danger and tragedy were close. Pressing on, though barely able to command his legs to move in front of him, he pulled the horses along as he desperately raced for the top of the rise. Stumbling repeatedly, his free hand and knees were sliced and raw by the time he finally reached the crest of the last hill.

He froze in place, his breath caught in his chest as a tear traveled down his cheek. Gasping, he tried to take in air and clear the dizziness in his head that was due to the shock at what his eyes were seeing. They city of his childhood was in ruins, as if a thousand years had passed since he'd last left only three weeks earlier. The houses, the ships, the shops and stores were all a massive decaying wreck. His eyes darted to the area he could best determine was where his home was but it too was in the same condition as the rest of the city. What could have done such a thing? What demonic weapon or creature could decay a city and its people in such a short space of time?

As if in answer, a far off cry echoed through the evening air as he dropped to his knees and wept.

Chapter Twenty

Slowing her horse to a casual trot, Jne gave her mount a short break from the speed she'd forced upon it for the past couple of hours. Though Tjal bred for quickness and endurance, no horse could maintain such exertion for much longer and survive. Squinting against the blinding sun, now setting directly in front of them, she scanned the area that was losing some of the rolling hills and patches of trees to a flatter, grass laden plain. It wouldn't be long before she entered the Enn. The thought filled her with both exhilaration and dread. Too long had she been away from her homeland living in the dysfunctional HuMan realms. She craved the logic and honor of the Tjal with its plainness of landscape, purpose and thought.

She breathed deeply the warm air that was now mixed with the scent of the grass that was growing more abundantly and marked the beginnings of what would, in another half day's ride, finally mark the boarders of her homeland. Suppressing a yawn, she hopped off her horse and walked along side it stretching the stiffness from her legs while giving her mount some deserved rest. She had spent almost two straight days in the saddle pressing her horse onward, anxious to complete her assigned task. Her mind wondered briefly down the trails of thought of what it meant for her to return to the Enn but she didn't allow herself to dwell on it much. She would succeed or not and that was all that mattered. What it required for her to be successful could not be helped, nor could the consequences to Thane should she fail and not return.

Her brief consideration of Thane drew him unbidden into her thoughts and clouded her mind with his face. Though needing to remain focused on her task, she allowed herself a few quiet moments of dreaming with him that she had always kept buried in the deepest caverns of her mind.

Suddenly she blushed as her reflections had taken her farther than she had originally planned to let them. She had finally allowed herself to admit that her admiration for him had begun the night she found him passed out in the mud beyond the Mogolth Mountains. She knew it was wrong when she discovered he was not Tjal but the longer she spent time with him the more her feelings grew no matter how unbidden. And finally it appeared that those feelings were shared and returned to her. She had been jealous almost to a rage when they'd found Tam and it was obvious that Thane's heart beat loudest for her. For that fact alone she would have killed the Chufa girl and claimed Thane to herself. But she had found a strange respect for Tam; had seen an inner strength that matched hers to where she understood and even respected Tam's desires toward Thane. She knew that only the strange Chufa custom kept him from Tam but that left him to discover his own respect and feelings for her. To the disordered HuMans it would have been an insult for her to be second in line to Thane's affections, but for a Tjal woman who understood such things it had been the highest compliment. Thane was hers whether he knew and accepted it or not.

Blushing, she forced thoughts of him from her mind as she continued to press forward toward the edges of what made up the vast Plains of Enn. She could ill afford the fog that such ideas created in her mind as she needed to concentrate on the realities that would soon force themselves upon her. Moving her hands deliberately, she forced them with an iron will to loosen the buckles that kept her weapons strapped like a part of her body to her back. Almost reverently, she secured them to her horse in such a way as to make them close to impossible to retrieve quickly. She felt naked and exposed but resisted the desire to take up her swords again. It was necessary to accomplish what she'd been sent to do. It was necessary to regain her place and her honor. It was the only way to save the lives of her people when she finally came upon them.

Running along side her mount, she quickly put miles behind her as she raced through the night and deeper into the plains that were her home. The air seemed fresher, the scent of the grass rejuvenating as she left the filth and stench of the HuMan world behind. It was exhilarating to pace herself with the strength of her horse as they sprinted forward going deeper and deeper into the Tjal realm. Her body seemed to waken with each lilting step renewing her strength of mind and body and filling her with satisfaction at being home again. How she ached to feel the comfort of her swords like an extension of her natural body swing precisely and with deadly accuracy in her hands. She wanted to feel that oneness that only was felt when flesh gripped steel in the dance that was beautiful and lethal all at once.

Suddenly she stopped. Her horse pulled up with her without the slightest touch or command as if sharing her thoughts and needs. All was dark save for the myriad of tiny pinholes that lit up the sky in a swarm of stars. No sound was heard but that of her horse's breathing as it stood rock still next to her. Jne's mind turned inward sealing the doors that had earlier opened to her emotions now leaving only instincts of survival to fill her corridors of thought. An outsider watching would have thought her strange to have stopped so quickly with apparently nothing to impede her way—but she knew. Her hands twitched and she had to mentally force them to remain at her sides instead of reaching instinctively for the swords that were no longer at her back. "I am *Jinghar*," she suddenly announced to the night.

"Then you are nothing," a voice responded in the grass not ten feet in front of her. Suddenly bodies seemed to rise from the very ground as four Tjal warriors rose out of the grass, eight swords at the ready to cut her down at the slightest provocation. The one who spoke approached, sheathing his swords as he did so.

"You risk all coming here, *Jinghar*," he said, the last word spoken as if by merely pronouncing it left a horrid taste in his mouth. "You know the law." Jne simply nodded and closed her eyes as the hilt end of a sword crashed deftly against the base of her skull rendering her instantly unconscious.

*   *   *

She woke with a terrible headache, her mind slightly swimming from the knock she'd taken to the back of her skull. It was what she'd expected, though that didn't lessen the pain any. Instinctively she tried to raise a hand to the spot to feel for injury but was unable finding both of her arms stretched out to either side and chained to a wall. This too, she'd expected but still her face flushed, not in anger but in shame. To be chained in such a manner was one of the ultimate dishonors to place on a Tjal-Dihn. Such incarceration was to openly declare one as not trusted; one without honor; a liar and deceiver. To even hint such a thing to a Tjal would invite instant retribution from the edge of a sword. But Jne was no longer Tjal. She had been labeled *Jinghar* and though her debt to Thane might have already been paid, she still owed those who once were her people.

Slowly opening her eyes, she took in the tiny cell that was now her home. It was rectangular, made of smooth stone and was no taller than half her height. In her current sitting position the ceiling was a mere inch above her head. Her arms were stretched out to either side and held against the wall with shackles. Her legs were crossed in front of her leaving only a few inches to the other wall so that she would not be able to stretch them out.

To her right was a tiny slit that let in air and a small sliver of light telling her it was daytime. On her left was a steel bared door that completely covered the opening and the only way in or out. She could just make out the form of a guard posted, the sight of his head and shoulders revealing that she was at least not on the bottom compartment of what she knew to be a multilevel cell block. Though she was seen as one without honor or place in Tjal society, the bottom cell was strictly reserved for those who took innocent blood and awaited execution in the most horrific and ignominious manners.

The fact that she was guarded was another sign of disgrace as if she did not have the integrity to accept responsibility for herself. It was almost more than she could tolerate as the marks of dishonor bit deeply into her pride. For any Tjal-Dihn, death in its most terrifying or painful manner was preferable to losing ones honor. How ironic that the man she loved was the one to place her here. But she held no malice. She had come voluntarily, knowing full well what awaited her as she did so. And it was still not over. Soon she would be free or dead and either was preferable to her current state.

"I request an *obed'ah*," she spoke to the back of the guard's head. Though he didn't move or acknowledge hearing her, Jne did not speak again knowing that to do so would weigh even more dishonor upon her already shattered state. She knew that she'd spoken loud enough to be heard and for the rest of the time she was caged she would not speak again. It was the last morsel of dignity she still retained and she refused to allow it to be stripped away with the rest.

The minutes slowly bled into hours and she watched as the blade of light from her "window" crept along the floor and up the wall until it was almost completely snuffed out. The door then opened and she took an involuntary breath of hope that she would be led out to her requested judgment, but instead, a small plate of food and a tiny cup of water were placed just inside her cell. The door closed but she was still unable to move her arms to reach her rations. Would they taunt her in starvation as well? Suddenly she felt slack in the chains that bound her and she realized that someone had released a mechanism on the other side of the wall at her back that allowed her to move her arms forward. Taking advantage of the slack, she first spread out her legs to one side relieving the cramps that had painfully formed in her joints as she had been forced to sit cross-legged for so long. Rubbing them frantically with her freed hands she did her best to massage away the ache.

It was long, slow minutes before she finally turned her attention to her food but when she reached out for the plate the chains were suddenly pulled back. In a moment of desperation she resisted, trying to get to her rations, but the chains continued to recede pulling her arms back as they did so. She wanted to call out that she'd not been able to eat yet, but knew that to do so would only further dishonor her so she remained silent and hungry. She would eat tomorrow.

The guard opened the door again and retrieved her plate and cup without the slightest look of surprise that nothing had been touched. Jne could only guess that many a Tjal chose death by starvation over the humiliation of being caged and that untouched food was more the norm than the exception. But she had no such thoughts. All she could think of was the task she'd accepted and whether it cost her her life to fulfill it she would complete her charge or die in the attempt.

Pulling her legs back as best she could she drew them up in front of her so her knees created a type of a table on which to rest her head. Ignoring the grinding emptiness in her stomach she tried to sleep but was only able to catch a few fleeting glimpses of the dream world as she was constantly awakened by her growling stomach or a sharp cramp. Night seemed to hold its grip against morning for an extended period of time before finally letting go its grasp and allowing the sun to rise once more. She hadn't slept hardly at all but comforted herself in the knowledge that her breakfast would come soon and that nothing would keep her from sleeping during the day should she get comfortable enough or exhaustion mercifully overtake her.

This time when her meal arrived and the chains were loosed she wasted no time in devouring the small portion on her plate and then quickly draining the cup. A small, empty bucket had also been left for personal relief that was no easy task. She was just finishing when the chains were pulled taut again.

Minutes passed slowly into hours that dragged into days that eventually reached a week with no change to her situation. She could now tell by the sliver of light and its position on the floor and wall when her meals would come. Though still not accustomed or comfortable with the cramped space of her confinement, she was able to finally sleep an hour straight at a time before having to move into a different position. Her body ached to be free and to move about to the point that it took all of her mental concentration to not cry out for pity and death. So far she had been able to hold onto her honor in at least that area but she wasn't certain how much longer she could hold out.

It wasn't only her discomfort at being cage that worked on her constantly but more importantly it was the time being wasted when so much was at stake. Her being there was not about retrieving her honor, though the possibility sent a thrill of excitement through her, it was now a matter of survival. She could not risk much more time before she would be forced to completely lay her honor aside and clamor for immediate judgment. The idea repulsed her soliciting a chilling shake that coursed through her body and tightened her stomach to the point of almost vomiting. It would be to go contrary to every moral fiber that was her; to give herself over as an animal bent on mere survival without consciousness or principle. Her stomach seized slightly and she forced the thought from her mind with effort. Today she would not compel herself into darkness but soon she would be left without choice. When that day came she knew she would never be able to find her way back again.

Another day passed, this one seeming longer than the rest as she continued to struggle with what she may be forced to do. She avoided setting a date in her mind of when she would completely lay away who she was and demand to be seen but by the time the light was snuffed out of her tiny window she'd resigned herself to three days hence. She was exhausted, both mentally and physically but she still held tenaciously to the core of what made her Jne. She was Tjal, she kept reminding herself, and though the horror of the *Jinghar* was her current state, it would not break her—for another three days, that is.

She was no longer able to make her own choices. Like the roc's sacrifice that carried her to Thane's people, she would do the same for the good of all. She comforted herself in the idea that it was what a true Tjal would do in such a situation. She sighed and finally understood what Thane had been facing all along. He had had to turn his back on his own people because they no longer carried the truth that once made them a great nation. Now she faced the same grim possibility.

She slept well that night but the following three days passed all too quickly. She now marked ten days since she'd been caged with no hint as to when it might all end. By this time, Zadok's armies could well be surrounding Bedler's Keep in its final assault that would then leave the Tjal exposed as well. She could wait no longer. Time and history would mark her without honor but the choice was no longer hers to make. When the evening meal came she would cast herself off forever and no longer be Tjal. She would join Thane as one without people or history and become a wonderer with him—if it didn't kill her to do so. For the first time in her life she felt fear. Fear so great that it seemed to cut off her breathing making it labored and shallow. Her head spun and she wanted to cry but only held back through sheer stubborn will.

The light from the window marked the well known spot on the wall that told her the evening meal was coming. The shuffling of feet sounded down the hall and finally stopped at her cell. The guard turned and she could hear the insertion of the key to unlock her cage. Jne took a deep breath choking back the tears that tried to well up in her eyes. A lump formed in her throat that she knew would make it difficult for her to speak past. In mere moments she would cease to be Jne and become someone she did not know or care to recognize. The door opened. Squeezing her eyes shut, she opened her mouth to speak but her throat constricted cutting off any sound. Steeling herself, she tried again but instead of hearing her own voice a deeper sound touched her ears. *"Jon't'obed'ah y'ud"*

At first she didn't understand what she'd spoken. It sounded nothing like her voice. Suddenly the chains holding her arms were released but even then the words did not register. It wasn't until her guard reached in and unshackled her right wrist that the words that were spoken formed again in her mind. *Jon't'obed'ah y'ud.* But they were not her words at all. She had not spoken them. It had not been her voice.

With one arm free, the guard moved back and started to unfetter her left hand and then her mind finally wrapped around what *he'd* said. *Jon't'obed'ah y'ud. Your judgment waits.* Her judgment waits. Opening her eyes, she stared at the guard for a moment finally realizing she was free from her chains as he motioned her out of the cell. They had accepted her petition. She was going to be judged allowing her to retain the morsel of honor she still clung to. Soon she would be full Tjal again, with her complete honor restored—or she would be dead. She took a deep breath and let it wash over her as if to cleanse her from the terror that had almost been hers.

The guard's eyes flashed at her slight hesitation and Jne found herself bounding for the opening before he decided she was not worthy of her granted request. Grabbing the steel door she pulled herself out and then up so that her legs could drop to the floor. The guard watched her closely as she fought to keep her feet and balance. Any faulting now would forfeit her chances for judgment. Though cramped and weakened by her incarceration, she found that she still had strength enough to walk as she fell in behind the guard that had since turned and led the way out. With each step she found her strength returning, and though her muscles spasmed with the sudden exertion, they seemed to welcome the chance at exercise.

The fact that she was not chained and allowed to follow the guard, his back given to her, was a subtle boost to her already fragile honor. No real prisoner, especially anyone of a different race, would have been afforded such trust.

It was only a matter of a few steps before they exited the prison. The Tjal had no real use for incarceration as any full Tjal would never think of fleeing should they be called to answer for breaking the law. And any offense that might warrant captivity was punishable by death so only a very few holding cells were constructed. Outsiders were under the same law though it was recognized that those not of the Tjal race had little to no honor so most of the time the cells were used for them until their judgment. Jne had been in a limbo state when it came to her sudden appearance on the plains. Having been marked as *Jinghar* she was no longer seen as a member of the Tjal but neither was she relegated to the ranks of a complete outsider. She was practically a non-person in Tjal-Dihn eyes and society.

Thankfully it was dusk, the sun having already dropped below the horizon while its influence was still visible in the western sky. Had it been daytime she would have been rendered almost completely blind having spent so much time in her mostly dark cell. She drew in another deep, cleansing breath. Though the jail was above ground, in a small building without exterior doors, the air still smelled sweeter and fresher.

Turning south, they walked the mile or so toward the location where her judgment would take place. The jail was a lone, squat building out on the plain away from contact with the main population. The distance was not to discourage any visitors, since no Tjal would ever debase themselves to visit a law breaker no matter what their relation, but to keep the "refuse", as it were, out and away. Jne welcomed the distance giving her muscles a chance to work themselves out of the slumber they had been forced to endure the past week and a half. As if aware of their deprivation and the exercise her legs were getting, her hands ached to feel the hilts of her swords.

Seeing the city pressed against the mountains in the distance, she was quickly able to determine where they were. There were only two permanent Tjal settlements, all other *Tja* preferring the freedom of a nomadic existence. This was *Kabu* of the *Kabu'ja* located on the northern tip of the Dorian Mountains almost completely removed from the plains of Enn. Those of the *Kabu'ja* were the masters of sword making and their city was situated to make trading for ore with the dwarfs a more convenient practice. Just like the best bred horses were offered by Jne's *Tja*, no finer swords were created by any others. The skill of the *Kabu'ja* was legendary.

The other permanent Tjal settlement was *Kufa* and was farther east near the plentiful groves of trees bordering the Enn. That is where the *Kufa'ja* made their home because they were workers of wood dealing mostly in exquisitely fine pieces of furniture.

Kabu was also the location of the only Tjal marketplace where all the *Tja* could be found selling their crafts and goods from all parts of the Enn. The *Kabu'ja* of course had their swords, while the *Kufa'ja* carted in their furniture and other wood pieces. Jne's people brought horses to trade while the *Svan'ja* and *Keno'ja* traded jewelry and fine clothing respectively. Outsiders were also allowed to sell and buy here but very few of them risked coming here to trade fearing there was too great a risk to losing one's life while in the company of the Tjal-Dihn. Those few who did come only did so because their greed was greater than their love of life, though rarely did any misunderstandings result in bloodshed.

It was almost completely dark by the time they reached the first buildings on the outskirts of the city. Unlike Calandra and other HuMan cities, those on the city's fringe were no poorer or viewed any less worthy than those who occupied the city's center. All were equal among the Tjal-Dihn. The buildings were almost all the same. Squat box shapes made of blocks coated in cement and whitewashed. Most had concrete steps leading up the front or side of the building to a flat roof that was used as a sleeping area during the hot months of the year. Some blue colored domed roofs were scattered about in no particular pattern marking the sword smithies and breaking up the monotonous white block houses that made up the rest of the city.

Few people were found on the streets as most were inside enjoying their evening meal. Those with whom they did come in contact turned their backs to Jne as she passed; some even spitting on the ground by her feet. Though she wore no badge to label her as *Jinghar* apparently word had gotten out. She ignored the reactions, expecting nothing less and knowing she would have done the same were she to watch a *Jinghar* pass in front of her. Such a person was seen as less than a dog returning to its own vomit to gulp down its shame. Ironically, these same people would welcome her into their homes with open arms and complete trust once her station and honor were returned by judgment. No stigma or label was placed on any who returned from being *Jinghar*; quite the contrary, most such people, though rare, were celebrated.

The guard suddenly stopped and knocked at a blue door outside one of the many block buildings. It was nondescript in its simplicity baring nothing that would mark it as other than the rest of the structures that surrounded it. A narrow stairway climbed at an angle from the right rising just above the right corner of the doorframe as it made its way to the flat topped roof. As another block house sat atop this one, the stairs also gave passage to the building above. A small, circular window to the left of the door was covered by a muted red cloth that was not so thick as to completely block out the light behind it and thus became illuminated giving it a warm feel against the starkness of the whitewashed outer walls.

The door opened easily revealing a Tjal woman of great age who merely beckoned the visitors enter. Jne caught her breath at the sight of her never having seen a Tjal of such advanced years. Though unmatched by any in skill with a sword, most Tjal did not live long enough to die of old age. Most found such a thought horrific and even bordering on dishonorable. As if reading her thoughts the woman suddenly turned and, in a movement as fluid and nimble as one half her age, had two swords instantly unsheathed and pressed against Jne's soft throat. "Lest you think me old and frail, young one, my ability, along with my honor, remains intact."

Jne didn't speak, knowing to do so would only invite the old woman's steal to sink deeply into her flesh. The woman watched her for a moment as if waiting for any excuse to do just that and then, as quickly as the swords had appeared, they were gone again. Turning her back to them, the woman shuffled over to a high backed chair situated in front of a small fire that danced gaily in the dome topped fireplace. No other furniture cluttered the small room that was obviously a foyer of types that allowed for visitors without giving them access to the rest of the house. Similar strips of cloth, like the one covering the front window, hung in doorways on either side of the fireplace blocking off any view of what might reside behind them making the room feel cramped and suddenly overheated by the fire. Of course, even should there have been another chair, or many, Jne would not have dared sit in one even had she been offered. The fact that she was even in the woman's home was like calling in a dung pile and giving it a place at one's table.

"So you come seeking judgment," the old woman said while staring into the fire. It was not a question but a statement so Jne did not venture to answer. "So tell me child," she continued, "how is it that one so young loses all honor and allows herself the disgrace of becoming *Jinghar?*"

Jne cringed at the words though spoken simply and without an accusing tone they still bit deeply. "I was beaten in the challenge of steal," she answered, the words stinging her like acid on her tongue.

"And you have paid the blood debt?" the old woman asked.

Jne felt surprised that the old woman skipped over her loss to Thane and went right to the debt she had owed to him. She expected to be shamed further by having to confess her defeat to an outsider and even more so by revealing that it was someone she loved. Such an admission would bring further doubt not only to her ability but to her motivation. The question of ultimate shame would then be asked as to whether she purposefully allowed herself to lose to save her lover's life. The idea made her suddenly feel nauseous. A barely audible "Yes," was all she could manage as she fought to control her stomach and her emotions.

Then her utmost dread was given voice. "And how is it that you were beaten at steal yet still live?"

So, her humiliation was to be drawn out after all. Jne felt lightheaded, her complexion draining to an ashen white and it was all she could do to keep from toppling over. She suddenly felt like it was too much to pass through; that she would rather have the woman take her life now and be done with it. Now, more than ever, she'd wished Thane had ended her life when he'd had the chance. Still, she was not bitter toward him for his choice, knowing he had been an outsider not knowing honor. And though he claimed the power that beat her came from one of his Tane, she would never think to try and make an excuse for her loss. Her shoulders noticeably sagging, Jne finally answered. "I was beaten by an outsider who knew not honor."

She felt empty. It took all of her strength to not fall to the ground in a heap and weep like a child. Any type of physical pain could not equal the anguish of soul she was forced to endure at that moment. She felt as if her soul, the essence of what made her Jne, was being ripped and shredded apart.

"I see," was all that the woman said. How she did so without a tone laced in disgust at such a vile admission, Jne could not know. The old woman merely stared into the fire as if enjoying an evening all alone with a cup of tea. "And now you come seeking redemption from your humiliation through judgment." Again it was not a question but a stated fact. Shifting in her chair slightly, the woman continued to stare at the flames as if she were the only one in the room.

Jne could feel the beads of sweat running a course down her back as the room suddenly felt stifling. She was on the edge of a sword's blade that at any moment could slice quick and true, ending her ordeal and possibly sealing their doom. All it would take was one word from her aged host and all would be lost.

The old woman sat silent for long moments, the sound of crackling wood as it burned the only sound in the room. Outside was quiet as if all of nature held its breath to hear the final decision. Jne began to dread, feeling certain that her petition for judgment would be denied. She'd failed already, and worst of all to an outsider. By all rights she should not even be here. Her corpse should be lying on the plains her flesh picked at by carrion birds while worms ate her innards for none who lost judgment were worthy of Tjal honors in burial. And yet, the irony was that she still may find herself in such a state should she be denied. But, having been stripped of any morsel of dignity, she found herself uncaring as to what her final state might be or how soon it should befall her. She had failed. She failed as a Tjal-Dihn being beaten by Thane in the first place and now she would fail in warning her people and seeking their help against the evil that would surely overtake them. She was an empty vessel to the point that when the old woman spoke, her words barely touched her. "You will have judgment in the morning."

Jne did not speak, her face an empty canvas, as she was led from the building and taken back outside the city. The old woman had merely spoken and then arisen from her chair, disappearing behind one of the cloth covered doors before the guard escorted her out. She knew that she should have felt relief at the decision but she had been stripped down so completely that she wondered if she would ever feel anything again.

As the guard took her back to the holding area where she had spent the last ten days, he directed her to a small chamber just across the hallway from the cell she'd occupied before. This time she was left unfettered, no guard was posted by her door, and a small cot with a blanket and a pillow were provided. A hot meal was left for her as well, but she ignored it even though her stomach was now as empty as her soul.

When the door closed behind her she simply threw herself onto the cot and wept bitterly.

Chapter Twenty-One

Jne woke with a start, the last wisps of the dream she'd been having quickly fading out of memory. Her eyes burned and her stomach ached, though from hunger or the heaving sobs that had almost completely overtaken her the night before she could not tell. Last night's dinner still sat untouched by the door no longer appetizing even in her state of hunger. She would not eat breakfast either when it came—if it came. She would not risk being judged with a full stomach.

Though in her current state of mind she almost yearned for death, she would not simply offer up her life without showing she still held to some bit of honor by fighting for every last breath. She would not give herself over to total loss of identity, nor would she shame the one who would judge her.

The door suddenly opened and Jne pushed herself up to a sitting position and rubbed the sleep from her eyes. The guard ignored the full tray of cold food on the ground and merely motioned for her to follow. No breakfast was offered and she smiled slightly, releasing a calming and head-clearing breath. She had barely slept the night before giving herself over to the extreme pain and suffering that was her lot at being completely exposed to the old woman in her status as *Jinghar*. Never before had she allowed herself to dwell on her position of dishonor and she admitted to herself that it had been too easy walking in the HuMan world to ignore what would have been a daily reminder should she have remained with Tjal society—albeit forced to exist alone on the perimeter. Even as *Jinghar* she held more honor then most of those she'd mingle with in the past months. But that was now behind her. Being here had almost crushed her in the weight of her guilt. The pain it yielded had almost been too much for her to bear.

Reaching around and pulling her braid to rest in front of her, she rose and strode out of the cell following closely behind her guard. It was a different person from the one the night before; this time a woman strode before her with ease and confidence giving off an air of assurance at who she was and the honor she held as a Tjal-Dihn. Her strides were fluid and sure as her feet, as if on their own, picked the path of greatest balance without any visible effort. Her swords were crossed against her back the hilts worn from use though obviously well cared for. Again Jne felt her hands almost reaching for the swords at her back that she knew were not there. She couldn't help but wonder if this woman was her judge.

The air was still as they made their way toward the city portending a hot day. Already she could feel the sweat gathering on her back though the sun had barely risen high enough to drink the dew from the grass. Entering the city she found its occupants strangely absent figuring that the streets would be bustling with people moving about on errands and the daily business of life. She soon discovered why.

Following a well-worn street they emerged from a darkened corner shaded from the low lying sun into a bright arena of open space that hailed itself as the famous Tjal marketplace of *Kabu*. It was a vast open space right in the heart of the city as if a great whirlwind had merely dropped down in the middle of the town and wiped it clean of any structures. A wave of people on all sides milled about pushing against one another as they vied for a proper spot to witness what would shortly take place. All the carts, tables, and covered wagons where usually goods were hawked and sold had been packed up and pushed aside against the outer rim of buildings leaving a large empty space in the middle where judgment would be rendered. Jne paused briefly becoming almost overwhelmed by the crowd that was gathered to witness whether she would conquer her shame or die. A loud hiss of disgust greeted her as she followed the guard out to the center of the area and then was somewhat surprised when she was left their alone. Apparently she wasn't to judge her after all.

Unmoving, she nevertheless turned her head about to see if her judge would soon present him or herself but all simply stared back in disgust as if she were something vile or contrary to nature. She took it all in stride though knowing that soon enough those stares would either become abruptly warm and welcoming or lost to her sight forever.

She suddenly caught movement to her left and turned in time to see the old woman from the night before extracting herself from the crowd. Jne felt her face flush at the thought that someone of such advanced age would actually be chosen to judge her. There was little to no honor to be gained from it. The thought threw a sudden cloud of despair over her mind and she could feel the steel grip she had on her emotions suddenly slipping. Even though the woman had certainly proven herself as able the night before, it was still an unnecessary slap in the face to both of them; to Jne as accusation that she would not pass judgment by anyone else and to the woman as if to mark her as no longer needed or of little importantance to the community.

The woman approached slowly until she finally stood at Jne's left side and turned about a full circle eyeing the crowd that gradually went silent and still. "We are here to judge this *Jinghar*," she spoke, her voice carrying farther than Jne would have expected from one her age. "Is there one among you who would give her judgment?"

Jne's eyes widened in. She felt certain that one had already been chosen to judge her. In this manner, if no one deemed her worthy of it, she would summarily be killed and the matter considered resolved. No one seemed to move as Jne's hope for vindication slipped slowly away. Death did not frighten her in any sense but a feeling that she was failing her people, failing the one she loved was a bitter cup too cruel to drink.

"Is there no one?" the old woman asked once more, slowly turning toward Jne while pulling a sword slowly from its scabbard at her back. Lifting the blade to Jne's throat, she turned her gaze back to the crowd who seemed frozen in place as they watched. Jne kept her eyes looking straight ahead, her hope draining as quickly as her blood soon would be upon the ground. She knew she was about to die but she still needed to speak of the danger that threatened. It would doom her further in death but they had to know.

"I must speak," she whispered just loud enough for the woman holding the sword to her neck to hear. Jne kept her eyes locked straight ahead not wishing to see the look of disgust the woman certainly must have been burning into her at the moment. "It is of great importance to all," she ventured once more as the blade pressed harder against her throat as if in warning. "I must speak."

"I will judge her," a woman's voice suddenly broke through the silence that had fallen as the crowd moved away to the right revealing her. Jne sighed. Not that she was to be given a chance but that her presumption in speaking may have forfeited the opportunity. Chancing a look at the woman who held her life in the balance she could see the rage in her old eyes as she stared back at her in shocked silence and fury. Jne sighed again, the last breath of one who was condemned to die and rightly so. She had failed.

"I claim judgment," the woman from the crowd cried again as she made her way to the center where judgment was already in the process toward execution. Jne closed her eyes and awaited her fate. She had heard that beheading was one of the least painful ways to die but it did not really matter to her what type of death was chosen for her. Nothing could match the empty pain she felt in her soul at that moment.

"Judgment has been given," the old woman spat, her blade suddenly leaving Jne's throat pulling back for the final deadly blow.

"It is my right," the other woman's voice sliced like steal and Jne opened her eyes to see her confront the old woman. "I have right to judgment here and I will not be denied." Jne stared at the two in confusion. The aged woman was poised to strike her down in a moment and this other woman, who was somewhere in between Jne and the elderly woman in age, wanted the task for herself. The crowd was deathly still, no one moving or making a sound, all straining to catch the exchange and see what would happen.

"What is your claim?" the old woman hissed, her eyes still holding fast to Jne and burning with loathing.

"I claim the right of *fersk*," she answered, her voice no less hard.

The elderly woman was visibly surprised by the answer, her sword hand relaxing slightly as she turned to regard the woman making the claim. "And what proof do you bring?" she demanded.

The woman smiled, pulling up the sleeve on her right arm until it exposed her shoulder and revealed a mark etched right into her skin. A long line crossed by another and then brought back creating a small triangle on the right side with a tail jutting out in the same direction beneath it. Jne gasped at the mark and before she could even react, the old woman was pushing up her sleeve to reveal the same marking on Jne's arm.

"Hello daughter," the woman said to her but without the slightest emotion. Jne's eyes widened at the revelation but she remained still as if uncertain as to how to react. Tjal children were raised by grandparents or other relations outside the *Tja* into which they'd been born. Jne had thus been given to her grandparents, who were part of the *Rena'ja*, when she was born. She had never met her mother until now. And this would be the last time they would see each other in this life.

Sheathing her sword, the old woman said nothing but motioned toward the crowd. The same guard who had escorted Jne the night before suddenly appeared carrying her swords and unceremoniously dropped them at her feet before turning his back to return to his place in the crowd. Jne looked at her weapons, the joy at having them with her again almost overwhelming. The Tjal were whetted to their weapons as soon as they were weaned from their mother's breast. To be without them was like to be without a piece of one's body so much did they become a part of them. Reaching down, she flashed a quick look at her mother who stood by emotionless. Though she never knew her, Jne could not help but suddenly feel a sense of loss. They were of the same flesh and blood and though they never shared other than a sanguine connection, this was the woman that had given her life and she felt an attachment that was soon to be severed.

Lifting the swords still secured in their sheaths, Jne strapped them to her back and let out a breath of relief and contentment. How uncomfortable she had felt the past week and a half without them there giving her confidence and reassurance. Without thought, her hands instantly reached for the hilts pulling them free in one quick, easy movement her body reacting to their weight with ease and familiarity. Swinging them in cadence and movement as if directing a symphony she flashed her blades in a complicated pattern weaving them together and then apart twisting her body as if in an artistic display before pulling them upright in front of her, a slight smile playing across her lips.

Her mother's face then came back into focus and Jne was snapped back into reality. The woman looked nothing like her, her hair was light in color and her eyes were dark. Her nose was slightly too large for her face and her skin was darker than Jne's. But that was where the differences stopped. Jne gleaned from her physique and the way she carried herself that her mother was not one with whom to trifle. Her stance was casual, yet balanced and Jne could see death in every move and nuance of her toned form. Neither was there any semblance of pity or care that the one she faced was her own child. But Jne did not expect any such thing. To show any mercy would be dishonorable to herself and to Jne. No, the one who had brought Jne to life did not enter the arena to give her own life as a sacrifice but to bring back honor to her family by also being the one to bring Jne death rather than to let that fall to a stranger with the simple beheading deserving a *Jinghar* who was unworthy of judgment. Jne knew that one of them would die this day only because the other had proven more worthy with the sword not due to familial pity or sacrifice—to do so was not the Tjal way.

Jne crouched at the ready, her swords out in front awaiting her opponent who had yet to draw her own swords. A hush fell over the crowd as all waited for judgment to commence. "I am Naye," her mother said, in a matter-of-fact tone. "I think it only proper you know by name the one who judges you that the memory of it might carry with you to the afterlife." She said it without boasting or jest but as one casually giving information to another as one might pass on the name of a horse.

Jne nodded her head slightly but did not reply. To do so would have been a sign of disrespect to the one claiming judgment. Also, her mother would already know her name having pronounced it upon her head in blessing before surrendering the child to her grandparents to raise.

Slowly lifting her hands to her swords, Naye removed them deliberately, her eyes locked on Jne as she did so. "Let the judging begin," she breathed and then shot forward with one blade slicing for Jne's neck while the other sought out her midsection. Jne's body reacted instinctively meeting the swing to her middle with both swords while ducking under the cut to her throat and then sliding a blade along her opponent's for a jab at her stomach. But Naye caught the thrust with a downward stroke with the blade originally meant for Jne's throat and then reversed it toward the back of her neck as Jne passed to her right.

Again and again, the two women thrust and parried, slashed and blocked back and forth as they mingled their swords in a rendezvous of death. The crowd having cheered with the first flashes of steel had fallen into a low rumble of activity as they watched intently to see which would retain or regain her honor. Side bets were suddenly being bandied about as an occasional cheer sounded after a particularly good attack or defense. The two women looked as if they had choreographed the whole fight and were now performing for the onlookers so close and quick were their assaults and parries against each other. And neither seemed the least bit winded by their efforts.

Jne ducked again and then crossed her swords in front of her and down as Naye brought up her other sword in an attempt to gut her. Turning to the side as she did so, Jne kicked the other woman in the midsection pushing her back and then followed after her with her own complicated windmill of slashes and reverse directional cuts and undercuts. But Naye was undeterred as she met each swing with her own steel often turning it back with an attack of her own.

Around and around they went, puffs of dust rising in the morning sun as each moved their feet to the rhythm of the dance. Sweat began forming on both women as their exertions, matched by the heat of the rising sun began taking their toll on their bodies. Both looked for advantage with the early morning rays but up to this point neither was caught by the blinding sun. Having been locked away for ten days, Jne felt the strain from the effort more quickly but the other woman's age seemed to equalize the difference.

Catching a sudden opening, Jne was able to pull a thrust and catch Naye in the face with her elbow drawing blood from her opponent's nose but paid for it when one of Naye's swords connected with her forearm slicing into the flesh just enough to draw blood but not so deep as to cause her to drop her weapon. Jne cursed herself for being drawn in knowing now that the supposed opening had been a ploy. She also knew that it was only her decision to attack with an elbow instead of a sword that allowed her to draw blood on Naye and actually possibly saved her life, otherwise the cut would have been in a different spot and most likely fatal. Both stepped back for a brief moment for a quick survey of the damage done to each before throwing themselves back into a hailstorm of steel.

Quicker and quicker the strokes seemed to come until it appeared that neither could possibly see nor react to the swing of the other. Only instinct born from years of practice could answer the question as to how either survived this far. Suddenly, Jne pulled back and the crowd roared with approval as a distinct slash along her right thigh revealed that one of Naye's strokes had gotten through again. Jne had only a brief glimmer of time to assess her injury before Naye, smelling blood and victory, advanced with another blur of complicated swings and cuts that suddenly put Jne on the complete defensive unable to turn back quick enough to mount her own attack.

Jne gave up ground as Naye forced her back, her swords coming at breath stopping speed. Jne parried as well as she could but could tell that her reaction time was becoming slightly slower and that her mother's blades were getting closer to meeting her flesh again. A sharp pain suddenly shot across her chest and she knew before the damp feel of blood registered in her mind that she'd taken another hit. Naye suddenly slowed her attack having felt the resistance of flesh instead of steel to her right hand. Backing a pace she inspected the damage she'd done giving Jne a quick opportunity to check for herself.

Just below her neckline a long streak of red was suddenly cascading rather quickly into her shirt where it mingled with her sweat. The strike had meant to take her head from her shoulders but Jne had been able to sidestep the swing just enough to make the sword miss its intended mark. Yet, still, it was a significant injury that would impede her ability due to blood loss if the judgment continued for too much longer.

Their eyes met briefly, neither showing any emotion yet both realizing that the verdict was almost all but decided. Raising her swords to the ready, Jne kept her eyes locked on her mother pausing only for a brief moment before moving quickly toward her, her swords already in motion. Naye watched Jne's approach as if she would simply stand motionless and be cut down. Only at the last moment did she move catching either sword easily and then turning the fight back on her daughter.

Jne's breathing was beginning to become more labored as the fighting continued, the minutes stretching out ever longer. Her wounds stung mixing sweat with blood though she had yet to reach the point where blood loss became a factor. Snapping her head back, Naye's blade just nicked the bridge of her nose and would have blinded her had she not reacted so quickly. Having done so though, she was thrown of balance and just barely turned away the counter slash that Naye had meant for her midsection that would certainly have spilled her intestines had it connected.

Recovering with some difficulty, Jne attempted to turn the attack back and go, herself, on the offensive but Naye seemed too fast. Every assault was met and turned back making her slip into the defensive and barely giving her time to react, let alone attempt another attack. She was losing and she didn't have much longer.

Strangely, even though this fight seemed already destined to end in her death, it exhilarated her at the same time. The power of arm against arm, steel against steel, and will against will was intoxicating even more so because her opponent seemed her better and that this was not a practice game where quarter would be given. Thane had cursed her with life because of his ignorance of honor and the effect it would have on her. Naye would not do the same and that knowledge made Jne strangely eager to see it through.

As she fended off wave after wave of slashing and jabbing steel, Jne found herself studying and finding beauty in the precision and exactness of Naye's form and she caught herself smiling at the privilege it was going to be to die at her hand. Again and again her mother's assault rained down on her, the clang of metal sounding almost like music as the tempo increased and waned. She found herself anticipating the sound, her movements settling in with the cadence that was a beautiful dance created by Naye as she moved about, her swords the instruments with Jne's making the music. The melody was almost hypnotizing as steel rang against steel in a crescendo before falling away in a diminuendo. It was the most beautiful melody Jne had ever heard.

Suddenly, she felt a jarring in her ears, an off note that invaded the serenity of her imminent death that felt so dissonant as to shatter the peace that had fallen over her. Again the music of the swords began, this time becoming even more harmonious as she anticipated the sounds; the melody certain now in her mind as her swords moved against Naye's adding her part of the symphony of death that had drawn her in.

This time the discordant sound was even more grating as Jne had caught up the rhythm and the harmony swinging her swords around as Naye continued her attacks. And again the melody seemed to restart and Jne suddenly realized what she had discovered. Naye had fallen into a pattern, the last part of which was an opening that she could exploit. She let herself drop back into the tempo waiting for the moment she was certain would come and wasn't disappointed when the discordant sound grated at her senses. It wasn't that Naye's motions were exactly the same every time and being repeated, but the way she moved together with her weapons had combined into a pattern that had left itself open at a certain moment like the bad note of a repeated song—and this time Jne would exploit it.

Jne crossed her swords over her head almost before the overhand strike had come and then pulled the right one away to deflect Naye's attack with her left. She stared at her mother with a look mixed of pity and triumph that Naye picked up on too late as she thrust forward with both swords at once. Jne pulled her eyes away as she stepped forward, ducking under the attack while raising her left sword to push it up. Carrying her motion around Jne swung counterclockwise giving her back to Naye while bringing her right sword around to place it squarely into her mother's chest cleaving her heart in twain as the blade slid out her back. Naye realized her mistake just as it was happening, the look of pride and disbelief mingled on her face now set as her eternal death mask. Pulling her sword, Jne watched as her mother dropped to the ground knowing she was dead before she hit the dirt.

Jne stared at her for a moment, uncertain what her emotions might reveal knowing she had defeated her mother in judgment and that she now lie dead at her feet. She was afraid that there might be sorrow and regret knowing she had taken the life of the woman who had given it to her twice now but those feelings never seemed to materialize. She had beaten an opponent with greater skill than she yet who had fallen prey to comfort in her own skills.

The crowd suddenly erupted in cheers of approval as Jne raised her swords in salute, her honor now fully restored. Those who only moments before had shunned her as an outcast now greeted her as one of their own and would welcome her as a member of their family to their homes without the slightest reservation. Unable to repress the smile that broke out on her face she shouted, "I am Jne of the *Rena'ja* Tja." Turning to each of the marks of the compass, she repeated her claim of heritage and honor as a full member of the Tjal people before turning back to her mother's body. Squatting down, she wiped the blood from her sword on her mother's pants before reluctantly sheathing them both. Her blood still pumped hot in her veins with the exhilaration of battle and though she was bleeding and tired, her hands still ached to hold her weapons.

There was no dishonor to herself or her mother by her actions and none would have expected any less. The spoils of battle and the laws surrounding them were very strict in Tjal society no matter what relationship there might be between combatants. Her mother was no longer there, only her shell remained, and nothing could be taken to the afterlife once one was dead. All her mother's possessions now fell to her. Removing the sash that wrapped Naye's waist, Jne moved to tie it around her chest to stop the flow of blood that was still seeping from the wound she'd received but a gnarled hand stopped her in the process. Looking up, she looked into the smiling face of the old woman who not too long before had been prepared to take her head.

"Welcome, child," she said. "Let us tend to that wound properly before it bleeds you out or you catch the fever from it."

Jne stood and nodded. "I would welcome that," she said gratefully, "but first I must address all who are present."

"Such things can wait, child," the old woman persisted, reaching out to take Jne's arm. "Come; let us see to you first."

Jne did not reply but pulled her arm away and shouted to the crowd that was already starting to break away; most anxious to get their tables and wares out for the day's bizarre, while others began moving away toward the lanes leading out. "Hold," Jne called out and then repeated herself three more times before every eye was finally turned to her and a relative silence had fallen on the gathered crowd. "A shadow has grown in the north and now threatens as it moves south and east of us on its way to the old HuMan keep named Bedler. It is not a trifle to be left to HuMans alone for should they fall, and they will fall," she added for emphasis, "we shall fall with them. I have come to warn and to call upon our people to action, to fight with the HuMans to defend against this great darkness that will surely encompass us all."

A rumble of voices echoed through the throng as sudden discussions of her claims grew up in all parts. "You have been too long with the ilk of dishonorable HuMans," one shouted to her though she could not lock on him from the multitude. "We do not meddle in the dealings of the HuMans."

"This is not a HuMan matter," Jne countered, "though they are the only ones engaged at the moment." Turning about, to assure the attention of all present, she continued, the heat of the recent battle lending her added adrenaline and strength to argue her point. "Many days past I searched out my people on the northern plains to ask their aid as a great army descended on the HuMan fortress at Haykon. It was as if all creatures of evil breed had gathered together as one to sweep the land free of any and all things good."

"And what concern is that of ours," a voice interjected, "should the HuMans battle their enemies behind their walls of cowardice?"

"It concerns us when that same threat finally turns its evil upon our heads as it certainly has already," Jne countered. "You are not hearing me!" she shouted, frustration growing. She did not come all this way to lose in the battle of mere words. She was one to act, not be acted upon. "Whether you feel there is justice in the wars of HuMans does not matter here. As I searched out my *Tja*, I found nothing but the signs of pitched and desperate battle and not a soul alive to tell the tale."

Her last statement created quite a stir in the people listening and it was long moments before she dare speak again so that all might hear. Another voice spoke out before her. "That does not prove that we face danger. Do you know for a surety that none of your *Tja* remains?"

Jne shook her head. "I did not have the time to search the area or scout out survivors," she admitted but added with gaining vehemence, "Do I hear that the Tjal fear to take up the sword to battle? Has Tjal blood grown so thin as to turn from a fight?"

A great shout of anger responded to her words and some had been offended enough to reach for their swords. Raising her hands, Jne called for quiet that came slowly and then not completely so that she was forced to shout above the din. "Along with an army of thousands, they have a wizard and giant creatures that rain death from the sky. I have seen and battled them myself. Their very skin is steel so that no sword can penetrate their hide while they breathe out death on all those who stand against them. It is such a creature that I am certain attacked my *Tja*, and if I am correct then there is very little hope that many, if any at all survived. This is the enemy that will overtake our own lands if we don't act now to gather the Tjal-Dihn in to fight back. The remaining HuMan army marches for Bedler's Keep where they make their final stand. Who will gather with me to give their life in head on battle rather than wait to be caught in their sleep and die in shame?"

Again, her words caused no small stir. The old woman at her side grabbed her arm forcibly and pulled her in the direction of her home. "Come child," she demanded in a tone that left no room for discussion. "You have spoken your piece and will have to know patience while your claims are discussed. The heated words that so easily flow when one's blood pulses from battle are not always chosen with the greatest care. Plus, your wound will have your life if you don't let me mend it straight away."

Jne resisted. "I will come," she sighed, the crowd breaking into smaller groups now to discuss her claims and whether or not they would accept them. "But not before I claim what is rightfully mine." The old woman let go of her arm as Jne turned back to her mother's body and gently removed her swords from her already cold hands. With some effort, she removed the sheaths from her back and replaced the swords that she now claimed as her own and carried in her hands. The body was then left for others to dispose of as was proper for a woman of her skill. Though she was beaten, Naye held no dishonor in her death and would be afforded all honor and dignity at her funeral pyre though none would come to mourn her loss. It was not the Tjal way to give ceremony to the dead but to burn the body quickly to keep disease in check and eliminate the smell of rotting flesh.

Jne followed the old woman, her thoughts suddenly dark dousing the inferno of joy that mere moments before had filled her at regaining her honor. The fires of battle were waning now and had almost completely been extinguished by the time they reached the old woman's dwelling. Leading her past the small foyer, Jne was taken through the cloth that covered the opening on the right into a large room in the back where she was invited to lie on a small couch while the old woman busied herself in gathering water, cloth, needle and sinew with which to stitch the nasty wound that still wept blood across Jne's chest.

Slipping down into the cushioned sofa, Jne was suddenly overcome with exhaustion. Whether from the loss of blood, the afterglow of battle or the release of so much emotion and worry she was not certain though the press of the cold, wet cloth on her wound brought her quickly back to full consciousness. The pain was enough to chase all wariness away as if demanding she fully experience the pain that came with stitching her up.

"I am Soyak," the old woman said with a smile as she pressed the needle through Jne's skin in the first of many painful pricks that were required to tie up her flesh. The pain was greater than she'd expected and more than once she whimpered as Soyak pressed the needle through her opened wound drawing with it the striped and dried sinew that acted as thread. How she wished Thane was there to use his Tane and close her gash with a single word. The thought of Thane brought a small smile to her face that was quickly replaced by a grimace as the needle again was pressed through her flesh.

Though her interactions with the crowd had been strained and difficult, she felt certain they would see the error in their thinking and send for others to come and help. It had been a risk to call in question their willingness to fight but she no longer felt like she had the time or the energy to speak with diplomacy. The Tjal were direct, never shying away from what was true and honest. She had merely followed those instincts though she admitted to herself that most likely Soyak had saved her life by insisting she leave when they did. Jne was in no position to fight another person on a question of honor. Another stab to her wound made her grip the cushion as if attempting to wrest the life from it. Each one seemed more painful than the last.

"How many more?" she asked through clenched teeth.

"Almost done, child," Soyak answered slowly, her full attention on her

217

work. "You will have a beautiful scar when it heals," she added and then bit off the surplus sinew she had just finished tying off in a knot. "There now," she said as she pushed herself up straight once more. "All finished. Just a little *eola* root juice to keep infections away and then a clean wrap and you'll be good as new in a week or two."

Jne forced a smile at the thought. A week or two could be all any of them had left if they failed at Bedler's Keep. Soyak disappeared into another room and then returned with the root she'd been looking for. No longer than her thumb, it was green and when she cut into it with her knife a thick liquid oozed out which she promptly spread over the stitches and then wrapped a clean linen snuggly around Jne's chest. "The *eola* will sting for a moment as it works itself down into the wound but will soon sooth away the pain to where you won't feel it much."

Jne's clenched fists were evidence that she understood the stinging part but soon she noticeably relaxed as the pain subsided into an almost numbing sensation. "Thank you," she finally breathed in relief, "I owe you much."

The old woman made a face and waved her off. "You *have* been *Jinghar* among the HuMans too long to forget the hospitality of the Tjal."

Jne smiled back and nodded but then quickly her mood returned to a serious one. "What do you feel about what I have spoken?" she asked without preamble. "Would you fight?"

Soyak's eyes flashed as if suddenly on fire. "Not would, child," she said, a warm smile creating added wrinkles to the many that already covered her face, "will! I have waited too long for the chance to leave this world in glory instead of—how did you put it?—wait to be caught by it in my sleep and die in shame."

"But will the others come?" Jne pressed, still a little desperate about their situation yet warmed slightly by the vigor of this old woman.

Soyak shrugged. "None can know. Each has to choose for himself."

Jne nodded, her face suddenly very pensive. "You speak truth but I cannot wait any longer to find out. I fear my time here has already been too great and that the battle might already have been fought and decided."

Soyak bounced on the balls of her feet like an excited child. "I will get my things then and we can leave as quickly as we retrieve our horses."

Jne gave her a surprised look that swiftly turned into a smile of gratitude and acceptance of her offer as a loud gurgle sounded in her stomach reminding her that she hadn't eaten for some time.

Soyak laughed. "After, of course, we bid goodbye with a small feast to fill the void that has apparently settled into your belly."

"And," Jne added, her eyes suddenly becoming distant, "a certain purchase I must make."

"What type of purchase?" Soyak pried.

"A *svaj* for the one I will marry."

Chapter Twenty-Two

It was dusk when the rocs finally touched down a safe distance outside of Aleron. What would have taken close to a week had been accomplished in two days thanks to the strength and persistence of their carriers. The birds were on the verge of exhaustion, as were the six people they bore. Domis fell from Azaforte's back and practically hugged the ground vowing he would never fly again. The excitement that had originally bubbled out of him at finally being able to ride was quickly sapped and drained from his mind just as the food had been from his stomach. Teek had warned him that it had taken him multiple rides before the changes in pressure and the sudden dips caused by wind flows ceased to bother him. Domis no longer felt the desire to reach that point. He was certain that he'd thrown up everything he'd ever eaten in his life that first day they took to the air. Only Thane's speech on duty and his part in saving thousands of lives got him onto the bird's back for the second day's flight; that and the threat of Jace's steel. He'd ridden Debipena the first day so switched to Azaforte the second thinking it might help but to no avail.

Jace and Ranse didn't look much better though neither of them had actually thrown up. Domis figured that Jace was too hardened to allow himself to be sick while Ranse, being royalty and all, probably was not physically capable of doing so in the presence of others. Neither dropped to the ground so unceremoniously as Domis had but neither did they move about much as if waiting for angry stomachs to settle.

The three Tjal clad Chufa, on the other hand, seemed almost unaffected save only for the scowl on Dor's face. Though he didn't have the ghost-like countenance shared by the others, he was still nothing like Thane or Tam who almost beamed with exhilaration and seemed sad that the ride was already over.

Thane stretched a bit looking north and then south down the hard packed road that led to and from Aleron. It was empty. "How far?" he asked, addressing no one in particular.

Ranse came up next to him while looking about intently. "From the last we saw it from the air and the area we are in now, I would say about a mile but no more than two."

Thane nodded. "Good. That will put us there just at dark. The fewer eyes that see us the better. We don't have time for the normal HuMan to Tjal rituals."

"We could always take these cursed rags from our heads," Dor snickered, his voice laced with mischief. "That would certainly eliminate any worry about Tjal-Dihn."

Ranse smiled while Jace just stared, his eyes cold and unreadable. Dor paid him no mind though, having become accustomed to death incarnate, as he liked to think of him. Jne was cheery and bubbling over with kindness compared to the prince's bodyguard who only seemed to find pleasure when blood dripped from his sword. Not that Jace was evil or bloodthirsty but more like a craftsman who was anxious to be about his trade; constantly at work to improve his skills.

"As long as there's a bath and hot meal at the end of our road tonight," Tam voiced her opinion, her tone still too cheerful for Domis and his angry stomach, "I'll be whatever race you want me to be." Domis eyed her questioningly but didn't put voice to his query.

Thane was surprised at the lack of security that met them when they reached the city's outer edge. Though the road that carried them was void of any vegetation, allowing the single guard a long look at whoever approached, there was no wall. The whole city was open on the north side. The only visible defensive measure was the river that ran past, which was, in its own right, wide and deep enough for boat travel, but not so much to stop an army with the will to sack the town.

Thane's questioning look was quickly addressed by Ranse. "The city wall is on the south side, for that is where the danger lies. It is not what might approach on the road but what might come out of the Underwoods that begs for defense."

"Until now," Dor spoke softly though all heard him.

They stopped short of the long and high bridge that spanned the water giving easy access to any who decided to enter the city. It was tall enough to allow rafts or oared boats to pass under but not so large as to permit ships of any grand size. Docks with signs touting different venders and wares dotted the south side of the river, though most were empty at such a late hour and a majority of the workers were already sinking their worries into a pint of ale at their favored pub. No other traffic passed them on the road as they met the guard left at the bridge's entrance.

"State yer business," he demanded with a sharp accent that Thane had not heard during his time on this side of the Shadow Mountains. He eyed Thane, Dor and Tam without showing much interest in the other three and it was obvious by the expression on his face that he didn't know whether to draw his sword or run screaming for help.

Though Jace looked as if he'd just as well put his steel into the man's gut as waste time squabbling with him, Ranse smiled slightly while producing the royal emblem from beneath his tunic. Upon seeing it, the man quickly snapped to attention sputtering out apologies and begging forgiveness while his eyes still darted back to the three Tjal clad Chufa. "My apologies, my Lord. We don't git, much of royal blood in these parts."

"I understand," Ranse said easily. "Where is the city commander?"

The guard hesitated, licking his dried lips while glancing at the disguised Chufa trio. "Well, that's right hard to say," he finally said, his eyes hardening as if he at last found a reserve of courage as he attempted to stare down Thane, Dor and Tam all at once. Dor's slight smile seemed to disquiet him though and his glare strayed quickest from his direction.

Ranse sighed. "I don't have time for your games or your peacock show of bravado. I am not a hostage to the Tjal, nor do I have the patience or time to sooth your ego, so I suggest you answer my questions forthwith before I have you brought up on charges for insulting the royal family."

Thane's eyes widened a bit to hear Ranse talk in such a manner. The prince had always been such a mild soul, especially when it came to his being of royal blood, though he did appreciate the response it solicited as the guard's face drained of all color.

"Beggin' yer pardon, my Lord," he stammered, stiffly bowing multiple times before standing as stiff as he could without causing himself injury. "The commander is most likely having his dinner at the Orc and Swine Inn right about now. It's just over the bridge and up the road here, you can't miss it. Best Inn in town, I'd say it were. Might even suit the likes of yer royal self, my liege." Suddenly catching what he'd just said, and clearly worried he may have offended the prince, the guard quickly added, "Though, I'm sure that nothin' could actually compare to yer royal courts as is found in our humble border town."

Ranse smiled at the man, his agitation gone. "Thank you," he said and then placed a gold coin in the man's hand. "This ought to cover any inconvenience that might arise from you letting my Tjal friends into the city armed."

The man looked greedily at the coin, not really hearing what the prince had said until they were already over the bridge and approaching the first row of buildings. By now darkness had almost completely fallen on the city giving way to the long shadows created by the occasionally lit street lamp. Splashes of light from shops that were still open or the infrequent inn or pub lighted the coble street sufficient to make ones way yet leaving many a dark alleyway the safe haven for those who would cause mischief or harm to the unwary passerby.

Thankfully the streets were already barren of those who bustled about making their trade or purchased goods during the daylight business hours leaving only the rare straggler seeking out refuge for the night or making his way to the nearest drinking hole. And even so, no one dared bother a group such as the one that strode boldly up the center of the street. If Jace was not enough to make one think a second time before harassing their small group, three Tjal-Dihn sent people running in the opposite direction.

True to the guard's word, they soon found the Orc and Swine Inn not too far away from where he said it would be. Two large oak doors with stained glass windows marked the inn as one of greater repute, though seeming somewhat out of place with its surroundings. Aleron was not a city that concerned itself with separating its citizenry into classes and areas as did Calandra. Anyone's money was good enough whether that person be wealthy or pauper. An orc decorated the window on the left side door, its face pulled back in a snarl while the right held a depiction of a large swine wallowing in the mud. What they had in common was lost on the Chufa as they followed Ranse and Jace into the inn tagging Domis along behind them.

The main room was hazy with the smoke of a dozen pipes that were being dragged on by various patrons throughout the large room filling it with the odor of various scents ranging from hickory to chickweed. Few candles dotted the walls and tables and the fire was somewhat low in the right corner giving the room a hushed feeling. The innkeeper, though maintaining a reputation of keeping to only the finest of clientele, knew that when gambling and ale were mixed, all too often, things got broken. He had discovered that a dimly lit room helped encourage a more mellow feeling in the patrons and so kept the candles to a minimum. Even so, the main hall was not so dark as to conceal the ethnicity of the newly arriving guests—three in particular. An immediate hush fell over the room as all eyes strained to stare at the newcomers without actually looking right at them. Being on the doorstep of the Underwoods Forest created a hearty lot of people in Aleron, but none were foolish enough to test the fragile line between honor and dishonor when it came to the Tjal-Dihn, especially when merely looking at one for too long or in the wrong manner invited steel to one's throat.

Ranse seemed to ignore the reaction that his friend's had caused and instead quickly scanned the tables until he found the person he was searching for. Over by the fire, sitting alone with an untouched plate of food and two pints of ale—one already empty—sat his quarry. It wasn't so much that he wore anything that might mark him as one employed by the crown or even as a soldier, for that matter, but the air he set about him seemed to scream authority as well as the fact that he was the only one looking directly at them. Such a man was either a fool or one accustomed to being in charge and having the responsibility of protecting those around him. Ranse could almost hear the thoughts that surely passed through the high commander's mind, trying to remember the duty roster and the idiot that allowed three Tjal to walk into town with their weapons displayed, as if in challenge, against their backs.

The prince led the others through the maze of tables leaving cringing patrons as they passed until he reached the commander and dropped into a chair at his table without the slightest word of greeting or a by your leave. "Fear not, commander," he said as the commander's eyes darted from him to the four figures that quickly surrounded the prince; poor Domis would not have been noticed had he jumped on the table and reeled a jig while singing *The Master's Coming Home*. "My friends will not cause any trouble, as long as none is visited on them," he added as almost an afterthought. "I am Prince Ranse," he said, using the title he no longer held while flashing the royal symbol that confirmed the station that went with it. "Is there a place more, private, where we can discuss matters of extreme import and urgency?"

The commander's gray eyes fell back on the prince, though his expression remained neutral. He was older than all of them, though not by too many years, yet his lifestyle had taken its toll on his features marking them hard and worn at the same time. Though probably once a handsome man, the luster of youth had been roughed away by the life of one set to protect the hostile boarders that were Aleron's southern fringe. The scars of that life were etched all over his body and were too many to count and less noticeable than the one that screamed for attention just below his left eye that ran down his check and finally ended at the side of his chin.

The commander regarded the prince for a long moment, his eyes barely moving to take in his Tjal friends as if trying to gauge what his chances might be to escape a fight with his life. Letting out a sigh, as one recognizing that his fate could not be altered, he leaned back in his chair. "Though the bauble you so easily flash would suggest you are who you say, I have to admit that I have never heard of a prince Ranse in the royal household."

Ranse's hand instinctively rose to motion Jace back though whether he did it knowingly or just as a reflex was unclear. The gesture was not lost on the commander who flashed a look at the prince's bodyguard as if seeing him for the first time. "Nor would you likely since my place in line for the throne is sufficiently distant as to make my life almost without general knowledge to the masses. But," he continued without the slightest tinge of anger at the commander's declaration, "this *bauble*, as you so call it," he said dangling the royal sign once more for added effect, "confirms my claims no matter whether you have heard of me or not. And the information that I have come to pass on to you is even of more import than my genealogy or your doubts regarding it."

"Be that as it may," the commander countered, "we here on the boarders have our own issues to deal with and can't be bothered with the intricacies of the court and its...excesses."

Ranse could feel, more than hear, Jace's hand reaching for his sword at the latest insult and he knew that at that point there was nothing he could say or do to stop his large friend from pulling his weapon in defense of his prince's honor. But what he hadn't counted on was the speed at which Thane suddenly leaped across the table, drawing his two scimitars while doing so, and then pressing them menacingly against the commander's throat. Those around the table stood frozen as if made of stone while a sudden rush of chaos filled the rest of the room as the Inn's patrons quickly fell over one another to reach the large double doors and the relative safety of the darkened city streets beyond. Even the innkeeper disappeared through the swinging door that led to the kitchen at the back.

"Enough of this talk," Thane breathed, a look of death overshadowing his face. Tam caught her breath at how much like a real Tjal-Dihn warrior he appeared at that moment, a shiver of trepidation shooting up her spine. The commander, to his credit, did not move as if having earlier conceded in his own mind that he would no survive this night. The look of surprise that crossed Jace's face at Thane's ability to move and unsheathe his swords before he even got his out brought a smile to Dor's face, his attempt to suppress it failing miserably.

"Well," Ranse said, almost masking the surprise in his voice, "it would appear that the room has suddenly made itself one of privacy for us." Leaning forward, he continued. "And now that I have your full attention,

I want you to listen carefully to what I have to say and I think you will find that my problems have, of a sudden, become your problems."

The commander tried to swallow to wet his suddenly dry throat but the press of Thane's blades made it rather difficult and nodding was out of the question. "I'm listening," he said in the half whisper he could just manage.

"Good," the prince said, and then continued. "To help you along, I'm going to ask you two questions first. What is the typical number of attacks you deal with monthly from orcs out of the Underwoods?"

Though failing to see how this would help him, the commander responded quickly. "About one per week."

"Now," the prince went on without the slightest indication as to how he felt about the commander's first answer, "I want you to think hard before you answer the next question. When was the last time you were attacked?"

The commander didn't move but his eyes betrayed the thoughts that passed like lightning through his mind. *How did the prince know*? It had been a welcome reprieve, yet had weighed heavily on the commander's mind for quite some time. While most would see the sudden end of attacks as a gift from above, the commander knew that more than likely it was an ill omen of even worse things to come. And now, suddenly, he felt that doom; not from the steel poised to severe his head, but from the words he anticipated coming from the prince's mouth. "It has been forty-eight days this very night," he responded. "And you know why." It was a statement more than a question. Why else would the prince have come to Aleron?

Ranse watched him for a moment as if judging the commander's resolve. He was right when he'd said that he didn't know the prince. No one here would. And Ranse knew that without the commander they wouldn't get the men to budge from where they stood. He needed to win him over and convince him to move his men to the Keep. "Thane," he finally said, waving him off. Thane only hesitated for a brief moment before putting his swords away almost as quickly as he had drawn them. "The orcs have left the Underwoods," Ranse said in a tone that left no room for argument. He paused to gauge the commander's reaction but his features did not change. "They have joined with troll and goblin under the command of an evil sorcerer who is intent on destroying all that resist him." Now the commander's face betrayed him. It was too ludicrous a statement to falsify since even the smallest child knew that never would such races spend even the briefest moment together without fighting amongst themselves. And now for the ultimate test. "Haykon and Calandra have already fallen."

"That can't be," the commander breathed, "Haykon and Calandra fallen?"

"In mere hours," Ranse replied, his face set like stone.

"How is this possible? How does one command an army that would kill itself off with infighting before they had the chance to attack anyone else?"

Ranse pressed him. "The questions of why and how are luxuries we no longer have the time to contemplate. It's what we do to counter that matters and the ability to resist is rapidly slipping past us." Ranse had the commander's full attention now and his training as a soldier was finally overcoming the overwhelming feelings of hopelessness that naturally followed such news as the overthrow of the capital city.

"We must make for Bedler's Keep," the commander suddenly interjected to the surprise of all. "It is the only place defensible enough to hold off such an army as the one you describe."

Ranse smiled, though his surprise at the commander's interjection flashed across his face. "That is precisely why we are here. How long will it take you to gather your army to march for the Keep?"

Chapter Twenty-Three

Domis stuffed a loaf of bread into his pack before deciding it would be a good idea to add another. The shop was empty save for him and the three Tjal clad Chufa who were busy filling their own packs. It had been like this all morning. Commander Garet didn't wait for morning after hearing what Prince Ranse had to say about the invasion. He immediately left the Inn with the prince and Jace to seek out his captains to ready the army to move. It had been determined that those able to fight would leave immediately while the rest of the city could come later or stay according to their desires. This mission needed speed and necessity dictated that they could not wait or be slowed down by carts, merchants or the elderly and infirm. Cruel as it was to leave the city almost defenseless, the fight would be at Bedler's Keep where no one would be safe should the battle go against them.

Thane's group, on the other hand, needed to ready themselves for a different journey and had the night to rest before preparing to leave the following morning. Domis had never laid down on such a comfortable bed in his life and was disappointed to the extreme that sleep seemed to elude him most of the night as the anxiety and excitement of what he was about to be part of overtook him. He found it strange that Thane and the others forwent the comfort offered by the best room and beds in the Inn to sleep on the floor. Apparently they were more than comfortable though as their snores quickly became his lullaby songs.

They were up with the sun the following morning and found they had to fix themselves breakfast as the Inn was completely empty of guests or service staff. Luckily, the kitchen was well stocked leaving them to feast on venison, cheese, day old bread, onions, peppers and even fresh milk that the innkeeper must have left early that morning before they were up. Even with armed Tjal-Dihn in the building, the cow still needed to be milked.

After filling themselves they had departed for the town center where they'd hoped to supply themselves for whatever might greet them in the Underwoods. Every shop they'd entered had been the same. At first sight of their garb and the wicked looking swords attached to their backs, the patrons and shopkeepers alike immediately raced from the store leaving it completely open to whatever they decided to take. They were so overwhelmed by this at the first shop that they waited for the merchant to return so they might pay him for the goods they needed, but it evetually became evident that no one was coming back. So, they left the money they thought was fair along with a little extra for the bother and went on to the next shop where the same thing occurred again.

"You'd better put in a third," Tam said, looking over her shoulder at him while stuffing a loaf into her own pack. She had taken to mothering Domis ever since finding out about his past and the events that brought him to where he was now. She'd asked about his parents only to find out that his mother left when he was very young and that his memory of her was only that her hair was long and deep brown. His father, who was employed as a guard at Haykon, raised him as best he could but was killed in a goblin raid near Nomad's pass when he was just five years old. From then on he worked in the stables and was cared for by the rough men that had made up Haykon's city guard drifting from home to home on occasion but finding himself sleeping most often in the warm hay in the stables with the animals he cared for. Tam felt a strong pang of regret for the boy that his life had been so filled with tragedy and difficulty. She had faced her own hard trials of late, but a loving mother and father were always in the back of her mind to give comfort when things got particularly bad.

"We will resupply at the armory before we go," Thane announced before tying up his pack and placing some gold on the counter for the baker.

Tam watched him for a long moment, the sudden sense that she was no longer seeing the childhood friend of her youth blanketing her in a shroud of sorrow. He was different now; especially since Jne had left. She supposed it was out of necessity to their situation and that need had hardened him to the tasks he was forced to complete, yet she longed for those days of greater innocence when a smile came more quickly to his lips than the seemingly permanent scowl that, of late, had taken up residence there. Dor, on the other hand, seemed unaffected. He was serious when the moment called for it, but his childish side was still ever present, the mischievous part of him lurking just behind his dark eyes. Cinching her pack she followed Dor, who flashed her a quick smile, before they all exited back onto the street.

It was obvious that word had gotten around about them as the street, that would normally be overcrowded in any other city this time of day, was almost completely empty. Thane turned to the left leading them deeper into the city's center while the others fell in behind without a word. She supposed that having the crowds dispersed at their coming was a blessing in that it allowed them to be quick about their business, but Tam couldn't help the feeling of eeriness it caused her.

Thane finally pulled them up short at a shop that was obviously an armory by the stack of swords in a barrel outside. Though simple on the exterior, with not even a sign to announce itself, the inside was a complicated mosaic of every sort of weapon anyone could possibly want or think of. Crowding the walls and more barrels throughout the space it was almost dizzying to look at. They all entered, eyes darting about and Tam almost missed a step when a form suddenly emerged from the shadows behind one of the display counters. A thin man, though muscular in build as would be expected of one who spent his days at the forge. He was clean shaven and nondescript in appearance though he exuded confidence without the slightest show of fear. Not the sort that was brought about by too much ale but the quiet assurance that ability and expertise brought to a person who had developed the skills to defend oneself in battle.

"Finally," Thane said, the slightest taste of derision tingeing his voice, "someone with the backbone to deal with us directly."

The man bowed slightly at the backhanded compliment. "Unlike the others," he said easily, "I understand the honor of the Tjal and welcome it."

For the first time that morning, Thane finally felt himself at ease. He hated pilfering through the property of others while searching out the goods they needed. Even though they paid them more than was fair upon leaving, it still left him with a dirty feeling that had placed him in a foul mood. He knew all too well the way people were and he imagined that more than one of the places they visited would make claim that their goods had been stolen by the Tjal while pocketing the overpriced amounts they received. Thane bowed his head slightly. "We need arrows and a sword and dagger for our young friend."

Domis' head snapped from the swords he was looking at to where Thane and the shopkeeper stood. Did he hear correctly? His own weapons? "Do not be so excited," Thane said, as if he'd heard his thoughts since his back was still to the young boy. "We fit you with weapons only because we know that more than likely you will need them to keep your own life."

Turning his head to look Domis straight in the eyes, he added, "Killing is a dreadful undertaking."

Domis dropped his eyes, his lips creasing into a frown. Tam slipped an arm around his shoulder while burning fire from her glare through Thane's skull but he merely glanced at her before turning back to the merchant. "Come and let's look at the daggers," Tam said pulling Domis to the far side of the shop.

"And the types of arrows?" the merchant asked, poorly masking his surprise. Tjal-Dihn didn't use arrows. "Where might you be using them?"

Thane turned back to the man, his face a cold mask. "We take to the Underwoods."

The man nodded slowly and then caught himself. "Then you will want something for close distances and maximum penetration," he said returning to the man of business who'd met them when they came in. "I have just the thing."

Though Thane had placed a slap of reality to Domis' excitement over getting his own sword, the stable boy could not help the extra bounce in his step as they exited the smithy's shop. Somehow he now felt older and of greater significance with the sword belted to his waist and swinging against his leg to the cadence of his stride. Thane routed them back toward the Inn and would have left them all behind had they not quickened their pace to keep up. Though the streets were all but empty it became no easy task as Thane was determined in his step.

They met Ranse and Jace just coming out of the Inn as they approached. "We were just looking for you," Ranse said after hailing to them. "We should be prepared to leave in the morning. I assume that is when you will depart as well?"

Thane shook his head. "We were just coming to see that all is in hand with the soldiers and then we are prepared to depart immediately."

Ranse reached a hand out and grabbed Thane's arm. "But it is nearly midday. You will be starting into the forest with most of the day behind you already. It would be best if you waited until the morning."

Thane shook his head again. "No, we are ready now and we have not the luxury of time to dawdle away. If there still are some of my people's trees left, we need to find them now and get back to the fight."

"But the forest is evil, Thane. Yes, the orcs are gone, but there are other things that lurk about in those woods that would give the bravest man pause."

"It will be just as evil in the morning as it is now," Dor interjected. "The forest is our home. We will be safer than most within its cover."

"Not this forest," Ranse countered.

"It matters not," Tam added, not willing to be left out. She'd been cowering for so long now since her captivity with the trolls that she was becoming sick of her own skin. It was time for her to tap into the feisty girl she once was and make a difference. "Our minds are set. We go now, and the mother help anything that gets in our way; within or without the forest."

Thane and Dor stared at her as did the prince until her challenging glare made them all turn away. "We will make the Keep as soon as we are able," Thane finally said. "There is yet hope in this war and we tend to bring it to you."

Ranse just nodded his head and then pressed a firm grasp on Thane's arm. "Stay well, my friend. We need you."

Thane nodded back but said nothing.

Then, to everyone's surprise, Jace spoke. "Keep your blades sharp and your enemies at your feet."

Thane nodded to the weapons master and then turned and strode up the road toward the south gate. Each in turned did the same until Domis, who bowed deeply, and then ran after the others, his sword flopping against his leg.

Reaching the others, and the secure arm that Tam draped kindly around his shoulders, Domis looked up at her quizzically as if he might ask a question but then dropped his head with a slight shake and a sigh. Catching his mood and recognizing that a inquiry burned in his skull, Tam gave his shoulder a squeeze and gave him an encouraging smile. "What is it, Domis?" she asked. "What has you so tied up inside that holds you back from the question I see desperately trying to escape?"

He shrugged his shoulders. "It's just that…"

"Yes?" she encouraged.

"Well, I don't quite understand what we're about, exactly. I know we seek some special sort of tree that makes special arrows, but I don't understand what Tjal-Dihn have to do with the Underwoods forest. Don't you come from the Enn?"

Thane and Dor turned to stare at the young boy as Tam looked up at them questioningly. All stopped in mid stride and Domis took a step backward suddenly fearful at having three sets of Tjal eyes boring into him.

Tam coughed, trying to dispel the sudden tension that seemed to come over them. "Well, Domis, that's an interesting question that…"

Thane cut her off. "Let us remove to a less conspicuous spot to discuss this," he said motioning to a nearby alleyway.

Domis had never had cause to fear his Tjal friends, always finding them friendly and nothing like the stories he'd heard—accept maybe for Jne. But he couldn't stop the shiver that suddenly seemed to take his frame in convulsing pulses. Had he offended them? Why the alley? Was he to be killed and his body left in the trash piled up between two buildings?

Tam flashed another questioning look at Thane but he ignored it and moved to lead them into the dim lighted alleyway situated between two competing bakeries. Checking to make certain they were alone, he regarded the young stable boy whose eyes darted back and forth between them.

Tam placed a hand on Thane's arm, as if to beg him to not scare the boy anymore than necessary but he seemed to ignore her. "You ask a valid question, Domis," Thane finally spoke, "and you deserve an honest answer. But, before I give it, I must have your word of honor on your life that you will keep what I am about to reveal in strict confidence and silence, agreed?"

Domis looked at Tam, who smiled warmly at him. "It's all right," she said. "We are your friends and would never harm you."

"Are we agreed?" Thane pressed.

Domis swallowed hard, but then straightened his back bringing himself up to his maximum height. "On my life," he breathed with only the slightest quiver to his voice.

Thane eyed him hard as if daring him to change his mind. "Hold him," he said to Dor.

"What?" Tam and Domis asked in unison.

"For his own protection," Thane replied. "We can't have him running into the street screaming."

"But why would I do that?" Domis asked, his voice less firm as Dor moved behind him and took a strong hold of his arms.

Tam flashed him a withering look but Dor just shrugged. "There is no reason to fear," Tam said to the young boy as Thane reached up and started removing his *Dihne*.

"We are not Tjal-Dihn," Thane said as he pulled the last of the cloth from around his head. "We are Chufa."

Domis' eyes widened as he took in the pointed ears that broke through Thane's black hair. Dor tightened his grip on his arms while Tam rubbed a soothing hand down his arm.

∗   ∗   ∗

Aleron's southern wall soon loomed over them as they approached the cities only real defense. Made of tall, sturdy timbers with mortar packed seams, it was twice Thane's height plus a little more making it impossible to overtake without hooks and ladders. In the past, such a wall may have served them well, but the war they now faced was something completely different. And should Bedler's Keep fall and they fail in its defense, the safest place to hide would most likely prove to be on the wall's southern side, in the cover of the Underwood's forest.

Domis almost skipped along next to them, the smile on his face barely contained as his eyes darted back and forth between his companions. His reaction to Thane's revelation had been a surprise to all of them. No screams of terror escaped his lips or struggling attempts to flee, but instead an overwhelming sense of awe had come over the young stable boy. In fact, it had taken them near one half of an hour to extricate themselves from the alleyway with all of the questions that had poured out through his lips. It was Thane's final insistence they be on their way that finally stemmed the curious assault Domis lashed out at them. If anything, he seemed all the more content now that he knew that he kept company with three Chufa instead of three mere Tjal-Dihn warriors.

As they drew near, the guard that had been at the bridge the night before stepped from the small building that marked his post and moved silently toward the gate. Apparently, Commander Garet had not forgotten the guard's blunder and as punishment was making him face the Tjal alone. Turning a wooden handle attached to a wheel next to the gate, he freed the mechanism that released the many gears and bolts holding the gate closed allowing the single large door to swing outward.

Standing a distance back, he motioned them through stating flatly, "I was left to open the gate for you and told to tell you that you should not try to return this way as the gate will be shut behind you and none will be left to attend it. The road into the woods is to the left about a quarter of a mile."

Thane simply nodded and without hesitation, walked through the large gate moving to the left. The others followed quickly until Domis, the last of their group, passed through, suddenly not so carefree and full of excitement as he had been mere moments before. Immediately the large gateway was pulled shut and the locks reengaged into place giving a sense of finality and irrevocability. And though the guard had said that they could not return that way, the sound of the locks against the closed entry gave Domis the distinct feeling that they wouldn't be returning at all.

A short fifty yards of dirt was the entire buffer offered between the wall and the forest whose trees looked dark and twisted. Those on the edge almost appeared tortured as if they yearned for the covering offered just beyond. Even the three Chufa, who were keepers of the woods, stayed almost pressed to the wall as they walked eastward seeking the road into the Underwoods. Thane kept his pace steady though he had the distinct feeling that they were not alone, that they were being matched in their strides by something just within the tree line.

All too quickly, a crack in the trees revealed itself as if made by a large wedge. Though not appearing as a normal road, or even a path, it was obvious that this was the entrance they searched for. Thane held them up shortly as he closed his eyes and sent himself forward, reaching out to the trees, trying to decipher what was just beyond that might threaten them. As his senses brushed past the first row of vegetation he immediately pulled back his eyes snapping open. He was surprised to find his swords in his hands and a look of shock on his friend's faces as they reached for their own weapons.

"What is it?" Dor asked just barely bringing his own swords to bear.

"Pure evil," Thane breathed, forcing himself to replace his weapons. "I have never felt anything like it before. This forest is tainted with hatred and malevolence."

Tam and Dor looked at him dumbfounded while Domis just nodded his head in agreement. Never had the Chufa ever encountered anything in the natural plant world that would even come close to being considered evil; angry they had encountered, but never anything that was actually evil.

"What do we do?" Tam asked.

Wiping a bead of sweat from his forehead, Thane looked at her and then turned and started walking toward the opening. "We go on," he said.

Closing the distance quickly, Thane paused a brief moment before passing under the Underwood's canopy. Immediately his eyes switched to night vision as the sun was almost completely shut out. The air suddenly felt thick and oppressive as if a wet cloth had been placed over his face making it difficult to breathe. The others followed him in, experiencing the same sensations then Domis cried out, "I can't see!"

Reaching in his pack, Thane produced a rope that he tied around Domis' waist and then attached it to Tam's. "I will lead," he said completing the last knot. "You will follow me with Domis attached to you and Dor will stay at the rear."

Tam felt a sudden surge of protest at being stuck in the middle like a child to be protected but she quickly brushed it aside, seeing the wisdom in what Thane was doing. It wasn't her that he was protecting, but Domis.

"Keep close," he said, almost in a whisper. "If need be, we may have to tie the rope around all of us to keep us together. We don't want to lose anyone in here. I've a feeling that only a few steps from the road would swallow any of us up in this darkness."

Moving forward, the road almost immediately curved to the right and them back to the left as if with purpose to snuff out the tiny light that the entrance had afforded. Even the Chufa trio were hard pressed now to see in the dimness. To either side the trees grew so close together as to appear almost as one trunk creating the illusion that they walked through a corridor. The air was oppressive, not only in its weight but also in the dank, stale smell of compost created by the decaying undergrowth that got little to no sunlight. Neither was there any airflow or movement creating a humid mire of damp that pressed against the body and made breathing difficult.

Thane's skin seemed to prickle with the desire to be free from this cage of massive trees that should have given him a sense of home. Their type and breed were foreign to him in the way they twisted at the trunks and limbs. They were so tightly wrapped together that it was difficult to determine where one tree ended and another began. It was as if they were locked in a timeless battle for supremacy over the small spot of ground they occupied. No foliage could be seen at ground level, the leaves keeping to the highest reaches where they were used to shade the rest of the tree from the sun. Thane wondered if they all wouldn't wither and die should the life-giving light be allowed to shine through the canopy high above. The road was no wider than what would be needed to pull a small cart though he couldn't imagine a horse that would enter such a place.

The others followed without a word though their thoughts of gloom fairly scratched at the back of his head. He could almost sense the fear that gripped poor Domis whose desire for adventure had been suddenly quenched with the grim deluge of reality. Straining his ears, Thane was disturbed by the lack of sound that should fill a forest full of life. This one spoke only of death and its still echoes of silence were unsettling. The dirt on the road seemed to absorb the sound of their footfalls as well, making it unnecessary for them to use their skills of silent passing.

Even with his night vision, he couldn't see that far in front of them. It was like walking in a cave with a lantern held before you, the passageway ahead revealing itself only as you continued to move deeper into its bowels. It was unnatural as if dark magic were at work. Thane did his best to brush away the uneasiness he felt as he pressed on deeper though his body remained tense and his mind shouted for him to turn and run back to the light. The feeling he'd had earlier of being followed continued but was now mixed with a sense of eyes all around tracking their every move. He tried to brush it off but it would not be denied a presence in his mind. He knew that something must be out there but resigned himself to the fact that until it revealed itself he was helpless to defend against it. He would not leave the road to seek it out. For the time being he must be content to be the hunted though it grated his nerves to feel he was at its mercy.

Time soon became a cadence of steps, one after the other, that passed into the sense of a never ending march that was void of purpose other than the placing of another foot forward. Though the road moved in gyrations from left to right, there was no way to determine the passage of time or distance as they continued on with a sensation of lacking destination. It dulled their minds and weakened their senses almost to the point of not registering their surroundings or the dangers they might pose; so much so, in fact, that Thane did not realize they were under attack until he felt the pain in his left arm from the needle-sharp tentacle that shot out like a whip, piercing him with its barb and then pulling back leaving the sack tip stinger in his flesh. The pain was like fire burning up his arm as the poison pumped into his body before he had his wits about him enough to pull it free. More tentacles lashed out, their stingers seeking like tiny daggers searching for openings to take down their victims. Thane felt his arm go numb as he called out while pulling free his sword with his good hand.

Tam reacted the quickest, cutting off one of their attacker's arms just as its venomous stinger was about to hit Thane's throat. They could all see it now, just at the edge of their sight, a large, black plantlike creature that consisted of a bulbous body with hundreds of thin arms that lashed out like whips at its prey. Dor quickly moved up next to Tam as best he could though there was little space with the trees closing in on either side. Thane was able to deflect more attacks with the sword in his right hand but his left arm was becoming alarmingly limp. Domis was pushed back behind Tam though he found himself relatively calm. He'd seen and faced battle situations before and was not afraid to fight, given the opportunity.

More whipping arms shot out at them and it was getting more difficult to deflect them as Tam and Thane pressed for the same position. "You're hurt," Tam shouted at Thane, "move back. You're getting in my way."

Thane cut another arm but knew that without his other sword he could not match the speed at which the creature attacked. She was right. Stepping back he gave way to Tam who instantly became a whirlwind of lethal steel as her swords spun, dipped and sliced through every arm the creature threw at her. By this time, Dor had given up his swords for the more comfortable and familiar bow. Loosing two arrows quickly in succession he buried both into what he thought must be their attacker's head. He then shot two more as Tam deflected more arms that had abruptly slowed down in their offensive. Domis and Thane could only watch impotently as Dor shot two more arrows while he and Tam moved forward on their slowing assailant. A multitude of plantlike arms lay in the road twitching slightly as if in their final moments they were still trying to imbed their stingers.

Dor shot one final arrow that must have hit a vital organ as the arms suddenly went limp. Tam wasted no time in hacking at the creature with her swords until nothing but a pile of oozing gel seemed all that remained.

Returning to Thane, Dor tore the sleeve away from his friend's arm and could immediately see where the venom had been injected. It was swollen, but only in the area next to the puncture. Dor gave Thane a worried look. "Are you faint or nauseated?"

"No," he breathed, surprised. "It's only right around where the stinger hit me that seems affected. It's almost paralyzed."

Tam came over, cleaning her blades as best she could before sheathing them behind her back. "Is it bad?" she asked, concerned.

"I don't know yet," Dor replied, "but one thing is for certain, we need to try and get the poison out." He pulled his dagger but hesitated, waiting for Thane's consent.

Thane nodded. "Do it."

Pressing the dagger into his flesh, Dor cut right into the punctured skin. Almost immediately a dark gel oozed from the wound dripping into a pile on the ground at their feet. Thane could feel sensation quickly returning to his arm and was encourage to the point that he began to squeeze the flesh around the cut until he finally drew out some blood. Though it still hurt, it appeared that once the venom had been extracted, the paralysis left and his feeling returned. Tam cut a small piece of cloth she retrieved from her pack and wet it so she could bathe the wound and then tied a strip around Thane's arm to stop the bleeding.

Thane nodded gratefully when she was done, and moved his arm about as if to test its strength. "It feels fine," he declared.

All looked at what was left of the plant, realizing how lucky they were that only one of them had been stung and with only one venom pouch. It was easy to understand now how such an opponent could quickly render its victim powerless so that it might devour its prey at its leisure.

"We better continue on," Thane said, motioning them forward, "until fatigue takes us. I don't want to spend a moment longer in these woods than is necessary."

No one argued as they fell back into their march quickly putting distance between themselves and the plant. Thane was fully alert now, as were the others, not willing to so easily fall prey to something else. Soon the trees began to spread out giving way to gaps and off shooting trails that beckoned to and tempted the travelers. At more than one place Thane had to stop and examine the ground to be certain they were remaining on the trail and not being led off into the belly of the forest to become quarry to one of its dark host or to be lost forever searching for a way out. Direction had become all but compromised without the sun to direct them so their trust was placed on the trail that was said to empty out in the southeast near Willow Wood.

In had been close to an hour before Thane suddenly halted them, motioning they all squat down. Using hand signals, he directed their attention up the road where at least ten black forms crowded the road from either side. At first they appeared to be moss covered rocks but all soon recognized them as the same type of creature they'd met before. Had they not had their first encounter, they would have walked right into the middle of them. Backing up slowly, they retraced their steps to what they felt was a safe enough distance away and out of range.

"We'll have to leave the road," Dor said.

"We could kill them with arrows at a distance," Tam offered, but Thane shook his head.

"We may need our arrows for something else," he countered, looking around briefly. The sense of being watched had still not left him. He feared now that it appeared that they would have to leave the road he would finally find out what was stalking them. He could see the uncertainty in their faces and added quickly, "We need to move off the road...just long enough to get past."

All nodded their heads in agreement but none liked the decision. But the choice was not theirs to make. There was no other option to get safely through. "Just as a precaution," Thane added, "we'll tie ourselves together with the rope." Quickly linking them all together, he left enough space should they need to fight or maneuver but not so much that any would ever be out of eyeshot. The ground was soft and loamy underneath their feet as they left the road's hard packed dirt and moved to their left into the forest. Thane's instincts warned him that leaving the trail was dangerous but he comforted himself in the fact that they were only doing so briefly; just until they made it safely past those deadly plants. The ache in his arm was proof enough that they could not withstand so many and hope to make it past alive. Just a quick circle around and they would be back to the trail again.

Glancing back at the path, he could still just make out the line it cut through the woods. Veering to the right he took them parallel to it thinking they surely were far enough away from the deadly plants to pass through safely. But only a few steps further and he suddenly halted seeing another rounded form, its tentacles laid out flat in a circle patiently waiting for the unwary. Cursing under his breath, he waved them back further into the woods. Looking briefly over his shoulder, the road was no longer visible. The trees had also become thicker again as if anticipating they would leave the safety of the road, forcing the group to turn to the left and right to pass through.

Again, Thane tried to turn along where he was certain the road traveled but only got a few yards when another black, swollen plant, barred their way. Should they go back? He found himself becoming desperate. The longer they were away from the main path, the more likely they were to be attacked or lost and the day was quickly waning. But the desperation of their mission and what it would mean should they succeed far outweighed the risks.

Putting the memory of the road to his back once again, he led his friends even deeper into the woods. Time seemed to be passing rapidly now and he wondered how soon it would be before they were left in almost complete darkness as the sun set. He did not want to be in the forest proper when that happened. Turning once more, he strode tentatively on a parallel course with where he felt certain the path led. Praying for passage, he was relieved when no more stinging orbs barred their way. Quickening his pace a little, he cast aside his caution for silence and tried to make up for lost time.

A short distance was all they needed to go before they could turn to the side once more and get back to the trail. He let out a sigh as surely they would be there again in moments. Turning again to his right, he made haste though kept himself vigilant of any danger. A couple of times he was forced to his left because of trees blocking their way, but all the time he knew he was getting them closer to the road. An eerie cry suddenly echoing off in the distance ahead brought them all to an unsettled halt.

"What was that?" Dor asked in a hushed tone.

All stared with eyes wide, trying to will their sight to reach further and reveal the enemy that threatened. Tam thought she saw a shadow move to her left sending a chill racing through her to match the pace of her pounding heart.

"Back to the road," Thane called, pulling them all into a run as he raced headlong toward the path and the unnatural cry heard only moments before. Finding another of the deadly plants, he veered to the left. A high pitched wail, different from the first one, came from close behind them followed by hissing and clicking sounds. Dor chanced a glance back and saw three shadows slipping easily through the woods chasing after them and gaining quickly. Tam saw two more shadows materialize on their left.

"I think I saw something move!" Domis shouted pointing to the right. Dor followed his arm and saw two more shadows suddenly materialize as if they detached themselves from the very trees. Thane abruptly stopped and reversed his direction while pulling his swords and cutting himself free from Tam. Dor and Tam did the same while Domis fought with his own sword before finally freeing it from the scabbard. Placing themselves in a tight circle with their backs to the middle they peered out into the dark as the shadows slowed and surrounded them. Another cry echoed in the distance and the shadows suddenly rushed in.

The dark forms materialized into insect like creatures with five spindly legs attached to long bodies. Three of the legs were affixed to the back body segment with one on either side and the third out the back. The two front legs were joined to the upper body and had hooked claws that looked to be able to rip the flesh from any victim caught in their clutches. All their legs had curved spikes protruding from them like thorns on a flower. A mantas like head carried large sickle pinchers that snapped together in front of a huge mouth full of sharp teeth that released a raspy hiss. No eyes were visible giving them the appearance of being sightless.

Not waiting, Thane rushed forward, slicing the head of one of their attackers, dropping it to the forest floor before turning on another, just barely ducking under its swinging claw. Hook and steal clashed filling the air with a great ring as all were thrust into a melee of death. Tam dropped another when she ducked beneath its forward swing before coming up under it and slicing through its neck. Dor was also able to kill another while Thane knocked away an attack on Domis who, though somewhat inexperience, was holding his own.

For a moment it appeared as if they might escape as Thane dispatched another assailant but, suddenly, more shadows materialized into the insect-like creatures. Now where four had remained, five more joined the attack. The situation was quickly becoming desperate as hooks slipped past the steel defenses and ripped at arms, legs and chests carving out wounds that, though not life threatening, were increasing in number and in lost blood. Thane searched for a way out but was so occupied with the attackers that nothing seemed possible. Even in the daylight, on level ground, he knew they could not outrun them. He'd tried to move the group closer to one of the large trees to at least give them protection at their backs but there were too many now to allow any movement as even more appeared. Their only hope was to stay tight together but even that was becoming less and less of an advantage. Killing yet one more, Thane lost count of how many there were as more seemed to materialize as if sensing the feeding frenzy that was sure to begin in mere moments.

His heart sank as he sensed the feeling of certain doom overtaking him. Tam's face, though determined, belied what he knew was hopeless. He chastised himself for thinking they could do this alone. An army was what they'd needed to succeed. Domis made squealed grunts as the fear and awareness of his assured demise sent its icy chill through his heart. Only Dor's face showed the calm acceptance that seemed to overcome him when death's specter came for him. It was something Thane envied in his friend. Though he did not fear to step into the beyond neither did he seek to hasten his journey there.

The hooks were too many and coming at a quicker pace. Soon one would get through and then each would falter in turn leaving them as nothing but a memory that would, of itself, be lost sooner or late with the victory or defeat of their friends. Maybe it would be better to let it all go now instead of prolonging the inevitable. There was not much hope anyway that they would even find the YeiyeiloBaneesh, if they indeed still existed. And what if they did? How was he to make arrows from them to save the others from the dragons? It was foolishness.

Blocking one hook, Thane was too slow to block another that nicked his collarbone opening up yet another break in his skin, the blood mixing with his sweat. It wouldn't be long now. Another howl broke through the woods, much closer now, and an audible grown escaped the companions' lips at the call of still more of their foe coming to feast. But then, as if by some unspoken word, their enemies suddenly just all turned and then raced away, once again dissolving into mere shadows that quickly disappeared into the forest.

Gasping for breath, the friends looked back and forth, trying to make sense of their sudden retreat at the moment of certain victory. Their confusion did not last though as different forms began to appear, slowly materializing out of the darkness. Night was coming on and it was obvious that this new threat posed even a greater danger and that their original enemies knew to run rather than become the prey.

They raised their swords ready to defend themselves to the last but the previous battle had taken much of their strength that would be quickly exhausted against a new foe. Only five forms materialized from the shadows as a thick mist began to rise from the forest floor with the last rays of the afternoon sun quickly retreating and plunging the forest into total darkness. They were large, standing on four great, powerful legs that rippled with muscle and sinew beneath a dark, thick, hairless skin. Their paws were almost hand-like with tremendous claws that dug into the dirt flexing as if in anticipation for the coming kill. As tall as Thane, their large heads stared down at them with glowing eyes that seemed unaware of the closing night. A great, dog-like snout pushed forward, big fanged teeth pushing up and down along the jaw line as a snarl escape curled jowls, a mane of hair cascading down their backs.

Chapter Twenty-Four

Gorbrak circled lazily as he took in the destruction and mayhem that had been his gift to his master, Zadok. Smoke still rose from many of Calandra's buildings. The city had been completely ransacked by the army in search of shiny trinkets that dazzled the simple minded or, more importantly, flesh for the cook fires. The moans and screams of days before were all but gone now as most of the occupants had been discovered meaning the supply of fresh meat had dwindled. Though he would have eaten the humans if the need where great, he preferred the tenderness offered by the sheep that were corralled outside the city. Sure he'd had to kill of few orcs to stake his claim, but word had spread quickly when the dismembered parts of their ilk were found scattered about the area.

Night was fast approaching and fires were beginning to pop up all over the city where pockets of Zadok's tremendous army decided to wreak their chaos for the day. The distant cry of a woman rousted from whatever hole she'd found to hide in lifted in horror as her fate would soon be sealed on an open spit. Apparently there still was feasting in Calandra. Banking left, Gorbrak allowed himself to descend on the once opulent city now reduced to refuse by its new tenants and glided toward the castle where Zadok had taken up residence while the city was being razed. He had a successful meeting with the town of Waterford that he needed to report before filling his belly with more mutton. It had almost been too easy and, like the others, he was wondering when Zadok would finally unleash their full power on the pitiful humans. He craved the fear that emanated from them and was so palpable and delicious to his senses.

Dropping easily into the spacious courtyard, he regretfully changed back into his pitiful human form and strode up the staircase that led to the main hallway and the thrown room beyond. Having captured the once king's favor so easily, he'd become rather adept at maneuvering his way through the many halls and corridors that was the governing seat of the land. How appropriate, he thought, that Zadok now filled the vacant throne where he commanded real power. His master looked up as he entered the grand hall, the damage he'd caused earlier a mere blemish on the grandeur of the room.

"Ah, Luvik," Zadok crooned, "back so soon?"

He hated it when Zadok called him by his human name. It was so demeaning to the powerful serpent that he really was. But, as other things, he patiently endured it finding the ultimate prize great enough to keep him loyal, not to mention Zadok's magic that was a constant tick in his head. "Yes, master, I have returned with another gift," Gorbrak hissed, preferring his own voice to his human one. He could at least hold to that. "The pile of rock and wood the humans called Waterford is no longer."

Zadok smiled, his grin so evil as to give even Gorbrak pause. He licked his lips as if tasting the victory in his mouth. "After the others report their successes we will then be ready to leave this dung pile for the real prize that waits us. I think the army has had sufficient playtime and that their bellies are plenty full. Tomorrow we will march."

*   *   *

Erl's constant growling finally brought Jack to his feet and to the tent's flaps. Erl beat him there but stood aside when Jack pushed at him with his leg. "What has gotten into you?" he practically growled back while exiting the tent. To his surprise, Tryg was setting out his bedding for the night his eyes narrowing fiercely at Erl who followed Jack out, his hackles raised.

"So, you've come back to us," Jack stated flatly.

Tryg released his glare for a face that was as close to innocent as he was ever able to draw up. "Yes," was all he offered in reply.

"So, where have you been to all this time," Jack probed and then added as an afterthought, "if I might ask."

Tryg regarded the old king for a long moment and then lowered his head as if in trouble. "It's still hard sometimes," he said with a somewhat melancholy voice though a touch of the typical acid still remained. "You know," he continued, "with what has happened to my people and all."

Jack just nodded though his eyebrows were knit in contemplation. He still could not figure out this boy. So much hatred for one so small. Though, he supposed that might be normal for one in his situation Teek seemed completely the opposite. "Don't know if you've heard, but Teek's missing."

He watched for a sign of shock or worry, or anything from the boy, but he just sort of shrugged his shoulders.

"Maybe he just needs some time alone. You know, like I did."

"Maybe," Jack said. "Anyway, are you hungry?"

At that, Tryg looked up at him and smiled sardonically. "No, I've already eaten."

Jack was about to press him but Wess suddenly appeared out of the chaos of tents that made up their camp. Rubbing Tryg's head, he completely missed the daggers the boy shot him before turning back to his bed roll mumbling something to himself that Jack figured could only be some type of threat.

"Good news," Wess announced.

"I could use some," Jack half smiled pulling back his tent flap and inviting him in. They both settled into the chairs that occupied the tent's first chamber while Erl dropped down in font of the doorway as sentinel.

"We're getting low on supplies," Wess stated to Jack's surprise.

"That's good news?"

Wess smiled, "No, but I figured I would throw that in at first when your spirits were up."

"It didn't help," Jack breathed pulling at his beard.

"Well, maybe this other bit will help. We're no more than a week from the fortress."

Jack just nodded. He'd guessed the same earlier in the day but with his Chufa friends gone there was no way of telling how close the enemy was or if they'd even left Calandra yet. With the slow pace they were forced to travel, he figured it wouldn't take too long for Zadok's forces to close the gap once they caught sent of their quarry.

"You're a hard man to please, Jack," Wess said when he didn't reply. "Well, I guess than this last bit won't be anything either, but we just got word from an advanced rider that Aleron's forces are marching at a quick pace and might even beat us to Bedler's Keep."

At that, Jack's face broke into a large smile. "Now, that is good news."

*   *   *

Soyak strapped her swords to her back, the worn leather almost becoming one with the contours of her body as if a piece of her returned. She smiled at how they felt, the welcomed return of a beloved family member. Reaching for the hilts, she drew her swords in one quick, fluid motion that would not have seemed possible for one of her advanced years. She relished their feel in her gnarled, old hands and swung them about in a complicated pattern before returning them to their scabbards just as quickly as she'd retrieved them. She breathed in the fresh plains air, taking in all her lungs would hold and then slowly let it out, knowing she would never have its scent on her nostrils again. She was going to war. She was going to die. But her swords would be bright with the enemy's blood when she did so. She was finally going to have her chance to leave this life with her honor intact.

Jne checked the supplies in her pack before hoisting it onto her shoulders. Placing a hand against a pocket on her belt, she felt the small lump that assured her the *svaj* she'd purchased just the day before was still there. Now with her honor and place returned she could pursue her purpose from the beginning when she'd first encountered Thane's limp form. It seemed so long ago now. The stone was a bright green emerald that she'd had the stone cutter shape into the sign of the five Tane and hung from a silver hoop. She would pierce his right ear with it as soon as they were together again and then on the day they married, he would remove it and pierce it through her left ear, claiming her as his own and she would remove the ruby *svan* from her left nostril and pierce it through his right nostril making him hers.

"You think of your man," Soyak stated plainly.

Jne looked at the woman now ready to depart and sighed. "And why do you say that?"

Soyak smiled knowingly. "Only thoughts of ones chosen can bring such a smile to ones face. I would see that glow in your eyes if we were in the deepest cave without so much as a spark for light."

Jne blushed slightly and turned away at having been caught. "I know not of what you speak," she said, though her voice seemed to say otherwise.

Soyak's smile only grew larger. "As you wish," she said simply and then dropped the subject. She would not shame Jne by forcing her to speak of something so private if she did not wish to. She gave her a long moment to compose herself and then ask if she was ready to depart.

"I am," Jne replied with resolve. The Tjal would spend a few more days discussing what she'd said before making any kind of collective decision. She'd done her best to convince them of the approaching danger and now it was up to each individual and each *Tja* collectively to decide their own path. They knew where to find the fighting if they so chose. Her path was set and she would not veer from it.

*   *   *

The pounding of drums was all Teek could hear as he raised his hands to his ears and tried to block out the noise; but it did no good. If anything, the pounding was louder and was now so intense as to shoot through his head like steel spikes. He had to get away but he felt as if he were shut up in a dark closet. *Boom, boom, boom* it came like a steady cadence that seemed to match the beating rhythm of his heart. Far in the distance he thought he heard a familiar sound; something that he felt he needed to find. Straining against the pounding he tried to focus on the recognizable noise that sounded again, but this time a bit more clear and near. Though it was no more pleasant on his head than the drumming, it filled him with a strange sort of warmth to hear it. Again it came, this time more demanding, more persistent. He wanted to race to it, to leave the drumming behind, but his body didn't seem to answer his commands. *Boom, boom, boom* it continued. He wanted to scream, the comforting noise, though grating, split through the drums again as if in desperation. He needed to get to it.

Consciousness suddenly crashed into him like a breaking wave, jarring him awake with such a jolt that he turned his head and threw up. He knew now what the drum sounds were as his head pounded with each beat of his heart. Again he heaved, his face screaming in pain as he did so. Tchee's screeching ignited the air with her cry as she called out in anguish over him and then suddenly cooed as she saw him moving. Darting her razor-like beak down she gently rubbed the side of her head against him while making what could only be exultant bird calls at his being alive.

Pressing the ground away, he forced himself into a sitting position and waited while the spinning in his head had completed its circuit and allowed him to focus once more. Tchee continued with her bobbing dance of exultant joy at his return to consciousness while Teek tried to grasp a greater sense of the reality in which he currently found himself. That his nose was broken was the first painful truth to force its existence into his mind as blood seeped from his nostrils, his sinus cavities aching. Looking down, he realized that he was covered in blood; some of it dried and flaking while most of it was set in the gel-like state of congealing. At first he was alarmed, thinking that perhaps he had suffered greater injury than he at first thought, but then he saw the dark, lifeless form of the large roc that had attacked them; the dead bird that he had killed in rage when it had swooped upon them from above.

A cold wind bit against his skin as he retrieved his fallen dagger and staggered to his feet. Anger pulsed through him at seeing the black bird as he remembered what had happened. Lifting his knife to the darkening sky, he let out a feral scream that reverberated across the mountain's face chasing vermin to their holes as it gained strength and then was cut short as his consciousness again betrayed him to the darkened corridors of oblivion.

Chapter Twenty-Five

The companions stood motionless as they took in their latest threat, all hope of survival with the coming attack gone. Dor found himself pushing back the Tjal head covering, not willing to give his life as anything other than the Chufa male that he was. He would not die pretending to be something else. As the material dropped to the ground, his short hair, wet with sweat dropped down just behind his ears leaving them in full sight. The snarling face of the enemy closest to him suddenly dropped to a look that almost appeared to be one of surprise as the beast abruptly sat back on its haunches and let out a strange whining sound. All the others did the same leaving the four defenders to wonder.

At that instant, Thane's mind was overpowered by the thoughts of the huge animal standing in front of him who had suddenly changed from a vicious and wild animal to something more akin to a favored pet. *"You have returned, forest child!"* his thoughts spoke cheerfully. *"Long now have we awaited your return to once again reclaim these woods. We are honored to be the first to serve."*

"I can hear him," Dor gasped in astonishment.

"So can I!" Tam added just as amazed.

"I don't hear anything," Domis complained. "What is happening? Are they going to eat us or not?"

Thane turned to the others sharing their wonder. "You can hear him?"

"We speak to all the forest children," the creature said. *"We are the* Kybara, *servants to the chosen. Has it been so long? Are we forgotten?"*

"What do you mean, servants to the chosen?" Dor asked.

"*We serve the forest children. We serve those chosen to shepherd the sacred woods.*"

"And we are the chosen ones you speak of?" Thane asked.

"*Do you not know your own ancestry? Are the days so long that memory has been lost?*" the Kybara asked, his tone turning from elation to sorrow. "*Have you not returned to make right the forest again; to cultivate what is left and return it to its former glory?*"

Thane looked at his friends whose faces bore the same confusion that muddled his own thoughts. Domis' calls for explanation had ceased as he determined that they would not be eaten today though he knew his dreams would overflow with these creatures in the coming nights; if he could ever sleep again.

"What do you mean cultivate what is left?" Tam voiced the question before either of the other two could.

The Kybara seemed to be getting somewhat restless and frustrated now by their questions. His growing sorrow was evident as he mentally replied. "*You are the tree shepherds, the keepers of the sacred woods, the cultivators of the great anchors. We thought you lost forever, but we have remained and protected what is left hoping someday you would return. And now you are here, but have you not returned to make what was lost right again?*"

Thane suddenly felt his heart begin to pound with growing excitement. If he understood the Kybara correctly then hope may not have abandoned them after all. Tree shepherds, sacred woods, and what had really made it seem clear, great anchors. Were not these all things that pointed to the once sacred woods of the.... "Do you speak of the YeiyeiloBaneesh?" he asked, the thrill evident in his voice.

He thought he could almost see the Kybara smile as his mental reply crashed into them, the sorrowful tone gone. "*You do remember! And are you here to make things again as they once were?*"

"So there are still some left?" Tam asked before the others could.

"Yes," the Kybara replied. "*We have kept them as best we could since the day of sorrow.*"

"Will you show us?" Thane gasped.

"*We will take you there. There are few that remain so their song is not as it once was to guide you but we know the way. Climb up and we will carry you as in the long ago days of peace.*"

As the others quickly scramble up the backs of the nearest Kybara, Thane turned to Domis. "Climb up," he said pointing to the great beast that had laid down to make it easier for him get on.

"What?" Domis asked in protest as the others seated themselves comfortably.

"Get on," Thane repeated. "They will take us to our destination. Your services as our guide have been given over to the Kybara."

"The Ky what?" Domis asked but was already moving to his patiently waiting carrier with Thane's prodding.

"Do not fret, my young friend," Thane soothed. "We will explain it all as soon as we understand ourselves."

That did not make Domis very confident but it was obvious that these great beasts meant them no harm and he was relieved that no longer would all eyes turn to him for direction, as if he could have given any. He understood that the only reason he was really even there was because he'd been promised he could go before Teek disappeared. The thought of his friend pricked at his heart. Where was Teek? He climbed onto the Kybara's muscular back; its dark skin was rough and felt thick. He reached forward and grasped the mane of hair that grew on its head, draping down its powerful shoulders brushing against its back.

Once all had gained their perch, the Kybara lurched forward, digging their sharp claws into the loamy dirt and pushing through the woods with the greatest of ease and speed. At first, all thought they might be immediately thrown only to crash headlong into one of the thick trees and break their necks, but the Kybara seemed to adjust to their movements so as to keep their passengers firmly attached to their backs. As if having memorized their surroundings, they passed through the close growing trees and thickets avoiding the great trunks and even the sting of the vine armed plants that had almost taken down Thane. The mist swirled at their passing as it continued to thicken with the darkness that crowded in as if trying to squeeze out any speck of light, but the Kybara didn't slow.

With night embracing the woods, the eerie quiet that blanketed the forest during the day was soon replaced by the sounds of the hunting and hunted as the struggles over life and death seemed to rise and diminish in a discordant symphony of death. None hunted the Kybara though as they raced through the killing ground unmolested or challenged. Looking back, Thane was shocked to realize that more had quietly joined their group increasing their numbers to near twenty that now fanned out on all sides as if a vanguard against anything that might dare challenge them.

Deep into the night the group continued its race through the woods as if chased by the specter of death itself. But neither did the Kybara slow or seem to tire. In spite of the constant jarring movements brought on by riding, all the companions at different points of the journey found themselves dozing off as the excitement of the ride and the possibilities surrounding their discovery faded into the exhausted recesses of their minds. All were jolted awake when they suddenly stopped allowing for a short rest and a quick meal. Others of the Kybara soon arrived with different carcasses of one type of animal or another leaving those who had been chasing through the night to fall upon the carrion and feed themselves. Thane was amazed at how organized the Kybara seemed to be. He also found, as the sun again battled to reach through the canopy overhead, that their numbers had grown even larger. All around were found the large, fierce looking creatures who had revealed themselves as ancient servants to the Chufa.

The one who had carried him approached, licking the blood from his jowls as he did so, and lay down next to him. "With all that happened last night," Thane said, cutting a piece of cheese from one of the rounds in his pack, "I did not have opportunity to thank you for saving us. We are fortunate you found us when you did."

"*It is I who should ask forgiveness,*" the thoughts flowed into Thane's head. "*We have tracked your progress since before you entered the woods. I should have come sooner.*"

Thane was somewhat taken aback. "So it was you who followed us?"

"*Yes. And had I known then who you were, we would not have waited to assist you. Though it is our custom to help those who travel these woods avoid the more vile creatures that make their homes here, we only interfere when absolutely necessary and when we determine that those we assist are deserving. And though your Tane called to us, it has been so long since we've heard the song in these woods, forest child, we wanted to be certain before revealing ourselves.*"

Thane found himself surprised again. "You can feel our Tane?"

"*Yes, chosen one, it calls to us and we respond to its voice. That is why so many have joined us in this chase. All have come to honor the return of the great one.*"

Thane looked around at all the other Kybara standing by watching them, and more particularly him. Even in such a horrific place he could feel the excitement in the air given off by those who had come to help. It suddenly hit him what his carrier had said. "The great one?"

"*You,*" was the simple reply.

"I am not the great one," Thane insisted, dismissing the claim with a wave of his hand. "Gelfin is. I'm Thane," he finished, though the remainder of his full name echoed in his mind unbidden.

"*Gelfin is no longer. You have come to replace him. You will make right what has been done.*"

"But why have you chosen me?" he argued. "I am one of many Chufa that still live."

"We have not chosen you, great one. The Tane has called you and is waiting to be loosed at your bidding."

Loosed at his bidding? He'd already done incredible things and wielded immense power through the Tane that coursed through his veins. The thought of there being more, and that even greater than what he'd already experienced, was almost too frightening to consider. It was a lot to take in. Not wanting to continue with this line of talk, he decided to turn it elsewhere. "How long until we reach our destination?" He couldn't bring himself to actually say the words that named the trees that were their last and only hope. As if to do so would turn luck against them and make it unreal.

"We have until this night, great one."

"Call me Thane," he returned, not wanting to be constantly reminded of the immense expectations that seemed to constantly fall to his shoulders to bear.

"And I am Aisig."

The group rested for a very short while allowing them to put something into their bellies and quiet the protests of hunger. The fog that had been their companion since the previous night was slowly seeping back into the forest floor as if returning to its diurnal residence to wait dusk's beckoning call. Though still ominous, the forest seemed somewhat less malevolent during the day when most of its predators had taken to whatever hole they buried themselves into to remain until it was time to hunt anew.

Tam fussed some over Domis, who secretly didn't mind but tried to put on a bothered demeanor, especially in front of Dor and Thane. He did not want to appear a child. He did have questions though, with which he pelted Tam while she cut some bread and cheese for them to eat. Not gifted with the innate communicative abilities that the Chufa and Kybara apparently shared, he was left to follow blindly while they discoursed freely with one another. Having caught half of the conversation from his companions, he had been able to follow somewhat but now was his opportunity to discover all he'd missed and he wasn't about the let this chance slip away.

Tam answered him patiently, with as much information as she could supply herself with Dor filling in the gaps when needed. Finally satisfied with where they were headed and why he turned his inquiry to the trees themselves. "Why are the Yei...yeilo...."

"YeiyeiloBaneesh?" Tam provided with a smile.

"Yes, those. Why are they so special?"

Tam shrugged, turning to Dor for help. He looked to be deep in thought for a moment and then shrugged as well. "None of us have ever seen them before. It's said they are what made us."

"And how is Master Thane to get arrows from them?"

Tam and Dor both shook their heads. "Again," Dor replied, "we don't know."

"What about Thane? Surely he knows, right?"

Tam smiled and looked at their friend in apparent conversation with the Kybara he was riding. "I don't think so. The fact that there are trees at all and that we're heading toward them is really more than any of us thought was possible. Certainly we held to hope but it was always the hope of the desperate. I don't think any of us expected this."

"But what if, after we get there, he can't draw the arrows out?" Domis pressed.

"Let us worry about that when the time comes," Tam said with a slight sigh, biting her lip when Domis briefly returned his attention to his food. What if, indeed? All of them knew how desperate their situation was and that any chance of survival depended on their ability to supply the arrows needed to bring down the dragons. Even Thane, with all of his abilities, was no match for the awesome power wielded by the dragons. Were there only one, none doubted that he would use his Tane to bring it down, most likely sacrificing himself with the effort, but he could not face them all.

Too soon, they were once again riding through the Underwoods toward whatever fate had in store. The Kybara seemed not to tire as the trees passed by in a blur of movement. Never did they pause or turn back but as if guided in their rush through the thick forestlands. Short stops were allowed, more for the passengers then their carriers, but only enough time to eat something and stretched. The day, though long, seemed almost to pass in moments as, once again, the woods grew dark. The slightest spark of excitement began to spread through the Kybara that only fed that of those they carried.

"*Soon, you will hear the song calling to you,*" Aisig's mind touched Thane's. Turning back to his companions, Thane could tell that Dor and Tam had heard him as well. Willing his eyes to see more and his ears to hear more, all that he could pick up was the waking sounds of the forest as death once more passed beyond its daylight barrier and unleashed itself upon the woods. The screams of the killer and the killed seemed to be all that broke through the normally eerie silence that ruled the Underwoods during the day making them all want to cover their ears to shut out the horrors of the night.

Pressing forward, the Kybara seemed unconcerned with the coming night and the desperate sounds that announced it. On they continued as if by a well worn path pressing ever closer to their destination. A scream to the right announced the dying cry of another life snuffed out and then sudden silence overcame them. Not the silence that had tickled them between the shoulder blades speaking fear and doubt to their minds, but a silence that felt almost reverent and harmonized with the best portions of their souls.

A welcome feeling of joy slowly came over each filling their senses with warmth and promises of peace followed by the slightest sound. The Kybara slowed and all cocked their heads to try and hear what it was. As they continued forward it seemed to grow with each step as if it called to them, pulling them closer. Whether it was a sound that touched their ears or, like their communication with the Kybara, was something more intimate, none could say but suddenly the most beautiful and peaceful song washed over them; one so hauntingly stunning as to draw tears.

"*You hear it now*," Aisig's voice pressed so irritatingly into their minds compared to the song. "*We will walk now.*"

Without argument, the companions dropped to the ground, the aches normally equated with such a ride not present. Even Domis seemed to sense something special as he slid off his mount's back and fell in line with the others as they walked forward, the song growing in their hearts.

Soon the woods began to thin, the trees in which Thane had sensed such evil began to diminish as if unable to bear the peace that washed over the area. Light grew steadily chasing away the Underwoods' shadows and those that had taken root like cobwebs in their hearts. Then a collective gasp broke through the tranquil air as all caught their breath. There they were. They could see them. The Underwoods had just ceased to exist giving way to a meadow in the center of which stood the YeiyeiloBaneesh.

None could pull their gaze away from them as tears flowed freely down their faces. The last five remaining trees that had once made up this forest, were all that stood as a reminder of what once was the majesty of the Chufa race. Straight up from the ground grew their trunks, the lowest branches growing out in a curved manner snaking back and forth was matched by those above them creating a large umbrella canopy that was open to the sun's final rays as it sank below the surrounding woodland. But the light did not seem to dim as if coming from the trees themselves.

The leaves were broad and full covering the branches in a kaleidoscope of colors mixing into a rainbow of the deepest greens, bright reds, oranges, violets and soft blues. The scent of fresh, clean earth washed over them eliminating the stifling stench from the Underwoods that had dull their senses leaving them refreshed and making it so much easier to breath. The song of birds was heard in the upper reaching branches speaking of life and renewal chasing away the last vestiges of the previous days' journeying. The tree's song cradled them, rising in welcome and beckoning them forward as they were just as excited by their presence as were the Chufa.

Thane felt his senses being pulled forward as he stepped ever closer drawing him into the largest tree that stood in the center with the other trees positioned at each station of the four directions. Suddenly he could no longer feel his body as his mind seemed to enter the tree becoming one entity instead of two. All of his feelings, his past, his dreams, were left bear as were that of the tree. He traveled through years of standing and waiting, doing what he could to protect the others, to help them grow even though the shepherds were no longer. Patiently he waited, hoping against hope that one day they would return and call others to life. And now, here was one like unto the great one who walked the woods so long ago. His need was evident, his desires, his heart—their heart—now beating as one, now one in all things and all purpose. The Tane sang to crescendo burning through the body that contained its power; its promise. Anchored as it was with the YeiyeiloBaneesh it became fully awake and the one who was once Thane was now part of it, no longer one separate, but the Tane itself.

The body that had been Thane suddenly lost all sense of itself while Dor, Tam and Domis watched with a strange lack of concern as it fell to the ground as if lifeless. Then, as if called to follow, they too lost feeling of themselves, falling as well as if feathers gently lifted and caressed by a passing wind.

Chapter Twenty-Six

Reks pressed his cheek against the horse's neck mixing its sweat with his own as he kicked its flanks begging for greater speed. The wind pushed against him, an enemy to his need. His body ached with fatigue, muscles crying for relief but he dared not stop to rest. His horse, he knew, was nigh unto its end but he could not let up. She was strong; it was just a little further. He could tell by the lay of the area that they had not passed more than a day before. With his speed, and their lack, he figured an hour more, two at the most. Patting his horse's neck he prayed to all the gods that she would make it.

*   *   *

Ranse motioned to the archers to fit their arrows and prepare to draw. Checking their position, hidden amongst the trees on the small rise, he felt certain they would go undetected until it was too late to react. Their enemy's confidence precluded them from sending out an advanced guard; they would pay for their mistake. Checking the skies as best he could he was unable to mark any of the dragons though it was impossible to be certain. Looking back, his heart sank at the size of the enemy. With a slightly elevated position he had a grand view of the massive line of soldiers snaking back as far as his eyes could take in. The ground fairly shook with their march. He hoped it would be enough to at least slow them some.

*   *   *

Reks almost cried out in relief when he finally spotted the tail end of his quarry and the rear guard that was now turning about and racing toward him. He slowed his horse to a trot, giving her a much deserved and much needed rest. Stroking her neck he whispered words of thanks, her flanks flaring and contracting with labored breaths.

*   *   *

Jack's expression lifted with the rising mountain that rose from the landscape like a lonely beacon in the distance. Bedler's Keep. It appeared they would make it after all.

*   *   *

Ranse's arm dropped and a volley of arrows shot out of the trees like a flock of birds scared into flight. The front lines, mostly orcs, dropped as a cry went up from the enemy who turned toward the trees in rage. Ranse sent another volley before ordering his men to their horses. Though they were on the high ground and could put up a good fight, hid in the trees as they were, it was only their intention to slow them. Falling back quickly, they disappeared into the woods and turned to the west while the enemy crashed through the foliage in search of their assailants.

That should at least buy us a half hour if not more, he thought

*   *   *

Reks was ushered through the throng in search of the king's party with a guard leading them and two others flanking him. He had news that could only be delivered to his majesty and he was not about to fail in that trust. His horse stumbled and he knew she had given all she was able. "Just a few more minutes," he soothed, his own body covered with aches and sweat. He was amazed at the number of people, both common and merchant, that marched toward the distant keep making his message all the more important.

Reks recoiled at the wolg that suddenly appeared amongst the refugees and called out a warning while reaching for his sword. The guard to his left grabbed his arm before he could pull it free as his horse whinnied in protest. "Don't be fearin'" the guard offered. "It be His Majesty's pet." Reks stared in disbelief, but didn't question as he returned his sword to its place.

Jack, having heard the commotion, turned his horse about and with a nod to the guard moved off the road. "What's the problem?" he asked, taking in Reks and his trembling mount.

"I must speak with a man named Jack," Reks said quickly. "I have a message from His Lord, Prince Ranse."

"Then deliver it," Jack said easily. "I am Jack."

"Sir," he saluted, "I was sent to inform you that the enemy is on the move and fast approaches."

"How long," Jack inquired.

"Half a day at most, sir. Maybe less."

Jack grabbed Reks' arms. "Are you certain?"

"Yes, sir. At your current pace and theirs, there's no doubt but that they'll reach us by the sun's setting."

*   *   *

Again positioned, but this time on the south side of the road, Ranse looked over the men he'd brought out of Aleron. All were focused, their visage fierce with determination. These were no mere honorific guard that had been dressed for ceremony or pomp, but men accustomed to the ugly truths of battle. Hardened by the constant assaults made upon their city, their hatred for orcs was only surpassed by their love of country and family. Ranse was proud to be amongst them. This was their only hope in giving Jack enough time to get Calandra's refugees safely to the keep.

Readying their arrows and waiting for the command to fire, they watched as once again the enemy's front lines moved into range. A bit more wary this time, they were still, nonetheless, easy targets as they pressed forward. A company of trolls had been placed in the front as if their massive forms would be enough to resist the coming onslaught. Dropping his arm in signal, the arrows whooshed past meeting their marks with deadly exactness. But this time the enemy was better prepared. As the trolls went down, two lines of orcs turned toward the attacker's position and loosed their own volley of arrows. Luckily, Ranse's men were not without cover, ducking behind the trunks of the trees where the orc's arrows were embedded with a thunk. Ranse regretfully passed up the order for a second volley as they no longer held the element of surprise and were forced to run instead. Another swarm of orc arrows broke through the tree line after them but fell short of their targets as the men quickly mounted and rode off.

Ranse glanced back as orcs, goblins and trolls alike rushed into the woods that had hid them. He cursed knowing that the next time would not be so easy and that their strategy of slowing the enemy was not working as well as he had hoped. Yet, they had to try again.

✳   ✳   ✳

Jack pressed through the refugee camp as fast as possible amongst the milling crowd that had suddenly been brought to an almost complete halt. Word had been sent through the camp that all but food and weapons were to be cast aside as they were forced to increase their speed. The expected outcry by the wealthiest among them at being forced to leave their most precious possessions when their goal was finally in sight had ground down their progress as they dug in their heels in protest. The frustration and anger that seethed through Jack was palpable as he ordered, yelled and then finally drew steel on any puffed up merchant who was unwilling to comply. Again he was reminded of how the wealthy seemed to be disconnected from reality when it came to their possessions. Too many were willing to not only risk their own lives, but those of their family and others all for a shiny bauble or trinket that was of no worth when gripped in lifeless hands.

Again he shouted, sword drawn, as the echoes of the soldiers could be heard up and down the line making the same threats. It was well into an hour since he'd received word before the column of refugees finally took flight, their speed, gratefully, increasing as they went. Carts and wagons that had been the label of many a merchant's wealth had been left to the side of the road, many filled with precious gems and metals or silks and fine fabrics not easily found in the kingdom. Guards were now set to protect the goods from greedy passersby who might be tempted to loot what had been left and in turn slow them all down again. Jack had made it clear that anyone who tried would be punished by death forthwith and their bodies left to rot.

He knew that he wouldn't be able to get the people to move any quicker until the enemy nipped at their heels. It was his hope that by that time they would be close enough to the keep for the desperate run that would be sure to ensue. A small detachment of men were dispatched to lead the refugees into the keep, while Wess and his command from Hell's End Station had been sent ahead to warn the city that rested in the keep's shadow to retreat into the mountain fortress. The remaining soldiers, who weren't protecting the discarded wealth, followed Jack to the rear to return in search of Ranse's party to assist with the hit and run tactic to help the Calandrians reach safety.

Jack bit his lip as they pressed their horses into a slow gallop. They needed more time.

✳   ✳   ✳

Brak smiled at the chaos that ensued once word had been shouted throughout the streets that all people were to gather as much food and weapons as could be carried and remove to Bedler's Keep. A drop of spittle escaped his mouth and dripped down his chin as he barely restrained himself from dancing about with anticipation. "He'll be comin' back nows, I jes knows it," he hissed, lifting his first to the skies. "And I'lls be here awaitin' to git 'im for yous Zel," he said and then punched a fat man waddling past with an arm full of potatoes, dropping him and his load into the ally. Shoving as many of the potatoes as he could into his pockets, he left the man unconscious as he turned toward the main street and pushed his way toward the front of the line wending its way toward the keep's main entrance.

*   *   *

Myles moved his company slowly toward the enemy lines. Looking to either side his eyes pierced the trees that cradled the road but he was unable to discover any movement. They were close; he could smell them as much as feel their feet pounding into the dirt. The horses seemed restless feeling the nervous excitement that gripped the men just before battle. But their purpose was not to engage the enemy directly—at least not yet. Raising his arm he signaled for a halt. They remained silent, waiting; only the occasional jingle of the bridle or a horse's restless stamp making any sound.

Around a slight bend in the road, not a hundred yards in the distance, the first line of the enemy suddenly appeared, wavering for a brief moment as their eyes locked on Myles and his men. Ignoring any sense of caution, the enemy's front lines broke from the rest and charged headlong toward the defenders. Myles and his men remained motionless, not even moving to draw swords.

Rushing forward, they got within fifty yards of their prey when a sudden rush of arrows cut them down from either side of the road. Angered and salivating for blood and revenge, others raced forward followed by even more as word passed down the column sending goblin, orc and troll running pell-mell toward Myles and his men. Coming around the bend as they were, most had not seen the ambush that had befallen their comrades and another volley cut down a good fifty of their number, piling up their corpses in the road.

The enemy swarmed into the trees in search of those responsible but was further enraged to find the woods were empty. Turning back to Myles and his men, they rushed forward. Waiting until they were almost upon them, Myles finally gave the signal and he and his men retreated back up the road at a fierce gallop, chased almost at their heals by a group of trolls, their long stride pulling them ahead of the group. They were easy targets for the men who had set up for another ambush and cut them down quickly with another flight of arrows.

Now they were out of the trees. Myles and his men passed through onto a large meadow area and were quickly followed by Jack and Ranse leading their own men out of the woods from either side of the road. Quickly forming a line, they all drew their swords and waited for the enemy to catch up. The men were anxious. Finally, the chance to meet them head on instead of hiding behind a branch.

They didn't have to wait long as the road released a flood of combatants rushing out of the trees and coming down the road howling in a frenzy with the scent of blood fresh and their quarry no longer protected. Jack quickly raised his sword and then cried out for the men to charge.

Breaking through the front line, the men cut down their opponents with ease and precision as they slowed to take on the second row. The clash of steel and the cries of the dying quickly erupted as blood soaked the ground. In the first moments, the soldiers held sway slashing and hacking to the left and the right, but where one went down, two took his place and the tide of battle was at the verge of turning. Calling out to those around him, Jack sounded the retreat as more of the enemy rushed forward anxious to join the fight. As previously decided, all turned and raced back angling their withdrawal in a northwesterly direction in an attempt to pull the enemy after them and away from the road.

A soldier next to Jack went down and was immediately trampled and crushed as the enemy pressed after them. Jack cut the arm from an assailant reaching to pull back on his bridle with his horse kicked in the skull of a goblin grabbing at its flank. Though able to extract themselves, it slow them just enough to leave Jack open to a massive rock troll's deadly swing. Spittle flew from the trolls mouth as he brought his club to bear, swinging with full force for Jack's turned head.

Chapter Twenty-Seven

Thane's eyes flickered open as his nose took in the scents of sweet grass and budding flowers. Stretching lazily, he suddenly became somewhat alarmed at what he felt; or more precisely what he didn't feel. All the fatigue, all the aches and pains, all of the cuts, bruises and injuries, both superficial and those somewhat more serious, were gone. Quickly checking the place where the vined creature had stabbed him and where Dor's knife had cut out the poison, he found healthy skin without the slightest discoloration or blemish. The innumerable other cuts he'd received from the insect-like beings were the same. He felt more whole and rested than he could remember ever having felt before.

Looking around, he found his companions stirring as well, their looks of astonished relief revealing the same sensations and healing he was feeling. "How is it possible?" Tam asked.

She followed Thane's gaze as it turned to the five sentinels that stood over them in silent majesty. He tried to remember what had happened to him after his first encounter with the sacred trees but all that came to mind was the floating sensation he'd felt and then waking moments ago. How long had they been out, he wondered. His stomach did not ache with hunger so he felt that it could not have been too long, but with the wounds he'd had now fully healed, the actual time was probably much longer than he'd wanted to originally stay. Scanning the Underwoods forest that made an almost perfect circular perimeter around the meadow, he could see the Kybara lounging lazily just inside the ring with more still lounging beyond.

"How long have we been out?" Dor asked through a yawn.

"I don't know," Thane said, "but it would seem too long."

Dor was checking his own wounds that were no longer visible and only nodded his agreement.

"Do either of you feel different?" Tam asked, looking at her hands and arms. "I mean, other than healed and rested."

Dor nodded his head quickly. "Yes. It's like I feel more whole than I ever have. More..."

"Complete," Tam said with him, then added, "more alive."

"Yes," Thane agreed. "It's like all things are at my bidding."

Domis looked at each of them in turn, his eyes growing larger with each passing moment before finally resting his stare on Dor. "You're glimmering, Master Dor," he breathed.

"What?"

All eyes turned to Dor as mouths open. "He is," Tam breathed.

"And you have a misty aura about you," Dor said.

They then turned to Thane. "It's amazing," Tam said.

"What?" Thane asked, suddenly feeling very self-conscious. He could see the patterns that seemed to dance around his two friends noticing that each was as different as the person they were attached to.

"You're glowing," Domis said, reaching a hand toward him and then pulling it back.

"It's like the sun itself is burning within you," Tam added.

"What about me?" Domis asked hopefully but was immediately disappointed when he could see by their looks that he was just himself. "What is it?" he asked, trying unsuccessfully to mask the frustration he felt.

"It's our Tane," Dor said, suddenly realizing that he recognized them in his friends. "We can see each others Tane."

Thane and Tam nodded their agreement. Of course that's what it was. Each suddenly became quite aware of the Tane that sang to them, running through their veins in a torrent, whispering to them, begging them to release its power and use their abilities. It spoke to them, revealing its secrets that none of them could ever imagine. It was like stepping out of the dark and into the light. They understood. Thane wiped at a tear that rolled down his cheek. It seemed so clear and simple now.

"We need to go," Domis suddenly said, breaking the spell that seemed to fall over the three Chufa.

They turned and stared at him for a moment as if not understanding what he was saying. "We have to go," he repeated. "We have to get the arrows and go. They'll be waiting for us."

Dor and Tam blinked and then looked at each other. He was right, but none of them wanted to ever leave this grove again.

Thane finally spoke, his words drawing them all out. "He's right. Domis is right. If we don't leave now, we may never leave. We are meant for this place but we can tarry no longer."

Dor and Tam nodded in reluctant agreement though their faces revealed the inner sadness that gripped at their hearts.

Thane opened himself to the song of the YeiyeiloBaneesh and was instantly one with the center tree.

"*Grandfather,*" what was once Thane spoke to the tree. "*We have great need of you.*"

"*I know your need child,*" it answered, "*but we also have need of you.*"

Their minds and spirits having congealed, as it were, into one entity, what was Thane instantly understood his responsibility as descendant of the great tree shepherds of old. And he would fulfill his duty but need pressed him to be away immediately though his heart desired to stay in the small grove forever. He felt more alive than he had ever felt before as his Tane called to him, enveloped him, and spoke promises of all that he could do should he but ask it.

"*I know my duty and will fulfill it to the least part…*" he said.

"*But for now,*" the tree finished for him, "*you must be away so that the victory of your return may be more than just a passing season. We will give you what you need, though only three are of a maturity to do so and I have already done so in the days of yore and cannot again.*"

They understood. Thane felt himself retracting, clumsily finding his way back to his body, though it was heartrending and almost painful to do so. His friends stared in wonder as his eyes blinked finding his body once again though feeling it a clumsy instrument compared to what he'd felt when part of the tree.

"They will help us," he explained, though Tam and Dor seemed to sense that on their own.

"But how will you get the arrows?" Domis asked.

Almost instantly he was answered as the trees position to the north, west and east suddenly moved their branches in a swaying motion, back and forth as if a great wind had come up, though the grandfather and the youngest tree to the south remained untouched. They watched in wonder as the limbs continue to move and sway, increasing their tempo back and forth and back and forth until reaching a crescendo. It was then that their limbs ceased to move and all at once they seemed to lean back bending at the place where the trunk transitioned from bare word to where their many limbs began. With a grown, the bark around the spot began to pull back as if cut by a sharp ax revealing the soft inner wood that was bright white in color. It too began to peal away, layer after layer until finally reaching each tree's heart. The hearts shimmered, vibrating with the song that filled the meadow, vibrating with the Tane that coursed through each Chufa.

They watched in awe, mouths agape, tears flowing like a river down their cheeks. It was like watching a birth as the mother writhes in the pain that will bring about such joy; an opposition of life that bespeaks all things in the world. A loud crack resounded from each of the three trees as their hearts were suddenly snapped from them followed by a profuse excretion of clear liquid as if blood flowing from their wounds. The hearts were then pushed forward through each of the tree's layers as they began to reattach themselves behind it until they reached the outer bark which closed after them, making the trees whole once again while holding secure the thin shaft of inner wood.

Hesitantly at first, Thane drew near to the closest tree, his hand raising, slowing to touch the gift that had been so painfully offered. It felt warm to the touch, just like the arrow that DaxSagn still held in his quiver. No longer could he feel anger toward his once mentor as his selfish disregard for what was happening had ultimately led him here. Gently pulling on the shaft, it freed itself from the bark and seemed to pulse in his hand. It was alive. Now he understood. The grandfather's heart was what Dax held onto. And now he would have the hearts of three others. Though he couldn't imagine that they could be destroyed, he also understood that to do so would also kill the tree to which they belonged.

Gathering the other two, he reverently bowed to the trees and then retreated back to his friends giving one to Dor and one to Tam. Dor smiled at the gift, running an appreciating hand along the shaft before staring down its length and snickering joyfully; perfectly straight.

Tam, on the other hand, hesitated, staring at Thane as if surprised that he would offer one to her. Instinctively, she understood the same thing about the heart that Thane had deduced and now she was not so certain she felt worthy to have one. She went so far as to open her mouth in protest but Thane hushed her.

"You are as equal a shooter as both Dor and I, possibly even better. We need your skill if we are to come off victors against the dragons."

Closing her mouth with a snap, she almost shone with Thane's compliment at her shooting skill, a wellspring of pride suddenly bubbling up with the realization that she was to be part of what could turn the war to their favor. But just as suddenly, the icy tendrils of doubt reached up and gripped her, stealing her breath as she took the shaft into her hands. All of her life she had wanted the opportunity to do something worthwhile, something that mattered, something that went beyond what her people saw as the proper place for a Chufa woman. Now that her dreams were about to be realized, she found herself hesitating. What if she wasn't good enough? What if she failed at the poignant moment when the lives of so many were dependant upon her ability to shoot true? What if Thane's compliments were mere words to force her in this direction out of need alone?

She stared at him while feeling the arrow's pulse that was now hers to guard and to use. In him she saw no doubt or falsehood as he held her gaze with his bright green eyes. It seemed to strengthen her resolve as she felt new life and added confidence suddenly chasing back the cold feelings of doubt. Smiling, she nodded once and then embraced her lifelong friend. She would do it. And when the hour came for her to perform her duty, she would not fail them.

Chapter Twenty-Eight

The troll brought his club down, Jack unaware of his impending doom as the full force of the troll's fury and bloodlust brought the weapon to bear toward the back of his head. A flash of white was all the troll saw before he felt himself suddenly flung backward, his club falling impotently to the ground as dragger-like teeth sank into his neck and tore out his throat cutting off his dying scream. Continuing with his forward motion, Erl's massive body collided with another troll, knocking it to the ground were it was trampled to death by its own before he again launched into the air, his claws raking off a goblin's face. Landing lightly and free of the pressing onslaught, Erl raced headlong after Jack who was none the wiser to his near demise.

The body of men regrouped quickly. Their small numbers, compared to the horde that poured from the tree cover like a disrupted ant hill, beckoned them on promising the thrill of the kill and fresh meat for the cook fires. Jack checked the skies, willing them to be clear, knowing that should the dragons come they were lost. Raising a hand, he signaled the archers to the ready. Arrows were nocked and pulled to cheekbones waiting for the sign to fire. On the enemy rushed, tripping over themselves to be the first to taste the warm blood that called to them as it sat ready in the open.

Jack dropped his hand and a hailstorm of arrows took flight shadowing their foe with the promise of death. The front line faltered as skin was pierced and muscles were torn dropping them in a heap to be trampled by those that followed. The few not struck by a killing blow were overtaken and crushed in the press of those that came in their wake as they cried out for help. Again Jack motioned his band farther away from the road drawing

Zadok's horde after them. It was working, and new hope filled them that Calandra's refugees might actually make it into the keep after all.

Bringing his men to a halt, Jack prepared them for another volley but froze in mid command, his face turning dark, his hope snuffed out. Erl growled, his hackles rising. "Draw swords!" he yelled. "Prepare to charge!"

Rushing out of the crowd of howling orcs and trolls, a large group of wolg riding goblins broke away from the throng and chased down the gap separating them. Somewhat disorganized at first, they coalesced into a rough line as they sped forward their swords drawn and faces fierce with rage. There was not time to send out a volley of arrows and then mount a charge. To be struck with the full force of the enemy's advance while standing still would be devastating. At the least they must meet them stride for stride.

Steel rang as it was drawn from scabbards and then heels were planted into horses flanks sending the men racing forward to meet the charge. Zadok's army continued to give chase, hoping to reach the fighting in time to get a taste of it. Jack knew they would have to be quick or risk ultimately being surrounded.

The two lines collided reducing their battle cries to rasps of steel and grunts of effort mixed with the screams of the wounded and dying. Soon the sweet smell of new grass and horse hide was mixed with the iron scent of blood and sweat giving the air a tang that stuck in the throat and nostrils. Though out numbered, these men were not fresh recruits having been vetted in war many times before, enjoying the kill almost as much as the enemy. Sharp teeth bit into horse flesh but was answered by razor hooves that lashed out while man fought goblin for the advantage. Bloodlust swept over the men driving them to greater strength as they pushed back against their foes, piling up their kills with such speed as to intimidate the enemy and force them back again toward the massive numbers of the approaching army. Though the men were in a battle rage and wanted to follow, they were still disciplined enough to hold back and retreat on Jack's word. The rest of the army was getting too close, and he was not willing to sacrifice such men to the slaughter that sheer numbers would visit upon them.

Kicking his mount, Jack led them away, leaving the field littered with the enemy, though not without some casualties of their own. Ranse galloped up next to him, his shirt covered in blood, his sleeve torn revealing a seeping wound on his arm. Jace was next to him, a slight smile pulling at his normally stone face. This was his element and he relished in it. A few of the wolgs and their riders gave chase for a brief moment but quickly slowed when they became aware that their numbers had been cut in half. Their courage was counted numerically not by a strong will or heart. Once they realized that the men outnumbered them, the fight almost immediately drained from them. They were natural cowards that preyed solely on the weak.

"They're stopping," Ranse yelled, pulling up next to Jack. "Is it enough?" he asked as they motioned to the men and pulled their horses back, turning to watch as the army halted, it's massive line turning back to the road that would take them to Bedler's Keep.

"I don't know," Jack answered, "but we had better make sure. There is still yet another long stretch of wood before they reach the keep and the city that sits at its feet. We best make for it quickly and see if we can't pull them up again. We'll know better then how the others fair in getting the people in."

*   *   *

Jne took a long drink from the water skin, scanning the terrain as she did so. The water soothed the dryness as it ran like silk down her throat. The day was hot and the terrain rough and dusty drying her mouth while wetting her clothes with sweat. They had taken refuge in the shade under one of the sparse trees that dotted the area along the road northwest of Bedler's Keep. Though anxious to overtake the remaining miles to the keep Soyak had convinced her that a slower pace would be best, thus allowing their Tjal kin time to come to their senses and catch up before they reached the castle. She'd argued, not wanting to miss any of the fighting, but more so because she missed Thane. In the end, Soyak's persistent logic and constant nagging had won out.

Passing the water skin to Soyak, Jne turned her attention to the road from which they'd come. "Do you think they follow?" she asked without need for explanation.

Soyak shrugged while drinking freely from the skin. "I cannot say, child, but I have faith that they will eventually come to the right decision. We are not so lost as to ignore the itch of a fight for too long. Whether they catch us or not, I think they will come."

Jne sighed, trying, without success, to suppress the thought that if the Tjal would come sooner or late, why then were she and Soyak traveling so slow? Let them catch up as they may.

Soyak smiled at her knowingly. "I too was impatient when I was young like you," the old woman said, a fire igniting in her eyes as she remembered. "What grand days they were throwing myself into battle without thought for any save the glory that would be mine. And I will have that glory again," she said, her voice strong, belying the age that had ravished her body. "But..." she let the word hang in the air, snuffing the blaze in her eyes and heart. "I have learned that sometimes it is better to wait for the betterment of all."

Jne glared at the piece of grass she'd pulled from the ground and was now shredding. "May age never take me," she cursed under her breath, though Soyak's ears picked up the near insult.

Instead of taking offense though, she laughed. "You may very well get your wish," she said. "And then where would your man be? Though I seek a glorious death as much as any, glory is not shared like a bed or a life with the one you love. It is a grand and selfish endeavor."

Jne suddenly regretted what she'd said. She didn't want to hear what Soyak was saying. She didn't fear death, and the thought of giving her life in glorious battle was almost greater than anything else she could ever wish for. But then Thane's face came to her mind and she felt the hole that had been left in her soul since she'd left him. It was all too confusing. Wasn't death in battle the ultimate that all Tjal sought after? But what of the man she would marry? Was not a life well lived with him just as glorious? She needed to change the subject. The thoughts and feelings that were suddenly bombarding her were giving her a headache. "And what of you," she finally asked, turning the conversation back on Soyak. "Was there one for whom you gave up the glory of battle or are you just too good to lose?"

Soyak stared at her for a long moment, her eyes suddenly sad. "His name was Karle."

Jne was surprised by his name. Certainly not a Tjal name.

"No," she confirmed, her eyes taking on a glossy look, "he was not Tjal. He was a blacksmith's son from Tigford, but he didn't fit there. He was a man born of human parents but with the heart of the Tjal. He hated the sea, and the forge even more, though I can tell you it certainly favored him." Soyak smiled at the red that suddenly flushed Jne's face. "It was so long ago," she continued, the mist returning to her eyes, "but I can still see him and the unruly locks of light hair that touched his large shoulders. I knew that moment I saw him that he would be mine."

Jne just barely controlled the gasp that tried to escape her lips. Thane had been the same for her, though she had originally thought him Tjal. When she'd found him unconscious on the dead plains north of the Mogolth she'd felt the certainty and rightness of it as much as the feeling of her sword in her hand.

"How did you meet?" Jne asked in an almost whisper.

"It was in the square at the market in Kabu where you regained your honor. He had come with his father to sell and buy. I wasn't even supposed to be there that day; one of the other girls was with fever so I had to fill in for her. And I have cursed and blessed her for it ever since."

"What happened?" Jne pressed, suddenly very interested in the old woman's story.

"We met and fell in love. One moment I was haggling prices with his father and the next I rested my eyes on him and they refused to look anywhere else." Soyak paused as if reliving the day, her face taking on a faraway look with the slightest smile curving her lips.

"And did you marry?" Jne prodded, the frustration evident in her voice at the constant pauses.

Soyak's face went slack. "No. I killed him."

Jne felt tears coming to her eyes to match those that suddenly rolled down Soyak's wrinkled face. "He left his father's care and employ that very night," she explained. "He seemed to find the same thing in me as I had found in him. The time we had together seemed so short," she whispered, remembering. "But the day came when he either needed to become one of us or return to his father. And, by fate's cruelest demand, the lot fell to me to test him at steel."

Jne could not keep back the tears now. She had been the one who tested Thane but it had been by her own choice. Once she'd found out he was not Tjal, she knew that there was no chance for them. And though she felt he was hers from the beginning, she felt it best that she be the one to test him. She tried those long days to hate him, to belittle him and see weakness in him; certain he could not possibly pass the first tests. And when he did make it to steel she had hoped that he would beat her and kill her so she would not be forced to live such a lonely life without him. She never thought he would spare her and shame her as he had. It had almost broken her, but she could never bring herself to despise him for it as she'd worried she might. And now they would have their whole lives to be together.

"I cut him down with the first swing," Soyak said, breaking through Jne's personal reminiscence. "I'll never forget the smile on his face as he bled out in front of me." Soyak suddenly wipe at the tears that washed down her face making Jne aware of her own. "After that, I threw myself into any fight I could find but the glory of battle had suddenly lost its glamour. It couldn't replace the void I felt inside." She stopped and looked at Jne who tried to look away and hide the emotion that had bubbled out of her unbidden. Soyak smiled. "And that is why I am an old woman all alone. And that is also why I embraced the chance for this last fight. I will give battle one final chance to bring glory to my name, one final chance to take me back to the young man that slew my heart."

Jne looked at her calloused hands where her swords fit so perfectly.

Everything in her life had been about glory and honor until she met Thane. Was it right for her to give up her life, her people, her culture, for love? Was the warrior's path so cruel and exacting in demanding the ultimate sacrifice for a life to be of worth? More importantly, would she give it all up for Thane's love? She couldn't deny who she was, but could she be more than that? Could she wed the two and be happy in her own skin?

Soyak's voice interrupted the debate raging in her mind and she realized that, for now, she didn't need to decide fore the choice was not given her as of yet. War was forced upon them and it would find her in its midst delivering death to the enemy.

"You see," Soyak smiled, pointing back along the road they had recently traveled. "They've come."

Chapter Twenty-Nine

Wess cursed at the casual pace taken by the Calandrian refugees as they swaggered their way toward the keep. No amount of threatening or force could get them to move any swifter as the line had come to an almost complete standstill. The fact that Bedler's Keep was created for defense and not for ease of entrance made the situation even worse. The only way in was toward the back of the peak that held the lofty castle above the stretching plain. One long, narrow stairway circled the mountain on its steep climb to the top. Wedged between great rocks that seemed to have broken away from the rest of the keep's base was the entrance that was only wide enough to admit a single wagon's width. The large oak doors that held fast the entry had been thrown open to admit the refugees but most were either too tired, too ignorant, or just plain too daft to rush through to the only place that offered any amount of safety. Few, if any, had seen for themselves the army that nipped at their heels and would soon be howling for their blood, creating a malaise in the refugees at having been forced from Calandra in the first place.

Wess checked the sun's position. It had been four hours since the first person entered the keep and the line hadn't seemed to get any shorter. The whole process had been further disrupted by the townsfolk adding to the confusion while jostling for position, but at least they had responded quickly and with fervor. Wess spat from atop his horse and glared at the people as they shuffled pass. At this rate it would be well past nightfall before they got them all safely in, if they even had such a luxury of time. He glanced at the distant tree line that marked the last sheltered area before the keep and felt instinctively that those woods would soon heave a froth of trolls, orcs and goblins; then he would see these people move, though he feared that by then it would be too late to save them.

Moving his gaze northward, he felt a sudden jolt of trepidation as the distinct form of a dust cloud began to appear and grow. From this distance, he couldn't make out the shapes that were creating it, but his nerves prickled with the promise of a coming fight. And whether they were friend or foe, he needed to raise the alarm that might, in fact, be the answer to get Calandra's lazy people moving. Turning his mount toward the keep he kicked his heals sending his horse into a quick gallop. Lowering his head, he pressed it harder to reach the front of the line where he hoped to place the proper amount of fear in them. To have done so at the back of the line would have only invited greater mayhem and the likely trampling death of far too many innocents.

Passing the soldiers spaced along the line to keep order, Wess finally reached the front where four men were stationed to try to keep the line moving up the narrow entrance. A merchant was stopped with his wagon, screaming at one of the guards who had confiscated some of the man's goods which had previously been ordered left behind. Wess, wanted to lop the man's head off knowing all too well that this was the type of thing that had kept the entry into the keep at a snail's crawl. The large heap of tables and chairs and other unnecessary items that littered the area testified that this certainly wasn't the first person to place his possessions over his own life or that of his family and the hundreds of people he held up in their escape.

"Get moving into the keep, now!" Wess shouted as he quickly dismounted and pushed the man forward. "The enemy is at our doors and you haggle over a rug?"

The man, who had stumbled forward and tripped on the first few steps, lifted his bulbous body from the ground with great effort and then, turned on Wess and his men. "How dare you touch my person!" he raged, his round face turning darker shades of red with every breath.

"I dare," said Wess, his voice dangerously low and venomous, "because the enemy is upon us this moment, and you are blocking the way with your rotund body."

The man was beside himself. "There is no enemy," he insisted. "Other than some false king trying to steal from his own subjects while herding them like cattle to a place he can better control them."

"No enemy, eh?" Wess countered, his hand gripping his sword's hilt so tight that his fingers turned white. "Then look to the north and behold the false enemy that chases," he said pointing to the dust cloud that was growing steadily larger and more ominous.

All eyes followed his gaze and a sudden howl went up as people started to cry out their doom. Wess barely got himself back into his saddle before the line of people that had been within earshot lurched forward in a sudden press to reach the entrance and safety. Looking back to where the merchant had been arguing only moments before, Wess just caught the flash of his back end as it turned passed the first corner up the steps, his wife and children crying after him as they tried to catch up. Turning to the guards, who suddenly found themselves almost overrun by the panic, he barked out his orders. "You best get atop your mounts so you don't get caught in the rush, but keep this line moving forward at a quick pace. If any slow to argue, direct their attention to the north, and if that doesn't work, pull them from the line and make them wait until the last. And if they try to cut back in, kill them." He didn't wait for the guards to respond before he was galloping back down the line calling for the rest of the shoulders to mount up and follow.

The refugees in the back suddenly became restless as the soldiers that had been spread out along the long column suddenly appeared at a hard gallop and started forming up behind them. Voices began to rise in confused discussion and fear when someone suddenly screamed above the din, "They come, they come! Look to the north! We are doomed!" All went silent as hundreds of eyes turned to take in the materializing figures that were fast approaching the line. Then, as deafening as thunder following lightning, all seemed to cry out at once and began to push forward. In moments it was bedlam as a crashing wave of bodies pounded against those in front swelling the column on either side as fear rippled through the line sending everyone forward in a rush.

Wess did not allow himself, or his men to sit and watch the horror as people trampled over one another as the fear of death finally gripped them. Barking out orders, he called the men to form up as others still galloped in and then turned to lead them forward to meet the enemy. His only concern was for the four men left behind who were now forced to fit a title wave into a bucket. *At least they're moving.*

Setting the pace to a quick gallop, he tried to put some distance between the refugees and the coming attackers to give them space enough to retreat as it was needed. Wess knew what they faced and held no fantasies that his small detachment of men could hold back the enemy, but loathsome as they were, he had to give the people as much time as possible to get safely into the keep. He was on the verge of calling for his men to draw arms when the dark shapes that approached suddenly began to materialize into men and horses. He held up his hand to slow the charge before finally calling for a halt allowing the others to close the gap that separated them. Soon he was able to pick out Jack and Ranse among the mass and raised a signal to hail them.

"Well met," Jack said, pulling up his horse next to Wess. Looking past him, he squinted. "I see the people are still not free and clear of the field."

"Not yet," Wess replied, "but your approach lit fire to their britches and they now fight one another to make the keep."

"Good," Ranse offered. "They will need to squeeze in quickly if they hope to survive."

"Zadok's army is soon upon us," Jack finished, answering the questioning look on Wess' face.

Wess' visage turned dark. "You know as well as I, Jack, that they will attack as soon as they break from the wood and see the exposed ground and the sheep's pen open," he said, referring to the remaining refugees still outside the keep.

Jack nodded. "We'll just have to slow them down then," he answered, the look on his face belying what all knew; this would certainly end with their deaths. They were close to a thousand strong, but Zadok commanded at least ten times that number and should the skies grow dark with his flying beasts, all would be lost in mere moments.

Wess nodded back, a slight smile breaking over his face. "It will be good to kill trolls with you again."

Jack grinned. "It looks like the raven has come for us at last. We will meet him with red blades."

"What have you got planned?" Ranse asked.

Jack looked at the prince and then at the men that surrounded them. All seemed anxious, but not with the anxiety of fear, rather, they held the look of men who were prepared to die and were restless to get to it. "No plan," he finally answered and then yelled so the others could hear. "We meet them on the open field and take them head on!"

A sudden cheer broke from the soldiers as swords rang out of scabbards and were lifted into the air.

The people were still fighting to squeeze onto the stairway that led to the keep and safety when Jack and his small army lined up a mere hundred yards from the trees that swallowed the eastern road. Carts and possessions that had moments before been worth more than life itself had been discarded all along the field where the battle would soon be joined. Though the people they were about to give their lives to protect didn't merit their blood sacrifice, these were men of honor who followed even greater men. They would see it to the last for those few that they loved but even more so for the duty that bound them to their country and king. It was one of the prime absurdities of war that the greatest among the people were the ones who gave their lives while leaving the dishonorable and morally bankrupt to live as they hid behind their self importance and cowardice.

"Wess," Jack called when the line had been formed, "when they first break from the trees, you take your men to the left flank while Myles, you take a third to the right." Gesturing to himself, Ranse, Jace, and those closest to him, he finished with, "and we will drive straight down their throats."

Wess merely nodded before breaking away and racing left to gather his men. Myles, on the other hand, saluted and then looked as if he wanted to say something more before merely bowing his head and turning to gather his men.

"Finally," Jace suddenly said, shocking both the prince and Jack. And when he noticed them staring at him he merely shrugged. "One tires of the diplomacy of the court and all its pretty talk when it's killing that needs being done. Some only understand the language of steel and blood and I intend to preach them a sermon they won't soon forget."

Jack felt the smile crawling across his lips and had to stifle a bellowing laugh that was suddenly rumbling in his chest. He didn't think he'd heard so many words put together by Ranse's bodyguard since he first met him in Haykon. And then, just as suddenly, he felt sad. Not because he knew that his life was about to end, but because he would miss out on getting to know better such great men as Jace and Ranse. He wanted to be able to share a pint of ale with them in some worn out, back alley pub where they could reminisce and tell stories of bygone years when all was glorious; where they could pick a fight with the locals and later laugh at how funny they each looked with broken noses and missing teeth. He wanted to see Thane again, the boy who felt more like a son than even his own flesh and bone had had time to before he was taken. He wanted to see Dor and Tam wed, and bounce upon his knee their babies and tell them the story of their parents and what they had been through together. No, it wasn't death that burdened him so much as the life that he would miss.

He finally let the laugh out, trying to add mirth to its sound but it still seemed somewhat hollow. "Now that is a language, my friend, that I can understand."

Jace stared at him briefly and then bowed his head. "Then we will speak it together!"

"And I," Ranse added, pulling his sword as the first of the enemy broke from the forest.

As one, the men along the line drew their swords and then, as if by some unseen signal, all leaped forward with a war cry on the lips as they galloped forward as if racing to be the first to meet the enemy. As the soldiers fell upon them, the font lines of Zadok's army were just beginning to start their own charge and were swallowed in the onslaught of men and horses, Erl taking down the first adversary with a quick snap to his throat. Like a clasping fist, Wess' and Myles' men converged on either flank as more goblins, orcs and trolls race out of the forest along the narrow road. It was easy pickings for the battle hardened men as they kept their line tight and their formation steady, the only thing impeding their death blows being the already dead bodies that were quickly piling up at their feet. It was a complete route as the unsuspecting army continued to move forward into the gauntlet of death that had already cut down many of their number. It seemed all too easy when suddenly the left flank bowed and then began to crumble as the enemy finally realized their predicament and started attacking from along the trees working their way around to the backside of the line. Wess recognized the danger his men were in as they were suddenly forced to fight along two fronts. Calling for retreat, Myles and Jack pressed their lines forward to pinch off the fight from the road and then all turned back toward the keep, retreating another hundred yards where they stretched out and formed the line again.

The refugees who had been in the back had a full view of what was coming after them out of the woods creating an even higher level of panic as it became obvious that the soldiers would not be able to hold long enough for them all to reach the keeps innards safely. Mayhem erupted as renewed effort was made to try to press those in front forward at a faster pace but no matter how hard they tried, the way was blocked by the mass of fear stricken Calandrians.

With increased determination, the men pressed forward galloping down the first line of offense before they were forced to slow in their progress as hundreds of enemy fighters spilled out of the woods, the promise of blood and battle calling to them. Though determined in their fight, the men were no match for the countless numbers that continued to press them while expanding to either side. They could not hold their line without risk of being flanked and then surrounded. Jack chanced a quick look behind him as Erl took down another goblin before attacking the wolg it was riding on.

The people were still so close to the fighting, the rush for the keep and the pressing of so many bodies making it almost impossible for anyone to move. They had to hold the line. Then he saw a group of orcs that had broken past the far right side and were no longer trying to fight the men on horses but instead were racing for the easy kill that waited them in those rushing to reach the castle. Already, one of the orcs had reached and cut down an unlucky soul who never knew they were there. Like a rippling wave, the people in the back suddenly shifted to either side, trying desperately to get away as more of their friends, family, and countrymen were cut down without mercy. They were like sheep when the wolf gets into the pen. Some broke off and tried to run away to the south but they were quickly run down and cut to pieces. Others just stopped where they were and cast themselves to the ground in fear, barely making a sound as they were pierced through.

Jack cried out to those around him and then quickly disengaged from the battle racing back and desperately trying to reach and save the innocents who were now falling like wheat to the sickle. The remaining soldiers gave way as well, as the word moved down either side of the line for all to fall back. Closing the gaps as best they could, the line formed again but was spread out too thin to cover the backs of all the people who suddenly found themselves pressed by the horses, soldiers and enemy on one side and their countrymen on the other. It was too late. There were just too many of them. Jack knew they couldn't hold for very long before the line would collapse and those still outside the keep would be lost.

The battle turned fierce. The men knowing they had no more room to give thrust forward with a low groan, temporarily pressing their opponent back and, for a brief moment, gaining the upper hand. Zadok's minions seemed to give way in fear to the fury the men unleashed as if suddenly tapping into a well of strength and determination that lent vigor to their arms. Jack caught sight of Myles who was desperately trying to fend off a barrage of club wielding trolls when one caught the side of his head and he went down. Jack didn't have the time to scream out as he suddenly found himself pressed to block the attack that was coming at him now from either side.

Their last surge was falling apart as there was no one left to fill the gaps that were quickly becoming larger. Ranse and Jace continued to fight near him, the large man and his prince dealing out death on every side, but even Jace was now covered in wounds across his arms and chest that seemed to be taking their toll as his sword swings appeared to come a little bit slower. Erl yelped, distracting Jack's attention as a pike thrust past his sword and cut into his thigh. It was over. All was lost.

Chapter Thirty

Helgar squinted against the fading light in an attempt to identify the large mass of bodies as to whether they were friendly or adversarial. Rangor, flanked by Bardolf, stood by their new king and peered into the distance at the long line that seemed not to move at all. After the devastating destruction visited upon their beloved Thornen Dar, the dwarfs had gathered all of their remaining strength and left their once safe mountain home to vent their rage on the battlefield. The long march down the Dorian Mountains had only fueled that fury into a berserker's need for blood and death.

"It's them from Calandra, yer highness," Rangor offered. "I'd bet me mother's beard by it."

"Then Calandra is fallen," Bardolf voiced the obvious. "They be seekin' the shelter of Bedler's Keep, the last bastion of hope."

"Aye," Helgar breathed, willing his eyes to see what the captain of his guard had so easily picked out while he was still unable to distinguish more than a glob of shadows. "We best be putin' a match to it then or we'll be missin' the whole thing afore it even starts."

"Wait," Bardolf called. "We may be missin' it already. Look over there." He pointed east of the column and Helgar followed his direction but couldn't make out what it was his friend was pointing at.

"There be movement there," Helgar agreed, "but I can't be seein' nothin' else."

"Cavalry," Rangor said, filling in the gaps for his seemingly nearsighted king. "Must mean there be trouble comin'. My guess is that it be just inside those woods."

"They be tryin' to start without us," Bardolf barked.

"Not if I can be helpin' it," Helgar fumed. "Call the charge!"

*   *   *

Jack felt himself weakening from his exertions and the loss of blood as the line bowed and then finally broke. Unhampered, a group of orcs shot through and started hacking at the unlucky peasants who were still pushing from the back in a desperate attempt to get the line into the keep moving forward. The cries of death and bloodlust erupted behind him. He could not turn to help or regroup as he was faced with the numberless wave of combatants pressing on him, trying to pull him from his saddle. His horse danced, kicking out, trying to protect itself from the jabbing spears and swords that had already marked it with multiply wounds. Erl growled and attacked at his side, but his fur was matted with blood and Jack knew it wouldn't be long before his long loyal friend would give way to the constant onslaught.

The remaining men fought to reform their line but the enemy continued to press them pouring out of the trees like a gushing artery. It was hopeless. Their only hope was to seal themselves in the keep but they were too few to protect the innocents who were now getting butchered. Wess suddenly appeared on Jack's left raising the cry, "To the king, to the king." Other men fought their way through, and the gaps were suddenly being filled, though their only chance for survival was to retreat. A small cluster of men suddenly appeared, gathering around him in a knot of resistance when a distant horn broke through the angry din. Jack chanced a quick glance back.

"Reinforcements come," Ranse called, suddenly at his side. Jace was with him, his sword flashing left and right with incredible speed and accuracy as the enemy dropped around them.

"Dwarfs!" Jack cried. "Helgar has come to our aid!"

A thousand stout, ax wielding bodies suddenly collided against the enemy pushing it back twenty paces before the sheer numbers that made up Zadok's army was finally able to absorb the impact and press back. The Calandrians lurched forward as they were once again separated from the fighting though by a short distance. Jack knew it was not enough to turn the enemy back, but it would at least buy them some more time to get the people inside the keep. They were still clumped in a clot of flailing arms and horrified screams, but it appeared that they were finally moving forward.

Helgar and his people crashed into the enemy like an iron first, swinging their axes and cutting them down like kindling for the fire. The dance of blood and death seemed to fuel something primal in the dwarves as they battled in fierce anger and hatred for the mass destruction that had been visited upon their beloved home and king. None would easily be called from the field of battle until their white hot rage had been sated. Shouts of "for Thornen Dar!" and "for the once king!" became battle cries of fury and rage to the point of turning into a battle frenzy as they dug out large chunks of Zadok's horde. Their axes cut deep into flesh and bone, their calls of war quickly becoming drowned out in the screams of death.

The once green grassland was now red and damp with puddles of blood filling the air with the scent of iron mingled with the stench of dirt and sweat. All around was the grating symphony of chaos and death peeling out its cacophonous sounds of violence and mayhem.

Jack blocked another sword thrust, twisting the attacker's assault and then pressing the steel of his blade through its chest. The dwarves had seemed to breathe new life into his men though far too many lay butchered on the gore soaked battlefield. He knew they could not maintain their sudden advantage for long as an endless stream of enemy fighters continued to take the field. Chancing a glance up thankfully there was still no sign of the dragons, though why Zadok had not sent his pets to destroy them, he could not guess.

The refugees gained fifty more yards as they continued to squeeze themselves through the keep's saving doors giving the fighters more space to retreat and regroup. Helgar's band had stopped its advance now and seemed content to take on combatants as they came, but soon they would all need to retreat back so as not to allow a turn in the fight and finally a route as had almost occurred to Jack and his men. He still didn't think they could save all of Calandra's people and he didn't want to contemplate how they would defend themselves once in the keep with most of the army dead getting them there. The flash of hope the dwarves had brought was quickly fading into reality's condemning certainty.

A large group of refugees suddenly broke away from the main body, the closeness of the enemy falsely convincing them that salvation could only be found in the distant woods south of the castle. Recognizing the easy kill, an equally large group of trolls and goblins split away from the main fighting and gave chase. Wess called out to Jack, pointing to what was happening. "Do we disengage to try and protect them?"

Jack swiveled his head back and forth between the fight that pressed him and the party of men, women and children who were about to be slaughtered. Swearing out loud, he shook his head. "We can't save them at the risk of the others. They are lost." Just as he'd spoken the words, the group was overtaken well away from the cover of the trees. Their screams were only muted by the raging fight that demanded the attention of those giving their lives to protect the main body.

*   *   *

Jne and Soyak crested a small rise giving them an unobstructed view of the battlefield below. They were followed by the hundred Tjal-Dihn who had raced to join them while runners had been sent out to the remaining *Tja* to call on all others who would add themselves to the battle. It took only a moment for her to recognize the precarious situation her friends were in as they gave their lives to save the mob of refugees fighting one another to enter the keep. She spat out the horrid taste it placed in her mouth to see the cowardly behavior of Jack's people. They were not worthy of the blood that was being spilt to protect them, but she would not shirk from the fight either. Preparing to lead her people forward, she suddenly paused as a dark blot inked the sky. Then another appeared and yet another. Even from this distance, she could feel the icy fingers of doom threatening to squeeze the courage from her heart. And then suddenly, the mass of refugees shattered into a multitude of pieces flying pell-mell in all directions.

*   *   *

"Dragons!" Jack cried, feeling them almost before seeing their horrific masses blocking out the afternoon light with their great shadows. Almost instantly many of his men suddenly broke away and fled as he called out for them to keep their courage and hold the line. Some obeyed, but too many, overcome by the almost supernatural fear that emanated from Zadok's Dren spawned creatures, broke away and fled, trampling fleeing peasants as they did so. The battlefield was quickly turning into a chaotic vortex of panic and confusion. Even Helgar's battle bred dwarfs were not immune to the powerful dread the dragons brought as they swooped down with their massive bodies to pick off any in their path.

The battlefield had suddenly turned into a desperate race for retreat as more and more defenders broke away trying to chase down the keep's entrance. The refugees who had been close to the saving gates finally fought their way in as the remainder of Calandra's people broke away leaving the door open and clear. Knowing they didn't have a chance, Jack called out for the retreat as more and more soldiers turned tail and ran.

In almost the same instant, Helgar called out to his own people whose lust for battle was suddenly sucked from their very marrow sending them chasing after the men who were mounted and leaving them behind to face the army and the dragons that were dropping from the sky, releasing their deadly breath in swaths of destruction.

"We can't leave them!" Jack shouted to Wess as he motioned toward

Helgar and his warriors still trying to break free from the battle enough to make an escape. Only a few of his men remained mixed with a group from Aleron who had mustered enough courage to stay with Ranse and Jace who still fought at the king's side.

"Rally to the king," Wess called out and then put a horn to his lips and blew out the notes to charge. To their credit, some of the men who had raced to get away, were suddenly turning back, responding to the order though the dragons still hunted in the skies above. Fifty men turned to face thousands as Helgar's people still fought to get free of the melee.

Preparing to reengage the battle, all of them paused in wonder as a blade of a hundred horses and riders suddenly cut through the enemy line from the north like a scythe through ripen wheat. In and instant, the dwarves were cut free like sharp scissors through cloth as Jne and the Tjal slit a large gap into the enemy. Not wasting the opportunity, Helgar called for his people to make for the keep while Jack led his men forward to help protect their rear. Though vastly outnumbering their attackers, Zadok's army seemed to stall with the coming of the Tjal that were like a swarm of hornets stinging them on every side.

Catching site of Jne, Jack was amazed at how majestic she appeared as she dealt out death on every hand, her face calm in the presence of such a chaotic storm. None of the Tjal seemed to feel the dragon fear that covered the field like a wretched fog as they plied their craft of death upon the enemy. Helgar's people quickly chewed up the earth between them and the keep, narrowly escaping the death that rained down from the dragons above. Though feeling cheated that they had missed most of the battle, the Tjal were not careless with their lives either, knowing that there would certainly be more to come as they broke away from the battle as Zadok's minions began to press their advantage of sheer numbers.

Using a hit and run tactic, the mounted men and Tjal covered their retreat as best they could while desperately trying to avoid the dragons that had already cleared the majority of the battlefield of any survivors and were now turning their eyes upon the remaining few on horseback.

Jack caught a quick glimpse of the keep's entrance as the last of Helgar's people passed through. He was amazed at how quickly and orderly they had entered the keep, unlike his own people who cared only for their own lives. "To the keep!" he shouted as the last assault was thrown at the enemy and then all turned about and laid heels to their horse's flanks. The trialing army was no match on foot to chase down the fleeing defenders and the wolgs had been held back as all eyes turned to the skies and watched as the dragons circled and then suddenly dropped from above.

Though the keep was not a hundred yards distant, anyone watching could tell that the dragons would reach them first. Pressing themselves as flat against their horses as they could, they willed their mounts to greater speed as the shadow of death descended. Any less disciplined would have turned away and chased after a different path desperate to escape and only sealing their fate in the process. But these were a group of the finest soldiers and fighters the defenders had and they knew to break away was suicide even in the face of certain defeat; still they pressed on.

Three serpentine necks extended in preparation as they readied to take out the remaining fighters in one foul breath. The horses strained, trying to find more speed as they could all see the coming promise of death. Suddenly, a cry went up from the parapets above and a torrent of arrows was released upon the dragons. Though their armor was too thick for any to penetrate, their wings were not so protected as multiple arrows made it through sending the closest one crashing into the next and veering them all from their course. The first rider shot through the open gate and up the stairs just as the dragons hit the ground crushing the last twenty Tjal riders as they crashed onto the field. Of the four soldiers that had been left to help at the gate, one had remained who now shut the great door behind the last rider, sealing them in and shutting out the cries of rage the dragons released at having been robbed of their quarry.

*　　　*　　　*

Jack pressed his horse up the winding stairway that changed from stone to wood for about a hundred yards before changing back to stone as they disappeared into a long tunnel and the final climb. Erl was at his side, followed by Ranse and Jace and what remained of the cavalry. Wess was nowhere to be seen but he felt certain his old friend had gotten free.

He stopped just inside the tunnel next to the large oak door that was propped open and dismounted tying off his horse's reins on a steel ring set in the stone wall just below a burning torch. Ranse paused long enough for Jack to give instructions. "Get everyone to the top and I'll fire the stairs once the last of them are through." Ranse just nodded, kicking his horse forward. Erl curled up next to Jack's horse who, though battle trained was still not too happy about having a wolg so close as it rolled its eyes and snorted.

A long line of weary soldiers trotted into the tunnel, none without some type of wound, their faces still flushed from battle. Jack watched them as they passed, when he caught sight of one face he recognized. "Aye there, Jack," an unkempt and foul looking man called out as he approached. "I see that ya still keep company with that mangy flea bag o' yours do ya?"

"He's a might cleaner and better company than the likes of you, Quin," he countered gruffly, but good naturedly. "Where's your master gotten off to?"

"Wess? He stopped to close the door and keep the riff raff from comin' in."

"Looks like he missed one," Jack argued, as Quin passed.

"I suppose he done that indeed," Quin agreed, and then moved up the tunnel.

More battle weary men filed by, their faces grim, their hands twitching slightly as evidence that the rush that takes a man during a fight had still not completely left them. These were good men all. Though not the type to invite to the table where proper folk ate, they were the cream, as it were, when it came to a fight. And a fight is all that was left for any of them now.

Soon there appeared a gap in the line. Jack waited expectantly as slow minutes passed before finally another rider appeared on the stairs. The faces and gear changed to that of the unmistakable Tjal-Dihn. Though happy for their assistance and well aware that had they not come when they did many of the men that had just passed him would have, in all likelihood, been left on the field to be gathered later for the cook fires, he felt a shiver of apprehension as to how he was to keep peace when the days passed with all of them tucked tightly and close in the castle. The treaty between men and Tjal was shaky at best and it wouldn't take much to ignite the tinder of their pride when close quarters were forced upon them.

"*T'oben'djen keah jal,*" Jack said with a slight bow as the first Tjal passed. His eyes were hard set, flashing a deadly look that might have caused a lesser man to soil his trousers. But Jack merely acknowledged the next rider knowing that courage was more respected in Tjal society than apologetics or weakness. He continued to greet them as they passed. Some returned his gesture with a slight nod or a word, but most merely ignored him as they filed up the stairway. It was clear that they had all preferred the freedom of the battlefield and felt it had been too early to come in from play.

Jack's face lit up considerably as Jne suddenly appeared among her countrymen. He'd hoped to find her in their ranks but had not wanted to hold too tightly to hope should he be disappointed. "Jack!" she cried, dismounting quickly and then throwing her arms around him. Jack stood stiff still, uncertain how to respond to a Tjal woman pressing herself against him in a bear hug. Suddenly pulling away, she eyed him and then abruptly demanded to know if Thane were in the keep.

Jack shook his head. "He's not yet returned, I'm afraid." He could see some of the light pass out of her eyes. "But," he quickly reassured, "I'm sure he's just a day or two behind in getting here."

Jne sighed, staring at Erl for a moment before reaching down to scratch him behind the ear. "Yes, he will come," she stated with finality and a hint of trouble should he not obey her words.

Soyak, seeing that they weren't going to be moving anytime soon, dismounted and pulled their horses to the side to allow the others to pass. Jack immediately addressed her in the same manner as he had the others knowing that Jne would not make introductions. Another of the Tjal-Dihn intricacies of honor and pride that demanded he introduce himself first and ask for her name.

"I am Soyak," she responded with a slight grin, pleased at the honor Jack had bestowed upon her by following their customs. Never in his life had Jack seen a Tjal at such an advanced age but he was able to hide his shock very smoothly, which most certainly save him a duel to the death.

"What are our numbers?" Jne asked.

He knew she was taking about those who could carry a sword and fight as her concern for the refugees extended only as far as that they stay out of the way and leave those who were able to the battle. "Not quite two thousand by my reckoning. Half dwarf half men and then what you brought with you. Any chance their may be more Tjal coming?"

Jne shrugged. "One can never say what another will do, but runners have been sent to the closest *Tja*. There is good chance many others will seek out the fighting as well."

Jack nodded, happy with the news but aware of the too many variables that might make it mute when it came to the actual fighting. Zadok's horde was no less than ten thousand strong with the added destructive power of his dragons. Should Thane not be able to retrieve the arrows he sought, they had no hope of survival. For the moment they were safe in the mountain fortress of Bedler's Keep, but how long could they hold out against a siege? He shook his head as the last of the Tjal riders passed into the tunnel.

"What?" Jne asked, watching him.

"They won't set up a siege to wait us out. Zadok faces the same problems as we do when it comes to feeding his army. They'll only last so long on the dead left on the battlefield. Not to mention that whatever power Zadok is exerting upon them to keep them from turning on each other will certainly wane should too many days pass in boredom. No, he will have to attack, and I fear that his dragons will be the ones to lead the assault."

Just then a crash echoed up the stairway follow by growls and the sound of feet ascending the stairs. "They've broken through!" called out Soyak, her swords already in her hands, a smile creasing her wrinkled face.

Wess suddenly appeared, racing up the stairway and calling out to them. "Set fire to the stairs and seal the door! They've broken through!"

Just behind him came the lumbering forms of two rock trolls followed close behind by goblins and orcs eager to reach the keep's interior. Before Jack could say a word, Soyak and Jne had raced down the steps to meet them, their swords flashing in a syncopated dance that cut down the trolls, one of them falling and somewhat blocking the way while the other teetered off the edge of the stairs and fell headlong toward the jagged rocks below. The goblins were hampered at first by the large body blocking their way on the stairs but Jne and Soyak jumped over it to reach the enemy dispatching four more as they continued down.

"Take the horses and get up," Jack shouted at Wess who hesitated at first, not wanting to be left out of the action. "I'll fire the stairs," Jack shouted. "There's not else for you to do but to get in my way!"

Wess nodded, and grabbed the reins to the other three horses, kicking his own forward into the tunnel. Jack turned back and yelled at Jne and Soyak while grabbing the torch from its sconce. "Get back! I'm going to fire the stair!"

Reluctantly, Jne and Soyak disengaged themselves from the battle and stepped lightly over the fallen bodies they'd left in their wake and raced up the stairs. The enemy followed, though not as quickly as they stumbled over their fallen comrades cursing the bodies for blocking the way.

"Have a taste of this," Jack spat, lowering the torch to the steps just past the tunnel entrance. Nothing happened. Glancing up at an approaching troll, he set the fire on the wood once more but he couldn't get it to catch. "It won't start!"

"There!" Soyak yelled, as Jne rushed passed her to meet the oncoming threat. Jack followed her finger pointing up to a trough running along the wall twenty feet above the stairs. "Must be oil to start the fire!"

Jack put the torch back into its sconce and looked around. "There must be a lever or something," he called out, but Soyak was already by Jne's side killing the enemy as fast as they came. It really was too easy with the small amount of space on the stairs but slowly they were being pushed back, step by step as the attack continued to press them. Soon they would be at the tunnel and passed the oak door. They could close it behind them, but without firing the stairs, they would just knock it in like they had done with the other. They had to burn off the stairs.

Jack moved his hands along the stone wall, willing himself to find a catch or something, cursing the builders all along at having hidden the main security measure for the keep. Erl growled making him aware that the fighting was getting dangerously close though he could almost feel it as Jne and Soyak continued to take on the enemy. Soon they would be forced to retreat into the tunnel and closed the door behind them or be overrun.

Then it hit him. "You horse's patute!" he berated himself. Grabbing the ring where he'd tied his horse not minutes before, he gave it a tug and it slid slightly out of the wall toward him. "Into the tunnel!" he cried, and then waited only long enough to see the two Tjal disengage before pulling with all his strength. There was a split second of resistance and then it released and he could hear the cries of surprise as the oil drained out all over the enemy filling the stairs. Handing the torch to Jne, she rushed forward, dispatching a goblin as she did so and then tossed the flame into the air. Turning, she raced back up the tunnel and through the oak door just as Jack was swinging it shut. A scream of terror and a whoosh of hot air carrying the stench of burnt flesh was shut off as the heavy oak door was closed and the thick bars set in place.

Chapter Thirty-One

It was dark when his eyes flittered open once more. Though the moaning sound of the passing wind called out in lonely retreat, it didn't chill him as he would have expected. Taking stock of his surroundings, he quickly discovered that he was covered in a downy embrace. Memory rushed back, as did the pain that was still demanding recognition as it pounded at his skull like two great fists. Raising a hand to his face, he gingerly touched his nose, wincing as he did so. His sudden movements brought a disapproving gurgle from deep in the throat of his protective guardian.

Pushing aside the great wing that had sheltered him from the cold, he let the mountain winds have him, tickling a shiver through his body as he breathed deep the frigid air. His nose was still sore and mercilessly clogged with dried blood, but the pounding in his head had subsided to a distant rumble leaving his stomach more at ease as well. Gaining his bearings as best he could, he looked to the east and caught the slightest twinkle of the early morning light seeping over the horizon in a slow, but deliberate fashion. So, he'd been out for at least a day, if not longer. His stomach grumbled, as if in response, and he felt comfort that it did so out of hunger rather than an angry need to empty itself.

Tchee rose up next to him, stretching her great wings and then flapped them briefly before tucking them back against her side and calling out in an angry screech.

Teek shook his head at the sound, recognizing the chastisement. "And what did you expect me to do?" he almost shouted in defense. "He would have killed you."

Tchee groaned in her chest, still unwilling to let him off so easy.

"We both would have died," he said more quietly. "Because you were protecting me and so couldn't fight back."

Tchee stood up straight, her majesty suddenly embraced by the first rays of sunlight.

"Never again," Teek said as he reached for his pack. Unstrapping the great axe that was still tied to the back, he released it and let it clang to the ground. "This is not a Waseeni weapon. I was foolish to think I could make it into one." Drawing his bloodstained dagger, he wiped it as clean as he could in a small clump of dewy grass that clung to a crack in the rock. Taking the sheath from his waist, he secured it to his leg and then used a piece of the strap that had once held the axe to tie off the sheath's bottom as well. Then, grabbing his blowgun from his pack, he loaded a dart. "This is more accurate," he said, placing the pack on his back and then climbing up onto Tchee. "No longer will the Waseeni be the people of the swamplands." Tchee flapped her wings and began to rise. "From now on, we are the terrors of the air!" he cried, shouting to the morning skies as he ascended to meet them.

*   *   *

Zadok peered through the stemmed crystal at the crimson wine that looked too much like blood for Resdin's tastes. Resdin gnawed on a chicken leg having avoided the meat that Zadok seemed to relish so rare and then tossed the bone over his shoulder. A young girl, having seen no more than twelve winters, scurried over to pick it from the lush carpets that blanketed the ground. She was a gift from the great capitol city that now stood in ruins, as were the other slaves that were stationed about anxiously waiting to serve their new master.

They were in a cavernous tent that was large enough to give the feel of being in a great hall; one of the trophies Zadok had taken from Calandra when he'd finally departed. It had belonged to a spice merchant who had obviously done extremely well in his trade, most likely gaining most of his fortune by dealing in illegal substances. A great table was placed in the middle that stretched out to a ridiculous length considering that Zadok and Resdin were the only two seated at it. Filled with delicious meats, pastries, breads, and vegetable dishes that were in quantity to feed a great banquet, the two lone eaters picked at their meals as if having no appetite at all. The food would be tossed out, deemed too great in worth for the likes of his Calandrian slaves who watched pitifully with the sunken eyes of the malnourished.

Four others occupied space to Zadok's left, all hooded and menacing, with an aura of darkness surrounding them that seemed to keep even the light of the many candles perched about the tent from reaching them.

"And so," Zadok's grating voice hissed as he swirled the wine in his glass. "You are telling me that on the eve of my greatest victory, the hidden entrances that I mapped out so carefully for you to use have all been sealed off!" His voice grew in crescendo to the near scream of a madman, as he brought his glass down hard, its contents washing over the side. "My army," he continued, his ranting voice maintaining its volume as spittle escaped his lips, "will not remain interested for long if they are forced to mill about on the valley floor with nothing but each other to fill their time!"

Resdin smiled, as he leaned back in his chair, his hands clasped behind his head. He enjoyed seeing Zadok's pets being brought to task. But the four hooded figures seemed unmoved by their master's ranting while the on looking slaves could not seem to calm shaking bodies. "Let *us* be about it then, milord," one of the hooded figures hissed. "They are no match for our power. Even locked away in their *mighty fortress*," he sneered.

"NO!" Zadok shouted, his hand banging the table, disrupting his wine glass completely. One of the slaves vomited from fear while another simply crumpled to the carpeted floor. Zadok visibly forced the calm back into his face and his voice. Finally, he spoke, a shallow, rasping whisper of a voice. "Wargon," he called and one of the hooded figures bowed slightly, his arms stretching out to his sides in obeisance. "I presume that the men of the keep have not let themselves be completely holed up in their rock cell. There is certainly another way in and I assume that you will not disappoint me in finding out where it lay."

"My only purpose is to serve you, milord," Wargon answered, the contempt in his voice not quite completely masked.

"Never fear, my pets," Zadok continued, his voice turned to honey. "You will have your play when the victory is assured and my army is reading to be dispersed."

*   *   *

Jack looked out over the vast army below that was a mass of bodies seeming without any order or discipline. Cook fires were beginning to pop up all over the field and soon the fetid scent of burned flesh would rise on the wind to torment the men in the keep with the knowledge that their fallen comrades made up a good portion of the enemy's meal. Jne approached him waiting for the answer to her question as they both turned their eyes to the distant Underwoods forest. Erl slept comfortably curled up on the floor.

The balcony could hardly be called such as its great size and expanse was really just a huge gap in the keep's outer wall. With a rock railing to keep the careless from teetering off the edge, the opening permitted an unobstructed view from the north to the south allowing those in the room a bird's eye image of the battlefield. The room itself was yawning with thick columns rising up to the distant ceiling its walls curving in a circular pattern with doors cut in at disparate locations that lead to varying wings of the keep. Few candles were lit giving it a dark and foreboding feel.

"He will come," Jack insisted. "And you know as well as I that there is no point in you getting lost in the wood trying to chase him down."

Soyak's voice drifted out from the near darkness behind them. "He is right, young one. In such a place you could cross mere feet from each other and be none the wiser."

Jne sighed, knowing all along they were both right. She didn't actually plan to leave and go after Thane, but she needed them to tell her what she already knew. Her blades were already wet with blood and she knew they would taste more before it was all over, she just wished to have him with her so they could fight together like the great romantic stories of her youth.

One of the doors burst open and all turned to the gruff sounds of Helgar's voice as he and Bardolf, followed closely by Rangor, entered the grand room. "Me axe be not sated with the blood o' the enemy as of yet, Master Jack," he bellowed as the three of them came out of the shadows to join them on the balcony. "And though we be folk o' the mountain, I tend to be findin' the sweet savor o' revenge upon those responsible for killin' me da."

"My lord, Helgar," Jack said, using the dwarf king's title as appropriate with a soothing voice to make an attempt at calming his rage. "We all have lost in this war and desire nothing more than to sooth our grief with the blood of the enemy, but, as you can well see," he motioned his hand toward the vast numbers below, "we can't afford to throw ourselves at our adversary head on."

"That might be so," Helgar conceded, "but me people already be gettin' itchy fingers and scratchy feet for the work o' the battlefield."

"We quite agree with you, master dwarf," Soyak broke in. "As our swords still hunger to sup from the corpses of the enemy. Not to mention, unlike our friends of the mountain, our people cannot abide the close walls of a keep such as this one, preferring the open air of the plains as our bed and the stars in the heavens our blanket."

"And that is all well and good," Jack huffed, a slight edge to his voice. "But none of us will be served by throwing our lives away for not in one glorious frontal attack. We are far out numbered and, against Zadok's dragons, have less than inferior weapons to do more than lay down and die at this point."

"And how will that be ever changin'?" Helgar demanded. "It be far better to be dyin' in a fight with the enemy than to be starved out behind a rock wall."

"I don't think that will be an option for us," Jack soothed. "The enemy is even more impatient than any of us for the battle to commence. They will manage a siege much worse than we."

Erl suddenly growled low in his throat. "He's right," Ranse's voice spoke from the dark as he and Jace materialized from behind a distant pillar, followed by Tryg who remained aloof and well distant from the others, especially Erl who seemed to focus his distaste on the young Waseeni boy. "Our enemy's army," Ranse continued, "will turn on itself in quick measure while we stand aside and watch."

"Aye," Helgar breathed disappointedly, "that be the truth of it for certain. But I fear that you have forgotten the true threat that be those flying rats."

"He hasn't used them so far except in the end as if trying to drive us into the keep," Ranse offered.

Jack's face turned dark. "But why would he do that?"

Tryg's voice suddenly broke from the shadows. "Like sheep in a pen," he said and then brought a hand to his mouth as if he'd meant the comment only for himself. The others stared at him for a moment before Jack finally broke the hush that had fallen.

"He's right! We've been corralled like sheep with nowhere to go."

"But why do that?" Jne asked. "Why, when he has the strength in numbers and the ability to destroy us all with his dragons alone?"

"Revenge," Tryg whispered as if the answer were obvious, again his voice carrying more than he'd hoped.

Jack eyed the young Waseeni boy, the hackles on his back rising with Erl's as a strange feeling came over him as it seemed to always do when he dealt with Tryg.

"The whys be unimportant," Helgar barked, "when the whats and the hows still be unanswered. We can be thinkin' o' that when the war be done and we be left with the cleanin' of blood from our axes while drinkin' a pint of ale. For now, all I wants to be knowin' is which way to be goin' to get me some more orc guts to be splattered on me axe."

All eyes turned when a door shut along the west wall. Wess sauntered through the columns and into the light, his face grim though his demeanor was relaxed. "Now, that won't be as easy as you might like, master dwarf," he spoke, bowing slightly to Helgar and then coming to rest next to Jack.

"Have you all forgotten that the stairs have been torched, affectively barring our enemies from entrance, while at the same moment, keeping us safely locked away in the keep?"

"And what of that?" Soyak demanded, her hands twitching some as if the walls themselves were suddenly closing in around them.

Jack held up and hand, flashing Wess a withering look. "What my friend has so conveniently forgotten in his moment of tongue wagging is the fact that the stairs are not the only entrance to the keep. That is to say, there are other ways out. Other, undisclosed ways to exit the keep."

Tryg suddenly stepped forward but then stopped as if he'd moved without wanting to.

"And where might those exits be?" Helgar asked.

"I know of them," Jack said, hesitant to reveal too many of the keep's secrets.

"And what if you should fall?" Soyak stated the obvious concern that was passing through everyone else's mind at that moment.

As if to confirm Soyak's concern, a loud screamed echoed through the chamber as a large figure dropped down from the sky above and landed on the balcony's edge just to Jack's right. The clattering of swords pulled from scabbards reverberated off the walls like an echo of the screech that had preceded the great bird's arrival. Tryg quickly slipped back into the shadows, his eyes burning with hatred, all other eyes focusing on their perceived attacker as Teek slipped easily from Tchee's back. A collective sigh seemed to breathe life back into the group as the quick shot of adrenalin dissipated through their blood and was brushed away with pounding hearts.

Teek hesitated at the sudden show of arms before turning slightly red with embarrassment. "I'm sorry," he offered shyly. "I did not mean to cause such a scene but we didn't want to be made an easy target for the enemy by making a long, deliberate approach."

Jack cleared his throat. "And where exactly have you been playing at these pass few days," he grumbled at the boy as Tchee hopped into the grand room away from a possible arrow shot from below. Strutting along the north wall, she peered into the darkness in its deep recesses, a slight rumble building in her throat before she settled herself to wait.

"I am truly sorry, your highness," Teek bowed in humble obeisance, "but the mind of a roc does not always match that of its rider. The good news though, it would seem, is that I think she has convinced others of her kind to help us."

"And what good are a flock of oversized birds?" Soyak complained.

"They keep the dragons at bay," Jne said, flashing one of her rare smiles on the Waseeni boy who blushed an even deeper red. "They will be most welcome," she added.

Jack's faced brightened at the prospect. Though they could only stall the inevitable, it might be just long enough to give Thane time to return and cause Zadok's army to lose interest. But how to deal with dwarfs, humans, and worse, Tjal-Dihn all boxed up in such close quarters? He couldn't be sure which side would break first. It very well could be those in the keep that lost interest—unless they were given something to do. Idle hands feed wrath's fires while those engaged direct its heat.

"And what of our way out?" Tryg's voice broke from the shadows though he kept himself hidden still.

Jack regarded those before him. "You are correct, as we have just witnessed, that I cannot keep such secrets to my grave. But, you must all give solemn witness to keep this one to yourselves until a strategy is agreed upon for engaging the enemy. We cannot afford groups sneaking out to fight and risk the hidden entrance be compromised over to the enemy."

All heads nodded in agreement as Jack turned his eyes on each in turn. "Very well," he continued, "just off of this hall, through the northwestern door is a room that in all appearances is nothing more than an antechamber filled with books. But by twisting the sconce to the left of the door, a hatch is revealed in the floor that leads down to a hidden opening out the northern end of the keep. At every level a similar room is come upon with the same hidden hatch until the bottom floor where the sconce opens a concealed wall out to the valley floor. It can be accessed from any level so it is of the utmost importance that it not be discovered since all can imagine the damage it would bring should the enemy discover it."

No one heard the very northwestern door Jack had spoken of open slowly and then close as an unkempt man with only one arm, passed through and was already turning the sconce that revealed the hatch. He suppressed a wheezing cackle as he took to the descending stairs, his mind having finalized the plan that would bring him his victory. He'd almost left his hiding place with his dagger bared when the boy and the bird suddenly appeared out of the sky. He might have gotten close enough, but with all the other weapons in the room, he'd let patience overrule his need for killing and now nothing could keep him from fulfilling his destiny. "Don't worry none, Zel," he crowed under his breath as he descended the second stair. "We'll be cuttin' 'im good and soon."

"Is that it?" Tryg demanded, drawing all eyes to the shadows where he stood, his voice suddenly changing in power and tone. Erl growled, abruptly standing while Tchee gurgled in her throat.

"What be ye playin' at boy?" Helgar demanded. "Come out from the shadows where we can all be seein' ya."

"Gladly," he hissed as a massive form suddenly rushed forward, the last appendages of what once was the Waseeni boy's body transforming into an enormous red dragon. The hall erupted in surprise and fire as he belched out a wave of flame scattering the hall in all directions as people abandoned weapons and scurried for cover. Completing his transformation, Tryg's great serpentine body rushed for the balcony edge, no thoughts on the easy kills that had flung themselves behind pillars or pressed in desperate retreat through the few closest doorways. He had the secret that would gain him favor in Zadok's eyes and place him above his brothers and sister and an easy escape had been afforded him to the open sky. No longer would he grovel in the form of the worthless Waseeni. No longer would he be forced to suffer the human's wolg or the strange stares he got from Domis or Teek. Should he ever meet either one again, he would take joy in devouring their flesh as he had the whole Waseeni people. He cried out in triumph as he cast himself out of the keep and into the air.

Teek was stunned by what he'd just witnessed as he peered out from behind a pillar as the last vestiges of Tryg's body were finally swallowed up in the form that was the dragon. The blast of fire seared into his mind as he remembered the charred remains of what had once been his home and family. With it came a primal rage that suddenly flared, equaling the heat of the flames with a vengeful desire to cut down the thing that had taken all that was dear from him. With a cry of his own, he leaped from his hiding place just as Tryg's dragon body cleared the balcony and dropped from site. As if reading his thoughts, Tchee moved with him, just a step ahead, jumping from the balcony right before Teek shot up onto the railing and flung himself into the air.

Opening her wings, Tchee caught an upward draft that lifted her slightly, catching the small boy as he landed softly onto her back and then she tucked them in and shot forward, giving chase to their foe. Jack's and Jne's faces peered over the railing and watched as they disappeared into the darkening sky.

*   *   *

The days seemed to all blur into one as they raced through the woods taking only the shortest breaks as needed for food and the least amount of rest. They were continually passed from one Kybara to another as fresh "mounts" were provided to allow them the greatest amount of speed in reaching their destination. The pack grew at an almost constant rate as others joined the race, the word spreading quickly that the Chufa had returned and war was at the forest's edge. Aisig had joined the group once again after having left for an extended period and was carrying Thane through the Underwoods' mist that seemed to hang on to the undergrowth.

The splendor and joyous feelings that had accompanied their reunion with the YeiyeiloBaneesh trees had still not diminished making the exhausting ride bearable as each reminisced in their minds and hearts the experience that had been a personal communion with their Tane. Each understood now the entity that was their birthright. The actual living influence that surrounded them on all sides was no longer a mere gift to be used but a living and breathing part of them that had substance and mass. Even Domis seemed to sense the sacred union that had been between the Chufa and their Tane. So much so, in fact, that he felt somewhat ashamed for having witnessed it.

Sadly, the promise of war and bloodshed was a dark specter that seemed to nag at their minds as well, picking away at the light and peace that each one so desperately fought to hold onto.

"*We are here,*" Aisig's voice broke into their minds, disrupting their silent contemplations.

Thane dropped from his back working life back into his legs as the others did the same. Walking stiffly, the four companions broke away from their Kybara friends toward the last remaining trees that marked the outer edges of the Underwoods forest. "It's almost night," Dor spoke as they all peered across the countryside.

Tam's eyes went slack as she cast herself, without hesitation, into the wind that brushed lightly across her face sending her spirit with it to scout the area. Though Thane could have followed, he didn't feel the need to baby her any longer, instead turning his attention to a piece of bread Dor pushed at him.

"How far away are we?" Domis asked between bites into an apple he'd gotten from his pack.

"It's hard to say," Thane answered, "since I'm not quite certain where we are. Tam will let us know shortly."

"*You are about a half a day's journey from the great HuMan mountain home,*" Aisig's voiced answered in their minds. "*I will take you there if you still wish it, though we generally do not leave the boarders of the woods.*"

"We may need all of you, I'm afraid," Dor sighed, knowing all too well the force that threatened them.

"It's begun!" Tam's voice suddenly announced, startling them as she returned to her body. "The keep is under siege."

"We're late," Dor spat.

"Maybe," Tam countered, "but we may not have missed our role in this fight. A dragon approaches."

Thane looked at his friend, a strange light glowing in his eyes. "Are you certain?"

Tam only nodded.

"You three take cover in the trees," Thane suddenly commanded while retrieving his bow and setting the string.

Dor grabbed his arm. "Wait. We can all help with this," he said, not willing to merely watch as his friend faced death alone. "We all have arrows."

Thane pulled the precious arrow the YeiyeiloBaneesh tree had given him and loosely fit it to the string. "I know, but we can't risk losing any of them should one of us miss."

Dor looked like he would laugh. "Miss?"

Thane's expression didn't change. "You will have your opportunity, Dor. But I can't afford the distraction of having you and Tam out there with me. Not to mention the fact that I want the dragon to come to me."

Dor was surprised to find Tam's hand on his arm gently pulling him back toward the forest. At the mention of the dragon, Domis had happily obeyed Thane's command and was already lost to view in the thick trees. "It comes quickly," she said in a soft hush. "We must be away."

Thane stared after her, his mouth agape, his face laid bare with surprise at her willingness to let him do this. Dor just shook his head and followed her as they strode back into the woods. When they were lost to his view, Thane turned and rushed out quickly onto the plains, his eyes scanning the sky for his quarry.

*   *   *

Teek and Tchee swooped down and then shot back high banking to the left as they raced after their lumbering prey. Tryg had the secret he needed and was turning east thinking to make a quick getaway and gain the praise of his master when Tchee's disdainful shriek caught his attention just as the large bird dropped down onto his back. It angered him that such an insignificant creature could cause such trouble to one of his majesty and power. Banking to the right, going south, he tried to shake his attackers cursing all along that Teek was not among the casualties from his attack on the Waseeni swamps. Again, Tchee pressed down on him, forcing him closer to the ground where he would have happily landed and fought, but he needed to get back to Zadok and he knew that Teek and his little pet would not face him head on.

Multiple times he made to turn east in an attempt to get back to his master, but Tchee's assault was relentless. Miles passed beneath them as the great dragon moved its colossal body with as much speed and agility as it was able but it was no match for the smaller, lighter bird. And yet, this stalemate was as grating on Teek as it was Tryg.

Teek screamed with rage at the boy turned dragon that he had befriended and defended for this whole time unknowing of the treacherous wretch he really was. Tchee dropped on him again but her claws were no match for the armor that was the dragon's skin and Teek knew his blow gun or dagger would have the same impotent affect. The frustration of not being able to mount a proper attack only fed his rage to the point of crazy abandon. He had to destroy this murdering menace not only in revenge for its killing his family and home but to save the lives of his knew friends. But he was uncertain in how to carry out the task. The only vulnerable spot was its eyes. Teek didn't hesitate. As Tchee made another pass, he slipped his dagger into his mouth and then jumped from the roc's back landing with a thud on Tryg's back just at the base of his skull.

*   *   *

Thane raced out onto the plain sprinting northward his eyes searching the darkening sky above for his prey. The arrow pulsed with life in his hand as if sensing its purpose and anxious to be about its business. He hadn't thought to quiz Tam closer on her discovery, the excitement of finally being able to fight against Zadok's terrifying creations had spurred him on without a second thought. It was now that he wondered if he'd been premature and if his race to meet the fight would turn out to be unfruitful.

He paused at the distant cry that could only be a dragon's wail and then almost leaped into the air with excitement when he spotted the inky black smudge taking shape as it drew closer to him overhead. He stopped and tested the line on his bow before nocking the arrow and waiting for the dragon to draw near. He didn't have to wait long as the form materialized and he pulled back on the bow and took aim. Taking a deep breath, he steadying himself and was just about to let fly his deadly bolt when his eye caught the flutter of wings dropping down just above his prey.

Slowly lowering his bow and releasing the tension he cursed at his luck. "Teek!" He couldn't fire and risk hitting the Waseeni boy and his bird. He watched as they raced toward him and then caught his breath as a small figure flew off of Tchee and landed on the dragon's neck.

*   *   *

Teek scurried up the dragon's neck and grasped one of the great horns that protruded back just above his ear holes. He slipped on the scales but regained his footing quickly as Tchee screamed at him from above. Ignoring his avian friend, he positioned himself as best he could knowing he'd have only one shot. Tryg shook his head and let out an irritate roar at having an uninvited rider. Tucking his giant wings, he raced toward the valley floor where he could better fight his insect-like menace.

Teek grabbed his dagger and raised it above his head. "This is for my family!" he screamed swinging the blade forward just as the large talons wrapped around his waist and pulled him free. His dagger hit something solid, jarring it from his hand as he was suddenly ripped into the air.

*   *   *

Thane watched in amazement as Tchee dropped out of the sky on top of the Waseeni boy and tore him away from the dragon just as it belched out an awful scream as if in great pain. He felt like his limbs were lead as the dragon's gaze suddenly focused in on him, a lone figure on a grassy plain with nowhere to run. As if by instinct, he raised his bow as the dragon suddenly bore down on him, its fierce head pulled back as it sucked in a tremendous amount of air in preparation to blow out its killing breath. He pulled at the bowstring using all of his strength to draw it back in time but the arrow was only halfway to his cheek when the dragon started to exhale.

Thane watched powerlessly as the great torrent of fire was released, its mass and speed too great for him to turn aside and escape. A distant scream echoed in his ears as he closed his eyes just as he was hit and engulfed in the dragon's flame.

Chapter Thirty-Two

Teek screamed in terror fighting desperately against Tchee's talons as he watched Thane disappear in an explosion of fire. Tam and Dor mingled their cries of disbelief and horror as they both broke from the tree line and raced forward in a vain attempt to reach their friend before he was reduced to mounds of ash. But their steps faltered as they both quickly realized that there was no hope of saving him. Teek's eyes dripped tears as Tchee swung away from the scene with a loud, mournful screech while the dragon turned about and descended to glory in his latest kill.

Tryg smiled, sensing the agony that envelope Thane's friends, burning them as completely with pain as his fire would Thane's flesh. Landing in a large spray of dirt and grass no more than one hundred yards from his foe, Tryg was somewhat curious to notice that Thane's body still remained upright as if the ash were held together in some way. His memory of the Waseeni was an almost instantaneous explosion of cremated remains that produced particles no large than dust that was quickly scattered by the tailing winds caused by his flapping wings.

*   *   *

Thane felt an instant of dread panic as the flames engulfed him, shattering against his chest and then wrapping around him like a new skin. He screamed in anguish expecting the searing temperature that would devour him in excruciating pain before leaving him a lifeless mass of charcoal. It wasn't until after the second scream that he realized his flesh was not burning though he could feel a tremendous amount of heat building up from inside. And then suddenly it washed over him like a pounding

303

wave, a feeling of power that threatened to overcome him, coaxing for control and a complete release to its will. He recognized it instantly as kin to the sensations he'd felt while flying. With the wind rushing past him, his ArVen Tane had come to life and sought his complete surrender. This time it was his QenChe Tane that had flared up out of dormancy. It called for his release, filling him with a sensation of ecstasy that was unlike anything he'd experienced before. It called to him, begged to be let go, cried and then demanded it be given absolute control. But this time he listened. This time he gave into the building sensation, forgetting who he was and becoming the Tane instead. Releasing the last vestiges of what had made him Thane, he opened himself up completely and let the rush of the QenChe overflow and then drown him in its power.

In an instant, the dragon flame was suddenly drawn into his skin, the fire still raging but sucked in under his flesh. His body lit up in a tremendous glow of light shining from within and making him a beacon in the near evening dusk.

Tam and Dor stopped in awe, their jaws hanging open as they watched in elated amazement to find their friend was not consumed but seemed to have devoured the dragon's fire. The forest behind them erupted in the eerie sounding cry of the Kybara as they lifted their voices in worship.

Thane was lost in the rapture of the Tane as it seemed to grow in strength, feeding on the fire that raged inside his body. No longer did he exist as a person but was instead one with the consciousness that was the QenChe. Heat. Fire. Burning. Flame. Purity. Clarity. The dragon's fire, now his own, was a molten river in his veins that suddenly rushed from his legs and into his core, gathering its entire mass and strength into one whole that was then directed up his arms and down to his outstretched hands.

Tryg approached, his amazement that Thane had not been destroyed quickly replaced with hot anger that a mere mortal dare steal his fierce power and not die from it.

The QenChe watched the dragon with an equivalence close to amusement as the massive serpent approached. The flames in its hands grew in strength materializing into two large orbs that peered through the near darkness like great eyes. Brighter and brighter they became until it hurt ones eyes to behold them, giving Tryg pause as he was forced to look away. And then, suddenly, they shot out, shattering the distance between them and the dragon and striking him full in the chest, sending him sailing back in a shower of sparks and embers.

Tryg's roar of pain and anger echoed across the valley as he crashed against rocks and dirt sending them shooting out in all directions before he finally came to a stop. Dark spots danced in his eyes, but other than his pride, he was uninjured. The flame had been his own. Even turned against him as it was, his scales could not be burned by his own fire.

"And what kind of sorcery is this?" he screamed clumsily regaining a standing position.

Thane found, with a jolt, that the rush and unity of the QenChe Tane was suddenly gone, leaving him as he was but without the slightest drain of energy. If anything, he felt rested without the least sense of fatigue. No scent of smoke clung to him or his clothing; neither dirt nor grime of any type. It was as if he'd just come from a bath, though he felt much cleaner than he could ever recall feeling.

The dragon loomed up on him, his great legs quickly overtaking the ground that separated them. "So, you have magic do you?" Tryg sneered. "Well, let's see how well you do with teeth and tongue!" Tryg leered over him, his mouth agape in preparation to swallow him, large fonts of saliva escaping his massive maw.

Reaching back, Thane pulled the heart arrow from his quiver and fit it into his bow in one fluid motion pulling it back in preparation to fire.

Tryg blinked at Thane's quickness, but then roared back with laughter, turning a mocking grin on his insignificant opponent. Puffing out his chest, he gave Thane an easy shot at his heart. "Go ahead, if it will give you comfort to know you tried to fight before you died. I'll even wait until you've fired before I eat you."

Thane smiled up at him. "You are too kind," he hissed and then released the arrow. Tryg let out another roar as he brought his head down, teeth bared, darting his head forward to devour his opponent. But his bellow was cut short as the arrow passed through his scaly armor like thin silk, piercing his heart and then continuing on through his back. The look of triumph in his eyes turning at once to shock as the light in them flickered out. Thane jumped to the side, just avoiding his great head as it crashed into the dirt the shocked disbelief permanently fixed in his visage.

Tam reached him first, her arms thrown with a vice grip around his neck chocking off his air as she rambled on about thinking him dead. Dor was close behind, adding his own asphyxiating grip while laughing almost uncontrollably in nervous relief. He was seeing small exploding dots of blackness before he was finally able to extricate himself from their deluge of exuberant sentiment.

"How did you do that?" Tam demanded, still holding his arm as if afraid if she let go he would fall down dead or disappear completely.

"It was my Tane," he stated flatly, as if it were the most obvious and normal thing. "Do you remember flying with the rocs?" he asked her.

Tam smiled. "Yes. I have never felt so alive in my life."

"It was the same for me. But take that and apply it to the QenChe Tane. All I had to do was give myself over to it."

"Completely?" Tam asked, a sliver of anxiety slipping into her voice. "I was afraid that to do so would cause me to cease to exist. Like I would become lost in the Tane's power and never return."

"I had originally thought the same thing," Thane soothed. "But now I understand better. It is in the surrender that true control is obtained."

"That's what makes using the Tane so difficult at times," Dor added as if fully understanding for the first time.

"The possibilities are endless..." Thane started but Dor finished for him.

"...if we'll allow it to happen instead of trying to wrest control!"

Tchee's exuberant cry brought all their heads around as she gently released Teek to the ground before flapping away and then coming back to rest near them. She cooed and bobbed her head in cheerful greeting bringing smiles to all their faces as Teek relinquished the reverent awe in which he held them and gave each a great hug in turn. "It is so good to see you all...alive," he finished, looking at Thane.

"As well as you," Tam said, tussling his hair. "We missed you."

Teek's countenance fell as did his eyes. "I am sorry I failed you." Then pointing an accusing finger at Tchee, he added, "but she is most stubborn at times with where she wants to go and who she wants with her." Tchee hooted in reply without the slightest hint of apology. Teek's face suddenly brightened. "But you were successful," he added gesturing toward the dragon's corpse that lay like an ominous mountain mere feet away. "You found the trees. Will this give us the victory then?" he asked with wide eyed innocence.

"I'm afraid not," Dor replied, "but it will even things out quite a bit."

"It was Tryg," Teek suddenly announced, the sorrow in his voice tinged with venom. "He was the dragon. He was the one that killed our people."

"Tryg was a dragon?" Tam repeated as if trying to convince herself that the idea was even possible. "But how?"

Teek shook his head. "I don't know. All I know is that one moment we were talking to him and then the next he was growing and changing into that." He pointed toward the dragon corpse, a look of disdain on his face.

"Zadok's sorcery," Dor hissed.

"That would explain the deaths in the camp with the merchant's family butchered," Thane said.

"So the others can change as well?" Tam asked the obvious question.

"I would think so," Thane reasoned.

"But then how will we know if one is among us?" Teek asked.

"We won't," Dor said and then looked back at Tryg. "That is, until they turn. But now we're a bit more prepared to deal with them."

"That reminds me," Thane said turning back to the dragon carcass and walking around behind it. The others watched for a moment as he got further and further away, his eyes stuck to the grassy plain.

"What are you doing?" Tam yelled, starting to follow after him.

Thane suddenly stopped and bent over and then rose again, the heart arrow in his hand. "Found it!" he smiled.

"Right," Teek exclaimed circling Tryg's great head and then clapped for joy. "I knew it! I knew I had hit him."

Dor followed around after him and nodded approvingly as he saw what had given Teek such a rush of excitement. Stuck in the dragon's eyelid, just below the crown of his right socket was a dagger that Teek reached for and then pulled at with some effort before he was able to dislodge it from its place. "A fine mark," Dor said with a nod of approval.

"I was trying to get his eye," Teek said excitedly, "but Tchee grabbed me. I bet I would have hit it square in the center had she not pulled me off when she did."

"Still," Dor encouraged, "it is no easy feat to wound a dragon with a mere dagger—especially while it's flying."

Teek smiled up at him, radiating with the compliment and feeling for once like a real warrior. Wiping the bit of blood from the blade on the grass, he then pushed it back into its sheath on his leg and silently wondered how he'd fare in a fight against something on the ground.

"We need to get going," Thane said, motioning toward the distant keep after placing his arrow back in its quiver.

"Tchee won't carry you," Teek announced dejectedly.

"Not to fear," Thane countered, his voice becoming somewhat distant. "We have our own ride." And then his eyes went dull as he caught the breeze and released his spirit to ride its many currents. Gathering strength and speed at once, he turned to the east willing himself forward to the place where they'd left the rocs outside of Aleron.

*   *   *

"And what now that the way in be compromised?" huffed Bardolf. All of them had been shaken by Tryg's sudden transformation from a seemingly insignificant Waseeni boy harboring a chip on his shoulder to a massive serpentine killer. The revelation was enough to explain how Thornen Dar had been infiltrated and how Jack's caravan of refugees had been attacked without anyone having witnessed it. This was dark magic indeed.

After confirming that everyone was uninjured they had regathered in the relative dark of the cave-like hall as the sun finally set beyond them, casting the grand room into deep shadow. A slight look of mistrust cast a pall over the group as none could any longer be certain who was friend and who was foe.

Jack looked out over the plains, the enemy's cook fires like dancing fireflies covering the basin floor. "You are right, master dwarf, we are compromised. And as I suspected, the attack will most likely come in the morning. Thankfully the entrance is small and should be easily defended by a small group."

"Then what do you propose we do as far as mounting an assault," Soyak pressed. "We still have the issue of too many warriors sleeping within the same tent. If they're not given something to do, they'll end up turning on one another for sure."

"I understand the predicament," Jack retorted, his voice rising slightly in anger. "But we still can't risk the casualties that will surely mount against us in an all out attack. Even with the unsurpassed skills that the Tjal command with the sword and our dwarf friends control with the axe," he soothed, "our strength in numbers in not sufficient to do aught more than perish in the rush."

"I agree with Jack," Ranse offered. "The enemy will break apart if we give them the time to do so. They will grow restless and mount an attack with hooks and ladders or end up fighting amongst themselves and dispersing. The walls are too high for hooks and ladders to be effective so that leaves them frustrated and their anger time to boil over upon themselves."

"And what about the army within?" Helgar demanded. "How long before we be doin' the same?"

"I would hope that we are greater masters of ourselves then orcs and goblins," Jne said, glancing at Soyak who nodded slightly in agreement though obviously not liking that it meant they would be forced to wait.

"For now, may I suggest we make certain our peoples are well taken care of…and well separated from one another," Jack said, "and take the rest we are able for now. The day will bring enough of its own evil, I am sure, to occupy us sufficiently with its demands."

The others reluctantly nodded in agreement, turning to their own and exiting the room through different doors. Jne whispered something to Soyak who glanced quickly at Jack before nodding and retreating through one of the south doors. Jne stayed behind with Jack who was now standing by Erl, scratching his friend behind the ears and saying something in tones too hushed for her to hear. "Am I wrong?" he asked her as she came to stand next to him taking in the sight below. The surprising thing was how beautiful the enemy camp appeared in the evening from such a vantage point. It was like the night sky had fallen and had decided to make its residence on the plains beneath the keep. They could just make out the distant rumbling that noised from Zadok's great host in their evil conversations.

"You speak wisely in what you say, old friend, but also do Soyak and the dwarf king. We cannot hold them all together for too long. There is vengeance in their blood; especially the dwarf people. And that is a fire that cannot be quenched without much bloodshed."

"And the longer the time passes, the easier it is to direct that bloodshed to whatever is closest," he sighed, stroking his beard and then pulling down on it in frustration. "Maybe the breach in our security is the best thing after all. At least that will give them something to be occupied with."

Just then three large shadows crossed the sky in front of them causing both Jack and Jne to stumble back as they reached for weapons, certain the dragons were upon them once more. Erl didn't move. Three rocs flapped back their wings and then gently perched on the stone railing before hopping forward into the great hall. Jack and Jne quickly returned swords to sheaths as Thane, Dor, Tam, Domis, and Teek dropped from their airborne mounts.

"Thane!" Jne cried, shedding all semblances of protocol and reservation as she bound into his arms.

Thane didn't seem to mind though as he enthusiastically encircled her in a bear hug and swung her around, Tam smiling brightly while the others simply gawked with opened jaws. None of them had ever seen Jne display anything but the strictest decorum that most often bordered on aloofness or outright rage. To most, the Tjal would as soon stick a sword in your gut as offer you even the slightest smile so to witness this was unprecedented indeed.

"You have returned to me," she said now holding his face with both hands, "and you are well."

Thane's whole body seemed to release in one breath the tightness that had cocooned him since they'd left the camp for Aleron. His face flushed with excitement and relief as his mind finally understood what his heart had known all along. He'd missed her. He knew that he had, but now he understood how much and that his life would never be complete without her by his side. "I have," he finally said, "and I don't plan to leave ever again."

Jne's head dropped to his chest, her eyes closed, as she soaked up his warmth taking in his scent like a dizzying intoxicant. Opening her eyes, she saw Tam smiling widely at her and just past, Dor, his mouth still agape. Pulling back quickly, she regarded the other people in the room that had become shadows when her eyes had fallen on Thane. Her face turned bright red, almost glowing brighter than the half light splashing on the outer walls from the few torches and candles. Taking a step back she bowed her head slightly to Thane and then to the others. "We are content to see you have returned. Was your mission successful?"

"Extremely," Tam offered while Thane fought to control the flush in his cheeks and Dor and Domis still couldn't seem to get their jaws to close.

"Uh, yes," Dor coughed avoiding Jne's eyes that had since become a challenging glare.

Quickly reaching back, he pulled the heart arrow from his quiver and displayed it for her and Jack to see. "We have three."

"And one has already proven effective," Domis added excitedly.

"Tryg?" Jack asked turning to Teek.

"Yes," Teek answered, his face confirming the anger in his voice. "The traitor is dead. Shot through the heart by Thane's arrow."

"So he didn't get away?" Jack asked excitedly. "He didn't make it back to Zadok's camp?"

"No," Teek said flatly. "He's dead, and no one will mourn his passing." Tam slipped an arm around Teek's shoulder and pulled him close in an attempt to comfort him but, after a brief moment, he pulled away and went to stand by Tchee.

"Then we are not compromised," Jack said with a grin. "The keep's secrets are still safe."

✳   ✳   ✳

Zadok stared at the prisoner like he would an insignificant bug he was about to step on with his boot. He was dirty and stunk in his ragged clothing, the look on his face revealing that he might have been just about as smart as a bug. He smiled dumbly, his yellow and black teeth separated by almost more gaps than there were teeth. A cloth that might have once been red was tide around his head holding back the greasy locks of disheveled hair. He had a soiled, threadbare shirt that half hung from baggy black pants that were tucked into muddy, worn boots that stretched to his mid calf. His right arm was missing.

"And tell me," Zadok hissed, while lazily staring at a hangnail on his index finger. "Why shouldn't I just kill you as a spy right here and now?"

The man bowed, flinging out his left arm in as good a flourish as he could imitate. "Because, my great lord, I can give ya what ya need. I can give ya the secret entrance to the keep." He paused. "For a small price."

Zadok's eyebrows rose slightly though he was very adept at hiding the sudden rush of excitement at hearing his prisoner's words. "And what might that be, if, in fact, you do have the information that you claim?"

The man smiled and his voice cracked into a near cackle. "I wants the boy that flies about on the great bird. I means to cut the eyes from his head an' give'm back to my friend Zel."

Chapter Thirty-Three

Thane stared out over the ocean of enemy fighters, their fires having burned down to a low glow across the plains. The camp was quiet now save for the occasional snort or jingle of mail as those on the night guard shifted their stance or exchanged their duty with another. Looking up, he stared at the bank of low hanging clouds that had appeared out of nowhere an hour before, blanketing the sky in ominous darkness as if nature could sense the evil brought on by Zadok's army and was covering its face in disgust. But these were not nature's clouds he'd realized. They were something created by Zadok's foul magic. Thane felt his anger sparked by the abomination and was tempted to use his own gifts to turn it away but decided that he didn't want to waste any of his strength on something so insignificant. Let Zadok play his theatrical games.

Stifling a yawn, he reached up and twisted the *svaj* Jne had pierced through his right ear only hours before. As she had promised, she'd brought back the male symbol of a Tjal man's marital status and placed it in his earlobe to signal he was yet to be wed. She also informed him that she had regained her honor and was no longer a *Jinghar*. As a full Tjal they could now be married when the war had ended. The thought had been intoxicating to his mind. His whole life he'd felt an emptiness that even Dor or Tam could not fill. At one time he'd thought that possibly Tam might be the one to make him whole, but she was right when she'd turned him away because they shared the same Tane. Because he held all five, he could never be chosen by a Chufa woman to wed. He was destined to remain alone—until Jne. She completed him in a way that he never thought possible. Just being in her presence seemed to fill the gaps he'd felt in himself his whole life. Together they were one.

"You must take your rest," Jne's voice broke through the silence.

He turned and smiled at her, touched by her concern. "And what of you?"

She shrugged. "I never can sleep the night before battle," she said, brushing it off as something slightly irritating but of little significance. "You sleep. I will watch for any movement in the enemy."

He sighed, looking down upon the army anew while twisting the *svaj* again. "Apparently, though my body might disagree, my mind is kin to yours when it comes to the eve of battle. I might lie down in my covers but I would not find rest there." He suddenly cocked his head to the side as if to trying to hear something in the distance but then just shook his head.

"What is it?" Jne asked, placing a hand on his arm.

"Nothing. I thought I heard something on the wind, but it's gone. Probably a fat troll snoring. I find that my hands itch for my swords and their flesh to meet."

Jne gifted him with one of her rare and beautiful smiles. His heart leaped in response as she drew herself up and gently kissed his cheek that suddenly felt hot with fire. "You are a true Tjal warrior, *Ne'va*. The heavens will sing of your honor and glory. And I will remain yours forever."

He gathered her into his arms, the warmth of her body filling him with light and comfort, chasing away the last vestiges of doubt or uncertainty that had plagued him for so many years. He knew who he was and where his life would go from here. With Jne, happiness was finally his to embrace. The light of dawn was just beginning to break the horizon as if giving its blessing to their union when he heard the sound again. But this time it was more distinct.

"I heard it too," Jne whispered as they reluctantly released their hold on each other and turned back to the balcony railing. Thane looked up and it hit him. The dark clouds Zadok had created were not to strike fear, but to hide what he intended. Throwing his spirit into the air, he shot above the cloudy mist, just in time to see one of the dragons pass, its heavy wings making the whooshing sound that had caught his attention before. Clutched in its great talons was what at first appeared to be a large tree but quickly materialized into a post with pegs shooting out in all directions each supporting an orc or goblin. He them watched in horror as the post was lowered onto one of the highest balconies of the keep. Not waiting to watch the cargo dismount, he returned to his body in a snap.

"We're under attack!" he cried, rushing toward one of the doors along the far wall, Jne at his heels.

Just as they reached it, Dor burst through, a bloody sword in his hand.

"We're under attack!" they yelled to each other as the clamor of steel and the cries of war echoed down the hallway.

"We have to get to the rooftops!" Thane cried. "The dragons are dropping orcs and goblins up there!"

"There are trolls coming up from the bottom floors as well where one of the secret entrances must have been compromised," Dor retorted.

"Where's Tam?"

"She must have realized what was going on because she said she was going up to one of the higher balconies to hunt for dragons," Dor said, with obvious concern. "I told her we needed to find you first but she left before I could stop her."

"You two go after her," Jne said, pulling her swords, "while I go find my people." A sudden grin played across her face at the growing thrill of the coming fight.

Thane turned to her, wanting to tell her to be careful, wanting to tell her that he loved her, wanting to hold her close one more time, but she'd already turned and, with a scream, was rushing headlong into the fight down the hall. Turning in the opposite direction, he gave one last look back at her and then followed Dor as he pulled him along saying something about a stairway.

The sounds of fighting grew louder as they turned right and then quickly left as they ran headlong down the hallway. Turning one last corner, the hall opened up into a great landing where, as promised, a flight of stairs rose to the ascending levels. A group of brown robbed figures were quickly descending when they reach the first step and started to climb.

Thane instantly recognized Bren and Kat leading the group as they came to a halt. "Bren," Thane hailed, "you need to get back to a secure area, the castle is under attack and we'll need you and your healers to attend to the wounded."

"We've taken care of that," Kat answered, flashing a smile at Dor.

"Then why are you running about?" he pressed.

"Thane," Bren started, giving Kat an impatient look. "We are here to help. That is to say, we want to fight."

Thane shook his head. "I understand your willingness, but we need you more to help the wounded."

"I told you, we've taken care of that," Kat said with a huff.

Bren gave her a withering look before quickly turning back to Thane. "What she means is that we have a group already in place to help with the wounded. Those who have not yet reached proficiency."

Thane was getting impatient now as Dor was motioning him toward the stairs. He didn't have time to bandy about with healers while the fight was in earnest. "What are you saying? Speak clearly!"

Bren seemed flustered at Thane's sudden irritation and merely stared back at him. With a sour look, Kat stepped forward and placed her hand on the water bag that hung from Bren's belt. "He's talking about this," she said as the water in the bag suddenly rushed through the skin soaking Bren's robe and creating an embarrassing looking puddle at his feet.

Thane's eyes went wide with understanding as he looked at the group of healers who were all nodding as if in answer to his amazement.

"That's right," Kat continued. "We've all learned to pull water. Probably better then you can," she smiled to soften her words, but her eyes revealed that she meant what she said.

"I knew your touch was dangerous," Dor said but immediately regretted his words as Kat glared at him while raising her wet hand threateningly.

Thane hesitated. It was one thing to pull water from a bag, but doing it in battle when the bag is holding a sword and trying to chop off your head was something completely different. As if in answer, just at that moment, a group of goblins turned a corner and almost ran right into their small group. There was a moment of surprise from both parties like the quiet breath before the scream and then it all broke open in a clash of bodies and steel as Thane's swords leapt into his hands and started cutting down the enemy. Dor was quickly at his side protecting his right flank as the healers suddenly rushed forward with a scream. Thane almost didn't duck in time as a goblin swung a mace for his head as he stared agape at the healers turned fighters, passing quickly through the enemy. In moments, the hallway was a mess of liquid and corpses. Though the carpets would have to be destroyed, the healers were all unscathed as they turned to Thane expectantly, their faces flush with adrenaline.

"Carry on," he said with a slight solute, the amazed look still plastered on his face as he slowly turned and started following Dor up the stairs.

"Wait," Dor said, turning back to the group. "Come with us."

"What?" Thane protested.

"The dragons are dropping the enemy on the top levels," he said, "where we're going. We'll need some protection so we can concentrate on taking the serpents down with our bows." Pointing to the anxiously waiting healers he continued, "They can help us. They can keep the goblins and orcs off of us so we can get a clear shot."

The stubborn part of Thane wanted to argue, wanted to keep everyone but himself out of danger. But he couldn't come up with an argument fast enough that would warrant the healers doing anything other than what Dor had suggested. His friend was right. Nodding quickly, he took the stairs two at a time as a shout of excitement escaped the healer's lips as they raced after him, all the while chanting his name.

*   *   *   *   *

Tam sprinted up the stairs gaining a large foyer that was crossed through on either side by grand hallways. Looking to the left she thought she caught a sliver of light cutting across the rug from an opening in the wall and turned toward it hoping to find the breach she needed to get a clear shot at one of the dragons. The distinct sound of trolls pulled her up abruptly as a group of five suddenly broke into the hallway. Turning in her direction, the leader saw her and quickly raised his club as he took a quick few steps forward and then stopped abruptly. Tam had her sword in her hand, ready for blood when the troll suddenly spoke, turning her veins to ice.

"Pet?" his gravely voice grated across her nerves. Tam's heart thumped in her chest like it was pounding on her ribcage trying to get free. It couldn't be.

"Krog," she said in a dazed whisper. Her muscles felt frozen as the troll that had been her master, the one who she'd become dependant upon for *dranlok*, the one she would have done anything for to get her fix, stood before her, a mocking smile playing across his dry lips.

He laughed at her while bringing his club down slowly to rest against his thigh. Then reaching back for something on his belt he produced a water skin and held it out in front of him. "I bet you want this," he sneered, waving the skin in front of her in a taunting manner. "Come. Get your drink, pet. I won't make you eat slug to have it."

Tam felt her right foot suddenly move forward as if on its own accord. Then her left as she slowly made her way down the hall toward the troll and his blessed offering. Her mouth felt dry and she licked her lips to wet them with a swollen tongue.

"That's it," he growled. The others watched on with interest at their companion's seeming power over the enemy and wondered if all of his earlier braggadocio had not held some particles of truth.

Tam lowered her sword and dragged it behind her as she covered the last few steps and came to stop right in front of her master. She looked at the skin, her tongue darting out to lick her lips once more before tentatively raising her other hand to take hold.

Krog smiled, pulling the *dranlok* back in mocking before finally yanking off the top and pushing the container forward into Tam's open fingers. "Yes," he said, his eyes narrowing slightly. "Your master returns."

She looked at him briefly, her eyes welling up with tears before she finally lifted the skin and pressed it to her lips. She could smell the strong odor that marked the liquid as the one she'd done unspeakable things to have. It seemed to awaken something deep within that got her heart pumping faster, her cheeks growing in color as she inhaled in anticipation. Closing her eyes, a tear dripped over her eyelid and slid down her cheek and she could hear the trolls laughing at her.

And then, in one fluid motion, her eyes popped open as her sword came up. Too late for Krog whose head was back just perfectly as he took in a breath preparing to snicker again as her sword sliced through his neck, turning his scoff into a gurgle as he dropped to the floor. She flung the *dranlok* at the nearest troll behind him while cutting quickly with her sword across his belly and then turned around and ran, knowing all too well that she could not stand against so many alone.

She could hear the screams of rage and feel the thundering of feet against the carpeted floor as she raced headlong down the corridor praying that she didn't run into another group of the enemy. Though she was quick, she knew she could not match the trolls' long strides that quickly ate up the ground between them. She could almost feel their breath on her neck when a stairway leading both up and down came into view. She knew that she needed to go higher to fight the dragons with her arrow, but to do so would increase the chances of meeting more of the enemy alone. She made her decision quickly, and without hesitation, bound down the stairs to the level below.

The trolls were almost tripping over one another to close the gap now as their quarry was mere feet away. She had to turn and fight or be bludgeoned from behind without a struggle. She heard one of the trolls cry out in pain as she whipped around with her sword, surprised that only one of the remaining four was bearing down on her. The others had turned back, as if suddenly engaged in another fight. Swinging her blade with all of her strength, Tam aimed for his neck, hoping to end the fight quickly but the troll blocked it easily with his club with such force that her sword went flying out of her hand and clattered harmlessly against the far wall. She reached for her other sword but the troll was too quick grabbing her and pulling her close, a roar of fury escaping his lips. His breath and odor were enough to gag her as he drew her in, his teeth bared as if he intended to eat her on the spot. Her hand pressed against the rough skin on his chest as she tried to wiggle her way fee, but the troll was too strong, and chuckled mockingly at her efforts.

Reaching for her Tane, she thought, at first, to create a blast of air to knock the troll back and free her, but she feared that the force of it might rip her arms from her shoulders should the troll not let her go. A whirlwind would harm her as much as it would harm the enemy, mostly likely bashing both of their skulls against the stone walls. There had to be another way.

The troll was looking at her now, a low growl in its throat, saliva escaping its slightly parted lips as it leaned forward preparing to take a bite out of her flesh. She struggle futilely when a sudden sliver of inspiration struck her. It seemed almost too absurd at first but quickly germinated into a logical conclusion as she reached out with her Tane into the troll's body. And why not, it worked with water. The connection was almost instantaneous, almost too easy, as she called to the air within him. With a forceful whoosh, the oxygen was instantly drawn out leaving his skin a sudden bluish color, his face frozen in a look of triumph as his grip slackened and he dropped to the floor. Not waiting to see if he would be able to recover by drawing in breath again, she quickly drew her second sword and pierced him through the heart, making certain he remained dead.

Almost at the same moment, the last of the other trolls fell back grasping its neck as it too, fell in the last throws of death. Tam was pleasantly shocked to find Jne and Soyak standing in front of her, both of their swords bloodied and wicked smiles painted on their face. "We saw you rushing past," Jne said, barely breathing hard, "and thought we might join in the fun."

Tam smiled. "I'm so happy you did," she said, and then quickly retrieved her other sword.

"What happened to this one?" Soyak asked staring down at the blue colored troll.

Tam looked at the troll with satisfaction with what she'd been able to do and what she'd discovered about the power of her Tane. "Let's just say, I left him breathless," she jeered.

Jne and Soyak glanced at each other in confusion and then turned baffled looks on Tam as if she'd suddenly spoken gibberish.

Tam sighed at her failed attempt at humor with the Tjal women, and instead of explaining, motioned back to the stairway. "I've got to find a balcony so I can get a clear shot at one of the dragons."

*　　*　　*

Dor and Thane had just reached the next level, with the healers in tow, when they happened upon Jack and Erl greatly outnumbered by a group of at least ten goblins growling and cursing as they tried to overcome the two fighters. Luckily, the corridor was too narrow to let more than a couple of combatants come at them at once but they were losing ground too quickly and soon would be forced onto the open landing at the stairway and then the attacks would come from both sides as well.

"Pull back," Bren called out before anyone else could speak.

Jack chanced a quick look behind him to see who it was while stepping back slightly allowing a third goblin to sneak past ready to cut him down on the left. But Bren was already beside him, pulling the water from the goblin's body and dropping him like a dried husk on the castle floor. His companions roared in anger but hesitated, understanding that some type of magic was at work that was far beyond their ability to counter. Then, as if by some unseen signal, they all suddenly turned about a raced in the opposite direction. The healers, without any encouragement, rushed after them, quickly disappearing around a corner, oblivious to Thane's calls after them.

Jack watched the brown robes rustling down the hall with a half amused grin before turning a cocked eye on the dead goblin at his feet. "How is it possible?" he asked turning his attention to Thane and Dor.

"We'll explain later," Thane said in a rush. "Right now we need to find a place where we can shoot down the dragons so they won't be able to drop more goblins on the roof."

"That sounds like a sound idea," Jack countered, "but the real problem is the enemy piling through the access on the bottom floors. I don't know how they discovered it, but they've got the secret exit I mentioned wide open and easily defended so that their soldiers can flow into the castle almost unchecked. We're quickly becoming trapped in the very fortress that was to offer us sanctuary."

Thane chewed at his bottom lip, thinking of what the best course might be. "I might be able to do something to stem the tide into the keep, but we still need to take down the dragons as quickly as possible."

"I'll take Jack and Erl with me," Dor offered, "and take out one of them. You go and do what you can about the rest of the army and then we'll meet up with you again on this level."

"Is there an access to the east side of the castle close by?" Thane asked Jack. "A balcony where I can see the enemy camp?"

"Down the hall our crazy brown robed friends just raced through. It's similar to the place we met in last night."

"Good," Thane answered already moving in that direction. "Take Dor to a higher area where he can have a good view of the sky and have a decent shot at one of those dragons. If I can do what I think I can, there should be a sudden shift in the fighting below."

Jack just nodded while grabbing Dor's arm and leading him in the opposite direction. Erl nuzzled Thane's hand briefly and then turned and plodded after them. Thane raced down the corridor leaping over a shriveled goblin's body that had obviously been too slow to outrun the healers now let loose through the castle. He didn't have much time to contemplate their success in drawing out water before Jack's directions suddenly brought him to a large platform that jutted out in a great circle from the small doorway giving him a spectacular view of the fields below. The sky overhead was still dark with the unnatural clouds Zadok had conjured up but their secret had long since been discovered.

Looking over the parapet he could see the enemy gathered in a large mass pressing toward the northeaster side of the mountain that must have been the location of the breach. Rushing to the balcony's northern side, he was cut off from seeing exactly where they were entering due to multiple towers and bulwarks blocking his view but he still felt confident that he could at least disrupt their easy access into the castle. Calming his thoughts, he reached out for the TehChao Tane and then threw his senses off the castle wall and plunged them into the packed dirt and rocks on the valley floor. It was like diving into a pool as the earth separated and then surrounded him, calling to him, promising tales of eons past as he called forth the ancient ground to rise and take form.

Almost instantly answering his call, the ground suddenly began to shake as the soil gathered itself into one spot and then burst upwards, growing at an incredible rate as a large creature escaped the valley floor growing arms and legs as it did so. Thane didn't wait to witness the complete formation of the TehChao warrior before dipping his senses into another area farther north and calling forth one more. Quickly the two formed and then moved slowly forward, gliding along the ground, their feet never becoming detached from the earth beneath.

The goblins, orcs, and trolls scurried away as best they could as the two focused their attention toward the breach, flinging bodies away with boulder hands sweeping the area clean. Thane watched in satisfaction as Zadok's army soon dissipated into full retreat, running in all directions as the TehChao warriors continued their cleansing of the area.

A shadow crossed above him, drawing his attention up as a dragon suddenly appeared with a rider on its back. Grabbing for the heart arrow, Thane eased it into his bow and was about to take aim when he realized that his target had moved too far away for him to get a clean shot. He watched with interest as it suddenly dropped from the sky towards one of the earth creatures drawing in breath for an attack.

Thane didn't wait, but sent out the Tane. A large earthen hand shot up, reaching for the dragon as it leveled off for its attack on the dirt warrior. But something fired from the serpent's back just as the hand was about to close around it, and it shattered into a shower of soil and rocks. The dragon released its breath on the TehChao warrior and then lifted almost immediately into the sky as another hand reached for it but missed. Thane watch as his creation suddenly stopped, its head blown off by the dragon's decaying breath. For a brief moment it appeared as if it was dead where it stood, but once again its boulder hands swung down, smashing the nearest troll into the ground.

He watched as the dragon banked and prepared for another attack, its passenger, who could only be Zadok, urging it forward. He knew he could raise more of the earthen beings to fight but he was unsure as to how much strength it would require and if he'd have enough to face the real enemy, Zadok, and defeat him. He had to make Zadok to come after him.

Raising his eyes to the skies above, he called to the ArVen Tane. Very quickly he was gathering his own clouds together swirling them through Zadok's abominations, devouring them in their path as the skies grew darker. Calling more and more masses of hot and cold air together, the thick clouds increased in size and power, crackling flashes of light shooting through them as they collected strength in preparation to release their fury on the enemy below. The air itself seemed charged with power as Thane gathered more power with his Tane.

And then, like a hailstorm of death, the electrical charges were released as lighting struck throughout the valley floor striking vehemently at the enemy. The crashing sound of thunder boomed through the army like a cacophony of war drums beating out their call for destruction. Again and again, the sky flashed until the strikes were coming so quickly as to leave the area lit up as if the sun were shining through at midday.

Scanning the sky, he quickly located Zadok and his dragon who had broken off their attack on the earth elemental and were now making their way across the valley. He watched with anticipation as a bolt of lighting struck them once and then was followed almost immediately by another that hit them again. But instead of knocking them from the sky, the lightning seemed to split and shoot around them striking the helpless fighters below. It was then that he saw the faint blue glow that covered Zadok and his dragon. Zadok's magic protected them.

"But come," Thane whispered, as he watched them get hit again without harm as they drew closer to where he waited. "Your magic will not save you from me."

*   *   *

A loud scream brought Teek out of a deep sleep almost throwing him from his bed as he desperately grabbed for the dagger tied to his leg. Scanning the unfamiliar surroundings it took him a brief moment to remember where he was as his heart pound angrily in his ears. Straining to hear what had awakened him he was beginning to think it had just been a bad dream when another cry rang out down the hall. Quickly gathering his backpack and blow gun, he cracked open the door to the small room he'd found the previous night after they'd returned from killing the dragon. At first he'd wanted to stay with Tchee on the balcony, having grown accustomed to sleeping under her protective wing, but Tam had convinced him that his own bed was what he needed and by that time he was too tired to argue with her. He did insist on staying close but the best they'd been able to find was a tiny room on the floor just below the great balcony.

There was a small slit for a window that let just enough light filter in for him to see by but from the looks of it, the sun had yet to break over the horizon for a new day. Peaking through the crack he could only see down one direction of the hallway and nothing presented itself to clue him in as to what was happening in the castle. He waited for a long minute straining to hear any more commotion but the castle seemed to have settled down into an eerie silence. Pushing the door further open, he snuck out into the corridor, crouching against the wall as he took quick stock of the hallway in the other direction. His breath caught in his throat as a figure shrouded in shadows wiped what could only be a dagger on the nightshirt of an old man in a crumpled pile on the ground. In the poor light, he could see a pool of dark liquid spreading out into the carpet that could only be blood. A cackling wheeze escaped the assailant and Teek found his blood turning cold. Slipping his pack off his back, he then set down his blow gun and reached for his dagger.

The attacker turned suddenly at the scraping of Teek's blade leaving its sheath and they locked eyes on each other. The ice that had filled Teek's limbs suddenly melted in a rush of fiery indignation as the one armed man faced him, stepping out of the shadows and into the pale light. "You!" Teek spat.

Brak smiled a wicked gap toothed grin and then brought his dagger up to his lips and licked it. "Oh boy, I been waitin' long time for this. And ye's all alone without yer stocky friends. We gonna dance long and slow you an' me."

Teek's eyes narrowed in rage and hatred for the man who had hounded him, who had tried to kill him. His grip tightened on his dagger as the berserker frenzy that had overcome him when he'd killed the black roc suddenly grew inside his gut and then quickly spread out to his limbs in anticipation.

"One of us dies now," he hissed.

Chapter Thirty-Four

Teek threw himself down the hallway toward the one armed assailant who had hounded him for these many months and who had threatened him with death, or worse, at every opportunity. Teek had only wanted to be left alone and it was Brak's own fault that Tchee had killed his friend and torn off his arm, but it didn't seem to matter. He was either just too dumb to see and accept the consequences of his actions or too evil to care. Either way, Teek knew that he would never be rid of the man until one of them was dead and he was not content to accept it be him.

With a feral scream, Teek jumped into the air, leading with his dagger as he collided with the man taking them both to the ground. Brak had been caught off guard by Teek's sudden attack and had barely gotten his blade up in time to keep Teek from running him through the chest. Using the young Waseeni's momentum, Brak was able to flip the boy over the top as they landed on the carpet and then both rolled up on their feet taking on a defensive posture. Brak's face broke into a silly grin confirming in Teek's mind that he did not have complete control over his mental faculties. "Eee hee hee, little one," he cackled. "Yous likes to plays now does you? Hee hee hee. I'sa likes to plays too. Come plays with mes so I's can cut ya."

Teek didn't wait for another invitation as he pressed forward with his knife, his eyes like pinwheels of fire, as he let his fury completely take over his senses. Brak was quickly put on the defensive as he brought up his dagger, twisting away and then falling back just barely avoiding having his guts spilled out. Teek was a demon of rage and speed as his knife cut, parried, jabbed and then cut again.

Sweat broke out on Brak's face and his eyes filled with fear at the realization that Teek was not the hopeless little boy he'd originally met and tormented. Turning Teek's blade away as it cut into his ribs saved his life for a brief moment but he quickly realized that it was only a matter of seconds before Teek would land a solid hit and it would all be over.

Turning quickly, Brak showed the true coward that he was. Dropping his knife he tried to run away and escape the boy turned demon leaving him for Zadok's minions to deal with, but Teek was too fast. "Wait!" Brak screamed in terror just as Teek's blade punctured his side cutting deep into his lung and then pricking his heart.

Brak crumpled to the ground as Teek pulled out his dagger and landed on top of him. Brak tried to scream for mercy but his throat was suddenly full of blood letting out a slight gurgling as Teek, without hesitation brought his knife down one final time burying it into his chest. Brak's body went slack, the horror of impending death permanently frozen on his face as his life quickly bled out of his perforated black heart.

Teek pulled his dagger preparing to stab again but caught the empty look in Brak's eyes and with great effort restrained himself. Standing up, blood sticky wet on his hand, he stumbled over to the nearest wall and let himself slide down to the floor. Soon the fire that blindly raged through him subsided with his labored breaths and he was able to once again gain control of himself and survey the damage he'd done. Looking at Brak and seeing the pitiful creature he'd become, Teek turned to the side and threw up while great tears poured out of his soft brown eyes. He had never killed a person before and the thought that he had with such ease sickened him. He tried to remind himself that Brak would have done worse to him, but it still didn't fill the void and emptiness he suddenly felt at ending another's life. It wasn't fair. All he'd ever wanted was…adventure. How many times had he heard the stories old Twee told about the adventures he'd had? And how many times had he wished that he could have some of his own? But in the stories, the killing had seemed so sterile and clean. No one got blood on them, or watched a person beg for their life before it was snuffed out.

He threw up again, emptying his stomach, and then the rage began to grow again; threatening to take over as it had with the roc, the dragon, and now Brak. He had not started this war. Neither had he hunted Brak down to kill him. It had been self-defense. He had not come looking for murder. The conflicting thoughts battled within his skull and he knew he could not fully justify either now. He allowed the anger to take hold knowing that the fight was not over and he would need it to carry on and fulfill his part. When it was all done he could mourn his choices or mourn the person he'd been forced to become. But right now, he needed the darkness that suddenly had become a part of him to guide his knife clutched hand and kill anything…or anyone that threatened him or his friends.

Forcing his legs to rise beneath him, he stood up, wiping the vomit from his mouth and smearing blood on his face as he turned down the hall and grabbed his pack and blow gun before going in search of the stairs that would take him up to Tchee. The battle had begun, and he was not about to turn aside now.

✳   ✳   ✳

Jack led Dor and Erl as they climbed higher through one of the northeastern wings of the castle. Though the sounds of battle could still be heard in the distance, the group had yet to encounter any opposition. They did, however, pass scattered groups of dead as they ascended; a jumble of orcs, goblins and men mixed together leaving grim testimony of the battles that had been fought in the castle heights. Jack did not waste time with the fallen though, pushing them forward feeling certain that a bridge connected the tower they were currently in with one that stood more to the north. It was on this bridge that Jack felt Dor would have the greatest chance at finding a dragon for his heart arrow.

"It should be just up ahead," Jack encouraged as he led them down another hallway that was somewhat indistinct from the many others they'd already passed through. Erl suddenly let out a low growl, his hackles rising along his back, his teeth revealed under his curtain of curling jowls.

Dor drew a sword, still preferring to fight with one blade while Jack and Erl took positions on either side of the hall in anticipation of an attack. The guttural sounds of anxious assailants echoed down the hallway as a group of orcs suddenly broke from an opening in the eastern wall not fifty paces from where they stood. Erl leapt to the front with one great bound ripping into the neck of the first fighter, taking him to the ground while, in a rush, Jack and Dor covered his flanks and met the enemy in battle.

Dor blocked the grisly axe his foe swung down and then grabbed his arm with his free ha•nd. Not to be outdone by the healers, he quickly made connection with the water in the orc's body and called it out with a thought, leaving his enemy a desiccated shell while wetting the ground and himself in his fluids.

Jack gut another with his sword, the grim look on his face a mask of death incarnate as he advanced on the next one easily blocking its haphazard swing and then dispatching it to join its fallen comrades on the bloodied carpet. The remaining three turned tail and ran but not before Erl hamstrung one and then pounced on another biting into its neck and shoulder ending its life while taking it down to the floor. Dor ran the first one through and then hesitated in chasing the last when Jack placed a hand on his arm. "We're here."

Pointing to the wall the orcs had just come from, a narrow corridor climbed up a small flight of stairs to a heavy oak door that stood opened to the outside. Dor and Erl followed as Jack led them up the stone stairway and out to a large platform that narrowed and then stretched northward across a great divide to a huge tower on the other side. Not waiting for his companions, Jack raced out onto the bridge taking in the spectacular view while Dor strung his bow and retrieved his heart arrow. This was exactly the spot he needed to find and kill his prey. And since they had just met a pack of the enemy, it was almost certain that one of the dragons was using this very spot to drop members of Zadok's army. All he needed to do now was wait for another to return.

Scanning the sky overhead, Dor stepped toward the bridge looking east in the direction of Zadok's army and the tiny black dots that made up each individual enemy. Drawing his sights closer to the castle he watched in awe as the ground started to bulge and then grow into what must have been a massive creature that suddenly started sweeping its great arms and wiping away those that got in its path. He smiled, knowing that Thane was at work here and a sliver of hope rose in his chest that they might, after all they had been through and suffered, come out the victors after all.

Erl's growl and Jack's yell brought his attention back around to the bridge as Jack suddenly rushed toward the opposite tower, his sword raised as if prepared to do battle. As he turned to watch his friend racing away, he just caught the slight movement in the air to his left warning him of the approaching dragon as it closed in on his position on the bridge. Turning to face it, he knew he didn't have time to take a shot and instead dove back to the platform as the dragon let out its terrible breath onto the stone where he'd been standing only seconds before. Erl rushed forward as if he meant to attack the dragon, or at least pass over onto the bridge and chase after Jack but he slid to a stop just as the rock where the dragon's breath had touched suddenly melted away like butter in a hot skillet.

Erl whined helplessly as he backed away and paced along the platform watching Jack cross to the other tower alone and cut off by the great gap in the bridge.

Dor regained his footing and quickly stood, his arrow ready now as he watched the dragon make a quick bank to the north and disappear behind the huge tower where Jack now stood. He thought he could see another person facing his friend, but the distance was too great to be certain and he couldn't lend his concentration to be positive as he was convinced the dragon would certainly circle back around from the west for another attack.

Erl was beside himself, still pacing and whining when the dragon reappeared in the sky just where Dor knew he would be. Dor stepped out onto the remaining bridge, facing the great serpent that tucked in its great wings and gained speed closing the gap between them. Dor pulled back the arrow, taking careful aim while praying that the dragon preferred to eat him rather then blow him into nothing with its caustic breath.

The sound of steel meeting steel echoing off the far tower grated at his concentration while Erl's constant whining threatened it as well. He could not afford to miss. The dragon grew quickly, only slim moments away as it continued to gain speed. Opening its mouth, Dor's heart sank as he realized it was drawing air to spit its decaying breath out again. He felt himself suddenly calm as death's presence settled his nerves into the still he'd grown accustomed to when it hovered about him with its promised finality. The sounds that had threatened to ruin his concentration only moments before were now erased with the slow beating of his heart. His mark became sure and focused as he pulled back on the string. The dragon took a deep breath in and paused only briefly. Dor knew that it was going dissolve him into nothing leaving only his memory as proof that he'd actually once existed, but he held his ground.

And at that very moment he released the string. The arrow shot forward and he watched as the first streams of decaying breath were gathering at the back of the dragon's throat as the heart arrow sliced through the the dragon's soft pallet and up into its brain. Its head was snapped back with incredible force sending a tiny amount of decaying breath into the air as the dragon flipped over, its massive weight and body colliding against the side of the castle tower before it dropped in a tumbling mass down into the fighting army below. A great boom sounded as it hit the ground crushing a multitude of combatants and sending dust and debris into the air all around its lifeless corpse.

Dor stood frozen where he was, death's presence having gone and with it the calm he'd felt as he'd face down the dragon. Erl's whine and the ringing of steel brought him out of his daze as he turned to see why Erl was so upset. Following the wolg's gaze, he looked back over the ruined bridge where he saw Jack more clearly now, locked in combat with a man dressed all in black.

*   *   *

Jack didn't hesitate as the man in black calmly walked forward, his sword at the ready. Though he'd not seen the man before, something was so familiar about him as to give Jack pause at first. But his resolve was not lessened any as it became obvious that the man was an enemy and had come prepared to fight.

Jack had spotted him almost immediately upon reaching the middle of the bridge and had originally thought him one of the commanders from the city. But as he approached his goatee covered chin curled up with his wicked smile as he pulled his sword in ready. Knowing a challenge when he saw one, Jack did the same though sorry that he couldn't at least find out who he was first and why he'd chosen to fight against his own. What sort of promises had Zadok made to win him over?

"And you must be Jack, the great and fearsome king," the man spat at him as he closed the distance between them.

"I'm afraid you have me at a disadvantage," Jack responded, "since it's obvious that my reputation precedes me while yours is yet to be spoken."

The man sneered at the obvious insult but did not let it fluster him. "Today you will learn of my reputation, old man, when you beg for me to finish your life more quickly."

Jack raised his sword in ready. "And whose name should I use when I am supposed to do this begging you speak of?"

"You may call me Resdin," he said with a mocking bow.

"Then I will be certain they chisel it upon your gravestone."

Resdin lunged forward with incredible speed that might have caught any other man off guard, but Jack had dealt with creatures more sinister than this boy had ever dreamed of. Blocking the thrust easily, he reversed his motion, catching Resdin's shirt and leaving a nice gashed in it across the chest. Stepping back, Resdin surveyed the damage that had only occurred to the linen leaving his skin unmarked. "You'll need to dig deeper old man if you expect to do more than ruin my clothing."

Jack didn't rise to the baiting but instead moved slowly forward with easy thrusts and jabs feeling out the boy's strengths and weaknesses without committing himself too far or using up too much energy. He would not be drawn into an all out brawl knowing that their differences in age would then most certainly put the fight in Resdin's favor.

Resdin moved forward and back with athletic ease as if taunting his opponent. Sometimes he left gapping holes in his defenses inviting Jack in so that he could quickly block and then score a hit, but Jack was not so easily baited or fooled. Resdin felt his ire grow at the insolence this old man dare show him in battle. Boring quickly to the juvenile clanging of swords that seemed to be his opponent's only ability, Resdin began to press his advantage trading caution for a quick end so as to be free to satiate his lust for blood on the levels below.

Jack matched the increase in tempo and daring, turning away Resdin's attacks while mounting an offensive of his own. As the battle became increasingly more intense, Jack could not shake the feeling that he knew his opponent from somewhere, that they had a connection some how. It did not thrill him to be fighting someone of his own race in such a battle as they had found themselves. It was one thing to kill off trolls and orcs and others of the evil races, but his heart was heavy thinking that he would be forced to end the life of a young man who might have a spark of good left in him.

Resdin feigned a jab to Jack's chest and then crossed his arm around cutting for his midsection. Distracted, Jack barely corrected his defense in time so that Resdin's blade sliced through his shirt barely nicking his skin. Resdin felt the slight pressure of connecting with flesh and smiled wickedly, feeling certain that the old man must be tiring and that his victory was sealed.

"You grow tired, aged one," Resdin teased, blocking Jack's over the top swing and flicking it back before turning to thrust with his own weapon. Jack was forced back a step to avoid being skewered while his mind still wrestled with Resdin's face in a bout to gain recognition.

"Ah," he retorted, "the foolishness of youth. They fight when they should talk and they talk when they should fight." Pretending to stumble, he easily turned away Resdin's thrust and then countered back with a slash of his own across the young man's belly. Resdin gasped as he stepped back, placing a hand over the cut that was seeping blood into the tops of his trousers.

Glaring back at Jack, he stepped away, while swinging his sword in a complicated pattern and then steadied himself. "Enough of this child's play," he spat. "We end this now."

Not waiting for Jack's reply, Resdin pressed forward in a full frontal attack that quickly left both of them with nicks and cuts all along their chests, arms, and legs. Both were soon breathing hard, their attacks becoming slower as the battle continued to wage on without a victor. Sweat beaded and then flew off of their bodies as they continued to press and retreat in a dissonance of steel banging steel.

With each passing moment, Jack felt that the mystery that was Resdin was coming closer to being solved, but his mind still could not wrap around the feeling that cried out in recognition of the man. And he was tiring. Never in his years of battle in the Shadow Mountains had he ever tired in a fight against even three trolls but suddenly he felt his energy diminishing and he feared that soon he would not be quick enough to turn away Resdin's attacks. With the skill the boy manifested, any little mistake would certainly prove to be his doom. He had to end this now.

Resdin shot forward with a thrust that he intended to turn back using Jack's block and then slice him through the middle, but Jack didn't block him as he'd expected. Stepping to his right, Jack allowed the blade to slice superficially across his left side while he brought his own blade around in a chopping motion into Resdin's ribs cutting him deep.

It was at that very moment, as they faced each other and Resdin's eyes widened in utter shock that Jack saw the strange little diamond shaped birthmark on Resdin's exposed shoulder finally connecting the last puzzle piece. "Cole!" he shouted as he pulled away from his son, drawing out his blade with a sickening smack allowing gouts of blood to pour out from the wound. Both Resdin and Jack dropped their swords as Jack rushed forward to catch his boy as he toppled to the ground, his hand trying desperately to stem the tide of blood.

"Oh, my boy," Jack cried out. "What have I done?" Smoothing back his dark hair he looked into the shocked face of his long lost son who so obviously favored his mother's features and for whom he had given up his thrown to waste away his life as a hermit chasing down the memory of his boy. And now, in a twisted game played by the gods his boy was to die at his own hand; the hand that cradled him as a baby; the hand that would forever be stained with his blood.

Resdin stared up at him, the shock at having been beaten by an old man more disturbing to him than the sudden babbling he took on as he sobbed over him. But Resdin was not without life yet. It was not over until the last breath was released. Seeing that his killer was now over occupied with a sudden attempt to save his ebbing life, he didn't notice as Resdin reached for the dagger at his waist. Drawing it slowly, he pressed it easily between the old man's ribs as he leaned forward, bathing Resdin with his tears.

*   *   *

Jne, Tam and Soyak raced through the doorway out into an open courtyard high in the upper reaches of the castle. A fountain claimed the center of the area, dried and in disrepair as was most of the keep that had been abandoned many years before and had only kept a skeleton staff to maintain it. The garden that must have at once been a beautiful retreat was grown over with weeds that were quickly turning brown in the early summer heat. The dark sky cast long shadows that were suddenly exploded in rapid bursts of light thrown off by Thane's lightning attack on Zadok's army.

Caught by the fierce wonder of the scene, their attention was stolen away for a brief moment as they watched the whole valley light up in the powerful blasts of the electric storm followed by the drums of thunder that broke across the sky reverberating off the castles giant rock. Almost too late, Soyak turned to meet the onrushing gang of goblins newly planted on the courtyard's far side by a large, black dragon. Meeting the first with the blunt end of her fist, she cried out to the others as her swords suddenly appeared in her hands and she jumped forward with a look of rapture as she met the enemy that far outnumbered them.

Tam joined the fight as well, swinging her two swords as best as she was able, meeting the enemy with a ferocity that fit well with her Tjal clothing.

Jne drew her swords in a flash, dispatching two overanxious goblins as they practically ran themselves through on the ends of her blades but then she hesitated, her eyes latching on the great dragon that eyed her evilly with its bright, blue eyes as if singling her out among the others. Suddenly, to her utter shock, the great leviathan began to diminish, reducing itself in size as its wings tucked back and then spread out, becoming garments that fit snuggly around what was now a dark haired Tjal woman.

Jne gasped, her recognition instant as the dragon-turned-woman strode easily toward her, two swords suddenly growing out of her black gloved hands. "Sireen!" she breathed as the woman came to stand in front of her, the goblins that had pressed about her, shying quickly away and turning their fight on Soyak and Tam. "How is this possible, my sister?"

Sireen laughed. "How is it possible that I am so much more than you? How is it possible that power flows through me like blood while you wallow in dishonor and weakness?"

Jne's eyes narrowed. "I am no longer *Jinghar*," she hissed. "I have reclaimed my place among the *Tja*."

"Ha!" Sireen sneered. "You have no *Tja*."

Jne felt as if someone had punched her in the stomach with a hammer. She remembered the search she had made for her *Tja* when they were threatened at Haykon, the memory of it coming back now in sickening detail with the revelation of what had happened. "It was you!" she breathed, still trying to understand; still trying to grasp at the strands of reality. "But why? How?"

Sireen laughed. "I think you can answer the how on your own. Though you are pitiful and weak, you at least can still conjure a logical outcome in your mind I would hope. As to why, well, let's just say I serve a higher power now," she spat.

Jne felt the rage building inside of her as it became clear what her sister had done. No, not her sister but something foul, unnatural and evil conjured by Zadok in his demented mind and using his twisted magic. "You are no Tjal," she said, the venom dripping from her voice. "I denounce you as one without honor. You are less than the dog that feeds on its own bile!"

Sireen threw back her head and bark out a laugh. "Possibly so, my dear little sister, but the bile on which I will feed today will be you!" She finished her last words like an oath as her swords shot out meeting Jne's in a loud ring as the two sisters became locked in battle.

Their swords became a blur of metal meeting metal as each wove a tapestry of death about her opponent with such skill as to have invited applause from any who might have watched. If death were not the ultimate outcome, it could have been labeled as a beautiful dance as their bodies moved with the motion of their weapons, cutting in and moving out while twisting and gyrating to an unspoken melody.

Tam pulled her sword out of the goblins neck letting it fall to the ground as she turned her attention back to Jne. She'd seen the dragon turn into the Tjal woman that now swung her swords with deadly precision at her friend and was anxious to be free of the fighting so she could take aim with her bow, but there were still too many goblins and only she and Soyak to deal with them. The old Tjal woman laughed as she met another goblin swinging its club for her head. A quick duck and then twist and both her blades pulled across the unlucky creature's center spilling its intestines onto the ground. The bodies seemed to pile up around her, as more and more goblins appeared, joining in the melee that was quickly becoming too large for even someone of her skill to outlast.

Tam ducked instinctively as the club whooshed past her head drawing her attention away again as she was forced to deal with yet another enemy. Twisting around to the side, she dropped one of her swords, drawing the goblin's attention away as she reached out and ripped the air from its body. A small boom accompanied the rush of wind that pressed her hand away as her enemy dropped onto the stony ground. Retrieving her sword, she threw herself back into the fray determined to eliminate her threats so she could take down Jne's dragon.

Jne threw back her head barely escaping a scissor cut that would have decapitated her and then threw up her swords to block Sireen's follow through as she sliced for Jne's midsection with her left while coming down with an overhand swing with her right. Jne was frustrated that she'd received multiple cuts while not yet having landed a single hit on her sister. She was not fatigued in the least, but her sister seemed just a fraction quicker to the point that she was starting to feel that maybe she was the rodent in a cat's cruel game. The pieces of what must have happened to her sister were forming in Jne's mind as her body seemed to move on its own as it deflected the constant attacks leaving her no chance to mount an offensive.

Her sister must have been taken by Zadok and then twisted to his will and changed in some unnatural way to create the creature that had turned on her people. Had she not been blood sworn to Thane, she too would have met the awful death that had been dealt out to her *Tja* by Sireen's...no, not Sireen's but the dragon's decimating breath. It made her sick to think of her friends and family cut down in such a cowardly fashion as was the lethal breath created by one she'd once loved and admired.

Jumping back she took another cut to her midsection though, like the many others, it was nothing more than a scratch. Crossing her blades in a defensive move designed to push her opponent's swords down Jne pressed in whipping her head forward and connecting with Sireen's sending the woman back. A trickle of blood formed and then dripped from the woman's eyebrow where Jne hit her, bringing at first a look of surprise and then one of condescending laughter.

"Well done, little one," Sireen mocked. "Finally you draw blood, though apparently your skill is more suited to your head than your swords."

Jne didn't answer but instead let her blades speak for her as she rushed forward throwing herself with abandon into the battle. Sireen met her rage with cool calculation, scoring multiple hits but this time sustaining some as well. She paid them no mind though knowing that when she returned to her natural dragon form that her powers of quick healing would turn them to distant memories. Blocking a wild swing she easily flicked it away and then brought her sword back down, slicing deeply into Jne's left arm rendering it useless.

Disengaging from the battle, Jne stared with wonder at her arm and then looked back at Sireen who merely smiled, dropping one of her swords in a show of dishonor to make the fight "fair" once again. Such an action was the lowest form of humiliation that a Tjal-Dihn could show to another. Fueling her body with her rage, Jne pressed in again sweeping her sword around, desperately trying to break through Sireen's defenses and score a deadly hit while blood rushed down her injured arm, dripping great drops to the ground. She screamed in anger and pain as Sireen's blade cut across her chest opening a large gash that quickly soaked her shirt with red.

Jne's breath came in short gasps now as her loss of blood was making her light headed and weak. The excruciating pain that throbbed from her arm and now across her chest was the only thing the seemed to be keeping her mind alert as she stared back at Sireen who maintained a look of boredom as she motioned with her hand for Jne to come and meet her doom. Raising her sword, Jne feinted right and then crossed left and down aiming for Sireen's middle.

Tam pushed the goblin off of her blade just as a loud scream rang out drawing her attention to the Tjal woman who crumpled to the ground, a sword sticking out of her chest. Tam stifled a cry as she dropped her swords and reached for her bow, quickly fitting an arrow and letting it loose on the enemy that was in the process of retrieving its blade with a sickening thwack. The goblin turned just as Tam's arrow reached it and embedded itself deep within its chest, knocking it to the ground.

Soyak was dead; of that she was certain. Tam scanned the courtyard but was only greeted by dead bodies. No more goblins pressed in on her. No more enemies growled with bloodlust or swung their clubs in an attempt to crush her skull. She felt slightly light headed and sick from the awful smell that accompanied death with all of its horrors. Remembering her main objective, she reached for the heart arrow and turned back to where Jne still fought the dragon woman but was suddenly frozen in dread as she watched her press her blade deep into Jne's chest.

Jne crumpled to her knees, her sword falling from her hand with a clank as it hit the stone covered yard. Sireen bent down and sneered at her as she mercilessly drew back her sword in a slow, agonizing motion that brought tears to Jne's eyes. A woman screamed across the courtyard and Sireen rose seeing the arrow drawn back and aimed at her. But she didn't try to move away or duck down. With a knowing smile, Sireen pushed Jne over with her foot and released her hold on her Tjal form allowing her body to change back into its natural shape just as Tam released the arrow.

Throwing out her chest, Sireen offered herself to the puny woman's weapon knowing that nothing could penetrate her thickly scaled hide. The shock registered in her mind for a brief moment when she was pitched back by the arrow's impact. Death rushed in to cradle her fall as the heart arrow, true to its name, shattered through her chest and ribcage severing her heart as it exited out her back.

Tam dropped her bow, the tears already pouring down her face as she tripped over the scattered dead trying to reach Jne who had flopped over, onto the hard ground. Lifting the Tjal woman's head onto her lap, she surveyed the damage that marred her body with the wicked results of razor steel meeting soft flesh.

Jne's eyes fluttered and she groaned in pain as Tam hurriedly went about tying off as best she could, the gash on her arm and then moving to stem the flow of blood pumping from the gaping wound in her chest. "Oh, Jne," she cried. "What am I to do? I am so sorry. I was too late. I couldn't get a shot in time."

Jne smiled up at her, pressing away as best she could the pain that clung to her face. "You honor me," she wheezed. "Hold no shame in your heart, for these are the payments of war."

"No," Tam balled. "You are not going to die. I will find Thane. He can fix this. He will come and he will make you whole again. You have to hold on," she continued to cry while she pressed on Jne's chest trying unsuccessfully to keep the blood from coming out. "You have to stay and marry Thane."

Looking up, Tam willed her spirit away, grasping the tiniest flow of air as it gently caressed her weeping face.

Chapter Thirty-Five

Thane watched as the dragon's head suddenly rose up past the railing. His bow was already pulled back, ready to fire as the dragon's massive body ascended, pumped by its great wings and lifting it onto the large balcony. It roared out a challenge, unconcerned with the arrow that Thane aimed at it. It rested its great mass on the parapet, tucking its leathery wings up against its body and then lowered its slender neck allowing a small, thin figure to slide off. Thane eyed Zadok with distaste, his arrow tracking his movements as the wicked sorcerer casually strolled over toward him.

"Now, now, now," Zadok said with the same warm tone he'd used on Thane the first time they'd met. "Is that any way to greet an old friend? Let's not be rude about this."

"This is not for you," Thane said, a cold chill in his voice.

Zadok looked somewhat surprised and then glanced back at his dragon before turning an amused look at Thane. "Surely you don't pretend to be able to shoot my friend here with your puny little arrow. Have you not witnessed the hardness of his hide that makes him practically invincible to any weapon?"

"If you are so confident," Thane offered, "then why don't you step aside and see whose weapon is of greater strength?"

The dragon hissed at him, but stood firm, all too confident about the armor that surround his body like a shield.

"Come now," Zadok said, his arms spread in a gesture of friendship. "Let us not squabble over such petty things when there are negotiations to be had." Zadok turned his head toward the dragon. As if on cue, it reared back and released a blast of scorching steam straight at Thane.

In an instant it engulfed him and would have left his skin cooked and peeling from the bone save for the fact that Thane had been prepared. As the dragon's breath receded, Thane released the pocket of air he'd gathered around him like an impenetrable bubble, his arrow still aimed at the dragon's heart.

"Well done," Zadok clapped. "I see that you have learned a few things since last we met, though I have to say that your earthen beasts are tiresome."

Thane didn't answer him.

"Now honestly," Zadok pressed, "why don't you put down the bow? I'm sure your arm must be getting fatigued with strain by now."

"That's a fine idea," Thane said evenly and released the arrow into the air right on target for the dragon's heart.

Zadok didn't move. His face was in the slow process of changing to a look of I-told-you-so when the arrow penetrated the dragon's thick, scaly shell. Its cry of pain and surprise was cut short as it toppled over, its head dropping mere feet from where Zadok stood causing the wizard to jump away in surprise.

Zadok stared down at the dragon, his face becoming a mixture of anger and shock at Thane's ability to kill one of his pets. "But how is it so?" he asked dumbfounded. "The trees no longer exist."

"Wrong," Thane said glaring at the man who had brought so much death and pain to his world. "Even your repulsive evil cannot completely destroy something as pure as the YeiyeiloBaneesh."

"You lie!" Zadok suddenly raged. "I wiped them all away a millennium past. None remain."

"If that is so," Thane taunted, "then why does your grand pet lie dead at your feet?"

"You will pay dearly!" Zadok screamed. "I will rip the filthy TanIs from your ankle just as I did to Gelfin so long ago. You have not known pain and anguish like that that I will visit upon you!"

"You are a child," Thane countered with a calm but lethal voice. "Your heart is darkness and your mind is clouded by your hate that will bring you nothing but ruin."

"No," Zadok hissed dangerously. "It will bring *you* to ruin." His hand's shot forward with incredible speed that contradicted his aged body as black light flashed from his fingers and shot out toward Thane.

Having thrown his senses into the native surroundings Thane could feel the pulse of the five Tane beating through his veins, drawing its energy from the natural world and lending it to him. Each of the Tane were at his fingertips to call forth and use as he willed to attack or protect. His mind and body seemed to act as one without being encumbered or slowed by thought. He didn't have to contemplate how to defend himself. He merely reacted as if his Tane were working on reflex.

Suddenly his swords appeared in his hands as he tore them from the scabbards at his back while the powers of the earth flowed up through his legs and out along the blades hardening the steel as he cut through Zadok's lightning as if it were water. Again and again, Zadok shot the dark light at him thinking to tire his foe or catch him in an error, but Thane continue to maneuver his weapons with confidence and ease.

"So you enjoy lightning?" Thane chided, as an onyx black cloud suddenly formed over his head rumbling in rage as bolts of lightning shot out at Zadok who was now placed on the defensive. Bolt after bolt shattered the air in an angry buzz as Zadok fought them away with his dark magic deflecting them past him or ricocheting them back at Thane where they simply disappeared.

Long moments passed as each attacked, defended and retaliated but without either of them scoring a hit on their opponent. Thane was quickly realizing that the natural power of his Tane and the unnatural nature of Zadok's magic acted as counter measures that seemed to cancel each other out. And though he was unwilling to test his theory, he was fairly certain that while he held onto the Tane that if one of Zadok's magical attacks should touch him that it would simply wink out of existence leaving him unharmed.

Thane felt like lightning himself, his limbs overcharged with the pulsing power of his Tane witch seemed to grow in strength each demanding his full attention with promises of victory. He was beginning to feel that at any moment they might explode from his skin scattering him to the four directions in invisible particles of dust never to be rejoined again as the entity Thane. It was excruciating while at the same moment euphoric as he continued to battle against Zadok and his vile magic.

Reaching out his hand he called forth fire and shot it from his fingertips in streams of molten death that merely collided with magic liquid that felt greasy against his hand leaving him feeling sick from its touch. Zadok retaliated by raising and then rifling missiles of rock which Thane called apart into dust fragments that exploded past him before being allowed to regroup again where they fell harmlessly at his back.

Thane then called forth razor sharp particles of ice that formed out of the moisture in the air and shot like a hundred thousand needles at Zadok only to be melted in a tornado of hot wind. Next, he quickly rejoined the stone ground at his feet as Zadok tried to separate them and cast him down from the mountain keep when something suddenly tickled at the outskirts of his hearing. He tried to give it ear, but with the massive amounts of power that seemed to rotate around him like a vortex of energy, he was unable to latch onto it or make it audible. Yet, even so, he could feel its urgency. He felt drawn to it, but he could not give it his full attention while he continued to battle with Zadok. Nothing could be so important as defeating the enemy before him. Should he fail, all would fail and fall in the crush of his massive army. Even now, he could sense that they were regrouping against his earthen warriors, picking them apart slowly as new promises of human flesh and treasure floated on the wind to their ears and hearts. Zadok. He was the one making the promises, whispering into the simple minds that made up his army at the same moment he raged against Thane.

The urgency was growing within him though he couldn't determine why or from where it was coming. One thing was for certain, neither the Tane nor Zadok's magic would rule the day in this fight. There had to be another way but he couldn't concentrate on it while his Tane danced about in his mind throwing fire and lightning or calling wind to shake off one of Zadok's onslaughts. It was all too much noise. The songs they all sang were disjointed and alone clamoring jealously above each other to be heard above the rest.

Though caught in the middle of so much power that seemed to answer to his every whim, Thane was beginning to feel his own strength being drawn away. Gelfin had warned him that without an anchor he was forced to give of his own self and energy to handle the Tane and now his reserves were beginning to fail him. He had to end this soon. He had to find a way. Again he felt an urgent rush pressing him to act but in what way he could not tell. It was like someone pounding on a distant door calling out in desperation but for what he could not tell.

Blocking another bolt of lightning he finally understood that only physical weapons would harm Zadok, and conversely, himself in this battle of wills. Zadok must have been tiring as much as he with the amount of power he was calling forth but he couldn't wait to see who would falter first. He needed to get close enough to use his sword, but he felt like he was welded in place, unable to move.

The disharmonious sounds of the five Tane rattling their individual songs in his skull was starting to become painful as he was forced to call on each one in his battle for ultimate victory. He wondered why he could not get them to sing together in harmony as they had in the grove of YeiyeiloBaneesh. Then they had all sung together in a united melody that calmed his soul while filling every fiber of his being with light and power. It must have been the anchor. It must have been the trees. No wonder the Tane drew out his energy when it lacked an anchor. It was not able to direct itself properly without the YeiyeiloBaneesh. If he could somehow get them all to coalesce in a harmonious reverberation he felt that he would have the key that would give him the victory he needed.

Again came the urgent banging somewhere outside his consciousness. It was so persistent this time that he'd almost let go of the Tane. He wondered what it would feel like to have Zadok's magic lancing through his chest without the protective covering the Tane currently provided. The thought of his arrow piercing the dragon came suddenly to his mind followed right behind by a glimmer of light and inspiration.

Swallowing a bog creature Zadok had suddenly raised by opening a gaping hole in the balcony, Thane sent out a strand of air searching for the heart arrow that must surely be still embedded in the dragon's chest while retaliating against Zadok with a swirling vortex of wind meant to shred his opponent with its battling crosscurrents of air. He didn't pay attention to how Zadok escaped the attack already knowing the outcome when he conjured it from the ArVen.

Back and forth they continued their colossal battle while Thane swept the area in search of the arrow. He could feel its presence calling out to him almost as much as the constant buzz that tried to steal his attention away with its now almost hysterical demands. He could feel the strand he'd sent to search almost like his own fingertips groping in the dark for a misplaced treasure and then he brushed up against something warm. He grasped his ArVen fingers around it and a shot of energy and exhilaration flowed through him as he felt its pulse and knew he'd located the arrow.

With barely a thought, he called the arrow to him and it became so clear in his mind what he'd have to do. He flinched, knowing the pain it would cause, but his resolve was firm as he guided the arrow with quick precision and tremendous speed as if he'd shot it with his own bow. Across the balcony it sped, its sharp tip leading the way until it penetrated its target right into the fleshy part of Thane's thigh. He cried out as it pierced his flesh and almost faltered as the pain seared through him, his own blood coalescing around the shaft, feeding it, uniting with it, matching his own heart rate with the thumping deep within its core.

Zadok quickly dove to the side, thinking they were under attack, remembering all too well the arrows that had almost killed him in a previous life. His magic faltered for a moment giving Thane a reprieve as he felt the Tane suddenly begin to align as their voices fell, one by one, into a harmonious union of power and song.

It was pure light radiating around him and through him; gathering all life into his pores and communing with it on such an intimate level that nothing was left hidden. It was at that moment, that the door seemed to crash open on the one that had been pounding along the outskirts of his consciousness and Tam's spirit suddenly materialized before him.

"Thane!" she screamed, "Thane, you must come! She needs you or she will die! You must come now!" And then she was gone, returned to her body, her desperate message delivered.

Through the peace that enveloped him like a cocoon, Thane felt a sudden welling of dread growing out from his heart as he understood who the she must be that Tam was calling about. Jne was in trouble and he had to go to her.

Zadok slowly stood, understanding that he must not be in any immediate danger from arrows as Thane turned his green eyes upon him, the power behind them making them spark with energy. Holding a sword in one hand, he forced his muscles to move him forward, the pain in his thigh that had, only moments before, been near excruciating was now gone. Still he felt stiff as he closed the distance.

Zadok called up his magic but this time Thane did not move to block or defend himself. Zadok smiled wickedly as black light shot from his fingers hitting Thane square in the chest but he was not even fazed in the slightest. The bolts seemed to go right through him, absorbed in the light that was the five Tane.

In desperation, Zadok continued to draw forth his magic, screaming in rage at its impotence against the Chufa boy. "I am the greatest!" he yelled, spittle flying from his mouth as he called forth more bolts of lightning. "You cannot defeat me!" he wailed, almost like a child throwing a tantrum as Thane closed the remaining gap to stand before him. Zadok reached behind him for something tucked in his belt and pulled out a knife that he tried to use but Thane merely reached out and grabbed his wrist twisting the blade out of his hand.

"You deserve worse than this," he whispered as he buried his blade up to the hilt into Zadok's chest.

Zadok's eyes widened as he dropped to his knees and then finally crumpled over. Thane's sword pulled free and he slowly bent down and wiped the blood off on Zadok's robe. Staring down at the pitiful man that had caused so much death, sorrow and pain he found that it was all he could do not to hack away at his flesh until nothing remained but the awful memory. Turning away, he replaced his sword in its sheath and then tore the heart arrow from his thigh. The pain came back in such a rush as to almost throw him to the ground. Tearing a piece of cloth from his sleeve, he wrapped the wound and then started for the edge of the balcony. Jne was in trouble, he had to find her.

A sudden sense of loss began to build in his heart and he felt a tear break from his eye and travel down his cheek. Peering over the edge, Zadok's army seemed in disarray as the enemy began turning on itself. A distant howl broke through the rumble far below drawing his attention to the south. Focusing his keen eyes toward the forest, he watched in wonder as hundreds of Kybara raced over the plain toward the enemy, breaking into the lines like a wave of the sea.

Their howls seemed to be answered by another call high in the heavens as a hundred or more rocs dove out of the clouds plunging toward the valley floor. Thane just caught sight of Teek riding Tchee as they lead them down baring claw and beak. Casting his spirit after them, he found Azaforte as he pulled a retreating troll from the ground and drove him into a group of goblins who had cast off their weapons and were running away.

Thane called out in desperation as the feeling of darkness that gripped his heart grew more intense.

*   *   *

It didn't take long for Tam to locate Thane as his battle with Zadok lit up the sky with spectacular and frightening light as they hammered at each other back and forth. The air itself almost seemed ignited with energy and power and she found it difficult to maintain a stream of wind as she approached. Ignoring the danger to herself, she pressed forward calling out to Thane with all her might but something seemed to be blocking her. She attempted to draw closer but was met by a wall of power that refused to give her passage.

Calling for as much strength of wind as she dared, she pounded against the invisible barrier again and again, screaming at the top of her lungs but to no avail. She was becoming desperate as she watched them battle, neither gaining the upper hand as they seemed matched in their abilities and power.

She saw the tendril of air that suddenly dispatched from Thane moving like a snake across the ground and then into the dragon's chest. She wondered at it as she mounted assault after assault against the invisible wall. She gasped as the finger of air suddenly snapped back, the heart arrow clutch in slim fingers that then plunged the arrow into Thane's thigh. Not understanding the significance at first, she screamed in agony with Thane and then found she was no longer held a bay.

"Thane!" she screamed, "Thane, you must come! She needs you or she will die! You must come now!"

Suddenly she was back in her body looking down at her friend who was now shivering. "Hold on, Jne," she cried, covering the Tjal woman's hand with her own over the gaping wound in her chest. "I found him. I found Thane. He is coming to heal you. Just please hold on."

Jne's face was pale, too pale, from the tremendous loss of blood. Her lips were tinged blue and her breathing was labored flashing pain across her face with every breath.

"Do not mourn...for me," she whispered up at Tam. "I have fought with honor. There is no...shame in my death. Thane can stand with his head held...high over me."

"No, Jne," Tam balled, her tears running down her cheeks and dripping off of her chin. "You are going to live to marry him. He is coming and will heal you. We can't go on without you. You two are meant to be together!"

"No, Tam." Jne said, her voice becoming weaker and harder to hear. "I die with honor...yet, I would trade...it away...and die...in...shame... in my old...age if it could be...with him." She took a deep, painful breath and then slowly let it out.

Tam screamed into the air, her sobs becoming uncontrollable as she wept over Jne's body. Suddenly a shadow passed over her face as a great bird landed with a screech in the courtyard. Through her tears she saw Thane as he flew from the bird and raced desperately toward them.

"Tam," he started to say, but upon seeing Jne, he pulled her hand away from the gaping wound in Jne's chest and placed his their instead. Calling for his Tane, the QenChe fires pulled at the dead space created by Sireen's sword, knitting the flesh together anew as it healed it from the inside out. Without pause, he moved his hand along the gash higher up and then finally placed his hand on her arm where the blood flow seemed to have stopped.

Finally looking at her pale face, he realized that she was no long breathing. "No!" he cried, pressing his lips to her ear. "No, Jne! You can't leave me alone. Please, don't leave me along."

Tam placed her hand on his arm, her tears racing in a deluge down her face. "She's gone, Thane," she said softly. "It's too late. You did what you could."

Thane stared at her for a moment and then looked down at Jne's lifeless form. She was still, and yet, even in her current condition, his breath caught in his throat at how beautiful she was and how much he loved her. His vision blurred, as the tears began to give form to his emotions, his heart aching in his chest. Was his god so cruel as to insist he be alone his whole life never experiencing the companionship and love of a soulmeet? Was his lot to be always cast amongst the outcast and forgotten, to live a life void of solace and warmth? Raising his face to the sky he screamed out his anguish and rage. "NO!"

Looking back at the woman he loved, the woman he had waited for to give his life and love, he froze as a dim light seemed to gather about her skin. Slowly at first, as if fighting to be free, and then with greater ease, he watched as her spirit released itself from her body and began to rise. "Jne," he called after her, but her face was lifted upward, seeing something afar off that was beyond his sight. "Wait," he called after her, but she seemed not to hear as she slowly began to rise into the silent air. Becoming desperate, he looked back down to her body and then over to Tam who was watching him quizzically.

"Air," he finally said. "She needs air."

Tam's face turned to one of concern at Thane's sudden babbling. "She's dead, Thane. She's gone."

"No!" he insisted. Pointing up he pled, "Can't you see her, Tam? Don't you see her spirit? I can call it back. I know I can, but she needs air."

Tam stared at him, her face changing from a look of concern to fear. "Please, Thane," she said, "I don't see anything. She's gone."

"No!" Thane shouted at her. "I won't let her go! She needs air, Tam. Use your Tane. Force air into her lungs while I get her back. She needs to breathe. Please, do this for me. Please." He was pleading now, the tears pouring out as he begged for Tam to help him.

Fearful that her friend had snapped under the strain, she nonetheless did as he requested, calling the wind in a stream to fill Jne's lungs and then allowing the natural weight of her chest to force it back out.

"That's it," he said, smiling through his tears. "That's it. Don't stop."

Throwing his spirit into the air, he shot upwards quickly becoming even with Jne's. Reaching for her arm, he felt her skin as they made contact, wrapping his fingers around her wrist and pulling her back. Her head was still raised, ignoring everything around her until she noticed that her progression had halted. Pulling on her arm, her face clouded as she struggled to be set free, but Thane held tight.

"Jne," he called to her. "Jne, wait."

At the sound of his voice she dropped her eyes and stared at him, her face blank as if not recognizing who he was.

"Jne," he begged, "it's me. It's Thane. Don't you know me?"

For a moment she just stared as if confused and then she smiled. "Have you died as well?" she asked.

"No, Jne," he smiled with relief. "No, and you don't have to either. Look," he said pointing down to her body. "Look, I've healed your wounds.

You don't have to go. See," he said, his voice cracking, "you're still breathing. You have to come back. I need you to come back," he said pleading.

Jne glanced back at whatever it was she could see overhead and for a brief moment he thought she was going to say no. But then she turned her beautiful blue eyes back to him and simply said, "Thane." And then she was gone.

Looking around, he became desperate, his heart dying within him as he felt he'd truly lost her when suddenly, Tam cried out. "She spoke! She called your name!"

Thane returned to his body in an instant reaching out and taking Jne's hand that suddenly felt warm and had less of a grey, waxy hue.

"She said your name," Tam cried, releasing her Tane and crying with joy as they watched Jne's chest rise and fall on its own. "You were right," she said, throwing her arms around Thane's neck and hugging him. "You were right."

Epilogue

With the dragons and Zadok dead, the battle took a quick and easy turn for those defending the keep. No longer did the enemy have Zadok's controlling magic to keep discipline and order and quickly the inbred hatred the orcs, goblins and trolls had for each other turned the battle against Bedler's Keep into infighting and brawls amongst themselves. And, with the added help from the Kybara and the rocs, even though they were still grossly outnumbered, the fighters in the keep were able to break through the hold over the secret exit and take, once again to the battlefield. Dwarf, human and Tjal fought individually and together creating a great wedge that forced the enemy away from the keep and then finally sent them fleeing for their lives back to the mountains and forests that were their homes. Detachments were sent after them to insure that they returned to their own lands while taking down any stragglers that might have fallen behind looking for an easy kill at a farm or small village.

Once the fighting was ended, the rocs returned to the skies, splitting off into all directions finding their way back to their homes, wherever they might be. The Kybara did the same, returning to the Underwoods Forest where they promised to await the return of their Chufa lords and guardians. The remaining Tjal gathered their few dead for the funeral pyre, save for Soyak, and then slipped away back toward the plains of Enn without so much as a nod of recognition or farewell. They had come to the aid of their human neighbors, even having fought beside them, but that was the end of their amity.

Helgar sent the majority of his people back to the Dorian Mountains where they were to rebuild Thornen Dar while he and Bardolf stayed behind to help with the clean up and to represent the Dwarf people when the new king was crowned. Rangor also stayed, ignoring Helgar's ranting about not needing a babysitter.

Ranse dispatched the remaining army to burn the enemy dead and bury their own before sending them back to their old garrisons at Calandra and Aleron. It took six days to complete the task. The warrior healers returned to their original skills and helped their companions minister to the needs of the injured as the keep was turned into a hospital for the rest of the summer until all the wounded had recovered and were able to return to their homes.

When Dor and Erl were finally able to reach Jack, he had long since passed into the next world. Only a trail of blood marked the path that Resdin had taken in an attempt to make an escape but it soon ended with his body slumped over in a nearby closet. Ranse ordered that both bodies be wrapped in royal garments and prepared for burial. Jack would be laid to rest in the tomb of his fathers there at Bedler's Keep with all the regalia and honor that was befitting a king, while Resdin was burned in a secret ceremony affording him as much honor as possible due to the circumstances. Though he'd fought with the enemy, none of those who knew the situation blamed him too harshly or objected to Ranse's decree of mercy.

It wasn't until the next morning when the men were gathering goblin bodies from the courtyard where Soyak had made her valiant stand that they were able to discover her body. Covered by the corpse of a huge troll, it appeared that both had impaled each other with the huge goblin landing on top of Soyak's withered frame. She still had a smile on her face.

With tears in her eyes, Tam helped Dor gather the Tjal woman's body, insisting she be the one that cleaned it in preparation for her funeral pyre. It was quickly determined that they would send her off with their respects that very night.

Jne was placed in a palatial room where she could be fussed over by at least two healers at all times. In the brief moments she was awake, she tried to send them away, insisting she was not in need of pampering, but thankfully she would almost just as quickly be overcome by exhaustion and fall back into unconsciousness. Thane had been able to heal up her wounds using his Tane, and he'd used his VerSagn blood to heal her from infection, but even he did not have the power to recreate blood in her body; at least not that he'd been able to discover so far. So, it was a matter of letting her rest and then forcing as much broth and liquid down her as she would allow in those brief and combative moments that she was awake.

Jack was interred that afternoon in a garden area that seemed a nice place to spend the afternoon. Even the tomb in its bright marble surrounded by spring flowers gave off a tranquil and peaceful feeling that didn't plunge the visitor into the lonely contemplations of death but rather a celebration of the life once lived. Ranse had insisted that Jack's body be paraded through the nearby town and then up the lonely walk toward his final resting place as was required to show respect when a king died, but he was quickly given over to agreement when the Chufa and Jack's other close associates asked that only they be allowed at the interment grounds. Jack was not one to make a fuss over proper protocol in life and he certainly wouldn't want to have to abide it in death either.

Tam, Dor, and Thane had kept to themselves on one side of the procession, walking in silence as Jack's body was pulled on an extravagant cart through the town by a lone white stallion. Erl followed right behind, his head down and his tail curled deep between his legs. Domis and Teek had been granted the honor of placing the body into its vault where both of them spoke of their love for the man who had shown them such care. When his body was finally sealed behind a marble wall where it would stay for his eternal rest, Erl lifted his head and called out a mournful howl that had all those present drying there eyes as his giant wolg gave his last good-bye. Thane stayed back for a time with Erl, trying their best to comfort one another while everyone else went to enjoy a victory feast that was customary to celebrate the life and deeds of the deceased individual.

Rubbing Erl behind the ears, the wolg turned and licked Thane's face in understanding and sympathy that brought Thane to tears as he reached out and touched the tomb. "Goodbye my father," he whispered. "For you are the only one who deserves that name from my lips."

*   *   *

A cold wind came up, rustling the cloaks of the three lone figures that stood beneath the clear midnight sky. The courtyard, that on the previous day had been the site of a great battle, had been cleaned of the bodies and blood that had polluted the now sacred ground where Soyak had given her life in defense of a people that were not her own. Ranse had dispatched a company of men to scour the area so that not the slightest evidence remained of what had occurred there. Gardeners had then been sent in to plant flowers and small trees whose beauty was lost on the trio in the darkness of night.

Thousands of stars looked down as if to pay their respects upon the lone pyre that had been put together for this very purpose. Ranse had wanted to build a tomb and monument for the Tjal woman so that people might visit it and remember her valor and deeds but Thane had refused, knowing that Soyak would not be happy, even in death, caged behind rock walls. No, she was to be burned as was customary for her people—for *their* people.

No one spoke a word as each remained comfortable in their own thoughts feeling it a greater sign of respect for her than if they tried to hail a woman all of them barely knew. Finally, feeling they had shown the proper honor, Thane placed his hand on the wood beneath Soyak's body and called forth fire. The dry limbs erupted into a blaze almost immediately, quickly catching onto the body and consuming it with its heat. Tam threw on sprigs of rosemary to cover the acrid smell and then they all stood back and watched for a moment as Soyak's body was given over to the flames.

Zadok's body was never found.

*   *   *

Teek stepped out of the small hut that hugged the base of the looming peak and looked out across the large, clear lake that had been his home for nearly a whole year. Spring was giving way to summer again but the morning air was still chilled, as it always was, high in the Dorian Mountains. His once sun-bleached hair had taken on a darker hue while, conversely, his skin seemed to lighten some as he lost the tan that once was the badge of those living in the Teague Swamplands. Today he would make the last lonely trip to his natal home and deliver the gifts to the ancestors that would appease his family's passing. It had not been his original intention to leave them until last but he wanted to give the best gifts to them and it had not been until the previous day that he'd found what he'd been looking for in Helgar's mines.

A great diamond, bordered by two others just as grand but smaller in size stared back at him in the burlap sack. For the previous eleven months he'd worked deep in the earth along side the dwarf people he now considered his family, stripping the mountain of its precious metals while working to discover its treasures that he had weekly taken to the swamps and dropped in the water near the areas of his people's homes as best he could remember. All along he waited until his gifts were worthy of the wonderful mother he still missed terribly, and the two siblings whose prattle he could still hear in the deep recesses of his dreams.

Tchee stood ready, a half eaten fish at her feet, as he greeted her with a quick hug before jumping onto her back. "We can't dawdle today," he said, stroking the soft feathers on her neck. "We need to get to the swamps and

349

then back so we can get you ready. They will expect to see us in our full battle armor."

Tchee squawked back at him. He knew she didn't especially like the dragon scales that he'd fashioned, with Thane's help, into a protective covering for both of them to wear. He supposed that it was because of the dragon's scent that still permeated the armor, but it couldn't be helped. No matter how hard or how often he scrubbed them with the yarrow roots found in plentiful supply around the lake there still remained a slight and distinctive smell that made Tchee murmur in her throat.

"Now, don't complain," he said. "I'm wearing mine as well. Plus, you look fearsome in it and everyone will surely make a great fuss when we drop into Calandra for the wedding. I'm sure that Prince Ranse and Master Thane will certainly be impressed. I know that Domis will."

He smiled at the thought of how his friend would react at seeing them. It had been too long since he'd enjoyed the company of his best friend and comrade in mischief. The thought of spending the entire summer as Prince Ranse's guest in such a large castle together had already brought to mind some ideas as to what they might do to torture pure Jace or many of the other castle staff that would surely be easy targets for their shenanigans. The idea lifted his spirits some from the sorrowful task he was to complete the following day at the Teague.

Tchee didn't seemed convinced though as she suddenly spread her great wings lifting them quickly into the morning sky and then turned to the south and the well known journey to Teek's ancestral homeland.

*   *   *

Thane didn't leave Jne's side for a month until her orneriness at being forced to stay in bed had reached such a level that he knew she was out of physical danger. He sympathized for those unlucky enough to be assigned to care for her. Kat seemed to pull more duty than any of the others. He felt that it was most likely because Kat could be just as cantankerous as Jne and because the Tjal woman's threats and rantings didn't faze her. Jne actually grew to like the healer woman, sensing her strength of will and character, something that Jne could respect.

During the afternoons when Jne slept the most, Thane spent his time in the gardens at Jack's tomb. He missed his old friend terribly and would often wet the marble crypt with his tears. The painful irony that Jack had spent his life searching for his son only to find him at the edge of his sword and then be killed by him as well was almost too awful to contemplate. Too often, he still found his rage building to levels of blind hatred for the man responsible for all of his sorrows in life—Zadok. That they could not find his body was somewhat troubling though he did not put too much thought or worry into the fact. The man was dead and gone. He knew it because it was his sword that had ended it.

Dor and Tam stayed at the keep for an extended period out of love and friendship to Thane and Jne, but also spent great amounts of time in the Underwoods with the Kybara visiting the YeiyeiloBaneesh grove. The keep was too confining for the Chufa, and though the Underwoods again hid the orcs, their numbers were so diminished as to make them almost an afterthought. And, with the Kybara as their companions, the horrors that were the Underwoods forest no longer seemed much of a threat.

When Jne finally showed signs of healing, they at last were able to convince Thane to leave her bedside for almost a week and return to the sacred woods with them. It was then that they returned the heart arrows to the YeiyeiloBaneesh trees and that Dor and Tam asked Thane to join them in the sacred FasiUm ceremony that would wed them for all time. He at first declined, feeling he did not possess the proper authority.

"You should wait until you return home and have the Kinpa do it," he protested.

Dor looked at Tam, both staring at each other in sad confirmation as if discussing the matter with merely their eyes and then Tam turned to Thane. "We won't be going back."

"What?" Thane asked, somewhat surprised.

"There is nothing for us there anymore," Dor explained. "Plus, we know that you will not be returning and," he finished with the old twinkle back in his eye, "what fun is there to be had if you are not there to have it with me?"

"With us," Tam corrected wrapping an arm around Dor's waist.

Thane shook his head and then looked up at them and smiled. "And where is it that you plan to live, here?"

Dor shook his head slowly. "Ranse has asked us to come and live in Calandra. He wants to replant the city with trees and flowers and has asked that we be his chief gardeners."

Thane smiled at the thought. What better use for a Chufa than to take charge of making things grow?

"He promised us that we could build our own hut on the castle grounds in the woods surrounding it," Tam blushed slightly, "where we can raise a family."

"I will visit you there as often as I am able," Thane smiled, though they could sense a feeling of melancholy behind his words. They were all growing up and the world was no longer the small patch of woods where their people still lived in ignorance. Their paths were separating and the thought of it hurt. Certainly, they would still be able to see each other whenever they chose but it would never be the same.

"Actually," Dor said, "we were hoping that you would come and make your home near ours."

Thane smiled at the thought, feeling the draw of friends and family but he knew that his destiny was taking him elsewhere. "That would be wonderful," he said drawing smiles from his friends that he quickly turned away, "but I have other responsibilities that I cannot leave for another."

Dor's countenance dropped slightly. "I understand," he said, though his tone said otherwise.

"Who else is there to tend to the YeiyeiloBaneesh trees and help them to flourish so that one day our people may return to their proper place?" Thane asked. Then his voice dropped as he added, "And who else is there that can find the other TanIs' Zadok stole and release their spirits into the afterlife?"

Tam reached out and touched his arm. "That is something we should all take part in," she said glancing over to Dor who nodded enthusiastically. "Ranse can find others just as suited to plant his trees for him."

Thane smiled but shook his head. "No, this is a task that was appointed to me alone and I will fulfill it. Plus, I will have Erl and Jne as company."

At the sound of his name Erl thumped his tail on the ground where he lay curled up enjoying the bit of sun that touched the meadow around the YeiyeiloBaneesh trees. He had not left Thane's side since Jack died; a comfort to both of them.

"Now," Thane said in a cheerful voice that only sounded slightly forced, "let's get on with joining you two as one."

*   *   *

The spring air was invigorating with a slight chill that clung to one's skin but with the promise of a beautiful warm day ahead. The tiny hill overlooking Calandra was carpeted with new grass springing up to meet the warming rays of the vernal sun and was mixed with a myriad of colors flashing in the breeze from fresh wildflowers that filled the air with a clean and soothing aroma.

Chtey's hooves marred the ground as he crested the rise giving Thane a clear view of the area from where he sat upon his old friend's back. They paused for a moment giving him an opportunity to scan the fields below and beyond. "It will be good to see everyone again," he said as Jne rode up to stand beside him, Erl stopping on his other side. "A lot has changed since last we were here."

Erl whined slightly and then nuzzled a cold, wet nose into his hand. Thane laughed, stroking the wolg's fur and then scratching him behind the ear. They had come for the coronation, of course, as well as the wedding that would follow. The real wedding would take place on the Plains of Enn, but the happy couple had been convinced by the soon to be king that the city deserved to celebrate with them now that they had become endeared to its citizens.

Thane brushed the hair from his face only to have it playfully returned by the gentle breeze. His eyes lifted to the clear skies in time to watch the giant bird dropping down out of the west, the small figure of a boy firmly planted on its back. He smiled, remembering the tiny warrior and his stout heart knowing that another brave lad would be anxious to greet his friend again and possibly be the death of the castle staff as they certainly would return to their former mischief. It reminded him of himself and Dor when they were younger and he couldn't help but wonder if they too wouldn't find some sort of trouble to earn themselves a scowl or two. He would welcome such innocence again.

Jne reached out and touched his leg, all visible signs of her injuries gone. "Well," she said, "shall we go and see our friends again?"

Erl turned a circle and yelped, his excitement to be on their way evident.

Thane turned his bright green eyes on her, taking in the beautiful smile that she seemed to reserve just for him. His heart leaped filling with the love that she offered him and that he shared with her. "I love you, Jne," he said softly, her face seeming to brighten with the words.

"I know," she replied, with her characteristic grin. "Now, let's get you and Erl off of this hill and into the city to reunite Dor and Tam. I'm sure that they are just dying to see you. You have kept to the woods too long."

Thane glanced at Erl who sniffed at the air as if finding in it a familiar scent. "Are you ready, boy?"

Erl slowly wagged his tail, not wanting to let go of the smell he'd latched onto but finally relenting as he turned and bound down the hill toward Calandra's open gates.

"Hey," Thane yelled, urging Chtey into full stride as he and Jne chased after him, just as anxious to be in the loving arms of friends once more.

THE END